Helen (Douglas) Mackenzie

Storms and Sunshine of a Soldier's Life

Lt.-General Colin Mackenzie, 1825-1881 - Vol. I

Helen (Douglas) Mackenzie

Storms and Sunshine of a Soldier's Life
Lt.-General Colin Mackenzie, 1825-1881 - Vol. I

ISBN/EAN: 9783337058838

Printed in Europe, USA, Canada, Australia, Japan

Cover: Foto ©Raphael Reischuk / pixelio.de

More available books at **www.hansebooks.com**

STORMS AND SUNSHINE OF
A SOLDIER'S LIFE

Colin Mackenzie

STORMS AND SUNSHINE

OF

A SOLDIER'S LIFE

LT.-GENERAL COLIN MACKENZIE, C.B.

1825-1881

FERENDUM ET SPERANDUM

VOL. I.

EDINBURGH: DAVID DOUGLAS

1884

Printed by R. & R. CLARK, *Edinburgh.*

CONTENTS.

CHAPTER VII.

CONVERSION—FURLOUGH.

(1836-1838.)

CHAPTER VIII.

" HOME AND OUT."

(1838-1839.)

CHAPTER IX.

CALCUTTA TO FIROZPUR.

(1840.)

" His crisp hair like ringes was i-ronne
And that was yalowe, and glittering as the sonne
His nose was heigh, his eyen bright cytryne
His lippes round, his colour was sanguine
And as a lyon he his looking caste
Of five and twenty year his age I caste
His voice was as a trumpe thunderynge."

CHAUCER.

CHAPTER X.

FIROZPUR TO JELLALABAD AND PESHAWAR.

(1840.)

> "To march o'er field and to watch in tent
> From his home in good Castille he went
> To the wasting siege and the battle's van."
>
> HEMANS.

CHAPTER XI.

PESHAWAR.

(January to June 1841.)

"The bursting shell, the gateway wrenched asunder,
The rattling musketry, the clashing blade;
And ever and anon in tones of thunder
The diapason of the cannonade."
LONGFELLOW.

"He loved chivalrye,
Truth and honour, freedom and curtesie,
And thereto hadde he riden, no man ferre,[1]
As wel in Christendom as hethenesse,
And ever honoured for his worthiness.
At mortal batailles had he been fifteen
. . . .
He was a very perfit gentil knight."
CHAUCER.

[1] Ferre = further.

CHAPTER XX.

ILLNESS AND DELIVERANCE.

"Now men see not the bright light which is in the clouds."—Job xxxvii. 21.

CHAPTER XXI.

MARCH BACK TO INDIA—REWARDS.

(October 1842-3.)

"It sounds like stories from the land of spirits,
If any man obtain that which he merits,
Or any merit that which he obtains.
For shame, dear friend ! renounce this canting strain,
What wouldst thou have a good great man obtain ?
Place—titles—salary—a gilded chain—
Or throne of corses which his sword hath slain ?
Greatness and goodness are not means, but ends !"
                                        S. T. COLERIDGE.

LIEUT.-GENERAL COLIN MACKENZIE, C.B.

CHAPTER I.

(1806-25.)

COLIN MACKENZIE was the youngest son but one of Kenneth
Francis Mackenzie, a junior branch of the Redcastle family.
No Scottish biography can be complete without a genealogy,
and whether the descent of the Mackenzies (sons of Kenneth)
is to be traced through the Fitzgeralds to the Geraldines
of Florence, or whether they are of unmixed Highland
race, it is certain that they are one of the most ancient
families in the North, and allied to the best blood of Scotland. Murdoch, the fifth Baron of Kintail, married Martha,
daughter of Donald, Earl of Mar, nephew of Robert the
Bruce. Kenneth, the tenth Baron, known as "Kenneth
of the Whittle," from his passion for carving on wood,
married Lady Elizabeth Stewart, daughter of John, second
Earl of Athol, by Lady Mary Campbell, daughter of
Argyll. To the third of his sons by her, Roderick Mór
(the Great), he gave the lands of Redcastle, cir. 1608.
Another Rory the Great, sixth Baron of Redcastle, married in 1707 a very remarkable lady, Margaret, daughter
of Sir James Calder, who had by her first husband,
Dunbar of Westfield, seven sons and a daughter; by her
second marriage she had seven more sons and a daughter,
and then another set of seven sons and two daughters,

making five-and-twenty children in all. Roderick died in
1757. His second son, Colin, seventeenth in direct male
descent from the first Baron of Kintail, married the beautiful Mary Cochrane, granddaughter of Sir John Cochrane of
Ochiltree, second son of the first Earl of Dundonald. To
this lady are attributed both the talent and the remarkable
personal beauty which characterised so many of her grand-
children ; and the subject of this memoir certainly inherited
not only the fighting qualities of the Mackenzies, but the
extraordinary dash and gallantry of the Cochranes. Her
grandfather, Sir John, the friend of Russell and Sidney,
on the death of Charles II., joined Argyll's hapless insurrection ; on the dissolution of that force he and Sir
Patrick Hume of Polwarth, with only seventy men, threw
themselves into a sheepfold, and defended its frail walls of
sods until they beat off double their own number of militia
under Lord Ross and Captain Clelland. Ross was wounded,
and Clelland left dead on the field ; but hearing that the
enemy was returning with strong reinforcements, Cochrane
desired his men to shift for themselves, while he himself, worn
out with fatigue, sought refuge with his uncle, Gavin Cochrane
of Craigmuir. The wife of the latter was the sister of Captain
Clelland ; and out of revenge for his death she betrayed her
nephew and guest, who was carried to Edinburgh, paraded
through Edinburgh bound and bareheaded, and lodged in the
Tolbooth, 3d July 1685. He was condemned to death. There
was, however, some hope that the old Earl of Dundonald,
who had rendered great service to both Charles I. and II.,
might succeed in saving his son's life, through the influence
of Father Peters, the royal confessor ; but the time previous
to the execution was too short for the negotiation. Sir
John's only daughter, Grizzel, though only eighteen, knowing that the warrant for her father's death was expected
from London, rode from Edinburgh to the house of her old

nurse, near Berwick. There she disguised herself as a lad, went to the little public-house at Belford, where the postman was accustomed to sleep for a few hours, watched her opportunity, and drew the charge of his pistols. She then waited for him on the road, presented her own pistol at his head, and demanded the mail bags. The man tried in vain to fire, and dismounted to seize the bold boy, when she caught his horse, galloped off with it, ripped open the bags, destroyed all the warrants, and made her way back to Edinburgh. This extraordinary act of heroism, rivalling the exploits of her great kinsman, Lord Cochrane, afterwards the tenth Earl of Dundonald, gained a delay of more than a fortnight, during which time a bribe of £5000 persuaded Father Peters to save Sir John's life. Her brother, another Sir John, had fought at Bothwell Brig when only sixteen, had been "forfeited" for it as soon as he came of age, and fled to Holland. He married a Dutch lady, Hannah de Worth. His daughter Mary was thus the niece of Grizzel Cochrane. Mary had two daughters and an only son, Kenneth Francis Mackenzie, born 1748, a man of noble and chivalrous character. Though a barrister, he too had his fighting days. His son thus narrates a striking episode in Mr. Mackenzie's life :—

"My father was, at the time of the first French Revolution, Attorney-General in the Island of Grenada, a prosperous colony of sufficient importance to attract the attention of the French fiends, who, as the propagandists of massacre, rapine, and anarchy, hated England, and strove in every part of the world to annihilate her prosperity, and by force or fraud to destroy the lives and property of her children. A servile insurrection broke out in Grenada, which nearly ruined the colony. Nothing could exceed the craft and skill with which it had been planned, so as to burst forth simultaneously throughout the island, except the fidelity of the negroes to each other, and the impenetrable hypocrisy of their demeanour towards their unfortunate masters until the time for their destruction arrived. I believe that the above features are common to the conspiracies of all savages. They certainly were conspicuous in the last great Indian Rebellion. It would be difficult to enumerate the horrors which attend a successful Jacquerie, whether the actors be white or black; but we well know that it requires, not devils, but men, to invent and perpetrate them. In Grenada numbers of the planters, with their wives and children, perished under circumstances of fearful barbarity (of which swift murder was the most endurable) before they could even attempt to reach George Town, a haven of doubtful safety, for the garrison was weak and ill provided. The arrival there of those fugitives who had escaped with their lives, roused up Mr. Home, the Governor, a gentleman much esteemed for his accomplishments, courage, and humanity, but unequal to the occasion, because he judged murderers and rebels by the standard of his own superior nature. Contrary to my father's advice he determined to proceed to the camp of the blacks and to endeavour to bring them back to their allegiance by appeal and remonstrance. The presiding genius of the insurrection was a French republican, called, I think, Victor Hugues, who had been sent from Paris, then the headquarters of the devil, to foment and guide the outbreak. This same rascal afterwards set a price on my father's head, and vowed that if he caught him alive he would lower his pride by cutting off his legs, because he refused to negotiate with one whom he looked upon as a leader of banditti. I have remarked that in all cases of misplaced humanity, and I am personally cognisant of many, the effects have been disastrous to all parties. Rose-water surgery never yet cured a deep-seated ulcer. But, 'revenons à nos moutons,' or rather to Mr. Home and his forty friends who accompanied him to the slaughter. On their arrival in the negro camp they were at once made prisoners, and a message was sent to my father, the chief authority left in George Town, that their lives would be spared if he surrendered the town and arsenal. His reply was to the effect that loyalty and honour made compliance impossible, and that he would visit with the severest retribution any injury done to Mr. Home and his party. The rebels immediately shot Mr. Home and his companions, with the exception of a doctor (named, I think, Campbell), and flung their bodies into one hole. Of course, had my father been weak enough to yield to their terms, these wretches would no more have kept faith than the Afghans did in 1842 with our army in the snow-blocked passes of Afghanistan, or the Sepoy rebels with Sir Hugh Wheeler at Cawnpore in 1857.

"The sequel of this long story is, that my father, having the blood of Seaforth in his veins on one side and of the Cochranes of Dundonald on the other, although a lawyer, stuck his pen behind his ear, girded on his sword, and for six months or thereabouts led his Britannic Majesty's troops in action, maintained his ground against overwhelming odds, and finally, by the assistance of reinforcements brought by the late General Sir Thomas Hislop, re-established the tranquillity of Grenada and the authority of the King. I am sorry to say that Victor Hugues escaped to France, but my father kept his word as to retribution by trying and executing a considerable number of the ringleaders of the insurrection. His reward was in inverse proportion to the service he had rendered. During the struggle he had, in furnishing the troops with necessaries, and in the public service generally, expended almost all his private fortune, not one farthing of which has ever been repaid to himself or his heirs. The Prime Minister offered

to make him a baronet, which he refused on the score of
insufficient fortune, but some years after, being in England,
and feeling the want of the money he had spent in his
country's service during so momentous a crisis, he had an
interview with Mr. Addington on the subject. The Prime
Minister frankly admitted the validity of the claim, but
added that, as it was not then of very recent date, parliamentary interest would be required to ensure its payment.
This my father did not possess, so that up to this day the
Government of the greatest nation in the world remains a
debtor of fully £20,000 to the estate of a brave and devoted
servant of the Crown."

There is no doubt that character is hereditary, so the
fact of descent from a long race of rulers and hard fighters
is likely to convey those qualities, while the consciousness
of aristocratic descent produces a feeling of equality, and
consequently of independence, towards men of high rank
or official position which is invaluable for the public service,
and which the Spaniard expresses when he says that he is
" as good a gentleman as the king, only poorer."

An assured position also raises a man above petty fears
of lowering his dignity. A gentleman will put his shoulder
to the wheel when the parvenu would fear soiling his newly-
acquired kid gloves. But the noble must have no privileges,
otherwise an aristocracy sinks into a caste. Let him start
fair and win the race if he can ; if not, let him be distanced
by the first man of the people who can do it. There are
as true gentlemen in the ranks as ever rose out of them,
and it is surely more honourable to be the founder of a
family rather than his twentieth descendant.

Colin Mackenzie valued his pedigree very little, but we
venture to think he owed somewhat to it. On the other
hand, he had the warmest sympathy for "a true man," to
whatever race, colour, or social stratum he belonged.

Kenneth Francis Mackenzie married a beautiful girl much younger than himself, Anne Townsend, the daughter of an English gentleman, the first English marriage known in the line of Kintail and Redcastle. She brought him a numerous family, of whom five sons and six daughters survived their father. Of these—

Colin, so named after his grandfather and his cousin, General Colin Mackenzie, was born in London 25th March 1806, and baptized at St. James' Church, Piccadilly.[1]

His was not a happy childhood. Every offence was visited with severity; flogging *ad libitum* was the rule, so that when the boys caught sight of their father they preferred escaping to meeting him; and yet he was a man of strong and ardent affections, who earnestly desired his children's love. He would romp with them, tell them stories, and make himself delightful to them, and was as tender in cases of illness as any woman. This harsh system was the fashion of the time, which seemed to interpret Solomon's warning against sparing the rod to mean—lay it on as often as possible; and it was not mollified by any interference on the part of their mother, though she was most tender to her children as long as they were babies. They never forgot how sweetly she would sing to them (without accompaniment) in the gloaming. At other times her husband would play his viol d'amour while she sang.

---

[1] Roderick VI. of Redcastle.

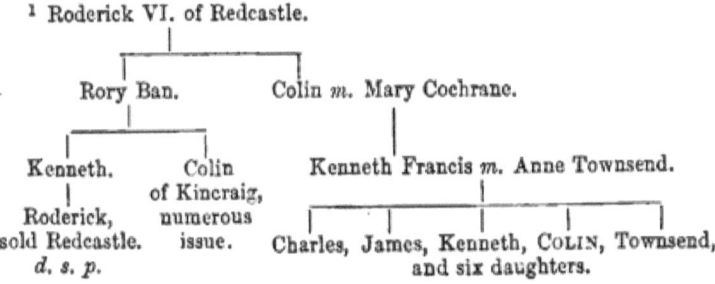

They were devoted to each other, and after his death she shut herself up in solitude, as if life and all its interests had come to a close for her. Naturally of a strong character, very shrewd and keen in judgment, the handsome old lady, with her high features, thin firm lips, and black eyes, sitting calmly and patiently in her solitude and increasing blindness with, by choice, no other companion than a little granddaughter of five or six years old, trained "never to make a noise," might have been taken as a fit representative of a Roman matron. Not even when the fate of her son Colin was a matter of uncertainty, nor when the certainty became one of the utmost peril, did her fortitude give way. She remained calm, though sorrowful, and quoted with proud composure as applicable to his conduct :—

> " But that I may not stain with grief
> The death-song of my father's son,
> Or bow this head in woe."
>
> *Gertrude of Wyoming.*

Latterly the whole character softened as she learned more of evangelical truth, especially from her son's friend, the Rev. H. H. Beamish who often visited her, and in her latter days she delighted in dwelling on the mercies of God in Christ.

In a letter, dated November 1816, Mr. Mackenzie thus addresses his boy, who was not yet eleven years old :—

"I am persuaded you love me dearly, as I do you ; but as you acknowledge that your giddiness makes you forget what I say to you, and that you therefore appear as if you did not care for me, would it not be well were you to lay aside this vile giddiness which does you so much injustice, and makes you look so unlike what you really are ? If you determine to do it I am much inclined to believe that you will get rid of that worth-less companion and his cousin-german, idleness, which I am sure have been, and, unless dismissed, will continue to be to you the cause of much more pain than pleasure."

This is certainly not the letter of a man who understands children, or who could make allowance for the "vile giddiness" which is so common in a lively high-spirited child. Colin often regretted the desultory manner in which he had been educated, and the inferior schools to which he had been sent. When about twelve he was placed with his elder brothers, James and Kenneth, at a school in Cumberland, of which he used to speak with horror, from the "brutal severity of the punishment." He became acquainted with some of the wild spirits in the neighbourhood, and the impressible boy imbibed from them a degree of sympathy for the smuggler which long after amazed his wife, who had been brought up in the principles of the Royal Navy, and looked upon smuggling as a crime.

He was then sent to the Academy at Dollar, and always remembered with affection his old French master, M. de Joux, with whom he was boarded, and whose favourite saying—"De woman has a cell more in de heart, and a cell less in de head"—he often quoted. Writing to his beloved sister Mary (1822), he rejoices at being able "to range at will among the most beautiful hills in Scotland," and mentions having become acquainted with Mr. Johnstone of Alva, "one of the most hospitable and kindest of men."

"How different it is here from what it was down in England ! For the two years I was at school in Cumberland not a single gentleman took the least notice of either my brothers or myself ; but no sooner do we come to Scotland than for the *very* reason of our being strangers, Mr. Paterson of Carpow, although he had never seen us, invites us to spend the holidays at his house, and others treat us almost as if we were their children. There is a Captain Scott, 91st Regt. . . . he gives me a lesson in broadsword every day."

He laments the departure of his schoolfellow, John

Halkett, who had got his commission—"the lad of all others, except our own family, I loved and esteemed the most, and during seven and a half years I have always found him the same."

About a year before this, Mr. Mackenzie had left Fife and settled at Llanforda, a beautiful place near Oswestry. After some time, Colin and his little brother Townsend became day scholars at the Rev. Dr. Donne's at Oswestry. The brothers were devoted to each other, though there was a difference of seven years between them.

Although the rod was freely used at this school, yet Colin never suffered from it. A false quantity was not to be forgiven, and an unfortunate fellow having commenced his copy of verses with the line, "O glorious Phœbus!" the Doctor gazed at him over his spectacles, and said "Mr. Conjuror! prepare for punishment!" Colin was a great favourite with Dr. Donne, though on one occasion, when he had expressed some opinion which, in the ears of the staunch old Tory, savoured of revolutionary principles, the latter sternly demanded — " Who was the first Whig, Mackenzie?" "Satan, sir, Satan was the first Whig."

When he left for India the good Doctor sent him his blessing, and furnished him with letters to several of his old pupils, among them Sir Richard Jenkins, the Resident at Nagpur. Whenever he returned to Europe, he never failed to visit his old master, whose picture hung in his dressing-room to the last. All his early friends were dear to him as long as he lived.[1]

[1] He kept up a lifelong intimacy with the families of Colonel Low of Clatto, the Spens's of Craig-Sanquhar, the Craigies, Mr. Cleghorn in Fife ; with the Johnstones of Alva, and his cousins the Taits ; and with his school-fellows at Oswestry, James King King of Staunton Park, Herefordshire, who afterwards became his brother-in-law ; Richard Jebb and his brother, Colonel Godfrey Russell, and others.

In 1790, Roderick Mackenzie being in embarrassed circumstances, had found himself obliged to sell Redcastle, and when his cousin Kenneth Francis wished to intervene as one of the heirs of entail, it was discovered that the original deed had never been registered, and was therefore worthless. It was probably after this that Kenneth Mackenzie purchased a very large estate, named Lusignan, in Demerara, which was, of course, subject to the usual fluctuations in productiveness and in the value of produce, so that towards 1825 he was in great straits for want of money, and full of the most gloomy anticipations for the future.[1] When, therefore, his son Colin asked to be sent to one of the Universities, he was unable to do so, but procured a cadetship for him in the Madras Army. The boy had been for two years champing the bit, very impatient to get to work in some way or other. His eldest brother had gone out in 1823 as Consul-General to Vera Cruz, and now generously paid the expenses of the younger's passage and outfit, which in those days cost no less than £500. The cadet was wholly ignorant of the value of money, never having had an allowance even for pocket-money—a fact which he often regretted in after years.

His father accompanied him to Gravesend, and he was followed by the most affectionate letters from his sisters. Perhaps the severest pang of all was parting from his young brother Townsend, who clung to him in an agony of grief. His father writes :—

"I do not doubt for a moment that you will exert yourself unceasingly in the road which leads to fame and fortune. To hear that you do so, and that your conduct does credit to your name and family, will bestow happiness on the evening of my life. . . . I place unbounded confidence in your principles

---

[1] Some time after the estate again gave a very good income.

of religion, integrity, veracity, and honour, and the only spark
of disquietude that remains on my mind is on the score of
temper, and tendencies connected with it ; but I flatter myself
you have sufficient manliness of character to resolve to conquer
and correct what is wrong."

On the other hand, Colin writes to the sister nearest to
him in age :—

" You must nurse my father and mother instead of me now.
Take care of them, dear Mary, and preserve them for my future
happiness." [1]

He sailed for Madras in the *Ganges*, East Indiaman, on
the 15th Nov. 1825, with a large and joyous party of
cadets, among whom were Captain Codrington, who fell at
Charekar, Colonel George Johnson, and, above all, one with
whom he formed an enduring and most tender friendship,
George Broadfoot, who was to fall in the flower of his age,
and with the most brilliant reputation and prospects at
Ferozshahar.

They reached Madras in May 1826, and Colin Mackenzie was hospitably received by Edward Elliot, Member
of Council, in whose grounds at the Adyar he fought a
duel ; but so great was afterwards his abhorrence of the
sin and folly of duelling, that he would never give any
particulars either of this or of one he fought at St. Helena.
On their arriving, his first commission and those of the other
Madras cadets were, by an arbitrary decision of Colonel
Conway, the Adjutant-General, instead of being dated 5th
Nov. 1825, the day they sailed for India (as was done with
all the Bengal cadets), was dated 8th January 1826, when

---

[1] It is a strong proof of their tenacity of affection that when these
two had rejoined one another in the Better Land, more than fifty-five
years after, it was found that each had preserved the letters of the
other, so that their early correspondence was complete.

they were in mid-ocean ; thus depriving them of more than two months' service.[1]

[1] This appeared of little consequence to the youngsters at the time, but when serving with Bengal officers in the year 1840, the injustice of the post date was forced upon Mackenzie's notice, and he laid a remonstrance before the Madras military authorities, who did not deny the hardship, but replied that as rectifying the mistake in one instance involved the necessity of rectifying it in all, nothing could be done. By this apparent accident, Mackenzie lost his Brevet-Captaincy in 1840, his Brevet-Majority in 1846, both being for length of service, and subsequently his Lieut.-Colonelcy, his promotion being thus retarded more than seven years. He appealed again in 1863, when Sir Hope Grant, then Commander-in-Chief at Madras, expressed warm sympathy, but could do nothing after so great a lapse of time.

CHAPTER II.

(1825-1830.)

WHEN Colin Mackenzie arrived in India he was a lad of nineteen, about 5 feet 10½, slender, agile, but very strong, broad-chested, perfectly made (so that fifty years after his friend Vincent Eyre spoke of his "Adonis-like form"), looking much younger than his age, with perfect features, blue eyes, and a superabundance of the most beautiful pale gold curls, like those of a young child. His hair retained this fair colour until his captivity in Afghanistan, when nine months' shaving turned it brown; but it remained extraordinarily thick almost to the last. The adjutant of his regiment declared he was the "most beautiful boy he ever beheld." He was quite ignorant of the ways of the world, and as bold as a young hawk.

He of course called upon the Commander-in-Chief, Sir George Walker, and after waiting some time in a room full of officers, he went up to the A.D.C. and said : "Can you tell me if I am to have the honour of an interview with the Commander-in-Chief or not, for I am not accustomed to kick my heels in a great man's antechamber?" The A.D.C., who was afterwards his fast friend, General Forster, repeated this to Sir George Walker, who was excessively amused, and asked the audacious young ensign to dinner. He

declined on the plea that he was already engaged. Some
one told him this was quite contrary to custom; that an
invitation from the Governor or Commander-in-Chief was
looked upon in the light of a command, and superseded all
other engagements; whereupon he wrote again, saying he
had not been aware of this rule, and apologising for his
breach of etiquette. Sir George answered very kindly:
"I invited you to give you pleasure, and not to interfere with any other engagement, and I shall always be
glad to see you at any time." Not only Sir George, but
the ladies of his family took a great fancy to him, and he
was often at their house alone. Sir George was a very
aristocratic-looking, handsome man, though small. He had
two daughters by his first marriage, one, a beautiful, noble-
looking girl, who made a great impression on the young
subaltern. Lady Walker was very kind to him, and the
Chief would tell him stories of his own military career,
which made him feel that he would like to live and die
under such a commander. Once he related that at the siege
of Badajoz, being then a captain, he and his company
forced their way to the top of the ramparts, and found
themselves, on turning a corner, in the presence of a superior
body of French troops. He called on his men to charge,
but they broke and fled. Captain Walker was left alone in
the midst of the Frenchmen, and having an old-fashioned
sabre (he called it sábre), he made a cut at one of them,
who drew back and fired at him. The ball shattered his
breast bone, in a moment five bayonets were in him, and
he was pitched over the ramparts into the ditch, where
his comrades found him. Colin said: "But surely, sir,
it was very unusual in British soldiers to desert their
officer. How do you account for it?" "The fact is,"
replied Sir George, "I was very unpopular; I had been
very severe with my men."

The young soldier was at first attached to the 10th Native Infantry and afterwards posted to the 48th.

One of his first adventures was on the march from Madras, when, in endeavouring to cross the Godávari river at Rajamundri, the strength of the current carried his horse off his feet. He disengaged himself and swam, accoutred as he was, to the opposite bank, landing with his whip in his hand. His horse found his way to shore lower down.

Being quartered at Aska, a place in the Northern Sirkárs, he made a trip to Jagganath in December 1825, his journal of which contains some characteristic observations. He passed through the magnificent station of Ganjam, then totally deserted in consequence of a virulent fever, which swept away almost every inhabitant. The houses and gardens were now infested by snakes and the woods by cheetahs and other wild animals, carriages were rotting in the stables, and the native town and public buildings were alike abandoned. At Jagganath he was hospitably received by a Norwegian named Mansbeck, formerly an officer in the German Legion. After describing the horrible image of Jagganath and his festivals, during one of which the monster is supposed to be sick and is taken to his garden three miles off, the writer adds :—

"The direct encouragement afforded by the Bengal Government to this dreadful superstition, and the support the people receive in every freak they take into their heads connected with their diabolical ceremonies, have rendered this district a turbulent one, by instilling into the minds of the natives the notion that we fear them, and that they are infinitely superior to the foreigners who are called their rulers, but who give way to them on every occasion. I consider the encouragement of Paganism and the almost zeal in favour of such degrading rites, for the sake of a little paltry revenue, as impious and disgraceful to a Christian Government. A slight proof of the little esteem the

Jagganath populace hold us in is, that a coolie of the lowest caste will, on passing a European of whatever rank, spit on the ground and curl his moustaches, which is accounted a greater insult among them, than at home it would be were a blackguard to give you a box on the ear. As I walked through the town with Mansbeck I felt much inclined to give several of the scoundrels a severe beating, but my companion told me that by so doing I should run the risk of being torn to pieces by the mob and also of losing my commission. The latter consideration withheld me, but I would hardly give myself up for lost were I beset by a hundred such ill-looking, squalid wretches as thronged round us.

" I shall not enter into a probably unwise discussion of the chief grounds of complaint with European settlers against our present rulers. It is sufficient that the same narrow policy which dictated the banishment and ruin of one (Silk Buckingham) who had the impertinence to bring forward stubborn facts and to judge of things as they really exist, has ever marked the conduct of the Court of Directors, influenced by those whose interest it is to keep them deceived with regard to a country of which, although its legislators, they know little or nothing."

He mentions reading Pope's *Essay on Man* while crossing the Chilka lake on his way back, a book to which he traced his first serious impressions after reaching manhood, and which he ever after took pleasure in quoting.

Leaving the lake, he came to a village where he found a crowd of people round the mouth of a small cave, who told him there was a tiger inside. He fetched his pistols, loaded them, and very rashly crawled in, the passage being barely wide enough for his broad shoulders. He fired at the yellow eyes that were glaring at him, and then, with some difficulty, worked his way backwards out of the cave; but, finding that the beast was not dead, he went in again and fired another shot, when the creature fell lifeless. No one would go in to bring out the carcase until he offered a rupee. With much trouble the animal was dragged forth, when it proved to be a huge hyena.

In January 1827 the regiment marched from Aska partly along the beautiful banks of the Mahanadi river towards Nagpur. Mackenzie kept a regular military journal of the march, noting distances, nature of the ground, state of roads, supplies, water, the health of the troops, etc., interspersed with notices of the romantic country, mountains covered with wood, and jungles full of tigers. There are continual notes—"Lad taken off by tiger." "Two old men belonging to regiment (*i.e.* to the families of the Sepoys who move with the men, mothers, grandmothers, and all) left in the jungle by the coolies, and devoured by wild beasts." "At night the Vakil (agent) and mess company attacked by several tigers at once, one bullock carried off. By torches and firing got back safe to camp. Great uproar. Strange assertion of the villagers that, in consequence of yearly offerings, none of them are carried off." [1] He often notes, "People suspicious," and sometimes "Village deserted." The officer in charge of a district generally sent out a "Bazar" (*i.e.* a set of shopkeepers) to supply the wants of the regiment, and entertained the officers *en masse* when they reached his station.

At one place they had to cross some very steep Ghâts (mountain or river passes) "composed of large blocks of gneiss, exceedingly difficult for carriage of any description." The march of nine miles took four hours.

"No supplies whatever. Water good. After breakfast returned with as many hands as we could muster to assist the

---

[1] Tigers are still generally worshipped in many parts of the country. Rude wooden images of them are placed at the entrance of the villages, and when one is slain, the people prostrate themselves before its body.

carts. With great exertion by 3 P.M. we got them all over the most difficult parts. Only one or two broke down. Suffered much from thirst, the water-carriers being very slack in bringing water. Lamentable want of spirit shown by the Sepoys in working. Obliged to bellow myself hoarse. Much pleased by the activity of two men of my company (the 2d), one very ugly, the other the best made, handsomest man I have seen for a long time."

It was owing to this habit of putting his hand to whatever work was to be done that he never found any difficulty in getting his men to do it. A few years later he was still more successful, as, instead of "bellowing" at them, he was full of jokes and encouraging remarks; so that, on one occasion in the Sátpura hills, wishing to make a garden-path for his wife, his orderlies (high-caste Brahmans among them) voluntarily toiled like day-labourers because the Sahib was the first to dig and to use the mattock. Even now, as we see, he never left zeal or good work unnoticed.

The extensive jungles near Nagpur abound in tigers and other wild beasts. Mackenzie used to go after them in company with a first-rate sportsman, Major Sheriff, commonly called "Tiger Sheriff." Once they went about 7 P.M. to a tree which had been fixed on in the heart of the forest, and in which a platform of branches, covered by a thin mattress and fenced round with boughs, had been made for them. Here they waited in silence for their game, an unhappy bullock being tethered to the tree beneath. It was a glorious tropical moonlight night. The jungle opposite had caught fire, and the flames were seen darting up the mountain-side, meandering along in swift rivulets, first in one direction, then in another, in a manner worthy of the most capricious of elements. The night-bird broke the deep silence of the woods with its melancholy whoo-whoo, and anon a bear was seen passing with

its loose, shambling gait, or a pack of wolves went stealthily
by, their tails between their legs, and their cunning eyes
peering hither and thither, and ever and anon the un-
earthly, ghostlike laugh of the hyena was heard.   All the
sights and sounds were of a nature to fascinate and enthral
the imagination.   At last they heard the roar of a tiger in
the distance, and then the dull, heavy plunge he made in
leaping the stream.   He soon drew near, and (as their
manner is) began gliding round and round the bullock, his
destined victim.   The poor creature, waving itself to and
fro, so as almost to touch the ground with its body, turned
and faced the tiger wherever he went, and at last broke its
rope, and the tiger bounded away.   Major Sheriff desired
his Brahman attendant to go down and tie his god, but
the bullock, suspicious of men and beasts in general, rushed
at the poor Brahman, tossed him in the air, made off into
the jungle, tail on end, and was seen no more.   They
therefore signalled for their elephants, and rode home,
passing a pack of wild dogs, one of which Major Sheriff
shot with a " plug."   The poor animal was nearly cut in
two, yet it ran on, and was lost in the jungle.

These dogs always hunt in packs, and will even pursue
the tiger.   When they overtake him, they make a simultaneous charge, and although he generally kills four or five,
yet he succumbs to the force of numbers.   The next night,
Mackenzie, Major Sheriff, and a friend took up their position upon another tree, where the latter had been stationed
the night before.   A tiger had killed his bullock, but he
had not been able to get a shot at it.   Before very long,
two jackals came up to the slain bullock, tripping along
silently ; one began to eat, the other placed himself as
sentry at the end of a narrow strip of jungle, which connected the forest where they were with the wooded mountain
opposite.   Here he ran to and fro, first peeping on one

side, then on the other, keeping the sharpest possible look-out, until he thought his ally had had enough, when he ran up to him, shook him by the scruff of the neck, and, after a short parley, the latter, seeming convinced of the justice of his arguments, padded away to his post, while the chack, chack, chack, of the little teeth of the late sentry was heard over the slaughtered bullock. Suddenly, without sound or warning, the jackals vanished, and in their stead stood a magnificent tigress, looking more majestic, soft, and beautiful in the moonlight than can be described. She fixed her large yellow eyes on the sportsmen, and they thought they were discovered; but she saw them not, and after cautiously circling round and round her prey, she began to devour it, keeping up a low, savage growl of satis-faction. Bang, bang, went the balls through her head. After a time, the hunters cautiously descended, pistol in hand, and found her quite dead. They covered her with branches, and returned to the tree, in hope of smaller game; but at last Major Sheriff grew weary, summoned his palanquin, and coolly departed, leaving Mackenzie and his friend to walk back four miles, in the midst of the night, through a forest filled with wild beasts of every descrip-tion; but by God's goodness, they were brought home in safety. It was impossible to describe the romantic charm of the scene. You saw man going home to rest from his labour, just as a new world was waking into life.

In those days home letters were not only six to eight months on the way, but their arrival was very uncertain. Mackenzie complains (August 1827, Kampti) that he has written twenty-five long letters to his family, most of which never reached them. He had received only two, and "know-ing the little care taken of packets on board ship, he is almost discouraged from writing at all." Speaking of his father's pecuniary losses, he writes to his sister Mary :—

"I never conceived for a moment that his fortitude could be shaken by any earthly calamity. The love and veneration I feel for his truly noble character make me wonder that I ever dared to offend him by word or deed. Among all the motives I have for exerting myself to rise with honour in my profession, the idea of giving pleasure to my father is infinitely the most powerful. Putting the naturally high and strong mind of my dear mother out of the question, the idolatry with which she regards my father would induce her to act as you so enthusiastically describe."

Mr. Mackenzie possessed a great degree of the self-denying habits and stoicism characteristic of Scotland at that time, and it is not astonishing that, with this noble nature before his mind, the young officer was filled with disgust at the low type of "old Indian," which was then only too common. He was at this time trying to get into the Nagpur Irregular Horse. Most of the officers in camp were attacked by fever, three died, and he rejoices that "his abstemious mode of life, joined to instant bleeding and sharp medicine, had enabled him to get on his legs again." As jungle fever is of a typhoid character, the marvel is that he survived the remedies. He continues :—

"You would laugh to see me at the head of my company. There is a curious combination of colours—red coats, white trousers, black faces, and blue turbans, with a brass ball at the top. They look very military, however, and their long moustaches give them quite a slaughtering aspect. Strange to say, in their manœuvres the Sepoys are generally much steadier than Europeans."

He describes his Colonel as a coarse, stupid man and a regular sot, but inoffensive :—

"I dislike him principally because he takes no interest in the Corps, and never exerts himself in any respect. But he is not a bit worse than the general run of old Indians, who commonly present an awful picture of the low state of degradation into which a man will fall by yielding habitually to vice, sloth, and enervating luxury. You would be horrified ! . . . Without religion, morality, or anything to check them in the indulgence of every bad habit, they dwindle into second childhood ere they reach what is usually considered the prime of life, and sink into the grave, their minds and bodies equally decayed, without even the power of feeling remorse for the past, or hope for the future. When I look at two or three examples before me in Kampti I shudder, and pray God not to suffer me to become like them. I wish the Army were cleared of the greater part of these persons, as they are quite ineffective in military matters, and set an awful example to those under them."[1]

His stay at Kampti was brought to a close by two very severe attacks of Nagpur fever, of which he would probably have died but for the unceasing care and attention of Colonel George Hunter, who brought him to his own house, sat up with him at night, fed him with his own hand, and, humanly speaking, brought him back to life. "None but my own mother," he says, "could have nursed me better."

In Europe good service can generally be bought, so that we have almost lost the habit of nursing our sick friends ; but in India, where men are not only isolated from their families, but where a good nurse is not to be hired, it is the universal custom to fly to the aid of any one who is ill, even though a perfect stranger. Officers or ladies take it by turns to sit up with an invalid. Those who have comfortable houses take possession of the sick bachelor ; those who are in a fine climate invite a convalescent to come and

---

[1] In the early days of the Company the Directors expressed anxiety for the conversion of the "Gentoos" and the morality of their own servants, but at this time religion and morality were at so low an ebb among the Europeans that on one occasion a Bible being required at a court-martial none could be found, until one was at last discovered in the possession of a lady.

share it ; and all learn to render many kindly offices with their own hands which are hardly required at home where good servants are to be had. Mackenzie was ordered to Europe, or, as he expressed it in a letter to his mother : " The doctors gave me the choice between a trip to England or indenting on John Company for certain cartridges.[1] I am afraid I will be obliged to obtain a temporary loan from my father on my arrival—a consideration that would effec-tually chain me to this country were it not for the extremity of the case."

It is curious to find such a purist in English grammar as he afterwards became, still adhering to the usage of the North in putting " will " for " shall."

After a journey of 900 miles to reach the coast, he embarked from Calcutta 1st March 1830.

[1] For the firing party at a funeral.

CHAPTER III.

(1830–1834.)

AMONG Mackenzie's fellow-passengers on his first home-ward voyage was a well-known Bengal civilian, Mr. James Pattle, with his charming wife, their eldest daughter Adeline, and two infant children. Mrs. Pattle, one of the most amiable of women, was a French lady, daughter of the Chévalier de l'Etang, who had been a page of Marie Antoinette, and who was sent out to Pondicherry to escape a *lettre de cachet*. There he married Therèse Blin de Grin-court, daughter of the Governor, and had three daughters, all brought up at St. Cyr under Madame Campan. The Chévalier, after the surrender of Pondicherry, removed to Ghazipur, and, his daughters having joined him, all married in India.

Mr. Pattle and his eldest daughter (then barely eighteen) landed at the Cape, but "propinquity" had already induced a tender feeling in the latter towards the handsome young officer. He accompanied her mother, who was in very bad health, to England. He found his parents settled in London, 18 Montague Square, and the father and son now mutually appreciated each other. The former said on one occasion: "Colin is a noble fellow; he will always acknow-ledge a fault." But they were not long to enjoy each other's society.

Colin's recovery was slow, for he had retarded it by nursing and sitting up with a sick kinsman, Captain Duncan Mackenzie, who suffered from epileptic fits. May in the following year, 1831, found him still an invalid, though a visit of some duration to Hampton Court was very beneficial. But he was dissatisfied with himself, and consequently with everything around him. He writes to his sister :—

"The races at Ascot are expected to be splendid, but the finest spectacles have no charm for me. Even Nature, in her most beautiful garb, instead of delighting, almost always suggests melancholy thoughts. I go on the principle that no species of happiness is worth having which cannot endure, and none but thoughtless people can succeed in deluding themselves into a belief of the durability of any of this miserable world's enjoyments. If ever a sensation of gladness crosses me, I am absolutely startled by it, and my mind naturally reverts on the instant to something which is sure to drive away the intrusive feeling. To have lost at the age of five-and-twenty, absolutely from disuse, the faculty of enjoyment, might seem hard to some, but I do not regret it, as by that means the most grievous calamity, though it may cause a feeling of grief mixed with anger, can never surprise me. Besides I have been so long accustomed to the society of difficulties and all sorts of annoyances, that were I freed from them all, I should miss them so much, that my mind would be constantly on the *qui vive* for a misfortune, which, trust me, would not be long in making its appearance."

At this time it seemed as if Poland were about to regain the freedom of which she had been so atrociously deprived in 1772. One of his brothers became Secretary of the Polish Association, and, fired with generous enthusiasm for a cruelly oppressed and gallant people, Colin pledged himself to join the Polish army. His father's health rapidly declined, but he kept his word and embarked on board an

English ship laden with arms. With great difficulty they escaped from the Russian fleet which effectually prevented their landing. The Prussians threatened to fire on them—the Hamburgers to sink the vessel; and in order to prevent the Danish custom-house officers at Elsinore from boarding, they were obliged to hoist the yellow cholera flag. All they gained by their expedition was positive information that the Prussians were sending arms, provisions, and men to the aid of Russia, and that they had allowed Paskewitch to march through their territory after a quarantine of three days instead of sixteen![1]

He received the news of his father's death while on this expedition; and one of his French comrades, seeing him sad and downcast, kindly endeavoured to cheer him by saying, *Mon ami burons à la mémoire de ton père!* In the autumn, after his return, Mrs. Pattle, who was then at Brighton, invited Colin Mackenzie to stay with her. He did so, and soon became engaged to her daughter Adeline. They were married, 28th May 1832, at St. Mary's, Bryanstone Square, and set sail for Madras in company with the newly-appointed Governor, Sir Frederick Adam, who was ever his fast friend. They arrived on the 23d October 1832, and rejoined the 48th M.N.I., then stationed at Madras.

The young couple stayed for a time with a very kind friend, Mr. Oliver, a Member of Council. The system of centralisation was at that time carried to such an absurd length as to paralyse the action of the Governments of Madras and of the Straits. A ludicrous instance of this occurred. Mackenzie asked his host one day "if much

---

[1] This affair brought Mackenzie into close intimacy with many Polish gentlemen, and Prince Czartorisky always retained a warm affection for him. After his return to India, he, with characteristic energy, set on foot a subscription for the Polish exiles, and remitted several hundred pounds to them.

business had been transacted in the Council Chamber?"—
"No," said he; "but Adam has been swearing fearfully."—
"Why?"—"Because, as is usual, our time has been taken
up in considering the propriety of adding one more sweeper
to the strength of a certain hospital; and, after all, we have
been obliged to refer the question of his pay—viz. 3½
rupees (7s.) per mensem—for the approbation of the Supreme Government. Moreover, we have received, as we
often do, a most insolent letter from one of the Calcutta
secretaries, which drove Adam frantic."

About this time Mackenzie made the acquaintance of
Captain F. Chalmers (afterwards Rector of Beckenham),
the first decided Christian he ever knew, and who subsequently became dearer than a brother to him. The circumstance is thus related by Mr. Chalmers himself:—

"My first recollections of my beloved friend would not have
counted for so much with a less remarkable man, but he made a
large opening for himself in my heart, and got deep down into
it, and stayed there; and there he will remain till we meet
again. My friendship with him began with one of the turning
points in my life, in the year 1833. A severe affliction had, the
year before, brought me to the knowledge of a Saviour, and I had
been just nominated to a political appointment in the Mysore
Commission, and was consequently to vacate the Cantonment
Adjutancy, with charge of the Police, at St. Thomas' Mount, the
artillery headquarters. It was a most pleasant appointment, the
officers of the artillery being superior men; and it was moreover
one of the best paid military appointments which a subaltern
could hold. I received a note from the Adjutant-General to say
that the Commander-in-Chief was about to nominate Lieutenant
Colin Mackenzie as my successor, and requesting me to receive
him and show him the routine of the duties, both on parade and
in the Cantonment Office. He accordingly came, and remained,
I think, two days. I at once perceived that he was a thorough
gentleman, and every inch a soldier, and was rejoicing in the

thought that I was leaving such a man amongst the many kind artillery friends I had at the Mount. On the second morning, however, a mounted orderly arrived very unexpectedly, bearing a second note from the Government Office, to say that there were too many officers absent from his regiment, and that he could not be spared at the present for staff employment. This was of course a great and sudden disappointment to him, especially as a young married man; and most men of the world would have met it with anger or impatience. Dear Colin, however, bore it *nobly.* He was getting much interested in what he believed to be his new and varied duties; but though naturally grieved, not a word of murmuring escaped his lips, and he declared that it was no more than his duty cheerfully to submit, and left me with some kind expressions of hope that we might meet again. My interest in him and admiration for him were, however, intensely awakened, and I inwardly resolved that, if it pleased God, such a man should be my friend.

"The opportunity was not wanting. Not long afterwards the Coorg war broke out, in which he distinguished himself. He then, to my great satisfaction, came to Bangalore for a short residence, and I made the most of the opportunity for further intercourse with him. At St. Thomas' Mount he had joined with me in morning and evening prayer, and again at Bangalore he was willing to meet with one or two Christian brother officers and friends, and remained for family worship, which he seemed to enjoy. Our friendship rapidly increased, but he was soon afterwards ordered to the Straits of Malacca, again distinguishing himself in some naval encounters with the Malays.

"We occasionally exchanged letters, and our Christian fellowship grew and ripened as the time went by."

In March 1833 Mackenzie's eldest child, a daughter, was born.

His wife was of a most affectionate, unselfish disposition and sweet temper; not pretty, but with fine eyes, a beautiful fair skin, and much of her mother's grace. She had received

some scriptural instruction from an aunt, and her Bible still
contains a list of passages on the necessity of regeneration.
She had naturally a good memory and good judgment, but
too little confidence in herself, and had never formed the
habit of reading anything beyond a novel.   The young
husband's letters are full of admonitions on the necessity
of mental occupation.   With touching humility she tells
him, three years afterwards, that her father had remarked
how much he had improved her since she became his wife,
adding :—

"This gave me great pleasure.   I cannot tell you how truly
thankful I am to the Almighty for having blessed me with so
pure and high-minded a man as yourself.   I am very careful not
to indulge in any scandal to which you have so decided an
objection."

She was devoted to her husband, who was sincerely
attached to her, and who doted on his infant children.
There is a pretty note from him when on guard at Bangalore,
beginning :—

"Mony braw thanks for the care you have taken of your
poor servant.   As far as bodily comforts go you have made the
main guard as snug as 'my ain house ;' but I have much missed
what forms at all times the chief pleasure of my life.   You may
guess what that is !"

In October he made a trip with a friend to the Gairsoppa
Falls ; and meeting General Cubbon, the Commissioner of
Mysore, who entertained them magnificently, they joined
his camp, shooting through the beautiful jungle.   Missing
his horse one day, Mackenzie had to walk several miles in
terrible heat ; but "fortunately," he says, "the missing
steed 'Jock' came up just as I had apprehended a footpad,
whom I found robbing an old woman.   Him I conducted

in triumph to the awful presence of Colonel Cubbon, who (in vulgar parlance) settled his hash."

This year was marked by a great sorrow. His young brother Townsend, a beautiful, fair-haired lad, had entered H.M.'s 46th foot. A cold caught in Fife settled on his lungs, no alarm was taken until too late, and he died on the 29th January 1833. Never was a young life more needlessly sacrificed.

When Townsend joined the army, Colin, knowing that English pay was insufficient, sent him an order on his agents for £50 a year as long as he needed it. Townsend, with equal generosity, resolved not to avail himself of the offer, and contrived to live on his pay. When he died a small arrear due to him was forwarded to his mother as his heir, and she devoted it to the purchase of a silver salver with the inscription: "For Colin Mackenzie, in remembrance of his dear lamented brother J. T. Townsend Mackenzie, from their affectionate mother."

Mackenzie always reverted with the utmost tenderness to the memory of this young brother. Long after he wrote, 17th May 1836 :—

"I have been thinking a good deal of Townsend. When I remember the strong ties of affection which bound us together, even during his early boyhood, the generous, noble traits of character that developed themselves constantly while we were in the daily habit of going to Dr. Donne's school together, where he found a protector in me, and I an object of anxious (almost paternal) love in him ; his burst of grief on my parting from him to come to India, and the matured good qualities and extraordinary excellence in one so young which gratified me on my return home ;—my heart swells almost to bursting, and my eyes overflow with tears, the bitterness of which is hardly lessened by my firm conviction that the Almighty called him in mercy so early from this most sinful and, through sin, most wretched world. . . I do not think even time can mitigate my feelings."

In 1834 the 48th regiment marched to Bangalore, and Lieut. Mackenzie, on being made Adjutant, rode up to the Adjutant-General and thanked him for the appointment. "You needn't thank me," was the reply — "There is not another officer in the regiment fit for it." The Colonel, though a kind-hearted man, was never satisfied unless he was in hot water with either one of his officers or the civil authorities, and the work his Adjutant had to keep him quiet is not to be described. In this he was heartily seconded by the good, kind wife of the Colonel, who was like a mother to every officer in the regiment, and who exerted all her tact and kind-heartedness to keep her unquiet spouse out of mischief.

CHAPTER IV.

COORG CAMPAIGN.

(1834.)

IN the meantime the misgovernment of the Coorg country had reached a climax which compelled even so mild and peace-loving a Governor-General as Lord William Bentinck to intervene by force.

This beautiful hill country, which lies to the west of Mysore, had been rescued from the tyranny of Tippu Sultan and restored to its native rulers by the British in 1792, yet it was completely closed to Europeans, and as even natives who once entered it were hardly ever permitted to leave, the insane atrocities of the Rajas were but little known. The last three of these petty sovereigns were monsters of cruelty. They were addressed as Máhá Swámi, or "Great God," worshipped not only by prostrations but by sacrifices, and implicitly obeyed, no one daring to question any command. General Welsh, who visited Coorg as the guest of the penultimate Raja, gives the following description :—

"The Raja, being acknowledged as the god of the country, exercised his supposed rights without remorse and without control. For instance, if a poor fellow standing in his presence with both hands joined in adoration as of the Supreme, and incessantly calling out Máhá Swámi, should be bit by a mosquito and loose his hands to scratch, a sign too well known would instantly be made by this *soi-disant* Deity, and the poor wretch be a head shorter in a twinkling."

This officer found an unfortunate native butler, who had somehow come into Coorg, and it was only by stratagem that he succeeded in carrying him away, and thus rescuing him from hopeless captivity. The last Raja, Virárája, was considered "less cruel than his father," as he was reckoned to have destroyed "*not more* than 1500 lives," yet his iniquities will hardly bear recapitulation. He had obtained the throne by the murder of his cousin, the acknowledged Ráni (Queen) of Coorg, and her sister, first putting their hands into boiling oil, and then hanging them. He destroyed every one of his family, and when his own sister and her husband contrived to fly to Bangalore for refuge, he demanded that they should be handed over to him. This being of course refused, he wrote letters filled with the grossest abuse to the Governor-General and the Governor of Madras, and finished by seizing a native Envoy from Government and casting him into prison.

Lord William Bentinck, though most averse to war, saw the necessity of putting an end to the terrible oppression and cruelty under which the people of Coorg groaned. He therefore formally deposed the Raja (15th March 1834), and sent a force of 6000 men to take possession of the country under Brigadier Lindesay, accompanied by Colonel J. S. Fraser as Governor-General's Agent. The force was divided into four columns. Of these one under Colonel David Foulis from Cannanore fought their way successfully up the Haggala Pass into Coorg ; another, consisting of only 500 men, under Colonel Jackson, had been despatched from Mangalore without a single gun. They were of course defeated, and all the sick and wounded, with many camp-followers, murdered by the Coorgs, with circumstances of horrid barbarity.

Colonel Jackson demanded a court-martial, and was honourably acquitted of blame.

The northern column, under Colonel Waugh, attacked a very strong stockade in front, and failed lamentably "from not properly out-flanking it." "Taking the bull by the horns they were, of course, miserably gored," losing 48 killed and 118 wounded. The enemy were commanded by a gallant Coorg, who afterwards became Head Sherishtádár (Clerk of Court) and a most loyal servant of the British Government.

The eastern columns (of which the 48th M.N.I. formed part), under Brigadier Lindesay, did the work. The Colonel of the 48th was absent, and owing to the incapacity and apathy of the acting commanding officer, the regiment was in "a shameful state, the men insubordinate, and not one duty properly performed,"—a state of things most galling to Mackenzie as Adjutant. It was therefore with delight that, a few days after beginning the march, he received the appointment of Deputy-Assistant Quartermaster-General under Major Steel. He writes to his wife :—

"Is it not an odd thing that I should always be so pressed for time ? At Bangalore I was called upon to enact Adjutant when there was barely time to get a steel scabbard, and here I am appointed to a Staff situation, which requires much peculiar knowledge and experience, at 5 P.M. to-day, and march to-morrow morning at 3 A.M. in my new vocation. My spirits are somewhat raised by the pleasant change in my situation, and by the excitement occasioned by the commencement of operations. Active employment heats the blood wonderfully."

The day before the force reached the Coorg frontier, Captain *Elizabeth*[1] Byam and Lieut. Mackenzie, attended by twenty spearmen, were sent forward to reconnoitre it.

---

[1] This was not a lady, but a very gallant officer, universally called *behind his back* Betty Byam.

They returned after a ride of four-and-twenty miles in the
broiling sun, much fatigued, and their faces "burnt to a
cinder." The next morning, on arriving at the Kávari (2d
April), Colonel Fraser himself rode forward and attempted
to cross the river with a flag of truce to offer terms, but
was fired on.

Our guns then opened a beautiful fire on the stockade
on the opposite bank, under cover of which the advanced
guard, led by three officers (Mackenzie being one of them),
made a rush through the river, which was about 200 yards
broad. Mackenzie had dismounted to lead on foot, and
got one or two tumbles from the slippery bottom of the
stream. He says :—

"Up the steep bank we sped, somewhat blown, but before
we could reach them the fellows evaporated, leaving matchlocks,
bows and arrows, swords, etc. Expecting to meet with a strong
body behind the steep eminence in front, we advanced, and
having surmounted the hill, found, to our surprise, that two
donkeys formed all the opposing force! The position was a
very strong one. . . . What a gallant veteran Lindesay is! I
saw his eye light up when the firing commenced, and the coolness of his manner and quiet promptness with which he hastened
across the river after us, and came on with the advance, and the
hilarity of his features showed that if the resistance had been
serious he would have looked on it as a piece of excellent sport.
I could not help laughing at Byam during the run up the Ghát.
Being exhausted, he hooked his fingers in the belt of a stout
private of the 39th, telling him to lug him along, and that when
it was over a stiff glass of grog should be his, to which, of course,
the man readily assented."

This was the first time Mackenzie was in action, and
he used to relate that leading the grenadiers of the 39th
across the river under fire of the battery, he felt his lip
quiver and bit it with indignation. Turning to look at

the men, he beheld them all as pale as death, but with
lips compressed, and nothing but determination in their
countenances. He said he never was more delighted than
to observe their pallor. More than twenty years later,
General Fraser wrote to him :—

"I view you still just with the feelings I did many a long
year ago when I saw you, sword in hand, rushing up the rocky
hill at Ramaswamy Kanáve in front of a party of H.M.'s 39th
to disperse the wild but brave fellows who opposed us."

Mackenzie's letter continues :—

"After breakfast on the 3d, Steel (who is a right good
officer), Byam, and I started to reconnoitre a stockade on a hill
three miles off. The moment we came in sight the worthy
gentlemen, piqued no doubt by having been thumped in the
morning, opened a fire of jingals (small cannon) and matchlocks
not only while we were advancing and reconnoitring, but even
after we were out of sight and had returned to camp ! There
was some stiff work when the force advanced on the 4th. They
were fighting and marching from daylight till 3 P.M. under a
burning sun. Took the stockade and pagoda early in the morning, an entrenched barrier in the afternoon, forcing many barri-
cadoes. Byam and I headed two storming parties, very fatiguing
work, and both escaped. Not a thing did I get to eat till 5 P.M.
I am most thankful to the Almighty for having shielded me from
the dangers of the day, which are not great or small, according to
our idea of them, but as He is pleased to direct."

He relates an act of heroic bravery on the part of a
Naik (native corporal). A party of native sappers were
ordered to cut down one of these stockades which the
troops had failed in scaling. It was at the top of a straight
steep path, a precipice on one side and a thick wood on the
other, with a tremendous fire of musketry pouring down
on the assailants. Nevertheless they went gallantly on,
till every one was shot down except this one naik, who

continued hacking at the gate with his axe. He received
a wound in the leg which brought him to his knees, but he
still worked on. At last a shot from above hit him near
the collar-bone, and passed through his body. He fell, but
in dying hurled his axe against the enemy.

On the 5th they marched towards Merkara, the capital
(called in these old despatches Mudkerry), "through
passes certainly insurmountable if properly defended. The
Diwán (minister) and four hundred of his best followers,
instead of defending the strongest stockade we have yet
met with, which would have cost us many lives, came over
to us, and after his surrender every stockade yielded without defence! The baggage did not come up, so I slept *al
fresco* beside Jock" (his Arab horse).

The following day the column took possession of Merkara. The Raja having fled to his stronghold, Nakánád,
about seventeen miles off, was summoned by Colonel Fraser
to surrender. He sent in his personal attendants and *cooks*
—a sure sign that he was coming—and then his women.
Mackenzie was sent to receive the Raja, with two companies under Captain Forbes to disarm his followers. They
waited from 3 P.M. till midnight at the "Gate of Execution," when at length the Raja arrived, "with an immense
suite of fifty-three palkies, and numerous torch-bearers, who
looked very picturesque winding up the defile. He alighted
from his palki on seeing us, and shook hands with all near
him, looking much dejected. He is short, with a good
aquiline nose, well-shaped face, and handsome mouth, but
low forehead, and a very debauched sinister expression, his
eyes (perhaps from the immediate circumstances) showing
the suspicious uneasy feeling of a capricious and ferocious
tyrant. His reception of Boppu, his Diwán, who came
over to us, was very marked, treating all his professions
and humility, while he grovelled before him in the dust,

with a sort of savage contempt. I did not pity the Raja,
but treated him with marked courtesy and respect, which,
I regret to say, was not generally done, that clown —— in
the absence of Captain Forbes presuming to ask the fallen
wretch a number of impertinent questions, assuming a dis-
gustingly vulgar and familiar air towards him. I was so
angry that at last I broke out and gave him my mind pretty
freely. Much as the man deserves his fate, he was an independent sovereign, and to behave with insolence towards
even a fallen tyrant betrays a soul that in the day of the
despot's power would have crouched before him; I could
scarcely refrain from kicking the blackguard!" which would
have been a very Irish way of teaching courtesy!

The Raja was eventually sent to Bangalore and thence
to Benares under charge of Captain Carpenter, 48th M.N.I.
The chief instigator and instrument of most of the acts of
abominable cruelty in this unhappy country, a man named
Básává, a Bádágá of low caste who had risen from the post
of dog-boy to that of Diwán, hanged himself in the most
determined manner, placing a second rope ready at the foot of
the tree in case the first should break. Colonel Fraser fully
believed that Básává had committed suicide, but after the
Raja had left the country the truth leaked out, that he had
been hanged by order of the Raja, who was thus able to
throw all the blame of his own atrocities upon him.[1] This
Raja was the man who afterwards handed over his
daughter Gaurama to the Queen, who gave her her own

[1] In 1857 the Raja often called on Major Mackenzie in London,
generally at dinner-time, and when asked what he would have, invariably replied: "Mutton chop and currant tart." He was staying in
England to carry on a suit against the E. I. Company to recover a
large sum which they had confiscated, but which was really the property
of his cousin, the young Ráni, whom he had murdered. It was curious
to see a man whose power had been as unlimited as that of the "Old
Man of the Mountain" going about London alone like any Englishman.

name in baptism, watched over her with conscientious care and kindness, and placed her in the charge of Mrs. Henry Drummond, who, to use Her Majesty's own gracious words, "fulfilled a duty of the most difficult and delicate kind with affectionate care and Christian solicitude, acting the part of a devoted mother to this poor girl."

Victoria Gaurama married an English officer and died young.

Mackenzie describes the whole Coorg country as "the most romantic and beautiful perhaps in the world, with splendid views, one of which, through an interval in the Western Gháts, gave a glimpse of the sea about thirty miles distant. The sea is intimately connected with all the principal events of my life, good and evil. I never look at it or hear its roar in tempest or its murmur at peace without deep melancholy, mixed with a sense of our complete nothingness, at the same time looking up with fervent trusting adoration to the great Creator and Preserver of all."

The active work of the campaign was now over, and Mackenzie, being on the Staff, lived almost entirely at Colonel Cubbon's, enjoying the society of Colonel Fraser,[1] of his own chief Major Steel, and of Lieutenant Robertson of the Commissariat. He used to mention an incident which shows the weight of even a few words from a man of high character and position. Some one at table was making a parade of infidel opinions. Colonel Fraser said shortly, "You have *not* read Paley's *Evidences*," which destroyed the effect of the unbeliever's assertions, and aroused a desire to read the book. He fully appreciated the advantage of being under so excellent an officer as Major Steel, and writes :—

"Old Seton and Cubbon are such fine fellows, and Colonel Fraser is as little chary of his carcase as any *preux* chevalier of old."

---

[1] Major-General James Stuart Fraser, afterwards the accomplished and high-spirited Resident at the Court of the Nizám.

He relates the wonderful escape of a soldier of H.M.'s 55th, who, after Colonel Waugh's disastrous defeat, was left in the jungle with two balls in his leg :—

"The Raja's followers murdered all our wounded and mutilated the dead. This man, seeing a Coorg approach with the amiable intent of smiting off his head, received the cut on his left arm, which was gashed from wrist to elbow. Too weak to make a lunge with his bayonet, he fixed it against his chest, threw himself upon his adversary, and the bayonet entered the Coorg's heart. At night the jackals scented the blood and ate up the Coorg's body as it lay at his feet. Two days and nights did the poor fellow lie in this horrible situation, unable to do more than turn himself a little. The jackals, after devouring the Coorg before his eyes, kept prowling round and round him. He was so weak that he could only faintly wave his bayonet and cry ' Ugh ! ugh !' whenever they came too near. At last some Coorg peasants found him, and, as a truce had been agreed upon, instead of slaying him, they took him to a hut and gave him milk, though they could do nothing for his hurts. The column again advancing found him in a most deplorable state, the maggots dropping from his wounds. The doctors pronounced amputation of both leg and arm necessary, but as the man was too exhausted to bear the operation, they fortunately only cleansed and bound up the wounds, and he finally recovered without losing a limb."

The last time Mackenzie saw him he was sitting up smoking a pipe and relating his adventure to his comrades.

In addition to a good deal of hard work at the desk, it was Mackenzie's duty to scour the country in all directions, riding thirty miles in a morning to explore roads or to endeavour to find the Raja's hidden treasures. The latter quest proved a bootless one, and although he was appointed one of the Prize Agents of the force, he derived no benefit from that usually lucrative office.

He records a curious instance of native flattery and the childishness so often characteristic of despots :—

" I visited a sort of Golgotha for the skulls of upwards of two hundred elephants, said to have been shot by the Raja or his father. Each skull had a hole bored exactly in the middle of the forehead, the fools wishing to make it appear (having stopped up the real shot holes) that the Raja has killed each by shooting him through a part of the skull which is really musket proof."

Not long after he had an adventure which shows the wildness of the country, and which might have proved very serious. Having lent a young officer one of his Arabs, they started for a ride and came upon a number of trees felled across the road (former work by the Coorgs for the annoyance of our advancing columns), whereupon they turned off into a path which led into the jungle, until they were suddenly stopped by a wall of thorns and all manner of obstacles. Prompted by the spirit of adventure, they with great difficulty pushed on for about two hundred yards, when they heard the evening gun, and, in endeavouring to re-gain open ground, completely lost themselves in the darkness and deep recesses of the forest. They struggled on, cutting down the sticks and creepers in their way to enable them to get through the jungle, until they were utterly exhausted. At length by God's mercy they reached a small open space, affording a little free air and some grass for "Jock" and "Waverley," the two Arabs who had contrived to follow their master. Mackenzie and his companion were bathed in perspiration, and their thirst amounted almost to agony, while the cold wind made their teeth chatter. There they passed the night, sometimes lying down close to each other for warmth, then walking about when quite benumbed with cold. The two horses were so tamed by fear, that instead of fighting as usual, they became so friendly as to pull the grass out of each other's mouths. Though the forest was full of wild beasts of all sorts, nothing came near them but a huge elk, which, after gazing at them in amazement, broke away through the almost impenetrable underwood with a crash which made them fancy for the moment that it was a wild elephant rushing on them. When at length the dawn rejoiced their eyes, Mackenzie climbed a tree, and spying the barrier outside the Fort in the distance, shouted with all his might and was fortunately heard by two of his friends, Robertson and Derville, who had been searching for them half the night, accompanied by Coorgs with torches and guns, but the jungle was so dense that they had neither seen the lights nor heard the shots.

Mackenzie writes :—

"Every day some fresh instance of atrocious cruelty and tyranny on the part of the ex-Raja comes out. Men, women, and little children seem alike to have been butchered by him or his minions on the slightest pretext. The interior of the palace must for years have been a perfect shambles."

When the Raja fled to Nakánád on the approach of our troops he carried with him the remaining members of his family, especially the children of the murdered princesses, and had these helpless women and children strangled in cold blood before he surrendered.

In a month the whole Coorg country was entirely quiet, the people showed no symptoms whatever of requiring coercion, and the force was withdrawn at the beginning of May. Mackenzie incurred his wife's gentle reproach by insisting on making a present of the wine and stores he took with him to the Artillery Mess.

Apparently it was on the return march that he met with one of those trials of patience which he used to refer to as unpleasant, but wholesome for a young soldier. In his duty as Quartermaster he had ridden on ahead of the force, and pitched the camp on the proper side of a river, *i.e.* with the river in the rear. · Whether it was that the Briga- dier was vexed at having to cross a river at the end of his morning's march, or from some other cause, he was exces- sively wroth, ordered the camp to be struck, brought back, and pitched anew, contrary to all military rule, with the river in front. The fatigue and worry to all concerned of doing this in the heat of the day may be imagined, and of course tended to heighten Mackenzie's satisfaction at returning to comparatively cool quarters at Bangalore.

At the close of the campaign, the Governor-General issued an Order (17th May 1834), expressing his thanks for the zealous and gallant conduct of the troops ; but it was not the fashion in those days to give medals or honours, and the Crown still more seldom noticed or rewarded service done by the Indian army. But the extracts given below[1]

---

[1] *Extract from Colonel Lindesay, C.B., Commanding Coorg Field Force, to the Adjutant-General of the Army, Fort St. George, dated Camp Mudkerry, 11th April 1834.*

"To the unwearied exertions of Major Steel, the Deputy Quarter- master-General, I am entirely indebted for the information and arrangement which by enabling me to concentrate the Force on the Capital, so speedily and satisfactorily effected the object for which it was employed. Lieutenant Mackenzie, Deputy Assistant Quarter- master-General, has performed the minor duties with great credit."

Copy of Letter from Major-General Sir Patrick Lindesay.

PORTOBELLO, EDINBURGH,
November 18, 1838.

MY DEAR MACKENZIE,—It is with very great satisfaction that I bear testimony to your merits and qualifications as an officer, which I had ample and constant opportunities of knowing and appreciating while your Regiment was under my command at Bangalore, and after- wards in the Campaign in Coorg, when you acted as an Assistant Quartermaster-General on my Staff,—your conduct then and at all times and in all situations, was that of an intelligent, enterprising, and show the estimation in which General Lindesay held his young staff-officer.

Mackenzie had never forgotten the impression made upon him by Captain Chalmers, and it was with great pleasure that he met him again at Bangalore.

By this time he himself had learnt to pray, to trust to the providence of God, and to feel gratitude for His protection. On the march to Merkara he wrote to his wife (28th March 1834) :—

"This is Good Friday, and fervently do I implore Almighty God, for the sake of Him who died for us on this day, to bless you and our darling child, and to protect you from all evils, especially those which may affect your immortal souls. Would that my practice were conformable to my feelings, for I dare not call those sensations principles, which yield to almost every bad impulse of my unworthy nature."

He thus expresses his feelings to her at the end of the campaign :—

"How little do I deserve the protection I have experienced from our Heavenly Father! Let us, my Addy, endeavour to evince our gratitude for His signal mercies by correcting the evil of which our consciences daily convict us. Repentance, which includes amendment, alone shows the really grateful Christian."

But he was still excessively ambitious, thirsting for opportunities of distinguishing himself. At Bangalore, he fell in with T. B. Macaulay, and writes to his wife, then absent in Madras :—

excellent Officer, and I know no one whom I can conscientiously or more strongly recommend for promotion and employment.

. . . .

Adieu, my dear Mackenzie, and with best and kindest wishes for the future, and in affectionate recollection of the past, believe me to remain,—Yours most sincerely,

(Signed)   P. LINDESAY.

" Conversing with that exceedingly clever man Macaulay has reawakened feelings and ideas which, for the sake of my own peace, I had partly succeeded in smothering. I am filled with a restless desire to go to Europe. Great events are gradually ripening there, and ere long opportunities will offer themselves to daring and able men which in all probability will not occur again for a century."

If, as it appears, these were Macaulay's forecasts of the signs of the times, they were certainly not fulfilled, and Mackenzie's ambitious spirit was soon to find a higher aim.

CHAPTER V.

MALACCA AND CALCUTTA.

(1835-6.)

Fecisti nos ad Te, et inquietum est cor nostrum donec requiescat in Te.
Aug. Conf.,

Mormora sempre e geme
Finchè non torni al mar
Dove acquistò gli umori
Dove dai lunghi errori
Brama di riposar.—Metastasio.

THE Regiment was next moved to Palaveram, the Cantonment of Madras, where Mackenzie was for a time station-staff to a very peppery old officer, nicknamed "Chili Vinegar," with whom, however, he got on well, partly because he always rode "like fury" on parade. He was then for nearly two years Cantonment Magistrate at Palaveram. The most atrocious villains were constantly brought before him, and he observed that, whenever a great crime was committed, the subsequent conduct of the perpetrator was almost invariably marked by some extraordinary act of stupidity or inconsistency so as to lead to his detection.

In July 1835 he accompanied his regiment to the Straits of Malacca, his wife and two infants going on a visit to her mother and sisters in Calcutta. They little knew they were never to keep house together again.

The period which followed was probably the most unhappy of Mackenzie's life. Separated from his wife and

children, with nothing to occupy him but the drudgery of
regimental routine, having no scope for his abilities, and
seeing no prospect of any, though he was now nine-and-
twenty, he found the monotony of his life intolerable.   He
had given away his favourite Arab "Jock" before leaving
Madras, and, having allotted the larger portion of his income
to his wife, he kept neither horse nor pony.   There was no
sport, and Malacca, though a pretty place and possessing
a delightful climate, "scarcely hotter than a very hot
English summer," was entirely shut out from the civilised
world.   A month elapsed before any opportunity occurred
of sending a letter to India.   Letters took from three to
six weeks to Calcutta, there being no regular communication, while letters for Madras had to go round by Singapore
and Calcutta.

He and his two friends, Lieutenants Lang and Compton,
lived (or, in Indian parlance, "chummed") together, and
trusted to their own legs for the enjoyment of locomotion.
They solaced themselves with a pet ape called "Phantom,"
from his white face and spider-like legs.   Lang and Mackenzie used each to seize one of its hands, and scamper up
and down like two boys—as they were.

Colonel Henry and his excellent wife were as kind as
possible to all of them ; but Mackenzie writes to his wife :—
" You can have no conception of the extremity of the dull-
ness of Malacca.   You would die of *ennui*."   He speaks of
"the morbid nature of my temperament"—"my usual
cynical endurance"—"my fellow brutes"—and says, "With
my usual miserable spirits, I cannot write letters in any
but a dismal tone," a description of himself quite unrecog-
nisable by those who knew the indomitable cheerfulness
he displayed in the very depths of misery and peril in
Afghanistan, or his happy disposition in later life.   So true
it is that joy is one of the fruits of the Spirit.   (Gal. v. 22.)

There can be no doubt that this trying period of inaction and apparent waste of all his powers was part of the discipline Divine Love saw to be needful for him. He had much opportunity for serious thought, and writes :—

"The imperative duty of placing ourselves and all belonging to us with implicit confidence in the hands of a most kind and merciful Providence is, at times, a difficult task. Convinced, however, as I am, that every event, not specially the result of our own free will, is controlled by the inscrutable wisdom of our Creator, whose sole object in conferring existence upon us was to enable us to attain everlasting happiness, I endeavour to resign myself and mine unreservedly to whatever may be in store for us,—accepting benefits with a sense of gratitude rendered deeper by my intimate knowledge of my own utter unworthiness, and submitting to calamity with the earnest wish, if not the power, to abstain from vain repinings."

In after years, when he held so strongly the doctrine that the will of God is supreme in His own universe, and that the will of man is never free until it has been freed from the bondage of sin by the Holy Spirit, he would strenuously have combated the theory here implied—that the results of our own free will are to be excepted from the control of inscrutable wisdom. He adds, almost as if by a presentiment :—

"With regard to affliction, I cannot but wonder at our extraordinary perverseness in that respect, inasmuch as, while submitting to a severe surgical operation, however the severity of our bodily suffering may extort groans and cries, we are not thereby shaken in our belief as to the good results of what occasions us so much present pain ; neither are we led to distrust the skill and good intentions of the operator. How much more ought hope, confidence, and resignation to be exerted when the eternal welfare of both body and soul requires a salutary, though perhaps grievous, infliction ?"

It was a good sign that he respected faithful missionaries and sought their society. He writes :—

"I am much interested in the Chinese College here. Mr. Evans, at the head of it, is a very learned, pious person, and indefatigable in the discharge of his duties as missionary. I cultivate him. He has given me access to the college library, which contains a great number of very valuable works."

A month later he writes :—

"My patience has at length failed me entirely, and if K. [his brother] would but inform me of the best way of disposing of our paltry inheritance [in Demerara], I would tear my red coat to tatters and be off to Van Dieman's Land. I would rather be a dumb animal or a reptile than lead the life I do at present and have led for years.

"My existence is at present a blank. But for the hope of again embracing you and my little darlings, and the consciousness that even my profitless life is of some value and advantage to those I love so dearly, I could wish it were the will of God that I should cumber the earth no longer. Nearly thirty years have passed since I first drew breath, and what am I ? what have I been ? and what am I likely to be ? Born with excellent talents, it pleased God to give me an inclination to excel, with an ardent admiration of virtue and a deep-rooted scorn of what is base and vicious. Thwarted by fate, to what has all this tended ? Only to make me more wretchedly sensible that the original purpose of my being has been utterly baulked. In my education, I may say that, as far as moral and religious instruction went, no fish was tendered me, but a serpent. In my journey through life I did not ask to be led by the inglorious path of ease and sensual enjoyment ; on the contrary, I longed to pursue the thorny and rugged route of—call it what you will —ambition, doing good to my race, exalting virtue at the expense of vice, obtaining deserved praise and just renown for myself. My choice would have been in favour of a life of labour and honourable exertion. To what was I condemned ? To a state of existence worse than that of a horse who wearily goes the round of the mill until he is utterly worn out, but whose misery is not troubled by the privilege (?) which our nature possesses—viz. the power of thought, with other faculties (oftener sources of wretchedness than of happiness), viz. memory and anticipation of the future. Every effort I have made to break my chain has only seemed to. rivet it more strongly, and I now despair. You exhort me to look on the bright side of things. I cannot create sunshine.

"My darling wife, I fear there are many passions of a dreadful nature pent up within me ; when they will find a vent I know not. That I may at all times be enabled to govern them is my fervent wish, but how can I reckon ! At times reflection fills me with a mixture of heavenly and diabolical sensations with regard to the world and my species."

With a full share of the *perfervidum ingenium Scotorum*, with feelings both intense and lasting, he was learning by bitter experience that the purest natural pleasures are but husks so long as the soul is far from God. The soul is made for God and is ever restless until it rests in Him. No wonder he said, "under present circumstances I cannot for the soul of me see the use of my existing at all !" However, next day, he is "quite ashamed of giving way to such an ebullition of discontent and moroseness."

About this time his wife wrote :—

"I have to-day taken the Holy Sacrament, and sincerely pray God in His mercy may make it a means of salvation to me. It is the first time I have done so since my marriage. You, I believe, have never yet ventured to do so, but I sincerely trust you will shortly. In an explanation of the Lord's Supper I have been reading, the author says : ' Our safety consists in resolving to take the best care that the performance may be accepted before God.' If we were to delay receiving this Holy Sacrament until a serious change had taken place in us, how long would many continue to do so ! I pray God to pardon my past and most numerous sins, and I feel a sincere wish to become better. And now, my own much-loved Colin, I trust you will endeavour to turn your thoughts towards the necessity of partaking of our Lord's Supper. You have led a quiet life, never been guilty of any flagrant sins, and your opinions on religious subjects are what they should be. Surely the Sacrament will strengthen your good resolutions, and enable you to resist the weakness of your natural dispositions."

There is here a sincere desire to serve God, with no knowledge of how to obtain strength to do so. Neither husband nor wife seems to have known clearly the good tidings of great joy that Christ died, not for saints, but for sinners, to make them into saints; that He offers salvation freely to all who will accept it, and, with salvation, grace to obey. Mackenzie writes to his wife :—

" No man ever experienced the strongest proof of his being an intellectual being—viz. conversion from a miserable state of scepticism to one of belief—without his heart having infinitely more to do with it than his head, the latter being unable, and the former fully able to appreciate the value of Divine Revelation." [1]

This is true, in so far that the real source of unbelief is in the heart and affections; but he as yet had only intellectual belief, and did not see the necessity of the new heart, the new birth (John iii.), without which a man cannot even *see* the kingdom of God. He knew God only as an earnest Jew or even Muhammadan might do, as his Creator and Preserver, not yet as his God and Saviour. He knew Him only afar off as " Jehovah, Jove, or Lord,"

---

[1] He said : " My faith, while yet an inquirer, was fully confirmed by the careful perusal of Leslie's *Short Method with Deists* "—a book for which he retained a special value.

not yet as "the Lamb of God who taketh away the sin of the world."

About January 1836 he rejoined his wife in Calcutta, and saw for the first time their youngest daughter, born the previous October. Mrs. Mackenzie had been exposing herself to the sun, which brought on liver complaint, and a severe course of bleeding and blistering according to the Sangrado medical system of the day, soon reduced her to such a state that a voyage to Europe was pronounced indispensable. Want of means prevented his accompanying her, for his West India property had been giving nothing for some years. She embarked with her three little girls in the *Catherine*, her husband accompanying her to the Sandheads. They parted on the 14th April 1836, at which time, though sadly weak, she appeared somewhat better. When he had to go on board the pilot brig, she saw by his face that he was come to take leave of her, and, springing up in bed, she threw her arms round his neck, and cried in the most entreating tone : "Oh, Colin, don't leave me !" He could only say, "It is God's will," laid her back, and went down the ship's side with a dry eye. Three miserable days followed, beating about in the brig, very ill, without a place to rest, to pray, or, if he could have done so, to weep. At length they fortunately fell in with a ship bound for Calcutta, on board of which he obtained a passage. She was so crammed with cargo that he had no place to lie down save in the midst of horrible filth and vermin (centipedes, scorpions, etc.). He therefore walked the deck for two nights, drenched with the heavy dew, and scorched through and through during the day by the sun, until the mate, seeing how utterly he was exhausted, gave him leave to lie down in his own cabin for an hour or two. On the third evening they ran aground on the famous shoal, the James and Mary, when he got into a fishing-boat, and reached Calcutta that evening, quite worn out with fatigue. He said: "I could but turn to my God for comfort, for earth could yield me none."

It is very touching to read the numerous affectionate letters he wrote to his poor young wife, which were never to reach her hand. Some extracts from them will show his increasing desire to serve God :—

"25th April 1836.—May He, of His infinite goodness, watch over you and our dear little ones, and reunite us speedily to part no more, until the awful (and may our lives render it the desirable) summons, which shall call one of us to precede the other a little way on the road to that blessed region, where, cleansed from the stains of sin and human frailty, we may, in the society of good men made perfect, for ever gratefully praise and glorify our God and our Redeemer, looking back on the pains, cares, and uncertainties of this life as on a troubled dream from which we have at length happily awakened.

"I have seriously considered the excellent arguments you make use of to persuade me to take the Sacrament, from which holy and paramount duty I have been so long deterred, partly from false shame, and partly from a fear which I am now convinced I ought never to have entertained. I shall therefore studiously endeavour to prepare my mind for it, and partake of the Lord's Supper the first convenient opportunity. I know this will be a source of great comfort and joy to you ; for what so dear to those who truly love, as each other's spiritual concerns ?"

He shortly afterwards called on Archdeacon Dealtry, and was admitted to the Lord's table. He writes :—

"Pray night and morning to Him, without whose help all human efforts to do right are vain, to enable you to do your duty to our darling children. I am sure you will, by God's assistance, cast aside your irresolution and indolence of mind, and fit yourself for the arduous duties now before you."

He gives a strong testimony in favour of water-drinking,

though less wise physicians afterwards prescribed wine for
him.

"I am very glad Dr. Garden enjoined me to drink no wine.
Since I left it off I am better in all respects and stronger than I
have been for a long time. While almost all around me are
complaining of the oppressive heat, I feel only comfortably
warm. The first five or six days after leaving off wine one is
strongly tempted to recommence by habit and by a certain depression of spirits; but be firm, and lo ! the bacchanalian spirit de-
parteth, and, instead of periods of exaltation and depression, a calm
equable flow of spirits succeeds. I have found it so, as all who
have followed the same course have done. The idea of any but
a worn-out old man having recourse to the bottle to promote
cheerfulness (as the plausible expression is) is monstrous and
abominable. My mind has also benefited by the alteration in
my diet. I am less irritable, and more capable of application,
than formerly."

He exhorts her to make the children her constant companions; to insist on "strict adherence to truth in small
matters; never to punish in anger; never to chide or punish
for a small fault as if the child had committed a gross mis-
demeanour."

"I remember accidentally breaking some china and being
punished for it as if I had told a lie, and I well remember that
the impression on my childish mind was, that my father and
mother were indulging their own passion most unjustly at my
expense. How fearfully a circumstance like that lessens respect
for a parent as well as confidence in any future decision.

"There is nothing I dislike so much as hearing children
·praised (especially before them) for their good looks, the pretti-
ness of their dress, etc. Such conduct on the part of grown-up
fools literally plays the devil with a child's mind. . . . I must
do you the justice to avow that I never yet met with any one,
male or female, so perfectly free from vanity and petty feelings

as yourself.　Do not persist in M.'s absurd plan of giving wine to the children.　*Never* give it, even on birthdays, etc.　It is begetting a vicious taste."

We now find conviction not merely of sinfulness in general, but of a particular sin, which is a sure sign of progress.

"I do hope to be enabled to conquer several habits which are directly opposed to my duty as a man and a Christian. Indolence and irritability of temper are my besetting sins, the latter causing me to break continually the third commandment, of the guilt of which I am more and more convinced every day."

He adds, almost prophetically :—

"Great tribulation may be in store for us, and we may never meet again, but we are not forbidden to hope."

CHAPTER VI.

(1836.)

"The stormy play and joy of strife."—HEMANS.

MACKENZIE'S "first dreadful state of suspense was relieved by the joyful intelligence of the commencement of his wife's restoration to health." A week after sailing she was able to write him a few loving lines, telling him that the Doctor thought her improving. He then sought out Captain Chads of H.M.S. *Andromache* (afterwards Sir Henry Chads, G.C.B.), who was then in Calcutta, and had just been appointed Joint-Commissioner with Mr. Bonham, the Governor of Singapore, for the suppression of piracy, and volunteered to accompany him on this service, the Captain kindly inviting him to share his cabin as his guest. This close intimacy produced the warmest affection and admiration for his gallant host, and he delighted to relate how this dashing officer—who had been trained under Nelson and Collingwood, and who, like his great leaders, combined heroic daring and endurance with a hatred of tyranny and great consideration for his men,—spent a part of every morning and evening in the study of his Bible and prayer. He had been prisoner both to the French (when he was very ill-treated) and to the Americans, having fought the *Java*, after the death of her Captain, with only a scratch-pack crew against the *Constitution*, of one-third greater tonnage and weight of metal, until the former was a helpless wreck, when the American Commodore Bainbridge showed his appreciation of his noble foe by returning Lieut. Chads' sword and complimenting him and his ship's company on the obduracy of their defence. Captain Chads was a man of transparent frankness and independence, combining much vehemence and absoluteness of manner with a most tender heart; rigid to himself, yet full of Christian gentleness to others; making little profession, but showing his Christian principle by his life.

Perhaps no other type of Christian character would have made so favourable an impression upon Mackenzie at that time.

He describes the officers and crew as first-rate, and their gunnery practice as admirable, Captain Chads' system being to have a short gun drill daily.

Mackenzie hoped to obtain command of a party of Sepoys on this expedition, but was eventually disappointed.

His anxiety regarding his poor wife was most painful. Months must elapse before he could receive news of her, and at times he lost hope. "This," he says, "I know, is sinful, and I trust I shall be enabled to bow submissively to the all-wise decrees of Him whose sole aim in afflicting us is to make us better and therefore happier. Excitement in the meantime is worth something. How strange it is that such a lover of ease and perfect quiet as I am should yet find such satisfaction in scenes of turmoil and excitement!"

The condition of the Straits of Malacca at that time may be judged of by Mackenzie's description during his former stay there:—

"The Straits swarm with pirates to a shameful extent. Small ships are obliged to sail in company to avoid the certainty of being plundered. If the crew escape murder they have no redress, as, even should the pirates be apprehended, they cannot be punished, there being no Admiralty Court in the Straits. Here, and at Penang and Singapore, convicts who have been transported for the most atrocious crimes have their irons taken off, and are hired as domestic servants at a rate of wages which they never could have received in their own country as honest men. Among the whole crowd of servants on the establishment of our Resident, Mr. Garling, I believe only two are free men, the rest being felons. At Singapore neither life nor property is safe for a single night, as far as the police of the place goes. Bands of thirty and forty desperadoes from the interior of the island plan an attack on a certain house (which generally terminates in murder). This is publicly known in the Bazar a day or two previous, but no measures are ever taken to lay hold of the villains. The unhappy object of the incursion is left to his own resources for defence, he being, perhaps, the last man to hear of his approaching danger. A case of this kind occurred the other day within a very short distance of the house where Lang and Ferrier were sleeping (during their visit to Singapore), and the poor gentleman having, in his hurry, taken up the wrong pair of pistols, was unable to defend himself, and was consequently cut down and left for dead. I could mention a hundred instances of the miserable insufficiency of the law here. It is a subject of sore annoyance to all honest men, and of exultation and triumph to rogues. I am told the Legislative Council in Calcutta have it in their power to remedy these crying evils, but there appears to be a strange apathy on the subject. At Malacca murder is not very frequent, but robberies are committed with perfect impunity.

"Lang and I nearly settled one fellow shortly after our arrival ; but the light being very dim, before I could get a fair shot at him the rascal dived under a low wall, and escaped. There have been no further attempts on any of us at night, owing to our alertness with our firearms, of which the convicts are fully aware."

He relates a characteristic trait of a Malay " who had murdered a whole family (the father and three little children), whom he had actually minced to pieces, and then taken all the plunder he could and attempted to sell it near one of our military posts. A convict undertook to secure him. He found the Malay coolly practising at a mark, and entered into conversation with him respecting the difficulty of hitting it. When the Malay had discharged his piece the convict offered him his, and, while he was taking aim, threw his arms round his body and cried for help. The murderer was secured, and a man set to watch him to prevent his committing suicide. He had nothing on but a cloth round his chest and a pair of drawers. He threw his cloth over his head, as if he wished to go to sleep. The watcher thought he slept very long, and gently lifted the cloth. He was quite dead! He had taken the string of his drawers, fastened it round his neck, and quietly pulled until he had strangled himself, without any movement to betray what he was about to the man who sat watching him."

The letter continues :—"Some three weeks ago, a vessel from the Madras coast was boarded and taken by pirates about forty miles to the north of Malacca. The blood-thirsty villains, after taking possession of the crew and cargo (which was very rich), cut the throat of a young Chinese on board for having exhorted his shipmates to resist. The cargo has been publicly sold, and the crew made slaves of, amongst them a poor woman and her child. The vessel itself is lying on shore, close to the piratical village. Ferrier volunteered to recapture her with forty men if Mr. Garling would take up a brig which was in the roads to convey him to the place ; but the answer was in the negative, as the Bengal Government allows no discretionary power to that of the Straits, and retrenches one dollar if expended without a previous reference. What a shameful state of affairs!"

It was to remedy these crying evils that Lord Auckland formed a plan for the suppression of piracy, and despatched Captain Chads to carry it out. Sailing early in May, the *Andromache*, after a tedious voyage, met the *Wolf* (Captain Stanley) at Penang. "She had had a good deal of boat-fighting with the pirates, and contrived to slay a good number without any loss. She brought some prisoners, whom she must take over to Madras for trial. Stanley caught the rascals in the very act of murdering some unhappy Cochin-Chinese whom they had plundered. The departure of the *Wolf* cripples Chads' plans for the present. As the Government steamer which was to have carried some Madras troops will not be ready until August, and the *Jardine* armed steamer at Singapore is totally useless, having lost her funnel overboard, and being unable to replace it, no Sepoys can be employed.

"*28th May* 1836, opposite the Ding-Dings.—Yesterday afternoon the pinnace and two cutters left the ship well armed and manned. I went in the second cutter with the second lieutenant, Gore. We pulled inside the Ding-Dings, proceeding up the river a long way, but met with no success. We searched from half-past 3 P.M. till 11 P.M., when we returned to the ship. On our arrival we were informed that a well-known large piratical schooner had been seen along shore some miles to the southward, and instantly made a fresh start in search of her. After a severe pull of about an hour, we descried what seemed to be the said schooner lying at anchor about a mile off. Availing ourselves of the obscurity afforded by advancing from under some high land, while she lay in the bright moonlight, we gave way in great style. The men stretched to their oars, and, as we rapidly neared the devoted prahu, not a soul on her deck seemed aware of our approach. Already we were within three boats' length, ready to pour in a double charge of round shot and grape, each man had put on his fighting face and grasped his weapon (I vapouring with a cutlass and pistol), when the side of the vessel was crowded with a multitude of dark forms, who flourished most primitive arms of all sorts, shouting in an eldritch fashion, and dancing about in what proved to be an ecstasy of fear. Our interpreter hailed in Malay, and we found that, notwithstanding the schooner's unfortunate resemblance to her buccaneering prototype, she was very harmlessly employed in the coast traffic. We boarded, and found the poor wretches as much relieved as we were disappointed, and eventually got back to the *Andromache* at 2 P.M., our crew perfectly exhausted by nearly eleven hours' hard work. So much for our first expedition. We are now hastening, as fast as a headwind will allow us, to the 'Arroa' islands, where Captain Vassal in the *Harrier* had a brush with some of the amiable members of society of whom we covet the acquaintance. There is an unpleasant circumstance connected with our pursuit of these Malays—viz. that, on ascertaining that they actually are pirates, we cannot give quarter (except under very peculiar circumstances) to prevent certain risk from their proverbial treachery and unyielding obstinacy.

"We arrived at the Arroas in the boats (the ship being some eight miles off) late on the evening of the 30th. The pinnace (with Lieutenant Reid commanding the expedition), mounting a 12 lb. carronade, and having a crew of thirteen seamen, four marines, the marine officer, a middy, and your humble servant, followed by the gig and jolly boats, with a brace of marines in each, took the west side of the islands ; the two cutters, mounting a long six and a three-pounder, received orders to pry into every creek and cranny on the east side, and to meet us at the other end. The gig was despatched to inspect a dubious-looking object some little distance out to sea, and, not returning immediately, the jolly was sent to look for her. The pinnace then proceeded alone. On arriving at the south end, and not meeting the cutters, we descried something like a boat at the end of a small creek, which had no outlet save the one by which we were entering. As we neared, loud voices hailed us in Malay. Our interpreter, Mr. Mitchell, called to them not to be afraid, if they were good men and true, as we were Europeans. Their consciences not relishing the condition, their answer to our peaceful overture was a loud, unmannerly shout—'Come on, sons of Malays, the boat is ours; let us board! let us board!' advancing at the same time in two large prahus, crowded with men (as we found afterwards about 130), beating gongs, and making altogether a most Babel-like uproar. Nothing abashed, though the presence of the cutters would have been acceptable from the enemy's overwhelming numbers, we pulled to within pistol shot, and commenced with grape, to which they replied merrily with grape and langridge.[1] Their first fire, by God's mercy alone, did not harm any of us, though it flew right in amongst us, knocking off Reid's cap, by whom I was standing. The pirates' great object being to board (which I think would have been destruction to us), everything depended on our accuracy and quickness of firing, so much so as to make it impossible to run out the carronade at every discharge. Reid's coolness and decision were admirable, and he was right well seconded by the men at the gun, who fired with the same *sang-froid* as if they had been at exercise, and with astonishing rapidity and precision. Repeatedly our antagonists endeavoured to close,

---

[1] Langridge then meant a canvas bag stuffed with bits of iron, gravel, old nails, etc.

and as often they were driven back.   Just as we had partly
crippled the smaller prahu and greatly shattered the larger,
the first cutter pulled round the nearest point, and let fly
into the midst of the rogues.   Forthwith, the smaller prahu
fled, the crew of the larger jumping into the sea and
making for the land.   The second cutter, commanded by
young O'Callaghan, coming up at the same instant with the
gig and jolly, Reid ordered him to chase the recreant with
the gig.   We finished our work by completely clearing the
big one, the Panglecmah (captain) of which, really a gallant
fellow, was the last man—although severely wounded—to
quit the vessel.   He remained at his post, fiercely flourishing his spear, until he was deserted by every one ; and we
were within a pike's length when, diving under the covered
part of the prauw, he reappeared at the bow, and plunged
into the sea.   He never reached the rocks, however, for a
discharge of canister at that moment among the crowd of
swimming wretches did great execution.   We now gave
three cheers, and, leaving the first cutter and the jolly to
slay as many as possible and burn the disabled prahu, we
started after O'Callaghan, who was coursing his prey as a
greyhound does a hare (it being bright moonlight), turning
her every now and then, which would have been much more
difficult for him to do but for the effect of some of the
pinnace's former handiwork.   Our men bent to their oars,
and, by cutting across, we arrived at the scene of action
just as the second cutter had overcome all opposition, the
enemy having at length, like a hunted wolf, turned to bay,
giving shot for shot as long as she was able.   The whole
crew having in their desperation jumped into the sea, the
work of slaughter began, with muskets, pikes, pistols, and
cutlasses.   I sickened at the sight, but it was dire necessity.
They asked for no quarter, and received none ; but the
expression of despair on some of their faces, as, exhausted

with diving and swimming, they turned them up towards us merely to receive the death-shot or thrust, froze my blood. My pistol and cutlass lay idle. One or two of them were seen through the clear water swimming desperately downwards to the bottom. I saw one man, a most muscular-looking savage, receive four shots and three thrusts from a pike, each of which turned him over, and still he swam and dived. A blow from a cutlass then laid open his head, and he was finished with a pistol. Such tenacity of life is almost incredible. A similar instance was exhibited by the chief of the prahu. He was desperately wounded in the water by three or four musket-shots, when, turning, he regained his vessel, and, seizing a spear, quietly sat down alone on the yard of the mast, awaiting the return of his enemies. A marine shot him again in the thigh, when he crouched under cover; but, on the cutter coming alongside, he rose and threw his spear with such force that, missing his mark (O'Callaghan), and glancing over the shoulder of the mid (Burrough), it was dashed to pieces by what it struck. He was at the same instant shot dead by two marines, who were watching for him. In that boat also lay dead the chief of the third prahu, whose crew had divided themselves between the other two, and which still lay on the beach of the cave, where we found and burnt it next morning. Having taken out some of the guns, O'Callaghan's prize was burnt on the spot, and we stationed ourselves round the islands to wait for daybreak. Morning came, and with it the *Andromache.* We sent the gig on board, received some provisions, and orders to scour the islands. In this we were employed till late in the afternoon, by which time we were all quite worn out, the jungle being to the full as opaque as the understandings of some of my acquaintance, and the hills very steep. Most of us had some queer somersaults. I saw one Malay bounding

along like an antelope among the rocks on the shore. I
was standing above, with Mr. Midshipman Slade. ‘ *Facilis
descensus averni*,’ thought I, and, followed by my companion, haggis fashion, we charged down hill. I value
myself chiefly on my speed of foot, and was within a few
yards of the active gentleman for whose sake I had risked
my neck, when a scoundrelly marine from above, in defiance
of repeated orders to cease firing, shattered his leg with a
musket-ball. Slade made a hasty tourniquet with a stick
and handkerchief, and, on sending him to the ship, the poor
fellow endured amputation with the same fortitude with
which he had borne his wound, and with which he would
have met with his death at my hand : a fate he greatly
wronged the mild expression of my countenance by evidently expecting on my approach. Altogether, we took
nine prisoners, about eight others are secreted in the
island, and the remainder, some 113, including three chiefs,
are slain. These pirates certainly fought with considerable
hardihood. I thank God that not one of our party was
even wounded, a most extraordinary circumstance, especially considering how hard the pinnace was beset at first.

“ Here is the confession of two of the prisoners, as taken
in my presence.

“ Saimba (the first captured, who showed the hiding-
place of the others) belonged to the largest boat, which
carried fifty-four men, twenty-eight oars, one large, and one
small gun. Two of her consorts are now cruising off Battoo
Pooty. Several other prahus are fitting out at Lingin.
The cargoes they take are sold anywhere on the coast, frequently at Singapore. This flotilla had no connection with
the Toomagong at Singapore (a Prince of Johore, actually
receiving a large pension from Government), but he knows
he has piratical prahus of his own. On capturing vessels,
if resistance is made, the prisoners are killed ; if not, they

take the best for slaves, and send the remainder away. Had heard that a man-of-war had taken a prahu (Stanley), which he knows was a pirate. They knew we were Europeans by our voices, and they wished not to fight, but the chief threatened to kill them if they did not. The chief beat the gong himself. It was their intention to fire and then to board, but they were prevented by our grape, which came among them like a shower of rain, killing a great number. It was a dreadful case of necessity, a stern example being absolutely called for, from the extensive loss of life and property this season by the hands of the Malay pirates. The most pitiable circumstance of the whole was that two male children were killed by our fire, their fathers having already commenced teaching the unhappy little beings their horrible trade of murder and robbery. Mansoor, another prisoner, confirms this same account; says all five boats belonged to the Sultan of Lingan, who sends as many men as he pleases in the piratical prahus. They must go, or be sacrificed with their families. Between twenty and thirty prahus come from his part of the country.

"Some days later, expecting to find a nest of pirates at the mouth of the Sookoot River, the place where the unfortunate Chinese had his throat cut a few months before, and favoured by the moon, we spent the night in the boats, searching every inlet where it was possible for a nautilus to lie hid, but in vain.

"7th June.—I shall have to leave the ship at Singapore. It is particularly provoking, as she then proceeds to Point Romania and Pahang, where she will be sure to meet with lots of pirates, some of great size and strength, with two banks of oars. The larger class come from Borneo and the small islands adjacent, and are much dreaded by the large seven and eight hundred ton China junks, and even by their brother rogues in the common-sized prahus, who vanish at the approach of these Brobdignags.

"10*th June.*—All yesterday we were in sight of Pulo Pisang, where we had every reason to suppose another batch of pirates was harboured. The man at the mast-head reported successively eight prahus off the island, but an unfortunate calm prevented our nearer approach, and the distance was too great to send the boats. In the evening a breeze came off the land, and we got near enough to boat it. The greater part of the night was spent most unprofitably in searching the little inlets and skulking-places of the above cluster of islets, and tired and vexed enough we were. We are again becalmed, but hope by the afternoon to have wind enough to carry us as far as the Cocos (about twelve miles farther to the south-east), where I sincerely hope we shall be fortunate enough to meet with, and give a lesson to some more of these 'vagabones.' These night-excursions are, however, even when we find nothing, pleasant in many aspects. The officers are all fine fellows, and the peculiarities and facetious absurdities of Jack's character are better seen in these situations, when naturally a greater degree of freedom and license prevails. At the 'Arroas,' while in hot pursuit of the pirates in the jungle, prompt and eager to shed blood, still Jack's kindness of heart and love of fun prevailed the instant a prisoner was secured, and resistance at an end. It was absurd to see a knot of blue-jackets assembled round a Malay, laughing and talking to him in English, and enforcing the meaning of their words by vehement gesticulations, ending by making the astonished captive eat biscuit and smoke cigars, which his queer amphibious friends assiduously lighted for him!

"Arrived off Singapore on the 12th June. Fearing lest secret intelligence of his proposed movements might be sent by the pirates' friends at Singapore to them, Chads determined not to go in, the ship being so much disguised as to have been taken for an Arab by the *Water Witch*. Chads communicated, however, with Bonham through a disguised messenger, and refused to allow me to go on shore, offering to be responsible should the delay prevent my joining my regiment in time. We proceeded towards Point Romania, off which we arrived early on the 13th. Started in the boats about seven, and as we coasted along, enjoying the beautiful scenery formed by the numerous romantic little bays, thickly-wooded shores, and occasionally bluff, rocky promontories, the last affording excellent shelter in all weathers to small vessels, the bowman of the pinnace, in which, as usual, I had taken my station, gave notice of something suspicious behind Point Romania. Telescopes were levelled accordingly, and we plainly discerned the masts of several prahus, apparently lurking in one of the aforesaid snug retreats. Reid made the signal to chase, and *more suo*, the pinnace shot gallantly ahead of all the other boats. On rounding the point the pirates (three large class and two smaller ones), who were on the other side of some rocky inlets about half a mile distant, perceived us, and made sail instantly, making towards a river in the mainland which affords good shelter, and across the mouth of which they have felled a huge tree, which lies just under water, and in a particular part of which a niche is cut sufficiently deep to allow their keels to glide over, those of the uninitiated, of course, sticking fast. Our object was to cut them off from this haven of safety, and arduous was the struggle for precedence. Meantime they opened a running fire on us of both grape and round shot, their chiefs shouting defiance and cutting capers on the poops of their vessels, brandishing their spears and shields. We only tugged the more strenuously at the oars, taking no notice of their more solid compliments, some of which were pretty well

directed, until we had gained so much on them as to be
able to give them back the like with interest, when our fire
told. Being forced to abandon their design of reaching the
river, they continued their flight along shore. Our running
fight was kept up at intervals, the other boats occasionally
getting near enough to join in the action. It was evident
that the enemy suffered severely, one of them especially,
which at length ran ashore, the crew of the two smaller
prahus having previously abandoned their vessels and got
on board the larger ones. As we passed the prahu on shore
we riddled her with grape, and a discharge of canister and
musketry among those of her crew who were swimming
away from her killed numbers. On we kept after the other
rogues, both of which at last also ran ashore, the crews,
'save those who ne'er shall fight again,' escaping into the
jungle. We took possession of the three large prahus, and
our work was crowned most satisfactorily by the release of
four Cochin Chinese (another swimming off to us afterwards
pursued by two Malays to the water's edge) who had been
taken with many others of their countrymen (some of whom,
I grieve to say, were forced into the jungle by the flying
pirates), and had been working as slaves ever since, their
captors intending to sell them at Pahang. By this time it
was past 1 P.M., but success prevented any one from feeling
fatigue. I then remembered my promise to James Prinsep
touching a specimen of a Malay *caput mortuum*. I accordingly got into a small canoe with three Malays belonging
to the gunboats and rowed away to the first prahu, which
had drifted a little out to sea. On getting on board I found,
among other relics of mortality, the body of the Panglecmah
or chief of the prahu, lying, still warm, on the poop, his
arms beside him. Not choosing to defile my own sabre,—
after admiring the corpse, which was that of a splendid
young fellow, being symmetry itself,—I made a Malay care-

fully cut off the head with the defunct's own sword and
wrap it up in a basket. I then possessed myself of his
sword, spear, and dagger, which I send with his head.
The human hair on the handle of the sword denotes the
rank of the owner, and, I believe, is that of a victim. I am
sorry I could not take the fellow's immense shield, my canoe
being too small.

"On my arrival, Chads was overjoyed at our complete
success. The pirates, who numbered nearly 130 men, lost
at least one third of their number, many more being so
severely wounded as to be scarcely able to crawl to the
jungle. I took advantage of Chads' good humour, and
showed him the chief's head. He was amazed and horrified, but gave me a small cask and sufficient arrack to preserve it. The doctor prepared the specimen, and in return
asked for one of the teeth, which had the enamel filed
away so as to make them concave outside, with the addition
of a black dye, and finally a St. Andrew's cross let into
each in gold, another mark of the rank of the deceased.

"Among the papers found in the prahus were actual
commissions from the Rajas of Rhio, Johore, and Salan-
gore to the Pangleemahs, authorising them to commit
piracy, and furnishing them with means to do so. Chads
hopes to be able to prove that one of the commissions was
given by the Toomagong at Singapore. The other books
and papers captured consisted of scraps of the Kurán, love-
letters, charms, accounts, and Malay poetry recounting the
heroic exploits of the pirates of former times, being a sort
of poetical history of the Malay islands and peninsula,
proving that piracy is esteemed among that race quite as
laudable a mode of obtaining a livelihood as it formerly
was among more northern nations. The old Norse sea-
kings were quite of this conscientious way of thinking.
After burning the prahus, we proceeded to Pulo Tingy,

and after that to Pulo Aor, employing two days in the
examination of these and of some smaller islands. We
found Pulo Aor partly inhabited by agricultural and fishing Malays. A small trade is carried on with Singapore.
The edible bird's nest is found in large quantities in all
these islands. The swallow itself, or gull, or whatever it
may be, is a most beautiful little white bird. They appear
to go in pairs. The inhabitants of Pulo Aor are annually
put in great dread by pirates from Borneo, who come every
July and August in enormous prahus, double banked, and
carrying from 150 to 200 men each, to plunder the poor
wretches, and carry them off as slaves. They (of Aor) have
small stockades along the shore in front of each group of
huts to defend themselves ; but they as often fly to the
jungle as fight. We are now *en route* to Point Romania
again to take another look at it, and thence to Singapore.
Is it not satisfactory as well as wonderful that none of us
have suffered in these little affairs ? Thank God for it !
The constant exposure to the dew at night and the sun by
day has not yet produced sickness. I am as black as a
crow. All this excitement has been of use to me in divert-
ing my mind from the misery of uncertainty with regard to
you, my best loved Addy. I find that the very effort to
be resigned to the will of God brings with it support and
consolation. Without religion what are we in this world ?
Rudderless drifts on the surface of a stormy sea.

"19*th June.*—The night before last we left the *Andromache* for a last cruise before reaching Singapore. We were
out all night and all yesterday (more than twenty hours of
it), but without success. Dropped anchor early this morning." Thus ended his six weeks' cruise. His friend James
Lang had been doing his duty as Adjutant during his five
months' absence from Malacca, and with characteristic
generosity had been hoarding up half the staff pay for him,

though, as Mackenzie was only "acting Adjutant," Lang might properly have retained the whole.

Thus Malacca, with the wearisome monotony which he had felt so keenly, was the means of procuring for Mackenzie that which he had long desired,—release from the drudgery of garrison life, and a field for active exertion. If he had not been sent to Malacca, he would not have joined Captain Chads' expedition, while at the very time that he was lamenting that, as a mere volunteer, he had no chance of gaining any credit, Captain Chads was reporting most favourably of him in all his public letters; and this brought him to the knowledge of Lord Auckland, who, in consequence, selected him for service in Afghanistan.[1] So

---

[1] Mackenzie subsequently received the following testimonials :—

Letter from Captain Chads, R.N., to Colin Mackenzie, Esq.

CHELTENHAM, *June 14, 1838.*

MY DEAR SIR,—It is with very great satisfaction I can bear testimony to your highly zealous and gallant conduct, whilst you were with me in the *Andromache*, when I was engaged in suppressing piracy in the Straits of Malacca in 1836. Although a passenger only, you were always foremost when any service was going forward, and invariably a volunteer in the boats when they left the ship, and as such always named in my public letters. It will be at all times a source of pleasure to me to hear of your welfare and render any assistance in promoting it.—Believe me, etc.

(Signed)   H. D. CHADS.

LIEUT. COLIN MACKENZIE,
   48th Madras Native Infantry.

Letter from the Earl of Auckland, late Governor-General of India, etc.

KENSINGTON GORE, *February 8, 1845.*

DEAR SIR,—In answer to the request which you have preferred to me that I would state my opinion of your conduct and character in the Indian Service, I have no hesitation in stating that I hold both in very

the Lord makes "all things," small and great, "work together for good to them that love Him," and even before
they love Him.

high esteem.   I had heard of you as early as in the year 1836, in the
war which was carried on by Captain Chads, under my direction,
against the Malay pirates, and I know that at that time, you gained
by your enterprise, and by your efficient assistance, the acknowledgments of that officer.   I was subsequently led, from my knowledge of
your merits, to name you for service in Afghanistan, and particularly
to recommend you to Sir William Macnaghten.   It will be for others
to speak of the courage, the endurance, and the ability which you displayed in that service more particularly than I can ; but every report
which has reached me has only tended to confirm the high opinion
which I had previously entertained of you. —I am, etc.

(Signed)   AUCKLAND.

To CAPTAIN MACKENZIE,
      Late Political Assistant, Afghanistan.

CHAPTER VII.

CONVERSION—FURLOUGH.

(1836–8.)

"Unter Leiden prægt der Meister
In die Seelen, in die Geister
Sein allgeltend Bildniss ein."

MACKENZIE had brought with him from Madras a servant named Jacob Augustine, a so-called "Portuguese Christian," that is, a Romanist. This faithful fellow accompanied his master in all his wanderings, and never afterwards left him, serving him with a degree of affectionate devotion that could not be surpassed. On rejoining his regiment after his cruise, Mackenzie writes :—

"Poor Jacob's joy at meeting with his old friends at Malacca was grievously interrupted by the afflicting news of his mother's death. He was quite overcome, and has been crying ever since. I sympathise most sincerely with the poor fellow, and he seems comforted by my feeling for his loss."

He was soon to receive a heavier stroke himself. On the 11th of October 1836 the fatal news at last arrived that the amendment in his poor wife's health had been delusive, and that she had breathed her last on the 28th May, the fourth anniversary of her wedding-day, aged only twenty-four, at the very time he was starting on his first chase after the pirates. She had been most kindly tended by Colonel and Mrs. Mackenzie, and Colonel and Mrs. King, and was buried at sea, as her beloved mother was ten years later. Mackenzie was so full of sympathy himself, that he attracted the sympathy of others to a remarkable degree, and, besides his friends in the Regiment, the good missionaries Mr. and Mrs. Dyer behaved like a brother and sister to him. He said afterwards of Mr. Dyer: "He was the man who raised my head when it was bowed to the dust." He used to spend every evening with them, studying the word of God, or discussing points of Christian faith or practice, and this was the time to which he always referred his conversion. The manner of it is not known, for so great was his fear of self-deception, that he was always very shy of speaking of his own feelings, but one stage was a very deep conviction of sin. He never again seems to have fancied that he could offer any "good work" to God, "whose eye is too pure to behold iniquity," but henceforth threw himself wholly on the free unmerited grace of his Redeemer, and from this time took his stand "on the Lord's side."

His friend Captain Chalmers wrote to him immediately on hearing the sad news of his wife's death :—

"Now that you have been wounded, may you look to the *only* Hand which can truly heal you. 'I, even *I*, am He that comforteth you,' saith Christ Jesus. Remember that you can only be taught to know Jesus as your *own*, your own particular individual Saviour and never-failing Comforter and Friend, by the Holy Spirit, who has been promised, and has *never* been refused to those that ask (Luke xi. 13). . . . May you be led to know the love of Christ which passeth knowledge."

Mackenzie was of a peculiarly nervous, sensitive temperament. More than one doctor declared that he "suffered a pound of pain where another man would suffer an ounce;" and mental disquiet or sorrow always told severely upon his bodily health, so that six months later (May 1837) he was ordered to sea for change, and went to

Singapore to embark for Manilla. The good Dyers [1] now write to him as to one who loves his Saviour. They look forward to "much profitable intercourse with him on his return," but this was not to be.

His voyage to Manilla was marked by one of those signal preservations from death of which he was to experience so many. Only two Spanish vessels go in the year from Singapore to the Philippine Islands, and he consequently was about to embark in one of these when an English ship, the *Harlequin,* unexpectedly entered the harbour. He therefore gave up his passage in the Spaniard, and took one in her. On reaching Manilla, he found that the crew of the vessel in which he was to have gone had mutinied and murdered the captain and all the passengers. Two of the murderers were executed in the Spanish manner, by the "garrote." The criminal is placed in a chair with an iron collar round the neck, which is crushed instantaneously by one turn of a winch. The effect was so violent that the blood had spurted from the forehead of one of them. The crime had been one of revolting barbarity, and the expression of one of the culprits was that of a fiend. Mackenzie had the curiosity to go with some friends to look at the bodies, which were left seated on the scaffold the whole day, and, to his horror, discovered in the hand of each a large roll of paper, being a regular passport to St. Peter! The Spaniards allow no one to enter the islands unless nominally a Christian. He was told that the former inhabitants of these isles, called Negrotas, still live in the interior, and resemble the inhabitants of Papua; the most horrid-looking race known. The only vestige of religion observed among them is the custom of prostrating themselves for a few minutes on entering a new forest; but

[1] The Rev. Samuel Dyer entered into rest in 1844 at Hongkong, his wife and four children being at Singapore.

they cannot explain their reason for doing so. The Manilla men, like the Islanders of the Western Pacific, are thought to have come from the Malayan peninsula, but are a much finer race than the Malays.

During his stay at Manilla Mackenzie in some way incurred the enmity of the Spanish Governor; in spite of which, he and a young Spanish officer, Don Francesco Jose Colubi, formed a warm and romantic friendship for each other, though one was a devout son of Mother Church, who had risked his life during an earthquake by crawling on his hands and knees, in company with the priest, into a tottering church "*pour sauver les images*," and the other was known as the "*heretico Ingleze ;*" but each recognised the chivalrous qualities of the other, as a knight of Castile and a noble Moor might have done. This was Mackenzie's first acquaintance with Romanism, and the arrogance and immorality of the priests made an ineffaceable impression on his mind.

The boa-constrictors at Manilla infest the houses, and are incessantly heard chasing the rats above the ceilings. While Mackenzie was staying with his hospitable friend Mr. Dyce, one was found in the fowl-house, where it had just swallowed a gamecock. It was fifteen feet long, and as thick as a man's thigh. Mackenzie rushed at the monster, and pinned it to a beam with his sword, while Colubi and Mr. Dyce kept it from turning on him by smiting it on the head, and after its demise the servants ate it up! They strike with the tail, and Colubi related that a soldier having gallantly attacked one which he found in the stables of the Governor, the creature struck him so hard with its tail, as to send him flying almost senseless against a wall on the opposite side of the court.

From Manilla Mackenzie went on to China to see his brother James. The absurd regulations of those days, counted leave at and east of the Cape as service, but not leave to Europe. Officers were therefore anxious to avoid going to England ; but, after spending a year in the Eastern seas, Mackenzie was at length obliged to do so, being pronounced by the doctors to be " suffering from general atrophy," and ordered home. Then Mrs. Dyer wrote again :—

" Having experienced the grace of God in your own heart, and that peace which the world can neither give nor take away, you will do your utmost to win all around you to accompany you in the path to Heaven."

CHAPTER VIII.

"HOME AND OUT."

(1838–1839.)

" Benedetto sia il giorno, e'l mese, e l'anno.
E la stagione, e'l tempo, e l'ora, e'l punto."—PETRARCA.

HE reached England towards the autumn of 1838.

At the beginning of December came a turning-point in his life, for which no rational explanation can be given, save the good old one—old as the days of Solomon—that marriages are made in Heaven. He had returned to Europe with an intimate friend (a partner of his brother's), Robert Douglas of Lockerbie House, and was naturally introduced to his friend's relations. First among these was one of the dearest of women, whose single state was a blessing to the whole family far and near, she herself being confidante, counsellor, and most sympathising of friends or of nurses, according to need ; one whose largeness of heart made up for smallness of means, and whose house was the trysting-place, and sometimes the refuge, of young and old for at least two generations. "Aunt Jane" of course invited Lieutenant Mackenzie to meet her beloved brother, Admiral John Erskine Douglas, his wife, and two daughters, at dinner. Mr. Mackenzie was then thirty-two, saddened by the loss of his wife, by ill-health, and a disagreeable lawsuit, yet he fell in love at first sight with the eldest daughter, a girl of nineteen,—to use his own words, — "as she came in at the door." He struggled against the feeling, " thinking it a temptation of the devil ;" but, though he soon became a favourite guest at her father's house, she was quite uncon- scious of his feelings towards herself. As she had been brought up in habits of frank intercourse with a large circle of male cousins, she " did not see why one could not be as good friends with a man as with a woman," and the acquaintance ripened into friendship and intimacy.

The Rev. H. H. Beamish of Trinity Chapel, Conduit Street, was then the best, if not the only evangelical preacher of the Church of England at the West End. He was most instructive as well as eloquent—an evangelical Calvinist, a stout controversialist and opponent of Romish heresies, who preached extempore sermons an hour long morning and evening, and whose chapel was crowded with men of influence, a large number being members of the Houses of Lords or Commons. He was a man who grounded his hearers thoroughly in the principles of the Reformation, taught most clearly the doctrines of the Trinity, of the Fall, of Regeneration by the Spirit, Redemption by the finished work of the Lord Jesus, and of His Second Coming to reign on the earth. Mr. Mackenzie attended his ministry with great interest and profit, and got into the habit of returning with the Admiral and his family to take tea at their house, 34 Charles Street, Berkeley Square. This practice was continued at Cheltenham the following summer, where he enjoyed the preaching of Mr. Close, Mr. Brown, and Robert Montgomery. He had now become a thorough Puritan in his views of both doctrine and morals. Though excessively fond of all country pleasures, a first-rate horseman, and a fair shot, he entirely disapproved of balls, cards, races, and theatres. Mr. Dyer had been of great service to him in many ways, and among others by showing him the strong objections to the theatre. Mackenzie said fairly, that he had no strong inclination for it but could not renounce it as sinful. Mr. Dyer used to state his reasons and leave him to think over them, and succeeded in convincing him that it must be sinful for a Christian to encourage any recreation which—irrespective of its effects on the spectators— places the actors in a position of so much temptation and peril. This was Wilberforce's view. But nothing would be farther from the truth than to imagine that he now became gloomy and morose. Though a Church dignitary warns us against the "savage sternness of Calvinistic tyranny," the fact is, that henceforward there are no traces of Mackenzie's former gloom and discontent. On the contrary, he seemed to have emerged into sunshine ; and as to his outward demeanour, there never was a more lively and cheerful companion.

When at Cheltenham, Mrs. Douglas, with the usual blindness of parents, asked Mr. Mackenzie, nothing loth, to ride with her daughters and a young friend. The quartette of course fell into pairs ; there was much delightful and interesting conversation on all sorts of subjects, which the young lady duly recorded in her journal. But there was no "love-making" in the ordinary acceptation of the word. They only learnt, in this unrestrained interchange of thought and fancy, to know each other thoroughly.

Here are some extracts from the above-mentioned journal :—

"*7th June* 1839.—He told me of the horrid cruelties committed by the Spaniards in their present war, which he had heard from an English officer on the Christino side. This officer entered a hut one day, in which he found one of his own men, an Englishman, who had been wounded so that he could not move, and had been left alone with an old Carlist woman, who had dragged him into the middle of the hut, laid him on some wood, with furze under it, to which she had set fire, and was roasting the heretic. The officer placed the point of his sword at the woman's throat and released his countryman, who was dreadfully burnt. General Evans had strictly forbidden reprisals, but he said his hand trembled with rage, and he was most sorely tempted to run her through.

"10*th June.*—During our ride we were speaking of duels. Mr. Mackenzie said he knew several men of the most undaunted courage whom nothing would tempt to offend their Maker by so awful a crime, one of which almost every man is guilty whether he has committed it or not, because his mind has been made up to commit it whenever he has an opportunity."

This, be it remembered, was at a time when duels were still considered "affairs of honour," and three years before the dreadful circumstance of one brother-in-law falling by the hand of another—the slain man's wife knowing of the impending duel—aroused the conscience of the nation. A memorial to the Queen, numerously signed by officers of the navy and army (among them, by Admiral Douglas), was the means of a change in the Articles of War, prescribing a course for settling differences and making any officer sending, accepting, or conveying a challenge liable to be cashiered.

"1*st July.*—I asked him if he thought brave men felt fear. He said undoubtedly, almost invariably, except a very few (if any) who were naturally insensible to it, and who had therefore no great merit in their courage. He had served with a man of the most dashing bravery, who frankly confessed that previous to action his hand shook so that he could hardly have signed his name. We came to the conclusion that courage was the effect of principle, and sometimes of other feelings, mastering natural fear. He

told me of one of Henry IV.'s bravest captains, a man of
almost incredible valour, who had defended a narrow
passage against 1000 men, and who, to escape from the
Massacre of St. Bartholomew, left Paris with a trusty band
of followers as brave as himself and completely armed.
They heard a voice behind a hedge, and such was their
panic that they all ran until forced to stop for want of
breath.   When they recovered themselves they began to
consult about what could have caused their fear, and came
to the conclusion (which Mr. Mackenzie said was the best
they could have arrived at) that God does not *give* courage,
but only *lends* it.   He said that the less fiction we mingled
with our ideas of sorrow and death the better.   We *must*
know the stern reality some time or other, and it will be
doubly appalling if we have never been accustomed to view
it stripped of poetical and sentimental colouring."

Feeling himself treated with such entire confidence by
the parents, a sentiment of honour withheld the lover from
taking advantage of it by betraying his feelings, until an
incident occurred worthy of a Spanish comedy.   A gentleman commissioned him to convey to Mrs. Douglas a
confession of attachment to her daughter.   Mackenzie
felt as if guilty of unwilling treachery towards his unconscious rival, and this impelled him to reveal his own
feelings.   The parents were naturally unwilling that
their daughter should marry a lieutenant and go to India,
so the answer was, that he must wait four years before he
spoke to her.   No difference was made in their intercourse,
they still rode and talked together; but Mackenzie made up
his mind to return to India at once.

"*5th August.*—Rode to the Seven Springs.   Mr. Mackenzie told us how, in spite of his unwillingness to return
to India, he was convinced that *all* was ordered far better
for him by the hand of God than he could order it had he

his own wishes, and this submission of his will to that of his Father was an enjoyment beyond any earthly one, 'for in keeping of His commandments there *is* great reward;' and therefore he strives to remember this, in spite of many rebellious uprisings in his heart." Then came his brother's wedding, more rides, and more walks; but, with all his ardour, his self-command and sense of honour triumphed, and he went out to India without having said a word.

The journal says:—"*9th August* 1839.—We all took a very sad leave of each other." Mrs. Douglas gave him a pocket Bible, in which she wrote the singularly appropriate verses—"He shall deliver thee in six troubles, yea in seven there shall no evil touch thee," etc., Job v. 19; words which were to be remarkably verified in his experience. It was only afterwards that the object of his love learnt the truth, owing to the mistake of a friend who thought she was acquainted with it. One effect of this knowledge was to enlighten her as to the meaning of some passages in the journal he sent home, in which he spoke of "dragging at each remove a lengthening chain;" another was to heighten her admiration and respect for his self-control.

October 1839. — Mackenzie made a hurried journey through France, going down the Soane. He writes:—

"At Lyons saw the Cathedral, the first temple of Anti-Christ that I had been in in that *soi-disant* Christian country, and my pity was strongly excited by the few worshippers I found there, who, trusting to forms and ceremonies as much as the Muhammadan, were, for the most part, not half so devout in manner. A good-looking priest came in and spoke to some workmen employed in repairs. His manner, even to these poor people, was most bland and insinuating, far beyond natural courtesy. The mien and tone of these blind leaders of the blind in France struck me as differing much from the undisguised arrogance of their brethren in the Philippine Islands, where priestcraft and spiritual tyranny reign supreme."

These expressions may seem harsh to those who have not tested Romanism by Scripture, but they illustrate a marked feature of Mackenzie's character — the intensity of his convictions. He cordially agreed with the Church of England that Rome "hath erred in her living, ceremonies, and in matters of faith." No one held stronger views of the soul-destroying nature of both Popery and Muhammadanism. He looked upon them as the Eastern and Western forms of Anti-Christ, one being a form of Deism, the other of idolatry, and recognised in the Papacy the Babylon of the Apocalypse "drunk with the blood of the Saints." He was, as he was so often styled, a thorough uncompromising Puritan, but he was no bigot. As soon as he was brought face to face with a Romanist or a Musalman he showed and felt nothing but friendliness towards the person, mingled with tender compassion for his errors ; as regards Christians, he appreciated and admired even those from whom he differed most widely in opinion, and, like most Christians in India, the question to what division of the Lord's people any one belonged was quite lost sight of. Instances of this were of daily occurrence in India towards Hindus and Muhammadans, while he was always foremost to show kindness or hospitality to a priest, and still more to a nun.

"The scenery down the Rhone to Avignon was picturesque, but savage and wild—the towering cliffs crowned with the remains of castles and strongholds, as on the Rhine. I posted with several comrades from Avignon to Marseilles, our road lying through high mountains, abrupt and barren, but whose pure, elastic air quite raised my spirits. Both men and horses are a finer race than any I have seen in France, and the women are handsomer."

Going from thence by steamer to Civita Vecchia he found on board a Papist Archbishop, head of the Greek College at Rome. "He was a Smyrniote, proud of his birthplace, dignity, and religious errors, being extremely bigoted against all heretics, especially his brethren of the Greek Church. All our Frenchmen attributed our bad weather to his presence. To me he was very courteous. We conversed a good deal in French, and parted such good friends that he made me a present of some peculiar snuff. My old friend Captain Baird Smith of the Bengal Engineers joined us at Civita Vecchia. He is a very gentlemanly and clever fellow, and most kind-hearted, which he evinced towards me at Malta; I was ill with spasms, and there being a scarcity of beds, he forced me to accept his, while he bivouacked on the floor.

"12th November.—Sailing along the shores of Greece, the sublime and craggy mountains of ancient Sparta rising summit over summit present the most magnificent masses of light and shade conceivable. Monsieur Grasset, a very pleasant Frenchman on board, gives a strange account of the Phil-hellenes who joined the Greeks during the war. They fought bravely, but were a most debauched and turbulent body. On board ship they used to get drunk, throw each other into the sea by way of frolic, fight duels every day, and commit all manner of excesses. The greater part of them were killed in the disastrous battle fought by General Church in the hope of raising the siege of Athens, or murdered in cold blood the day after. Surrender, when fighting against barbarians, is ridiculous. The Turks tortured their prisoners. The unprovoked massacre at Scio, with its attendant horrors, alone ought to have raised a crusade for the extermination of every Turk bearing arms.

"Syra.—A few days ago a Greek lady returned here

under very touching circumstances. She had learnt that her boy, who had been carried away during the Revolution, was alive and well, and had become the adopted son of a Turk of rank. She sought him out, was received with great kindness by his patron, and identified her lost child, whom, to her grief, she found a Musalman. Nature appeared to work in the young man; but to her entreaties that he would 'Dash the turban to earth' and again embrace the faith of his fathers, he answered that he was accustomed to luxury and ease, and that 'he could not dig, to beg he was ashamed.' Still, he promised that he would endeavour to prevail on his infidel father to give him sufficient to support him, and allow him to rejoin his mother, in which case he would renounce Muhammadanism. The poor mother has come back broken-hearted.

"17th *November.*—Arrived at Piræus. Drove immediately to Athens. In the evening I had the pleasure of joining in social worship at the house of the Rev. Mr. Hill, an excellent American missionary, who, with his wife, does much good here. Saw the Greek Lancers exercising. They are wretched cavaliers, on most rat-like steeds. The irregulars in the Albanian dress are active, stout fellows, and good soldiers after their own fashion. Otho has sent away most of his Bavarians, to the joy of the Greeks. Experience has shown that against Greek mountaineers the Bavarian troops are useless. When sent to quell some insurrections, they were picked off in the mountain passes at a terrible rate. Eventually, most of their detachments were taken prisoners, when their captors used to strip them naked for the sake of their arms and clothes, and then take them to the outposts of the Bavarian force and sell them for a drachm each, jocosely requesting a further supply. I stood on the Areopagus, and remembered who had stood there before me. How all the mighty remains of human art and perseverance sunk into utter insignificance as the toil-worn figure of the chief of the Apostles rose before me, when, with holy boldness, he delivered God's message to the surrounding multitude !

"Otho is entirely ruled by Bavaria. His prime minister's wages—for salary it cannot be called—are about £456 per annum. His chief aide-de-camp's, £62, out of which he must keep his horses. This extreme poverty, of course, leads to corruption. The country is overrun with banditti. To-day fifteen more 'gentlemen of the shade,' vulgarly called robbers, have been brought in. There were already fifty men in prison under sentence of death, which they have not been able to carry out from the impossibility of finding an executioner. Some little time back a Maltese accepted that situation. He had got quite into the way of guillotining people ; but, by ill-luck, the night before he had to perform on two glaring offenders, a friend of the 'unfortunate brave' crippled justice by slaying him. With much pains a man was procured to take his place ; but at the Piræus (the Tyburn of Athens), he bungled so that the criminals felt themselves called upon to enter a protest against his continuance in office. At last he declared that he neither could nor would fulfil his bargain. The chief civil authority sent to the Commandant for some soldiers to shoot his charge, which request was indignantly refused, and the tragicomic scene ended by Otho's reprieving the vagabonds. This story is vouched for by what ought to be good authority.

"Infidelity seems to be spreading widely among the Greeks from the revulsion of feeling natural to a long enslaved and now disenthralled people, at all times inquiring, shrewd, and fickle ; who, true to their kind, run from one extreme to another, and think it necessary, in escaping from civil and political oppression, to shake off at once the spiritual tyranny of their priests and revealed religion in the lump. This deplorable tendency is greatly increased by the habit of sending the young men to study in France— the last place where they can learn that the only perfect freedom is that of the Christian.

"*26th November.*—As we neared Alexandria the forest of masts indicated the continued presence of the Turkish fleet, through which we passed. It was a noble sight. There were eighteen Turkish sail of the line (one of 140 guns), nineteen large frigates, and fourteen smaller craft, arranged in lines so as to be commanded by the Egyptian fleet.

"Found that there was a very remote chance of overtaking the Suez steamer. Waghorn was most energetic, and in three hours after landing we were on board a very comfortable passage-boat on the Mahmoudy Canal. . . . This evening a large boat being moored on the wrong side interrupted the progress of our horses. An altercation ensued, when the Reis of the stranger took on himself the unfriendly office of beating our riders, who forthwith dismounted and fled. Our crew caught up their arms, and, headed by a wild Suliote servant of Bushby,[1] made a furious onslaught on the aggressors. Cudgels and sabres were freely used.

> 'With many a stiff thwack, many a bang,
> Hard crab-tree and cold iron rang.'

No dangerous wounds, however, were inflicted, and a brace of pistol-shots sent the enemy to the right-about, when a volley of emphatic Arabic abuse concluded the victory.

"After a long, long night we arrived at Atfeh, where the canal terminates, disembarked with our baggage, and, crossing a narrow neck of land, found ourselves on the banks

---

[1] Mr. George Bushby, B.C.S.

of the Nile, looking very yellow and majestic under the newly-risen moon. I and two others of the party embarked in a pretty good boat.

"*28th November.*—Walking along the bank we were accosted by two respectable Arabs, who, hearing that we were Ingleez, devoutly thanked Heaven that it was so, and then begged for a little snuff. Even taking that creature comfort between sunrise and sunset is unlawful during this severe fast of the Ramadan.

"The discipline of the crafty old savage, Muhammad Ali, both in his army and navy, is dreadfully severe. The wild birds are here more than usually fearless, from the rarity of firearms, the Pasha, wisely removing all the instruments of rebellion lest temptation should arise from their possession.

"Our boatmen, in common with their class, hold the superstition that asking or answering questions is alike unlucky. We contrived, however, to wring out of our Reis his opinion of Muhammad Ali and Ibrahim Pasha, which was most unfavourable. Touching the former he said nought, but made a drawing cut with the edge of his hand which spoke volumes, accompanied, as it was, with a most sinister scowl. He had been a boatman on board the yacht in which Ibrahim Pasha used to take his pleasure on the Nile. Before our interpreter came to our aid, he had made us understand by the most extravagant pantomime the particulars of that personage's drunken and then too often blood-stained orgies. A few days back one of the Pasha's ministers being disgusted at the loose life of his niece as regarded Franks (sin with a Moslem being venial), had her accused,—her large fortune being the bait in reality,—and obtained her condemnation. The miserable lady was carried by night in a boat to the middle of the Nile, opposite Cairo, when the executioner literally twisted her neck round till it broke, and then threw her into the dark waters.   It is too horrible!

"At the fork of the river the expanse of water was very fine.   Population and villages seemed to increase, judging from the now distinct sound of the discordant drum warning all conscientious men to gluttonize no more, and to smoke their last pipe before daybreak.   Shortly before the sun rose—which it did with a cloudless majesty not to be described, its coming forth having been heralded by a gleaming vanguard of tints and hues, so glorious, so chaste, and so varied as to defy the painter's art—we arrived opposite Boulac, the port of Cairo ; the tall minarets of the latter glancing in the distance, and the huge paper, gun, and other manufactories of the former, conveying a certain idea of national prosperity, which, however, receives a check from the after-thought that their cost is human misery in its most aggravated degree.   The country all round looked like a garden when compared to the uncultivated wastes we had left behind ; but the hollow eyes, emaciated bodies, and utterly joyless aspect of the inhabitants, seemed to plead to Heaven against the ruthless means employed to produce this flimsy mask of agricultural prosperity. Muhammad Ali has for ever alienated the affections of his subjects, not only by his cruelties, but by his short-sighted plan of forced labour in all departments.   When visiting the citadel, the abominable massacre of the Memluks was dwelt on with horror by my guide.   Muhammad Ali is now building over the scene of the carnage, as if by doing so he could obliterate the remembrance of the darkest of his dark deeds.

"I visited the slave market.   This was done under the cloak of my Musalman companion's meditating a purchase. In this way we entered the inner chambers, and certainly I was disgusted to satiety.   Besides natives of Nubia and

Dongola, chiefly girls, there were Abyssinians, nearly as fair as myself, and the way in which they were uncovered and examined, like so many animals, was shocking. Some of these poor creatures shrunk from these insults to their natural feelings, and were rudely checked for their untimely modesty. The treatment they receive after being kidnapped during their long voyage down the Nile induces many of these unfortunates to jump overboard. I bought some of the whips of these traders in human flesh, called Korbash. They are of the hide of the hippopotamus, and cut like a knife. One little Nubian boy took my janissary aside, on my noticing him, and begged that I might not be allowed to buy him, as I was a Christian. Doubtless he had heard many of the horrible stories circulated among the Musalman population as to our ferocious propensities.

"*30th November.*—Spent some hours in the enchanting gardens of Shubrah, which present a delightful combination of Oriental and European taste. I only required the presence of those to whom my soul is bound to have been chained to the spot.

"Visited with great interest Mr. Lieder's mission at Cairo, which is doing good preparatory work.

"*4th December.*—Went with Mr. Bell, R.N., to the Mosk of Sultan Hasan. Bell is a fine looking, daring man, and speaks Arabic, French, and Italian with fluency, possessing also a knowledge of Romaic and Turkish. Besides his escape from drowning when the *Tigris* went down (on Colonel Chesney's expedition), he has gone through many scenes of equal peril. On one occasion he was conveying despatches from Chesney, accompanied by a Nubian servant and an escort of friendly Arabs, to Aleppo. They pushed on through the desert during the afternoon in safety, and resolved to travel all night. About midnight they arrived at a very wild and suspicious-looking spot, when a shrill yell was heard, and a large party of banditti pounced upon them. The escort, without exchanging thrust or cut, fled incontinently, so that Bell and his servants had also to trust to the swiftness of their beasts. The keen vision of the desert robbers marked their proper prey on the instant, and for some time the headlong race for life and death was well contested, the advantage being in favour of our adventurer, who was right well mounted, but unfortunately his servant, in whose saddle-bags the letters were, was not so. Bell partly reined up to relieve him of his charge, which enabled the foremost pursuer to close on them. Already the Bedouin's lance was quivering within a few feet of the Nubian's back, when Bell turned round in his saddle and levelled his carbine to shoot him. At that moment his girth broke, he fell with stunning violence to the ground, and before he could jump up and draw his sabre, the Arab, throwing his horse back on its haunches, had sprung off, plucked from his girdle a heavy mace, and dealt our prostrate friend three tremendous blows on the head. Bell knew no more until about three hours after, when he awoke as from a deep sleep, and found himself alone, drenched in his own blood, stripped to his shirt, and in the midst of a howling wilderness infested by troops of hyenas and other unpleasant nocturnal ramblers, without even a stick to defend himself. But the same Providence which had abated the force of the Arab's blows, and had watched over him as he lay senseless, was still his friend. Looking about he spied to his great joy the despatches, which, unperceived by the robbers, had been thrown down in the scuffle. These he secured, and then for six hours pursued his toilsome and dreary way, tormented by the thirst of a wounded man, and under no small apprehension of being met with again and presently despatched until he reached the tents of a peaceful tribe. There the women bound up his head, he drank some stinking water, which was all they had, mounted a horse of the Sheikh, and with a guide set out again for Aleppo, which he contrived to reach in safety. He has still a deep dent in his forehead, and two other large scars from the cudgel play of his adversary. The Nubian, who was bound on a camel and carried off prisoner, but who escaped some days after by plunging into the Euphrates and swimming across, on rejoining Chesney's party, related that the banditti tried to carry away Bell also, but, seeing his head fall back when they lifted him up, they threw him down again as dead.

"*18th December.*—Left Cairo in a small waggon drawn by two horses, with two dromedaries as leaders, rather a novel team. The dromedary drivers sometimes rode and sometimes ran, their beasts at times exhibiting fits of extraordinary obstinacy, lying down and biting like furies. One black Arab ran with his dromedary thirty miles. I never saw such a sinewy vagabond."

Mackenzie suffered extremely from a Nile boil on the right wrist, which made the arm swell to an extraordinary degree, and brought on sharp fever. He embarked at Suez on board the Berenice steamer on 22d December, having been detained nearly a month in Egypt. He mentions the curious history of Boghos Bey, the Accountant-General, "the shrewdest man in the country, possessing a blandness and courtesy of manner most difficult to resist. It is said of Boghos Bey, in whom the Pasha has long placed unbounded confidence, that many years ago, having offended his patron, he was summarily shoved into a sack and sent Nilewards. *En route*, fortunately, his most intimate friend, also at the time blessed with the despot's dangerous friendship, met the grim cavalcade, and asked who was in the bag. Struck with horror at the response, he had recourse to the most effectual mode of entreaty, and bought Boghos

at a fair price from the soldiers, who reported that they had
committed him to the keeping of the water-kelpy.   Some
time after, Muhammad Ali's accounts got entangled, and
aloud did the Pasha deplore his rash indulgence of bad
humour.   The friend of the supposed defunct, with due
caution, acquainted his master with the real state of the
case, ever since which Boghos has basked in the hottest
beams of Satanic favour.

   "*29th December.*—Reached Aden, taken about a year ago
by orders of the Bombay Government (the first conquest of
Her Majesty's reign).   It then contained between 700 and
800 inhabitants, but that number is now nearly trebled. Six
weeks ago, on the morning of the 11th ultimo, while yet dark,
five thousand Arabs made a desperate attack on our troops,
in all scarcely four hundred men.   They were repulsed
with a loss of three hundred, none on our side being even
wounded—a wonderful circumstance.   One of the Bombay-
European regiment, commonly called the 'Toughs,' was,
some time back, murdered by the Arabs while picking up
shells on the seashore.   He was unarmed ; but with that
truly British weapon, the fist, he knocked down the first
assassin, and was trying to strangle him when another
stabbed him in the back.   His comrades, in the late affair,
consequently gave no quarter.   In the wars of these Arab
tribes among themselves, a battle in which they lose two or
three is looked on as a bloody one.   Such a slaughter
generally produces overtures of peace, which, being accepted, the families of the slain find out the slayers, and a
deadly feud is kept up between them till the price of blood
is paid.   The loss of three hundred, therefore, astounded
these good folks ; and a day or two after, the sheikhs of the
tribes, who had been urged on to the attack by our principal
enemy, the Sultan of Fandli, assembled and took an oath
on the Kurán to avenge their slain comrades or die.   Not-

withstanding, an embassy has since made its appearance with overtures for peace.

"Returning from viewing the Turkish wall yesterday, one of my companions, being mounted on a horse of the kind called 'man-eaters,' had a narrow escape. The beast made a furious attack on the horse of a lady (a Mrs. Moore) who was passing by, threw my friend off, and commenced trampling on and kicking him in a way that made me give him up for lost. He and the lady (who only screamed once) were in infinite peril, and I could assist neither, as I was mounted on a dromedary specially inclined to bite. By good luck a sailor gallantly rushed forward, and although trampled down, and severely cut across the forehead, secured the bridle. The lady would not leave the field until she had ascertained the extent of my friend's damages, which were pretty severe. This same heroine was, on the night of the attack, behind the Turkish wall in a tent with her husband, who, on the first alarm, armed and ran to his post. The advancing columns of Arabs came creeping in silence on their hands and knees towards our batteries, but on receiving a volley, sprung up, and yelling hideously, contrived, in spite of the murderous discharge of grape, to throw some two hundred men within our lines. Two privates of the European regiment made a dash for Mrs. Moore's tent and, catching her up in their arms, escaped into the battery, just as a party of the enemy gained the tent, which they attempted to burn. The poor lady sat wrapped in a cloak close to a great gun during the whole affair, with balls flying round her, but preserving the utmost calmness and presence of mind."

On the 2d January the voyagers witnessed a curious phenomenon. There was no moon, but the sea became white as milk as far as the horizon, and appeared like a boundless plain covered with new-fallen snow. "The captain told me that once in the Persian Gulf he saw a most wonderful sight. The whole sea was as one sheet of liquid fire, the billows of which rolled up from leeward, the vessel rising to them, and shot out on the windward side in tongues and forks of flame.

"On the 10th January 1840 we arrived at Bombay. Public works were going on on the Sabbath. This was not permitted by Mr. Farish, when acting Governor. The very natives look with contempt on *soi-disant* Christians thus violating their first obligations. The old practice of worshipping the statue of Lord Cornwallis is still in high value among the natives of Bombay. Little did he anticipate divine honours being paid him after death. Many of the statues of our deceased great men all over India are reverenced in the same way by the superstitious natives. After being hospitably entertained by my old friend Gray, left Bombay on 22d January.

"At Puna (23d January 1840) received much kindness and hospitality from Captain Rudd, commanding the Police Corps, which is in excellent order. Among them are a number of that notorious tribe of robbers, the Rámushis. These men are skilful in detecting marauders to a degree incredible to Europeans. Let a thief double like a fox, they can track him by his footmarks for upwards of twenty miles over ground where the unpractised eye cannot discern a trace, and they can frequently determine who and what he is from his mode of walking, the almost imperceptible peculiarity in the shape of his sandal, etc. Two sons of the celebrated Umiah (whose terrible exploits and magical dexterity in escaping the fangs of justice are still a theme of wonder among the villagers) are, notwithstanding the execution of their father, active members of this gang in our service.

"*27th January*, Aurangabad. — Warmly welcomed by

my old friend Captain Hugh Inglis, now commanding a
regiment of Nizám's Cavalry. The tomb of Aurangzeb's
daughter was shown to us by an old Hadji, who was
accompanied by a most interesting child, his only daughter,
who trips by his side, her sweet, olive face, intensely lustrous
black eyes, and fairy figure, contrasting well with the grave,
wrinkled visage, long white beard, and toil-worn but still
sinewy form of her father. I took some notice of the
child, for my heart warmed to the little creature, and gave
her a small piece of silver. The old man looked at me
with real emotion, and said : 'Surely my lord has children
also.' He was right as to the nature of my feelings, for
the images of my darlings were, as they constantly are,
before me.

   "At the famous fortress of Doulatabád Inglis told me
the legend that one of the caves had been the residence of
a famous 'Pari' (fairy), a great friend of King Solomon's,
and a promoter of the true faith. He (Inglis) once modestly
hinted his doubts as to Solomon having been a Musalman,
which heresy greatly offended his informant, and called
forth a severe reproof for so hardened a display of misbelief
on the very spot which had been sanctified by the presence
of the orthodox elf. Even his Orderly (one of his own
spearmen) showed unequivocal symptoms of disgust at his
leader's spiritual depravity. When visiting the caves of
Ajanta Inglis asked his Musalman Orderly the names of
some of the images. To be supposed learned in such a
diabolical nomenclature rather ruffled that worthy's dignity,
and he replied : 'Your Highness, I really do not pretend to
distinguish one Shaitán from another, but one thing I can
tell you, viz. that these are the identical scoundrels who
hollowed out the caves, which they fully intended to carry
away to Ellora to perfect the suite of the devil's apartments
there, but just as they placed their backs to the walls to

lift their accursed burthen, a stronger Shaitán than themselves, who owed them a grudge, transformed them into stone, as your Excellency beholds!'

"One of the sculptures represents all manner of beasts assisting in the creation of the world—huge tigers, less bloodthirsty than the present race, are laying out gardens, a most extraordinary taste for the feline genus! and giant apes are arranging the position of the various chains of mountains; but our guide cheerfully acquiesced in any improvement in the details of his traditions which our levity prompted us to make—such as that these caves were actually in existence before the present world was thought of.

"Now that the horrors of Thuggism have been exposed, three figures which were brought to our notice possess interest—viz. a great fat Brahman kneeling before the altar of his god, a truculent Thug tightening a rope round the neck of the pious man, and Brahma himself rising suddenly out of the shrine, and, with a villainous leer, thrusting his foot with apparently a forty-horse power into the pit of the stomach of Káli's disciple, to the great detriment of his respiratory organs." This group is an appalling proof of the extreme antiquity of Thuggism.

Mackenzie now started on a march across India in company with Mr. George Bushby, afterwards Resident at Haidrabad; his nephew, Henry Bushby, now a magistrate in London; and Dr. Metcalfe, a son of Sir Charles, who was to perish at Gandamak. He writes:—

"Passing through the Haidrabad country it is impossible to shut one's eyes to the evident consequences of the tyranny and misgovernment of the Nizám and his minister Chandu Lál. Large tracts of land once highly cultivated are now covered with jungle, the people are wretched and discontented, frequently rising in insurrection, in which they would certainly succeed but for our power,

which is employed to uphold the wretches who thus grind
their unhappy countrymen to the dust.

"Near Karanjah the elder Bushby, Metcalfe, and I
were walking about half a mile in advance of our palanquins,
enjoying the cool moonlight after the oppressive heat, when
we came to a nallah [1] bordered with long grass and several
suspicious-looking thickets. The water being too broad for
a leap, we turned aside to find a narrower place. Bushby
remarked that it was a famous cover for a tiger. Hardly
had we gone a dozen steps when a huge individual of that
truculent family rose up within a few yards of us from the
water's edge, where he had been drinking. We 'halted,'
but did not 'stand at ease,' and he did the same, apparently
selecting the fattest of the three, in which case I should
have got off. We were without arms, having foolishly left
them in the palanquins, and the only way was to out-face
him, my mind running on the fact of a fellow, when I was
stationed at Nagpur, having, on being seized by a tiger,
thumped him on the head with a pebble with such perseverance as to induce him to let go. Thank God, the
creature thought better of it and took his sullen way into
the recesses of the forest. He probably was gorged. Our
palkis having come up, we armed and went on again. A
few hundred yards beyond the nallah, near which, the day
before, a man and his horse had been killed by a tiger, we
encountered two of the Raja's sawárs, whose path had just
been crossed by another tiger to the consternation of their
horses. They turned back with us, vapouring in front with
their long spears ready for a charge (which their horses
would never have executed); and, as our palkis again
lagged behind, to my amusement they ordered one of our
guides to walk last, that being the post of danger in case of
a lurking tiger, an injunction which the honest man obeyed

[1] Stream.

with, to my mind, unnatural alacrity! The jungle on the
hills was blazing magnificently, probably set on fire by Bhil
marauders—a most brilliant and imposing spectacle. At
Karanjah we found our people had been scared out of their
senses by another tiger. A spearman mounted guard while
we slept, his martial equipments and picturesque dress as
he sat on his equally wild-looking charger, appearing to
great advantage in the bright moonbeams, which glanced
coldly off the steel head of his long lance stuck upright in
the ground beside him.

"Leaving Karanjah, we came upon the body of a poor
man who had been killed two or three hours before by a
buffalo. A short way from the village we perceived a huge
hyena intent on pouncing on a terrier belonging to our
suite. Bushby fired his pistol at him, and I pursued him
at speed and chevied him in the moonlight across the plain
with murderous intent, but a ravine, into which he plunged,
saved him, my ball whistling close enough to admonish him
of the danger of again meditating evil against small doggies.

"14th February.—At the Nagpur Residency met with
a warm welcome from Major Wilkinson, who, in his present
exalted situation, is the same friendly, kind-hearted man I
knew eleven years ago.

"Nagpur looks very different from what I had left it
in '28. The European officers were withdrawn by Lord
W. Bentinck's order from the Raja's service, to the complete disorganisation of the matured plans for the better
government of the country, originated by the present Sir
Richard Jenkins under the direction of Lord Hastings. It
really looks as if we delighted to produce the greatest
possible misery in these dependent States by leaving them
to the uncontrolled mismanagement of their native rulers
(the natural remedy of assassination and revolution being
withheld from the oppressed by our presence) in order

to give us finally a pretext for seizing on the whole country.

"18*th February.*—Remembering my dangerous illness here, I bless God that I have been spared, as, even in my shortsightedness, I can plainly perceive His abounding mercy therein ; and I know that when the awful moment does arrive when my soul shall be required of me, all the pains and sorrows I have felt or may be still called upon to endure will appear in their true light, viz. as messages of love from my Redeemer.

"At Jabalpur I was in thought carried back to the time when, more than ten years ago, I last went this journey. How different now my thoughts, sentiments, and opinions ! but inanimate nature had undergone no perceptible change.

"Reached Calcutta on the 7th March 1840."

CHAPTER IX.

(1840.)

DURING his stay in Calcutta Mackenzie was selected by Lord Auckland for political service in Afghanistan, and employed himself in studying various matters, a knowledge of which was necessary for the career on which he was about to enter. He left Calcutta on the 15th July in a flat towed by a steam-tug up the Bhágarati and Ganges, in company with his friend and brother cadet, George Broadfoot, of whom he writes:—

"What with his extensive acquirements in languages, both Asiatic and European, in science, and his thorough knowledge of his profession, Broadfoot is the most accomplished officer I have met with. As a cadet, he promised to be an ornament to the service, which he has since become."

So tedious was their passage up the swollen river that they took four weeks to reach Allahabad. Mackenzie and an excellent man, Mr. Cahill, an indigo planter, succeeded in establishing Divine service on board on Sundays.

At Ghazipur he for the first time met the old Chevalier de l'Etang, his wife's grandfather, now eighty-four, who had been for many years at the head of the Government stud, "an excellent specimen of a French gentleman of the old school, who received him with affectionate *empressement*." He spent three days at Benares with his sister and brother-in-law, Captain Carpenter, then in charge of the various captive Rajas residing at Benares. Under his sister's roof the kindly affections had full play. He had some long conversations with the unfortunate Raja of Satára, not long before deposed by the Bombay Government, who, he says, "took mightily to me on account of my expressing some sympathy with his misfortunes. The impressions I had received in Bombay and Calcutta, that his supposed treason towards us was the result of a foul conspiracy to effect his downfall, were greatly strengthened." At Cawnpore all H.M.'s 3d Dragoons sought to be hospitable to the two travellers. They bought camels, seven of the Kabul breed, at only 55 rupees, and nine of the larger Indian race for 82 rupees each. Cawnpore, being famous for camp equipage, they furnished themselves with tents, Mackenzie presenting his faithful servant Jacob "with a stout, active pony, on which he pranced forth with infinite satisfaction." At Alighar he received instructions from Sir W. Macnaghten to hasten onwards to Lodiana to take charge of the blind Shah Zemán, with his family, and that of Shah Shujah, and to march them across the Panjab to Kabul. He explored the field of Lord Lake's defeat of Perron's cavalry, and the monument to the gallant officers who fell; and adds : "If military glory consists in the consciousness of having been enabled to perform duty, and in feeling unfeignedly thankful to Him by whom alone we can prevail, I covet it; but if in the ignorant applause of my fellow mortals, long may I continue indifferent to it. Our kind host, Mr. Neave, reads prayers on Sundays ; but, although there are some thirteen officers and divers civilians here, the congregation consisted of two or three half-caste drummers, one woman, and a few children. The Sabbath is habitually desecrated, being devoted to amusements such as billiards, etc. Two of the officers are married to sisters, a third sister being the wife of a Musalman gentleman, a most extraordinary and unhallowed connection for a Christian lady !

"11th September.—Agra:—put up with my friend Thomason, secretary to the Lieutenant-Governor." Then follows a graphic description of the well-known Táj and of the orphanages containing 160 boys and about as many girls, saved from the famines of 1837 and '38, brought up as Christians and taught different trades.

"18th September.—News from Afghanistan gloomy. Every soldier who ventures one hundred yards from the sentries is pretty sure to be attacked. Many have been murdered. The animosity of the entire population against our puppet king, Shah Shujah, increases every day. Letters constantly intercepted offering to join in a general rising and slay the Feringhis, if Dost Muhammad, now at Kulum, will make his appearance once more among them, the Sikhs intriguing and supplying the rebels with money.

"22d September.—Started in my palki for Fattihpur Sikri to rejoin Broadfoot. The principal entrance to the Mosk is by an enormous gateway, to which you ascend by a flight of steps on the same scale. Broadfoot says that nowhere on the Continent has he seen arches that can be compared to these for gigantic beauty. Our guide, an old gentleman named Bishárat Ali, asked leave to say his prayers, and after going through the proscribed prostrations, offered to wrestle in prayer for us, albeit we were in the wrong path, especially if we had set our heart on any particular object. Broadfoot desired general prosperity, but I, having no faith in the process, politely declined his offer. He set to work accordingly on Broadfoot's behalf, remarking that he might as well say something for himself, and that was, that Providence would lead a host of generous gentlemen to Fattihpur Sikri, by whose bakshish he might benefit largely. Such, in sober earnest, is unassisted prayer, even though it be made in Christ's name.

Our guide informed us with much mystery that the evening before the Musalman public had given thanks in the Mosk for Clibborn's defeat, and had rejoiced greatly over it, he alone remaining faithful. There is no doubt that every little reverse of ours occasions much joy among the majority of the natives, especially the Muhammadans. Much gratified by our presents, he besought us to turn to the true faith, or at least not to get drunk, to abstain from the flesh of 'a certain animal, to pronounce whose name would fill him with shame and disgust,' and not to put our feet on books containing the name of God.

"*24th September*, Bhartpur.—At daybreak met a messenger of the Raja who had been apprised of our coming, and who, with his invariable liberal hospitality towards our countrymen, had sent an agent to Fattihpur Sikri the evening before to take our commands. Leaving a guard of troopers with matchlocks to accompany our palanquins, we now mounted an elephant and proceeded by a circuitous route through the forest with four very handsome hunting leopards (cheetahs), who, as they stood erect in their carts waving their long tails, and making a sort of complaining noise from time to time—for the creatures divined what we were after—looked very noble and graceful. Came upon some antelopes, but were unfortunate in not getting near enough. Good lodgings had been provided for us in the city, with servants, etc. Our courtyard opened into one of the Raja's gardens, whose shady walks stretched down to the moat of the citadel. It was taken by the Bengal European Regiment, who had been ordered to attack the smaller breach to draw away the enemy from the real point of attack, and who not only gained the walls, but forced their way through a fierce opposition right into the citadel. Out of this Lord Combermere, on the cessation of resistance, forthwith marched them, to make way for the 14th Foot; and to crown this piece of wretched partiality and injustice, omitted to mention the former gallant corps in his despatch! We were fed sumptuously by our exalted host, and received a native gentleman on his part, who came to pay us the usual compliments, and to present trays of flowers and fruits, with a whole bazar of delicacies. To this was added in the Eastern mode two bags of money, which we courteously declined. Our friend Vinkátásu, a Guzerát Brahman, was most intelligent and polished, frank in affording information, and full of the praises of the Raja, who appears to be a just and proper man, who understands English and looks into his own affairs.

"*25th.*—Started before daylight for the Raja's Ramna, or hunting-ground, which embraces forest, cultivated ground, and unreclaimed wastes, with plenty of tanks and marshes, and consequently abounds in every sort of game except tigers, which generally keep to the hills in the vicinity of Deeg. Mounted elephants, and sent on the palkis. Our object being to course the antelope, we passed with indifference all else that might otherwise have induced B. and myself to waste powder and shot,—both being wretched marksmen. The stately and magnificent peacock, and his scarcely less beautiful mate, with her train of chicks, as a matter of necessity in this part of the world, where slaying one is sacrilege, stalked by unscathed. Bands of gobbling pelicans and groups of tall cyruses [1] in their half-Quaker, half-lancer plumage consulted and conferred together, in seeming perplexity as to the nature of our intentions. The partridge and hare kept close in their grassy retreats; companies of quails burst away with a

---

[1] A sort of crane with gray and scarlet plumage.

whirr from under our feet, but we were set on disturbing
the peace of several large herds of deer which, encouraged
by the constant companionship of the harmless cultivators,
cropped the tender herbage or frolicked with agile bound
in fancied security. Not to alarm them we stopped the
elephants. The four carts, on which the cheetahs were
slightly tied, then moved on in different directions with
seeming carelessness, and an appearance of being engaged
in the every-day work of the field, calculated to deceive the
incautious antelopes. Meantime the cheetahs were kept
with their eyes hooded, notwithstanding which they expressed their consciousness of what was going on by a low
grumble rather than a growl. At last, the requisite distance being reached, one was unhooded and unbound.
Glancing round with an eye of fire, he slipped down from
the cart, and singling out his victim, in an instant he
dashed after it. The swiftness of the antelope is proverbial, but although it was exerted to the uttermost, it
was of no avail. In less than a couple of hundred yards
the last fatal bound was made, the death-stroke fell, and
at the same time the cheetah's fangs were sunk deep in the
jugular of the unhappy deer. Hastening up, we found the
conqueror lying on his prey, of which he retained his hold
with the tenacity of a thorough-bred bull-dog. To loose
him it was necessary to obtain a ladle full of blood by cutting the throat lower than his grip, and pushing the cheering cup against his nose. The smell and taste overcame
his obstinacy, and after lapping the seductive draught with
great gusto, he allowed himself to be reconducted to his
cart, on which he jumped of his own accord. We killed
another, a fine black buck, in the same way; but the
cheetah was more savage, and objected to returning to his
cart. The keepers told us that they seldom show either
caprice or ferocity towards them, and that the utmost mild-

ness is necessary, or the animal is spoilt, and becomes dangerous. This kind of leopard is, I believe, only met with in the deserts of Rajputáná.

"26th Sept., Deeg.—Early in the morning discovered that the taste of our master of ceremonies had lodged us in the most romantic spot possible. It was an old palace, built by the founder of the present Bhartpur dynasty on a magnificent scale. Our apartment looked out on a beautiful piece of water, surrounded by trees and temples, beyond which part of the town appeared, with the remains of the old wall and fortifications, amongst which the Shah burj (assaulted and taken by Lord Lake) stood conspicuous. Cool tanks and shady trees contrasted with the dismantled but still firm-looking citadel, which towered above all, lowering, as it were, in huge discontent at its own fallen importance, and at the cheerful independence and peaceful prosperity of the humble dwellings that formerly barely existed by its permission.

"Visited the Raja's principal garden, which contains an abundance of beautiful fountains, in which I delight, which were made to play for our gratification.

"I am bound to mention, with the praise due, the flourishing state of the Bhartpur territory, owing to the mild and judicious administration of His Highness Balwant Sing, of whom his respectable subjects, both Musalmans and Hindus, speak in the highest terms. In India, where the principal part of the revenue is derived from the land, the prosperity of the country and the character of the ruler may be pretty well estimated from the state of agriculture and the appearance of the peasantry."

At Delhi Mackenzie met with a real Highland welcome from a cousin, Captain Kenneth Mackenzie of Kincraig, and hurriedly visited all the principal sights—"the palace, now quite shorn of all its ancient splendour, and filled with the idle, dissolute relations and hangers-on of the poor old emperor, who sits moping in his solitary corner from one year's end to another."

Broadfoot describes "how Colin lost himself at night in a jungle, and was hunted for with elephants and torches; how we were objects of great curiosity throughout, for I had been recognised by some who remembered me a Musalman! how Colin (with indignation he heard it) was, if *not my son*, a very young warrior setting out under my auspices. He is very much better, but still far from well. I was at one time very apprehensive about him."

Mackenzie continues:—"Rode and dawked (*i.e.* travelled in palanquin) from Delhi to Lodiana, arriving on the 10th October; found that the departure of Shah Zemán and his family was indefinitely postponed owing to the continued disturbances in Afghanistan. Put up with Lieutenant Joe Cunninghame, Mr. Clerk's assistant. I wish for immediate employment, but would rather shirk the charge of nearly nine hundred female inmates of two royal scraglios. They and their attendants form a body of some six thousand souls, requiring, for the march to Kabul, upwards of fifteen hundred camels. Some sixty of these ladies are of sufficient rank to claim palanquins, the remainder travel in kajáwahs or panniers, swung on either side of a camel. I have looked at these kajáwahs, and certainly it requires the supple limbs of an Asiatic to travel a mile in such a conveyance without dying of cramp, especially with the rough jolting pace of an ordinary dromedary. Most of these poor girls have been born in Lodiana since the exile of the two Shahs from Afghanistan; and I fancy, if they ever do go to Kabul, exposed, as they most likely will be, to all sorts of fears, fatigues, and anxieties, from the perpetual state of warfare in which that unhappy country must remain for years to come, they would be too glad to return to the dull repose of the Zenana here. Met Mr. Ball of the Indian

Navy, who commanded the first steamer ever seen on the
Satlej. He told me the attention of most natives on the
banks of the Indus seemed to be more excited by the spectacle of the fowls confined in coops, than by the engine, or
aught else about the ship.

"The chief political authority here is Mr. Clerk (subsequently Sir George Clerk). His predecessor, Sir Colonel
Claude Wade, was too well acquainted with the intrigues and
rascality of the Panjabis to suit them. To disgust Lord
Auckland with him, they affected, during his lordship's late
visit to Lahore, to treat Wade with studied neglect, avoiding
all communication with him, as if he were so utterly dis-
tasteful to their Government as to make it a sheer matter
of policy to replace him by another Agent, through whom
negotiations might be carried on more smoothly. Lord
Auckland left this, without appearing to be overcome.
The Sikhs supposed that Wade had obtained a victory, and
forthwith returned to their former friendly mode of trans-
acting business with him, and actually gave up to him the
strongly-contested point of allowing one of our convoys to
pass through their country. Meantime, Lord Auckland
suffered ill advisers to prevail, and superseded Wade;
thereby affording a great and unexpected triumph to our
subtle enemies, and holding out but little encouragement to
the honest servants of the State. Clerk's course is rendered
more difficult by the weak conduct of Government with regard to his predecessor. Hitherto he has reported the
Sikhs as more favourably disposed towards us than Wade
did, thereby coming violently into collision with Sir William
Macnaghten, whose letters to Government affirm them to
be the prime movers, not so much in favour of Dost
Muhammad as against Shah Shujah.

"*November* 1840, Firozpur.—Met with a warm welcome
from Mr. Clerk, with whose manner and appearance I was

as much pleased as I was struck with the ease with which
he despatched business of every description, a tithe of which
would greatly oppress most men, even of more than ordinary
capacity.

"Strange intelligence from Lahore. Kharak Sing dead,
and burnt with his principal wife and three wretched slave-
girls. The new Maharaja, Nao Nehál Singh, going to the
ceremony, was passing under a gateway, when a beam from
above fell on and killed him and his companion, a young
son of Guláb Singh, one of the two chief Diwáns. With
Clerk's approval, Sher Sing, an acknowledged son of Ranjit,
started to take possession of the throne.

"I was introduced to Shelton as a stranger; we recognised each other, although neither acknowledged it. He
has been very civil; but I shall not join his brigade."

He records his first meeting with Henry Lawrence.
"Met Captain Lawrence, Assistant Political Agent here,
and dined with him. Clever and good man. Town improving wonderfully under our auspices. Inhabitants
pouring of their own accord into our territory from the
neighbouring petty states. The chiefs jealous, and punish
those they catch emigrating. Clerk gave me many curious
details as to the social state of the motley multitude of small
states over which he has the chief control. There are
between three and four hundred vakils or ministers from
these independent kingdoms, constantly waiting on him,
and tormenting him out of his life, besides an incredible
amount of other work. He cannot stand such uninter-
mitting fagging much longer. But Governments always
spur a willing horse to death. One community, consisting
of about twenty thousand persons, has been for some
hundreds of years literally without a government, each
man being his own chief. This they have great pride in,
and, strange to say, although pure Sikhs, and surrounded

by neighbours of the worst character, they actually refrain from the indigenous vices of India—viz. lying and stealing. They shed blood, however, without remorse, and are a habitually warlike race, always going to their labours in the field armed to the teeth. The Raja of Patiála, about ten years ago, was in the habit of attacking these people, under the pretence of some long forgotten, if not fictitious, claim to their homage. The British Government, to stop the effusion of much blood, interfered, and placed this now sole specimen of the pure original Sikh under the management of Mr. Clerk. Clerk was sorely puzzled how to deal with a tribe in which the son was wholly independent of the father, the labourer of the landlord, etc., who acknowledged no system of laws, and none in the wide world as their superior. After some years, he persuaded them to elect fifty representatives, whose decisions, in which Clerk should agree, they promised to obey. But it was all in vain; for day by day the rising generation asserted their rights as they came to man's estate, declaring they could not obey, as they had had no hand in the election of the representatives to whom their fathers had given their votes; and, indeed, the elders themselves, when a case was decided against them, sturdily asked what right their equals had to lord it over them. They would resist unto blood any attempt to enforce the observance of any rules whatever; to save which extremity, the supreme Government prefer leaving the management of them to the ingenuity and tact of the Political Agent.

"The Panjab is infested by a set of Sikhs called 'Akalis,' signifying 'immortals.' To this any reckless vagabond may belong, if he chooses to give himself up entirely to harassing his neighbours by depredations and wanton shedding of blood, and to destroy himself by drunkenness, eating bang, and throwing his life away in any mad quarrel or adventure. They were useful to Ranjit Singh in heading his most desperate attacks on his many enemies ; but he himself was frequently in danger from their ferocious habits and fanaticism. One of them even attempted to cut him down in the presence of the Governor-General. Old Ranjit ordered his nose, ears, and hands to be cut off; but, when a little cooler, fearing to disgust so powerful a body, he reprieved him. Clerk mentioned that at times large bodies of Akalis found their way across the Satlej and ravaged the protected Sikh States. Once, while he was at Ambala, one of these destroying parties picketed their horses and pitched their camp in a field of corn. The zamindar of the neighbouring village sent civilly to request them to remove to an uncultivated spot. Their answer was, cutting the messenger down. He then sent his son, whom they also killed. The villagers then despatched a party towards Ambala to ask for assistance. These were immediately intercepted by the Akalis and slaughtered. A messenger, however, contrived to steal quietly away, and reported these monstrosities to Clerk, who forthwith sent a circular post through the country, warning the various Rajas to assist in capturing the brigands, he himself making with a party of horse towards the spot. All, however, seemed in vain, for the Akalis had dispersed and could not be traced. They, were, however, rather premature in reassembling (while still within the limits of the protected States) immediately in the vicinity of a Musalman chief, who sent out a strong body of Patán riders, who longed for nothing better than to cut up idolaters. The Akalis, being summoned to surrender, requested a conference with one of the attacking party. The young khan bravely went forward, and was straightway shot through the head. Some days after Clerk was surprised at Ambala by the appearance of the Patáns with several carts, which stank afar off ; and no wonder, for they were filled with the decomposed fragments of the Akalis,—all but one

having been literally made mincemeat of by the followers
of the poor young khan. The survivor hastened to Lahore, where he had the insolence to demand vengeance on
the British from Ranjit Singh, who, to quiet him and his
tribe, gave him large presents, and sent him to Peshawar.
Clerk not long since had to take notice of a frightful murder
by a Sikh woman of rank, who, to ensure her having a child,
in compliance with a brutal superstition that prevails in
these parts, enticed a little girl who was playing by a tank
into her house, where, with the assistance of an old woman,
she sacrificed her by sticking sharp nails into her temples.
Again, about three weeks ago, a Rajput lady, the wife of a
chief, having a child very sick, enticed a fine young man
into her house, where, with the aid of some Brahmans, she
sacrificed him to the idol Devi, and then, with her own
hands, washed the child all over in the blood of the victim
to restore it to health! Pity these wretches cannot be
severely punished.

" Heard of the melancholy fate of Lieutenant Loveday.
He had been sent in a political capacity to Khilat, where,
some little time back, he was taken by the Beluchis. The
other day the marauders started to sack Dádur, carrying
Loveday in chains with them. They spoiled the place ; but,
H.M.'s 40th foot and the 38th B.N.I. coming up, they were
obliged to evacuate it, after losing a great number of their
men. Our lads, on coming to the place where poor Loveday
had been left chained to a kajáwah (camel pannier), found
his body naked, his head cut off, and his servant sitting crying
at his feet. To be murdered in cold blood, bound hand and
foot, with his victorious countrymen in full career to deliver
him and almost in sight, must have tried Loveday's resignation and fortitude. On our first taking Khilat, Loveday had
been kind to the widow of the chief, who was slain in the
assault ; and she, in turn, had protected him when he was

captured. I should not be surprised if she were eventually the means of our being enabled to punish the murderers, for women are most earnest in their friendship when their feelings are enlisted in behalf of a generous enemy, even against their own people.

"A strange letter has been received from Sir Wm. Macnaghten, in which he warns all European officers and men not to attempt to bring hams or any other part of the unclean beast into Afghanistan, as all such abominations will be destroyed. No Muhammadan state, however arrogant or powerful, not even Persia, ever asked for the establishment of such a rule as that now laid down by Macnaghten."

CHAPTER X.

(1840.)

MR. CLERK having obtained the consent of the Panjab Government to the march of our troops through their territory, the Sikhs built a bridge of boats about four miles below Firozpur for the passage of Shelton's brigade.

As Mackenzie had lost some time in waiting for the family of the two Shahs, he was now allowed to push on, and this onerous charge was eventually fulfilled by George Broadfoot. On the 14th November Mackenzie rode down to see the troops pass. "The spectacle was very picturesque. The column[1] was seen winding slowly along the deep sandy ground which there forms the left bank of the Satlej, followed by countless strings of camels, pack and led horses, with an enormous multitude of camp-followers, etc., of every tribe and costume,—Afghans, Sikhs, Rajputs, Hindustanis, and others,—among whom the trains of several natives of rank accompanying the brigade, in all the pride and pomp of Eastern horsemanship, pranced along or wildly scoured the plain with a most reckless disregard to the comfort, and even safety, of their pedestrian fellow-travellers. It was with mingled emotions of pleasure and pain

---

[1] Consisting of 1st Troop Bengal Horse Artillery, 5th Bengal Cavalry, H.M.'s 44th, and the 27th and 54th Bengal N.I.—all in high order.

that I recognised among these chiefs Martaba Singh, the famous Nipál leader, whom I had seen in Calcutta in 1836 at the head of the finest regiment of light infantry I think I ever saw. Then he was in high favour with his own Court, was caressed beyond measure by our Government, and was apparently the most powerful and prosperous man of his nation. Since that he has gone through all the trials a man suspected by a native Court is subjected to. His family has been ruined; his uncle, Bhim Singh, put to death in the most cruel way; and himself not only degraded and despoiled of all he had, but absolutely tortured after a frightful fashion. He is now a fugitive at Lodiana, under the protection of the British. I knew his athletic, martial figure and his honest, open countenance; but, on taking a nearer look, I detected deep traces of care and suffering. Poor fellow, he battles bravely with his misfortunes. One Afghan nobleman who accompanies us is a nephew of our opponent Dost Muhammad. The filing of the troops across the bridge, the bands playing in front, had a fine effect. I fancy troops and followers are in all about 15,000 souls." When Mackenzie gazed with admiration on this fine force he little dreamed the brigade was marching straight to death. Within little more than a year they were lying slaughtered or frozen to death in the Khurd Kabul Pass.

"*18th November.*—Shortly after 6 A.M. overtook the advanced guard, commanded by Colonel Chambers[1] of the cavalry. My new horse is fat and saucy, and if a loose horse rushed past him, or a quick movement and clang of arms took place, he made him ready for battle, rearing, plunging, and bolting up in the air."

On entering a comparatively unknown country, Mackenzie's journal becomes full not only of graphic descriptions, but of minute details of the road, distances, nature of

[1] Fell in the Khurd Kabul Pass, 12th January 1842.

ground, crops, kind of trees, supplies, or their absence, etc.,
etc., forming a complete military itinerary up to Kabul,
invaluable at that time, but now unnecessary. A few
extracts illustrating the state of the country may be given.

"19*th Nov.*—Few wells and almost no population; no
supplies on the banks of the Rávi or Hydraotes. Sikhs impertinent, except one old man, who apparently never had
seen a European before. I made out his barbarous Panjabi
idiom with the help of my Lascar, who carried my ammunition. He asked if only gentlemen in my country were
white like me, and was astonished to find that the lower
castes were the same. He then asked if many of the
Sepoys going with us to Kabul were not Musalmans, and
commented on their iniquity in assisting Feringhis against
their brethren in the faith, adding that, if we were not at
peace with Lahore, the villagers would soon send us to the
right-about. He concluded by a friendly warning not to
stray so far from camp by myself, and especially not to be
abroad after sunset. Reason good, for we were beset with
thieves all night. Two rascals entered my tent : one seized
my brass washing basin and other utensils, and the other
my carpet-bag. I was so astonished at their cool way of
doing it, that I thought it must be my servants coming to
load the camels; but the truth flashing on me, I jumped
out of bed, seized a pistol, and gave chase to the lad with
the carpet-bag. I gained on him in the dark, and let fly,
then first remembering to call out 'Thief!' I cannot tell
if my ball took effect, but he dropped the bag and disappeared down a ravine. Heard the chink of my brazen
vessels vanishing in the distance. I picked up my bag, and
came back with my feet cut by my chase over sharp stones.
During yesterday's march our flanks and front were, so long
as it continued dark, infested by troops of armed plunderers,
who took advantage of every mistake in straying from the

main body, darting out of the scattered thorny jungle and long grass, cutting down the servants, and bolting with the camels and baggage. Riding on in front with Rattray (all whose clothes had been stolen) and a sawár, I came on one poor fellow sitting very melancholy and cold, stripped by the thieves, and bleeding fast from many sabre cuts. I did what I could for him, and left him in charge of a chaprási. Hodges of the 3d Cavalry had two servants wounded in like manner. Arriving in camp, found that even Cunningham's people had been attacked, and two camels taken. This was disgraceful, as several well-armed and mounted Sikh sawárs were present as a guard."

Mackenzie records a marvellous instance of an officer trying to become a Hindu. "M. of the Cavalry has performed pilgrimage as a Hindu devotee to Goburdhan and other sacred places, going through all the usual prayers, ablutions, etc., to the great scandal of his race, the infinite damage of his own soul, and exciting the contempt and disgust of the Hindus themselves, who looked on him as quite as unclean after as before all his serious tomfoolery."

He mentions reading part of a minute drawn up by Lord Auckland two years back, *i.e.* in 1838, when, "in defiance of all probability and the opinion of nine-tenths of those who were capable of forming a judgment, he determined to replace Shah Shujah on the throne, and thought the task would be so easy that it was certain we should be able to withdraw from Afghanistan in the spring of 1839 !" He pronounces the Governor-General "a good, well-intentioned, hard-working man, of shallow judgment," and his premises "vague surmises, almost all, to my knowledge, unfounded ; " and points out the almost impossibility of Shah Shujah being able to maintain himself or to raise a revenue, now that the Sikhs had possession of the most fertile provinces of Afghanistan.

"Colonel Shelton is a wretched brigadier. The monstrous confusion which takes place in crossing the rivers of the Panjab from his want of common arrangement is most disgraceful, and would be fatal in an avowed enemy's country."

"30th November 1840.—Having at length obtained a guard of four troopers—one of whom, as he belongs to Mr. Clerk's peculiar troop commanded by our noted spy and partizan, Suleymán, would probably stick to me—I have made up my mind to push on ahead of the brigade. All this morning the cold excessive."

Leaving the great plain, extending fourteen hundred miles to Calcutta, he entered the wild mountainous country in the west of the Panjab.

"No wells. The country almost impracticable, and supplies hardly to be procured. At the Jelam welcomed by one of the Sikh agents sent from Lahore to assist us. He procured me everything I wanted, but I suspect oppressed the poor in so doing. The shameful extortions of men in power among the Sikhs are quite abominable. Captain Bellew,[1] the Quartermaster-General, overtook me. We spent a very pleasant evening together. Encountered a Panjabi faqir, sitting apparently absorbed in thought, a wild, squalid, miserable man; but on my approaching him he suddenly sprang up, rushed towards me, and commenced shampooing my horse's shoulder, then my leg. Leaving me, he performed the same office for my sawár, and lastly condescended to pinch the attenuated calves of my old horse-keeper. The sawár explained to me that this was the mode in which the faqirs of the Panjab ask charity. I had no money, the sawár had none, and my sais could only produce a pais (less than a halfpenny), with which, however,

[1] Captain Bellew was to fall in the Khurd Kabul Pass less than fourteen months later.

the pious beggar appeared to be contented. Scenery of the most savage kind, until a sudden turn to the left brought the famous stronghold of Rotás suddenly before us, its black walls and bastions showing in strong relief against the sky."

Fortress of Rotás.—" The silence of this savage region oppresses the visitor with a sense of desolation, only equalled by his thankfulness that Providence has so ordered it, that good government and civilisation are, all over the world, making the construction of such wild retreats, in which lawless violence found safety from the just indignation of its victims, unnecessary and in fact useless."

On one occasion, after a thirty mile march, he says :—" Except a draught of milk I had fasted all day, and to encourage my people had walked most of the way, but at the end of it neither food nor forage were to be had." Again :—"I am fagged and sleepy at 11 P.M., but just about to take my watch outside the tents for two hours. It is shockingly cold."

It was this practice of sharing every hardship and labour with his followers which gave him such power over them. Men will do anything for a leader who will do everything with and for them.

7th December.—He notices the great accuracy of Elphinstone's work, which he seems to have carried with him. " Here the Chowdry (head of the shopkeepers), like many other Musalmans with whom I have conversed *en route*, expressed his earnest wish that we would take the country from the Sikhs. In this he was seconded by the elders of the village, who gathered round me to hear the news in the absence of my Sikh guard. Rawal Pindi : Halted, it being Sunday, and feasted my little camp."

Near the Margallah Ghát " crossed a stone bridge built by Shah Jehán, the only thing of the kind I have seen in the Panjab, of which this is the real boundary, the country from this to the Khaiber being a conquered province taken from the Afghans by Ranjit Singh.

"*8th December.*—In front of us is the great mountain of Gandghar (the castle of grief), part of a range inhabited by these bold freebooters, the Gakkers, whose Sultan does homage to the Court of Lahore by sending a 'Heriot,' viz. a fine horse, to the Maharaja every year. On one occasion he sulked, and refused the tribute. Ranjit Singh sent General Allard to reduce him to obedience, a difficult matter among the almost inaccessible mountains, where the Gakkers, formerly the lords paramount of the country from the Indus to the Jelam, preserve a sort of lawless independence. Allard tried negotiation, but failed; nevertheless, he persuaded the Sultan to send a Vakil to hear what he had to propose. On the arrival of the Envoy, Allard very quietly dismounted him, seized his horse, reported the success of his mission to Lahore, and sent the vexed dignitary back to his master on foot, 'with rusty spur and miry boot.'

"Ranjit Singh's passion for horses induced him to commit many absurdities. Witness his two years' war with Sultan Muhammad Khan of Peshawar, for the possession of the latter's gray horse 'Laili,' whose great excellence was a fast amble and great endurance.

"At Hasan Abdul a Sikh officer, Gopal Singh, commands the guard of the 'sacred proof' of the sanctity of Nának Ram, the founder of the Sikh sect. This 'sacred proof' is the deeply-indented mark of an outspread hand on a huge rock, which the Sikhs devoutly believe happened thus: Nának was busy with his religious duties when a demon took a mean advantage of him, and cast at him the great stone, which would have taken a hundred such as Ajax or the Douglas to have 'putted' so far. The saint,

however, was wide awake, and seeing his danger, merely
opposed his open hand to the shock and stopped it. Close
by is the dwelling of Nának Ram, into which I was permitted to enter and gaze into the little pit into which he
descended at night. The temple is kept with great care,
and a Sikh had the civility to show me the way in. As I
stood on the platform before the tank (which was of beauti-
fully clear water and full of fish), a cry was raised that I
had profaned the place by entering with my shoes on. I
had on cloth overalls, with leather soles. I pretended not
to hear. The people thronged about me, and one old rascal
especially pointed out the fact of the leather soles, but
others took my part, said I looked like a good fellow, and
insisted on my remaining. My jemadar[1] was close to me,
and his being a Brahman may have influenced the mob in
my favour. Meantime my Sikhs and others were, in spite
of the cold, ducking themselves in the tank, and performing
all manner of fantastic ceremonies before the abominable
sign. Jacob joined me shoeless, and, to the astonishment of
the surrounding listeners, I gave him the history of what
he saw, and enlarged on the folly of idolatry, in English.
Gopal Singh had now come up, and the respect he was
pleased to show me exalted me in the eyes of all, and I was
escorted about with great consideration.

"My appearance, arms and accoutrements, horse, and
mode of riding, as usual called forth many unceremonious
remarks, some for, others against me. A fat vagabond of a
faqir exhorted me to ensure my own welfare by giving him
a rupee. I, being moved by a spirit of levity, replied by
'taking a sight at him!' The novelty of the action did not
prevent its being understood, and the crowd applauded me
and laughed at the impostor. Along the green sward by a
rippling brook outside the town some women were pre-

---

[1] A lieutenant or headman either of troops or of a household.

paring yarn for the loom. It looked like home. They
stared at me in great wonder, and seemed much amused
when old Nadir Bey called out as I turned the corner : 'The
show is now at an end.' So we parted in good humour.

"Met many strings of camels, bullocks, asses, etc., some
with supplies for camp, others with grapes, apples, etc.,
from Kabul for Lahore. Every man armed.

"*9th December* '40.—Twice crossed a small river which
ran rejoicing in its purity over its pebbly bed. How
charming are these pellucid sparkling waters after the
turbid streams of Hindustan! My very horse seemed to
perceive the difference as he plunged his head deep into
the wave, drinking and snorting with evident rapture. Saw
for the first time in the East a small water-mill, only
excepting the large floating one moored at Agra.

"Passed a very large 'baoli' or well, with descending
steps (for the benefit of travellers who have no string to
draw water with), of very ancient date, shaded by trees with
enormous trunks. It is esteemed most meritorious in this
country to furnish water and shade for weary pilgrims, and
justly so. These works of charity are generally performed
by some wealthy stranger, who may have suffered from heat
and thirst during his journey through the country. The
ancient fort of Attok, built by Akbar the Great, seen from
the opposite side of the river, is most picturesque. At the
very baoli I passed this morning, an unhappy 'baniah' or
shopkeeper has just been murdered with one of his servants
as he journeyed, and three thousand rupees carried off.

"*10th December.*—Marched at 4.30 A.M. Our road lay
through a defile of a most difficult and dangerous character
if beset, being very narrow and rugged, cut frequently
through rocks which rise perpendicularly on each side, the
ascents and descents being very steep, and every hundred
yards affording excellent places for ambuscades. The high

mountains through which it winds are infested by an
'Afridi' tribe, who do little else but plunder. A number
of Sikh soldiers, who, from the little neighbouring fort on
the right bank of the Indus, had acted as watchmen all
night (to the great relief of self and people, who could
thereby sleep uninterruptedly), started along with my party
to see us safely through the pass. A small party of my
Sikhs, with their pointed turbans, closely-fitting underdress,
and long scarfs loosely flung over the shoulder, plaid
fashion, their round shields slung at the back, long matchlocks at 'slope arms,' with their glow-worm-like fuses, and
their broad *talwárs* (sabres) with the hilt brought close up
to the left breast in all readiness, formed my advanced
guard, and I really believe they apprehended danger (which
I did not), from the anxious manner in which they peered
about, especially round corners. Others of these valorous
men led the string of camels, which answered with groans to
the injunctions of their drivers not to stumble among the
sharp stones and difficulties of the path, while a third
detachment brought up the rear. I could not help mar-
velling how many of these heroes would remain to assist
myself and servants if a single shot were fired from the
hill, and almost wished for such an occurrence, for the fun
of the thing. 'Nothing came on't,' as Sam. Johnson said,
except that we laid hold of two unhappy varlets who were
rushing along with the public letter-bag, and fiercely inter-
rogated them as to their intentions. These miserable two-
penny postmen professed their innocence, so I examined the
contents of their packet and let them go. At the end of
the pass I gave my guard (!) the expected reward, and was
glad to get rid of them.

"There are watch-towers and stations along the road all
the way to Peshawar, for the protection of travellers, being
part of the arrangements of le Général Avitabile, Governor

of this province, under the Sikhs. He is a famous man in his way, and certainly keeps his province in better order than any other Sikh governor.

"From the end of the pass up to Peshawar, some forty miles, is one great plain, the eastern boundary of which is the Kabul river. Passed quantities of graves. In these parts, when there is no tomb, the common graves are adorned with rows of light and coloured stones, presenting the appearance of a skeleton—viz. backbone and ribs, ghastly enough in early dawn on the long black hillocks under which repose the dead, as my horse's weak nerves testified. People much more civil than the Sikhs.

"11*th December* 1840.—Reached Peshawar about 2 P.M., after twenty-four days' march from Firozpur. On our march hither, two armed horsemen suddenly dashed up at full speed from our rear. My sawárs were not backward, and we bustled up to them, under a strong impression that there was a scrimmage on the tapis, especially as six or seven others were seen galloping up with the same suspicious haste. My hand was on the butt of my pistol; and, in spite of the assurances of the two first that they were true men, their fate would have been doubtful, had not their followers, in answer to their shouts to them to halt, reined up at a short distance. They then told us that they formed part of a body of horse kept in the neighbourhood to check the inroads of the Afridis, of whom a small band was at that moment on the look-out for travellers; that they had heard of my being weak in fighting men; that their Sirdar's name would suffer were I to meet with harm, etc. All this proved true, although for some time I distrusted the whole batch, especially one fellow, with a preposterously long spear, who kept in my rear. I disdained to keep turning my head; but I felt that it was very possible he might poke at me unadvisedly with his foolish weapon.

"Near Pabbá, came on the tomb of a saint of this country, styled 'Hajrat' (His Highness), on which, if any one afflicted with the toothache lays, as an offering, a bunch of the parwah (a tree I took for a fir, a useless wood, except for burning), forthwith the pain will depart. As the sun mounted higher in the heavens, and we approached Peshawar, cultivation increased, and the hitherto wavy blue outline of the Khaiber hills became more sternly distinct, their inhospitable rugged character (which accords well with that of the hitherto unsubdued banditti who dwell therein) developing itself more and more. Far beyond arose in lonely beauty the snowy summit of the Safed Koh (or white mountain). To the south were the tents of Colonel Wheeler's brigade, guarding Dost Muhammad Khan, who will leave for Masuri as soon as his family arrive from Ghazni.[1]

"Do not fancy the Dost is anything of a hero. Just before he left Kabul, Sir William Macnaghten presented him with some shawls, and of course sent the shawl merchant with his bale for the Amir to choose from. He accordingly selected the best, pricing them himself. When our people had gone and left the coast clear, he sent to the shawl merchant, and insisted, as he had, in pricing the articles, made the Feringhis pay double their value, on going halves in the plunder. I could give you lots of instances of his mean rascality.

"He would have given himself up at Bamián, and on many occasions before and afterwards, but for deadly fear of his own people. He said so himself, and related how, in the charge at Parwán Darra, he cunningly kept in the rear, and, as soon as he saw his men well occupied in

---

[1] It was to the fact that the Dost's family were in our power, that our captive ladies afterwards owed their safety. Akbar dared not allow them to be in any way insulted when his own mother, and all the female members of his family, were in the hands of the British.

slaughtering those calves of troopers, how he addressed himself to flight so dexterously as to pass his own people without being recognised.

"Found the tent of the Political Agent, Captain Mackeson, and pitched close to his.

"*12th December.*—Rode to call on General Avitabile, the Governor, at the very extraordinary house he has built for himself in the city. It is large, but disfigured by the tawdry ornaments and villainous paintings of the Sikhs, the latter representing much of their hideous mythology. Avitabile is an absolute prince here, and his pomp and magnificence are unlimited—*e.g.* all the housings of his horses are of solid gold. He is evidently a man of great talent and dauntless determination, but capricious, somewhat cruel, and most unscrupulous in increasing his already large fortune by heavy fines, which are the perquisites of the Governor. He is very hospitable to the English, and popular accordingly. He is a Neapolitan, and was introduced to Ranjit Singh by the late General Allard. He had served as a lieutenant in Napoleon's artillery, and afterwards under the Shah of Persia, whence he wandered to Lahore. He hangs a dozen unhappy culprits, looks to the payment of his troops, inspects his domestic concerns (especially his poultry-yard, in which he takes much pride), sets agoing a number of musical snuff-boxes, etc., all by way of recreation before dinner. He seems, withal, to be a good soldier and a just man—that is, impartially stern to Sikhs and Muhammadans. His appearance is rather *outré* : a tall, burly man, ordinarily apparelled in a magnificently-laced Horse-Artillery jacket, wide crimson Turkish trousers drawn in at the ankle, a golden girdle, and very handsome sabre ; his large Jewish features and bronzed countenance adorned with fierce mustachios, which look like twisted bayonets, and a thick gray beard ;—the whole surmounted by a gold-laced forage cap, which he never takes off. He has greatly improved the large city of Peshawar, and has repressed crime, but the one, at the expense of much oppression, and the other, of innumerable executions. As a Sikh officer he is obliged to conform to many usages of his masters; but when he alleges that, by having hanged upwards of sixty Muhammadans at once for the offence of killing oxen and eating beef, he prevented a more wholesale destruction of life by the enraged Sikhs, I cannot think the excuse sufficient. He himself is of no religion. It is unpleasant to have to pass day by day the bodies of poor wretches who have been hanged by his order, sometimes for no moral offence. Latterly, he has become rather sensitive as to what we Englishmen think of him, which may tend to soften his iron rule. Breakfasting with him another morning I observed that a large box, secured by a padlock, was let down by an iron chain outside the window into a much frequented thoroughfare. This is to receive all petitions, none of which can be intercepted *en route*, as the General himself keeps the key."

As Shah Shujah used to avoid the extreme cold of the winter at Kabul, which stands 6200 feet above the level of the sea, by spending it at Jellalabad, which is 4200 feet lower, Mackenzie proceeded thither to report himself to his chief, Sir W. Macnaghten, leaving Peshawar on the 17th December. At Jamrud, at the entrance of the Khaiber Pass, "I counted five bodies on one gibbet, two of which were hanging by the heels, a favourite mode of dealing with Avitabile, whose ingenuity in these horrors will not bear repetition. This is the man who, on taking leave of me, said quite sentimentally, with his hand grasping mine most affectionately: 'Remember that in Peshawar you have always a friend.' But 'ami,' after all, is not equivalent to the English 'friend.'

"18th *December.*—Entered the Khaiber with twelve of
Ferris' corps and fifty Afridi matchlock-men as a guard.
Sent some fifteen ahead, and lined the camels with single
files, the rear being brought up with a strong party, keeping one whom I could trust with me at the head of our
little column. Met several Kafilas all bristling with arms.
The European features, fair complexions, and sometimes
blue eyes and red beards of the people, especially of those
from Kabul, are very striking, but the real inhabitants of
the Khaiber have a very rascally expression.

"Found a dry spot in the bed of the stream where the
width between the opposing precipices did not exceed fifty
paces. The sheer height above was at least 400 feet, and
seemed to overhang us, suggesting the dreadful condition
of those who in the last day shall call on the mountains to
fall on them to conceal them from the Divine wrath.

"On the left arose the lofty hill on the top of which
stands the Fort of Ali Masjid. I climbed the steep and
rugged path, and after much puffing and many halts, gained
the entrance to the first of Shah Shujah's strongholds I
have yet seen.

"My tent below looked like a pocket-handkerchief
spread out to dry, and the men like mice. All around was
one great jumble of bare craggy mountains. The native
Governor (for young Mackeson, whose post is here, had
gone to Peshawar) was most urbane. He was sick from
continued low fever, so I felt his pulse, inspected his
tongue, and promised him some pills, which I afterwards
sent. In his gratitude and politeness he sent me a dish
prepared by his wife of a sort of sweet vermicelli, which
was rather nice. The sun can never get a good look into
the valley below, the cold of which, as the night breeze
rushed down, was excessive, making me appreciate the comfort of a sheepskin cloak Mackeson had given me.

"Late at night, gazing up far into the heavens, between the rocky walls on each side, the contrast between the bright stars and lovely deep blue sky and the gloomy abyss into which I appeared to have fallen, made me think of the valley of the Shadow of Death.

"Met a string of women, with asses and goatskins, coming for water from a village nearly three miles distant. The old women looked as wretched as their condition actually is; but a number of the younger ones, more gaily dressed in spotted dark petticoats and large blue scarfs flung loosely over the head and upper part of the body, seemed to enjoy the brightness of the day—'I knew they were talking of me, for they laughed consumedly.' No part of my motley dress (for I am not at present under military control) seems to attract more attention than my top-boots. Next to them the caps on my pistols and gun excite speculation.

"Each village has a square tower in which are stores of water and provisions, besides being the arsenal of the village. Into this in extremity men, women, and children retreat, all ascending to an opening near the top by a knotted rope. As a specimen of the word-and-a-blow system so prevalent among this race, this morning one of my guards—one of Ferris' regulars, who carry firelocks—asked a man who was travelling with us for protection, where he was going to. The other refused to gratify his curiosity, and forthwith a contest ensued, the inquisitive man belabouring the other furiously with the butt of his musket. I interfered, and, having summoned these fierce savages into my presence, I was mildly and sensibly expounding that 'their little hands were never made to tear each other's eyes,' when another of my guards became suddenly so moved by my discourse that, to show how strenuous an advocate he was for peace, he began thumping

the chief offender with his musket with all his might.   I
again interfered, and finally gave them up as incorrigible.

"Here a couple of Shinwaris, representing themselves
as employed by the Shah's Government, officiously proffered
themselves as sentries.   My Afridis roughly turned them
away, telling them they were thieves come to spy.   I
rebuked this incivility, and calling the men back, thanked
them courteously, and excused myself from accepting their
offer, but not before they had in their wrath declared their
intention of bringing their comrades at night and treating
us to a volley.

"19th, Ali Masjid.- The native guards at this place
told me that they had never been to the top of the moun
tain from the certainty of being shot, using a very strong
expression to denote the insecurity of their post.   It was
too late, or I should certainly have gone myself (for I place
little faith in their exaggerated reports of danger), especially
as they said they had heard there was an inscription over
one of the gateways.   About six miles from Landi Khána
the Khaiber Pass ended, and we emerged into a small
plain hemmed in by mountains.

"The Momands are the principal clan here, the chief of
whom, Turábáz Khan, raised up by us at the expense of a
disaffected grandee of their tribe, lives in a fortified vil
lage near by.   I breakfasted in the small camp of Captain
Watt, late chief of the Commissariat in Afghanistan, en
route to Hindustan.   Mrs. Watt was with him, and their
child, with all the roses of England on his little face.   It
was delightful to meet them.   Turábáz Khan paid me a
long visit, and I conversed much with him about the state
of the country, through the medium of my munshi, who
translated his half Pushtu, half Persian, into Hindustani.
He, poor man, is troubled with many Radicals among his
tribe,—those in the plain, who can muster a thousand guns,

peaceably obeying his rule; and those in the mountains, some seven thousand fighting men, not only refusing tribute, but extorting blackmail from him. Thus his income, instead of being seven thousand rupees per mensem, is, he says, not two thousand. Like most of the men of this country, he is a stout handsome mountaineer, with a more than ordinarily honest look—his brown eyes have really a very sweet expression—and we became great friends. If I would have permitted him he would have overwhelmed me with presents, his own sword (a splendid blade) and a very handsome cloak among them—the first a very great temptation—positively refusing any acknowledgments in return, except a few flints for his pistols, which were given him by Colonel Wade. A box of grapes had been sent him from Kabul, which he insisted on transferring to me, with pomegranates, fresh fish, sheep, etc. Really a kindly, good fellow.

"*20th December* 1840.—This being Sunday, I, as usual, halted. While Jacob and I were engaged in the morning service,[1] Turábáz Khan came again. My munshi explained matters to him; but the length of our devotions so astonished him that, on entering my tent after the congregation was dismissed, he asked me if I had not been asleep! He thought with the friar : 'No conscience clear, and void of wrong, could rest awake and pray so long.' I gratified him by asking him for a pair of Khaiberi sandals, made of the leaf of a shrub, which looks like the branch of a very diminutive palm; and I presented him with a letter in Persian, acknowledging his kindness, which he placed on

---

[1] At Malacca Mackenzie had placed a Tamal Bible in his faithful servant's hand. This, with his master's daily explanations, made Jacob not only a Protestant, but, so far as man can judge, a conscientious Christian. When at home his master sent him to the Colonial Society's School, so that he became a fair English scholar.

his head, pressed my hands in both of his most affectionately, bade 'God bless me with peace of mind,' and departed, leaving me quite sorry so good a fellow should be a Muhammadan.

"Dismissed my fifty Afridis, retaining only the twelve Jezailchis (musketeers) from Ferris' corps. One of these, the sentry outside my tent, is at this moment, 10 P.M., whiling away the time by marching up and down, giving the word in English to himself, 'Right, left, Right, left,' and then stopping to sing, *sotto voce*, in the funniest falsetto possible. With the vices of the savage, these people have a childish simplicity which is very amusing. I think kindness and firmness might make something of them.

"*21st December.*—Still met strings of camels and mules, bringing fruit from Kabul, as also crowds of emigrant labourers, avoiding the extreme cold of the upper regions by retreating to Peshawar. Occasionally met well-mounted travellers, their attendants following with their baggage, perched on the top of stout yábus. These yábus are stout little horses, peculiar to this country and Turkistan, and will carry from four to five maunds (320 to 400 lbs.) with perfect ease, making journeys of thirty miles per diem. Those which are ridden and which amble are called yurgas. The Afghans tie a knot in the middle of the long tails of their horses, which, they say, strengthens the animals' backbone !

"*22d*, Jellalabad. — Reported myself to the Envoy. Received by him and Lady Macnaghten most kindly. Formed several agreeable acquaintances, among them Captain G. St. P. Lawrence, Military Secretary ; Captain George Macgregor, Political Agent here ; and Captain Trevor, in charge of the Jánbáz regiments. Found my old schoolfellow and friend John Halkett Craigie in command of one of the Shah's Hindustani regiments. Afghan chiefs here in abundance, the Shah being present—generally great rascals. One, by name Ajíz Khán, some years ago invited some sixty of his nearest kith and kin to dine with him, having previously laid bags of gunpowder under the apartment. During the meal, having gone out on some pretext, he blew them all up. Dost Muhammad, then ruler, compounded the matter. Another virtuous magnate, by name Saiad Faqir, deliberately stabbed his brother and smothered his father, for the sake of the inheritance. He avows the first iniquity with much self-complacency, but evades the other question. He is a fat, big man, who swells about with a train of disgusting-looking desperadoes after him. I hate to look on him.

"The king's band, which plays morning and evening, and in the middle of the night, being close to my tent, is a great nuisance. It consists of several most discordant drums, and some trumpets, which are blown alternately, bass and treble, and sound exactly like the braying of a most vociferous 'cuddy.'

"People under small control in many respects. Since I came here a sawár was cut down close to camp; and, during the night, matchlocks loaded with ball are discharged in all directions."

Sir W. Macnaghten having appointed Mackenzie to act as Major Mackeson's Political Assistant at Peshawar, he marched back with Captain Macgregor, who was to have political charge of Shelton's Brigade, starting on 28th December.

"Close to the Mosk, where we took our meal, is the tomb of a famous saint or Darwesh. Here people bring madmen, who are chained to a post near the saint's resting-place, until the efficacy of his sanctity is evinced by the return of reason. As many of the insane persons of this country are so from the too free use of opium, and as, during their confinement, that drug is inaccessible to them, cures are often effected.

"Several Afghan chiefs are with us, among them some very fine men. They are cheerful, pleasant companions, and the most intelligent no longer believe the monstrous reports that the English are demons incarnate, child-eaters, etc. But even these comparatively sensible persons retain the idea that 'London' is an earthly hell, and have not at all shaken off the absurd dread of being sent there as prisoners.

"*29th December*, Lálpura.—The ranges of caves hewn out of the rocky side of the mountains, which are the ordinary dwellings of very many of the people, not only in the mountains of Khaiber, but throughout Afghanistan, looked like embrasures in a natural fortress. Many persons came to make salam to Macgregor, in whose district all this part of the country is. Among them a stout Patán appeared to prefer a complaint. This was that, twelve years before, the wife of a fellow-villager had come to live with him; that during Dost Muhammad's time he had absented himself, dreading the vengeance of the injured husband; that latterly he had been unable to resist his wish to live again among his friends; but that he was day and night obliged to be on the watch and to be armed to the teeth, as the plaintiff in this *crim. con.* affair continued resolutely to refuse all offers to accommodate matters in the usual way, although he had offered him much money and a beautiful daughter—'blood, blood,' being still the reparation demanded. Assassination is winked at by all Muhammadan authorities in such cases, and even the peaceably inclined of our party seemed to admire the husband's inflexibility. Macgregor sent for this worthy, who came after being assured that the destroyer of his peace no longer polluted the presence, and, after coolly listening to Macgregor's exhortations to abate

his excessive choler and to follow the mode of obtaining
redress pointed out by the Kurán, declared that the Kurán
had one way of adjusting these matters, but that his tribe
had another and a much more satisfactory one, and that
slay his enemy he would. Macgregor told him that in that
case he strongly doubted his being a sincere Musalman.
This alarmed him: he repeated the Muhammadan confession
of faith with great fervour, and seemed inclined to relax a
little, when all of a sudden, from behind a tree close by,
stepped out an aged man with a long white beard, his
features swollen, and his voice hoarse with rage, and altogether a most wicked-looking old sinner. This proved to
be the father of the murderer-in-intention before us, whom
he reproached furiously for relenting, and protested that, if
he failed, he himself would avenge the honour of the family.
Macgregor reproved the old incendiary sharply, reminding
him that he must shortly appear before his Eternal Judge,
and that such a crime, in addition to the doubtless already
long catalogue, would probably ensure his going to hell.
He replied with a frightful expression of countenance that
he did not care if he did go to hell, provided he could first
kill the offender ; so we drove the bloodthirsty pair from
the judgment seat, and Macgregor reported what had passed
to the Vizir. The unhappy Lothario again came forth,
more nervous than ever ; but we could do nothing for him.
He had with him a young child, part of the fruit of his sinful exploit, whom he caressed with great affection ; and it
was affecting to think, as the young thing toddled after him
and clasped his knees, how soon its father might be a bloody
corpse, and his soul gone to its account.

" Found Shelton's Brigade near Lálpura. As I expected,
Shelton has marched the brigade off its legs, and has
brought the troops into the field the next thing to being
wholly inefficient. The artillery horses are quite done up,

those of the cavalry nearly so, and the beasts of burden, camels, etc., have died in great numbers, and will continue to die from overwork. A bad feeling also exists between the Queen's 44th Regiment and the native troops. Swords and bayonets have been drawn between them. Shelton's gross want of arrangement, and the unnecessary hardship he has exposed the men to, especially during their passage through the Khaiber, have caused much discontent. Part of the horse artillery on one occasion mutinied and refused to mount their horses ; but Major Hodges of the 5th Cavalry, who commanded, reasoned them into obedience.

"31*st December* 1840.—Rode into Peshawar, about forty miles."

CHAPTER XI.

(January—June 1841.)

" We are the voices of the wandering wind
  Which moan for rest, and rest can never find ;
  Lo ! as the wind is, so is mortal life—
  A moan, a sigh, a sob, a storm, a strife."

ARNOLD's Light of Asia.

THE province of Peshawar had been conquered from the
Afghans by Ranjit Singh, dread of whose power had induced
the Amir, Dost Muhammad Khan, to seek the alliance of the
British. Sir John Cam Hobhouse had rejected his overtures, and preferred to invade Afghanistan and restore the
deposed Shah Shujah, who had been living in exile with
his brother, the blind Shah Zemán, at Lodiana on a pension from Government for about thirty years. They were
grandsons of the first king of their family, who had conquered the Panjab and overrun Northern India about ninety
years before. The rulers of the Panjab (or Land of the
Five Rivers) were Sikhs, a Hindu sect of modern origin.
The British Agency at Peshawar consisted of Major Mackeson ; Lieutenant Colin Mackenzie, Political Assistant ; and
Dr. Reid in medical charge. They lived at the Vaziri Bagh,
near the city, which Mackenzie describes as in " sad dis-
repair and most uncomfortable. My little domicile, in
another part of the garden, has one ground-chamber, a bed-

room overhead, and chambers underground for the hot
weather.   It is, however, a vile place.   Took charge from
Caulfield, and a preciously troublesome one it is.   Accounts
to keep sufficient for a thoroughbred merchant.   Grievous
to me, who hate figures.

"26th March.—I have now settled down in my place.
Mackeson and I have to keep the peace of the Khaiber
Pass, and to maintain amicable relations with the principal
chiefs of that wild region.   This is difficult from the savage
nature of the people, who have never yet been conquered,
not even by Baber, Teimurlang, Nadir Shah, nor any of
those powerful monarchs who overran India; from their
right to plunder having always been virtually allowed;
from the innumerable conflicting interests and feuds of the
host of clans; from the circumstance of several of these
lawless tribes possessing no chief, each man being wholly
independent, and uniting only in the common cause of
plunder, etc. etc.   Stipends are distributed monthly among
the principal clans through their Máliks, or leaders, to the
amount of some 12,000 rupees.   Stations have been established throughout the Pass, garrisoned by reclaimed robbers,
who receive our pay; and a large band of the same repent-
ant sinners is always at the mouth of the defile, who by
detachments accompany such travellers as carry a passport
from this Agency; and when any one is robbed, the stipend
of the clan within whose jurisdiction the offence has been
committed, is cut.   They are better than they were, but
still arms must be resorted to occasionally.   Mackeson has
just made a most successful expedition against the Sangu
Khail, and, in spite of the almost inaccessible position of
their valley, completely defeated them, levelled their numerous forts, and destroyed their vines and barley crops,[1] etc.,

[1] The Jews were forbidden to destroy the fruit-tree.—Deut. xx. 19,
20.   Can it be right for Christians to do so?

with trifling loss on our side, the heaviest part of which were the deaths of Captain Douglas, Assistant Adjutant-General, and Lieutenant Pigou of the Engineers, both valuable officers. Elphinstone is wonderfully correct in his descriptions of these tribes, but was led to form too favourable an opinion of them.

"The Khaiber tribes are individually the most savage of the savage. I have examined many of them, and I do not think one per cent is unscarred with sabre cuts and other wounds. Stealing is so much a part of their nature that you cannot convince them that it is morally wrong. For instance, the Sangu Khail hostages are lodged over the great gateway, leading into our gardens. The other day Mackeson's old shepherd made his appearance quite beside himself with indignation. 'What!' said he, 'after serving you so long, am I to be so misused? Are we in Khaiber?' It appeared that, as he was driving his flock through the gateway in the dusk, one of the hostages, unable to resist the temptation, nimbly slid down from his perch, grabbed the last sheep, and vanished with it before the astonished pastor could knock him down with his crook. The hue and cry sent some of the guard to the rescue, who found the unfortunate *bakri* (sheep) on the point of being made 'hálál,' *i.e.* lawful, most unlawfully, and the thievish brotherhood showing the most unsophisticated joy at the prospect of a feast. The culprit, on being brought before Mackeson, smiled, and seemed to be only abashed at the failure of his enterprise. The independence of the chiefs is great—I mean the savage pride commonly called independence, for they can sneak, lie, cheat, and practise any other of the smaller virtues to attain an object. Ghazn Khán of Dira, a magnate whose goodwill is of some importance to us, was invited to visit Shah Shujah. 'Why,' said he, 'should I stand before the King? he is not a better man than I ; he can give me nothing that I want. I have dogs, hawks, horses, and a house,—what can I wish for more? I will not go.'

"They have a curious sort of etiquette and rules for retaliation, which, strange to say, they observe as if they were playing chess. For instance, Mackeson was returning from the other end of the Pass in the middle of the night, for the sake of coolness, when he was suddenly surrounded by a host of armed men and boys (these imps being always foremost in murder and robbery), who evidently were out on some devilry. Ascertaining who he was, they allowed him and his horsemen to proceed. They belonged to the Koki Khail, and said they were on the look-out for some Shinwaris who had done them a mischief. A little farther on he came on these very Shinwaris, about a dozen stout fellows, who rushed up to him crying out for justice. It seemed the Koki Khail had lied to Mackeson, having already robbed their enemies, who of course, although well armed, had offered no resistance, being in the territory of their spoilers, such being the custom in regular cases of 'Barhampter.' In cases of other feuds, however, the love of shedding blood is quite fearful among the Khaiber tribes. I conscientiously believe that not an hour in the twenty-four passes without libations of human blood being poured out before Moloch, even among the clans immediately within our ken.

"The position of the British Agency is by no means a secure one. Our policy is to maintain peace among the tribes, still it is a comfort that, in case of extremity, we could always set the Afridis to thresh the Orakzais, or *vice versâ*.

"The troubles in Afghanistan seem lulled for a season since the surrender of Dost Muhammad Khan last November; but the idea of withdrawing our troops for the next ten years, *if ever*, is perfectly chimerical."

He describes the misery inflicted on the Panjab by the frightful oppression of the Sikh governors :—

"This province of Peshawar is certainly happy in its ruler compared to the rest. Avitabile is accounted a just man by the natives, is both sagacious and firm in his efforts towards improvement, and, except that he is wholly insensible to human suffering, he does not seem to have an actual pleasure in cruelty for cruelty's sake. Hordes of plunderers from the mountains no longer descend and devastate the plain, and cultivation has increased greatly. He has also reduced the revenue system to something like a fixed rate. But if a village refuses to pay tribute either from contumacy or the provocations of the inferior civil officers, troops are immediately sent against it, who burn the village, destroy the crops, cut down all the trees (a strange gusto in all Sikhs), and of course slay the inhabitants, no attention being paid to inability on the part of the defaulters, or to their having been stung into resistance by oppression. Avitabile himself owns that for one thousand rupees of revenue collected by the troops, two thousand rupees' worth of property is destroyed, to say nothing of the loss of life among the working classes. All fines being the perquisites of the governor, he is not chary of their infliction. Almost all crimes, even murder, may be atoned for by money, to extort which, torture is always applied.

"The tender-hearted creature confessed to me that, suspecting a small chief of playing tricks, he seized him and condemned him to a heavy fine, and to enforce payment had him stripped and cold water poured over him night after night. He added : '*Figurez vous, mon ami, ce brigand est mort sans me rien donner !*' The hands, noses, and ears of offenders who are either poor or obstinate are constantly lopped.

"Two days since an Akali (Sikh fanatic) murdered his wife and then ran through the streets with his drawn sword like a Malay, killing and wounding eight persons. He being a holy man, Avitabile only chopped off his hands, whereof he died in the evening. Even the bodies of the crowds who grace his gibbets must be bought by their friends. In cases of murder a thirst for private vengeance is encouraged, contrary to the spirit of true law, by the relations of the deceased being permitted to kill the guilty person. One revolting instance of this took place a short time back. A man had assassinated another. To obtain the price of blood, Avitabile kept him in prison for some time, and then exposed him stark naked to the scorching heat of the sun, the attacks of insects, etc., with half his body painted red. As he continued obstinate, the mother of the slain was permitted to use her right of slaughtering him with a knife, which she not only did, but, in her delirious and savage joy, stooped down and drank two handfuls of his blood as it welled from the death-wound. This vile custom prevails far and near. Some two months back in Afghanistan a woman complained to Shah Shujah's eldest son, Taimur, that her husband had been killed by the paramour of his other wife. The thing was proved, and the gentle widow's request was granted to be allowed to avenge herself. The guilty person was brought into the presence of Taimur and a large assembly, his hands tied, and his breast bared. A broad dagger was then given to the woman, who instantly plunged it into his heart. The other day I was riding with Avitabile. Passing a village, we came upon an old woman standing between two graves, who assailed us with vehement cries for justice, pointing to the graves, each of which contained a murdered son. She entreated to be allowed to drink the blood of the two homicides, who are now in prison. Avitabile very coolly told me that as he had no hopes of being able to extract any coin from these men, he should grant the old hag's request, and finished by inviting me to come and see her cut their throats !

"Some Afghans, having refused to pay tribute, Avitabile seized them, shut them up in a little room about twelve feet square, and began gradually to brick up the door, telling them they should never come out until they had paid. He fed them on bread and water; and although they could have paid the sum at once, they chose to remain there in the most dreadful heat until one of them died. They sent to beg Avitabile to have the body interred, but he refused, saying that they must all stay there until they had paid the money. The bricking up of the aperture proceeded gradually, and the odour became so insupportable that the men who brought their food flung it in and fled away in haste. The prisoners stopped up their noses and ears with shreds of their clothing; for the horrid result of keeping a body unburied in that tremendous heat may be faintly conceived. Still they bore it, and it was not till the door was bricked up to within a few inches from the top that they gave in and paid the money. Avitabile then had them bathed and their nostrils sponged with vinegar, and having dressed them, made them sit down on their heels over some beds of stocks in his garden, '*pour se rafraichir*,' as he said. For some horrible crime a man was sentenced by the judges to be thrown from the top of a minaret. Avitabile, who *never* pardons, confirmed the sentence. The man was thrown off, but alighted on a projection not very far from the top. In vain they called to him to throw himself down, neither did any one dare to go out at a little door opposite the projection on which he lay to push him off, as, being a very athletic man, he would certainly have dragged his assailant with him. They therefore represented the case to Avitabile, thinking he would pardon the culprit; but not a bit of it.

When they had finished, he waved his hand and said: 'I have not heard a word that you have been saying. I gave you orders; they must be executed.' Upon this they drew up a Persian paper, put Avitabile's seal to it, and showed it to the culprit, telling him it was a pardon. He came in at the little door, they seized him, and flung him over the battlements effectually."

Of course the political officers were brought into constant intercourse with the Governor, who on all occasions proved himself the fast friend of the British, especially by facilitating the passage of our troops. He formed a great affection for Mackenzie, and told him a good deal of his life. He said of all the troops he had commanded he preferred the Sikhs '*perchè sono semplici*'—'because they are simple-minded,' and have no religious prejudices against the Europeans as the Persians and Afghans have.

Avitabile asked him one day what he usually did with himself in the morning. He replied that he generally read. "Ah!" said the General, laying his hand impressively on his arm, "*ne lisez pas, mon ami! Cela est très mauvais pour vous. Vous avez tort de lire!*"[1]

Part of Mackenzie's special work being to keep open the Khaiber Pass, he often had to ride through it to settle matters with the chiefs, and more than once a ball whistled close to his head from some enemy hidden behind the rocks. He formed a special friendship with Turábáz Khan (the Momand chief already mentioned), who proved himself a most faithful adherent of the British.

Mackenzie was at this time in constant correspondence with his brothers-in-law, Mr. H. T. Prinsep and Mr. C. H. Cameron, Members of Council, giving them full information of the distracted state of the Panjab, where the

---

[1] "Ah! don't read, my friend! It is very bad for you. You are quite wrong to read!"

lawless soldiery were supreme. The strong rule of Ranjit Singh had given place to that of the feeble Sher Sing. The two brothers, Guláb and Dhyán Singh, were almost in rebellion ; the provinces Ranjit had conquered, particularly where the population was chiefly Muhammadan, were long- ing for deliverance from the grinding oppression of the locusts in office, and were looking for it to the Government of India. Sher Sing was secretly negotiating for our protection.

The foreign officers in the Sikh service were in imminent danger, and anxious to get out of the country. Mackenzie writes in March : "The idea of restoring discipline among these Prætorian guards is absurd. The spirit of license has been suffered to proceed too far. They must be utterly crushed like the Pindáris, for, like them, murder and plunder are now their only bond of union. They are ousting all their officers, European and native, and substituting others chosen from among themselves. In Kashmir they have mutinied and murdered their kind-hearted old governor, Mián Sing. With the exception of three regiments and some artillery, all Avitabile's troops have, like their brethren, long disdained submission to authority, as a weakness un- worthy of disciples of the Guru. The Maharaja dares not let Avitabile march against his mutinous regiments for fear of irritating them, and desires him to do the best he can for himself, as he can give him neither help nor countenance.

"10th April.—Things have come to such a pass that Avitabile has arranged a plan with Mackeson and myself for his escape, should the worst come to the worst. For myself, I should prefer sticking to my post, and going out of the world like a gentleman, sword in hand ; but if the Agency is attacked, I suppose I must obey orders. Macke- son is a very good soldier, and will doubtless do what is right. Poor Colonel Steinbach came to me yesterday to ask my advice. He detailed sufficient to show that his men are only postponing his death, so I told him to sell his life dearly, but he was obstinate, and would not return to his camp. Life to some men is very valuable.

"The Sikh soldiery hate the British as the only power they fear, and not long ago at Jamrud fired upon Mackeson, killed some of his followers, and nearly finished him. Four Sikh regiments broke into open mutiny, marched off to Attok, where they looted the treasure coming from Lahore for the payment of all the troops, leaving Avitabile without money to pay the regiments at Peshawar."

Broadfoot had undertaken the charge which had been at first destined for Mackenzie, of conveying Shah Zemán, and the enormous harems of both Shahs, from Lodiana to Kabul. Mackenzie writes with enthusiasm of his friend's "long head and stout heart," and of the extraordinary combination of tact and intrepidity which enabled him to accomplish his difficult task. He writes :—

"*6th May.*—I cannot help thinking of poor Broadfoot. He has already done wonders. His march through the Panjab is a second 'Retreat of the Ten Thousand.' His position requires many qualities in which he greatly excels me—such as a perfect knowledge of the language, unrelenting severity, combined with a perfect command of temper, while dealing with knaves. The escort given him by the Sikh Government is entirely hostile. They were chosen at Lahore out of Ranjit Singh's most trustworthy veterans, but had rapidly deteriorated into lawless banditti, over whom their most influential leaders had lost even the semblance of control.

"As soon as the enmity of the Sikhs became unequivocally manifest, Broadfoot assumed a sternly defensive attitude. On one occasion the Sikh troops demanded that

Broadfoot should place his camp in a position which would have left him and his helpless charge at their mercy. They had openly avowed their intention of plundering the harem, and had frequently threatened Broadfoot that they would "rip him up." Shah Sing and the other commandants entreated him not to sign their death-warrant by persisting in his refusal. Of course he remained firm, and the soldiery were baulked of their design.

"The only men whom he could trust, in case of actual conflict, were some two hundred Hindustani recruits he had raised for the Shah's sappers. The Ghurka recruits were continually deserting, being seduced by the Sikhs, and twice the little rascals broke out into open mutiny. Once near Lahore the Sikhs were actually present ready to support them. Broadfoot forthwith turned out the Hindustanis, and preceded them to the scene of the *émeute*. The Ghurkas were handling their arms, and the Sikhs collecting in their rear. Broadfoot ordered one man to ground his arms, and on his refusal, knocked him down with the butt end of his pistol; gave the same order to the next, and on the same reply, broke the pistol over his thick head, and on his endeavouring to use his weapon, floored him also with the remaining pistol. At this moment the Hindustanis marched round the corner, and drew up in front of the mutineers, who forthwith threw down their arms and cried 'Peccavi.' Broadfoot then inquired into the circumstances of the case, seized a ringleader, and gave him five hundred lashes on the spot. The effect was wonderful. The abetting Sikhs being astonied, departed in all haste. Without the power to flog, which we have in the Shah's service, what can be done in a case like that? Death is the only alternative. Avitabile's four revolted regiments are lying in wait for Broadfoot, with the avowed intention of plundering the kafila, and have sworn to do his business.

"On arriving near Attok Broadfoot took up a strong position in the Gidargalli Pass, to await reinforcements. All Avitabile's letters and messages were treated with the utmost contempt by the mutineers; they even attempted to seize his munshi, and Avitabile was obliged to announce officially to our Agency that he could not ensure the safety of the kafila or the tranquillity of the province in any respect. The mutineers were in open communication with the regiments at Peshawar, and with Broadfoot's precious escort, with whom they had arranged a simultaneous attack on the kafila, the garrison of the fort at Attok having promised to fire on the unwieldy cortege and its few defenders. To avoid the cannon, Broadfoot was obliged to shift his position among the mountains, to a place where he contrived to make himself pretty snug, and to communicate with the Khattak tribe, who had been warned by Avitabile to assist him, and where he was joined by Captain Davidson and a regiment of the Shah's Jánbáz, who came over a mountain-path, but from whence the kafila could not escape."

Mackenzie, who had been excessively anxious about his friend, rode through the Khaiber to bring down Shelton's brigade—though Broadfoot had not asked for their assistance. It came no farther than Jamrud, at the Peshawar end of the pass (fifteen miles from Peshawar), for their approach had the desired effect of putting the Sikhs in a terrible fright, and making them forthwith raise the blockade, on Broadfoot.

Mackenzie then accompanied the kafila through the Khaiber. The garrison of Jamrud, who had been very "mild and polite" while Shelton's brigade was there, immediately they had marched showed their teeth at the kafila, but were checked by Broadfoot's firmness and Shah Sing's exertions, Avitabile's authority being laughed at.

Broadfoot's continued exertions ended in a severe attack of fever, followed by smallpox. Mackenzie continues :—" I was introduced to Shah Zemán, who still assumes regal state, having his titles as king proclaimed before him by a multitude of retainers in scarlet liveries, with fool's caps on their heads, surmounted by horns, making them look like red-hot devils, and also by parading a preposterously big drum, which must from its appearance have belonged to Nadir Shah. By dint of dyeing his beard and other artificial aids, he still looks almost handsome, and he struck me as possessing a simple and, at the same time, an extremely dignified demeanour, not rendered less so by the somewhat tremulous accents of venerable old age. My habitual reverence for an old man, and my recollections of the former condition of the fallen monarch in whose presence I stood, may have worked on my feelings. Though Zemán has been blind for so many years, he still goes through the ceremony of having a glass held up before him during his toilette. So great a man cannot be vulgarly blind ! This trifling trait shows the animus of his race, which is that of insane pride.

"As I was returning from escorting Broadfoot's kafila at Gharri Lala Beg, where I had halted, my horror and indignation were strongly excited by a base murder committed under my very nose. At that place there are several villages and small forts, two of which are inhabited by two brothers of the Zakar Khail named Alidád Khan and Faizlalab Khan. These two unnatural monsters have for years been at death-feud with each other, and many murders have been committed. Although it had been tacitly agreed that women and children going to fetch water from a small tank between the *gharris* (towers) should be respected, the more savage of the two, Alidád, a short time back, caught two little children from Faizlalab's house and cut them to pieces. Well, we have been obliged for some time back, in addition to the monthly stipends of these two big thieves, to entertain Alidád's son, Firoz, and three followers, and Faizlalab's brother, with the like number of ragamuffins. Guess my disgust, while these fellows were actually eating, as it were, their daily bread out of our hands, at its being reported to me that Firoz and another had, in a house a short distance from my tent, just murdered four persons in their sleep in the middle of the day. Two of these were mere boys, and a poor little child had received a frightful gash. My munshi found one of them coolly wiping his butcher's knife. He said it was ' all right,' as the deceased favoured Faizlalab. Firoz came out at the head of a band of cut-throats to make salam to me as I rode by, but I refused to receive him, expounding my ideas pretty freely at the same time. I fell in with his ruffian father afterwards, and reproached him bitterly with being a child-butcher; but the old savage merely rolled up his forehead into a more remarkable mass of wrinkles than usual, glared at me like a wolf, and seemed quite unabashed. Were I to put the hundredth part of the monstrosities committed here on paper, you would look on me as an awfully mendacious character."

The British Agency was surrounded by an enormous burying-ground, and as the hot weather approached, Mackenzie's health began to suffer. By the end of March the early rains were nearly over. "The climate begins to be hot, a flood of verdure covers the plain, which waves with the most luxuriant crops I ever beheld. The gardens and orchards (that is, such as these destroying demons, the Sikhs, have left), what with blossom and foliage of every tint, and loads of all kinds of fruit,—plums, quinces, oranges, apples, grapes, and huge mulberries,—surpass the fondest dreams of the most enthusiastic horticulturist. The sod is thick and elastic, as in England, and docks, dandelions, and other dear English weeds, flourish."

General Elphinstone arrived at this time on his way to take command in Afghanistan, and as he rode through the grove of orange trees in full blossom which led to Mackenzie's abode, in order to return his visit, he remarked : " You have a strange mixture of sweet odours and stink here, Captain Mackenzie."

In June the thermometer under canvas was from 106° to 110°. He writes :—

" There is little difference between a tent and this doghole. The only place in which I can breathe is the underground chamber, which is dark and unwholesome in the extreme. Part of Mackeson's house came down with a crash, just missing his head. I and my cheerful companions, the bats, rejoice in our dwelling being the safest of the lot ; but oh ! the swarms of mosquitoes, sandflies, and reptiles in this dark swampy retreat."

No wonder that, with Mackenzie's extremely sensitive organisation, he suffered from swimming in the head and constant attacks of severe fever.

" To a Christian every dispensation, whether for apparent good or evil, comes direct from the hand of his Heavenly Father ; but our nature is weak, and grief will occasionally find vent in complaints, even when the heart is perfectly resigned. I can say with the utmost sincerity that, however I may groan under the infliction, there is no trial to which God, in His infinite wisdom and mercy, may expose me which I could wish removed, for I *know* He does not willingly afflict us."

The doctor warned him that his life was not worth a day's purchase unless he betook himself to Kabul, or some other cool region, until the intense heat had passed away. But the aspect of affairs at Peshawar was so full of danger to all of them, that nothing would induce him to go.

13th June he writes :—" Avitabile has latterly been in a peck of troubles. The Najibs (irregular troops), about a fortnight back, broke out into open mutiny, which was put down with much difficulty by granting them a considerable increase of pay. About five days ago the mutinous Kashmiri Regiment, the colonel of which, Steinbach, has gone off to Lahore, was summoned to Avitabile's residence to be paid their arrears. Avitabile was taking his morning ride when his treasurer sent him a note saying the battalion had mutinied for further gratuities, and entreating the General not to return. 'I on the contrary,' said Avitabile, thought I ought to return. I dug the spurs into my horse, and galloped to my house. The guard turned out at the gateway, and as soon as the troops heard the roll of the drums they knew that it was the General, and fell into their ranks. I galloped past the line, went into my house, summoned their chiefs, and asked what all this commotion was about. They looked at each other, but nobody would answer. I then summoned the paymaster, and made him relate what had occurred. I then said : "What is the amount the troops demand?" He said : "Altogether ten thousand rupees." I said : "Very well, make out an order for it." I signed it, and he began paying them.'

"Their demands grew more and more exorbitant. They treated him and the king's letter with great contempt, and ended by wearing out the Italian's patience. He ordered them out of his presence. Then they threatened him with the fate of the Kashmiri Governor. Fortunately, some still faithful Najibs were at hand. By their help the rioters were expelled the town, some, however, remaining. Of these Avitabile seized about a score, whose muskets were loaded. He also confined some officers of artillery and privates who had adventured to carry off the guns to the enemy. In the evening, Mackeson and I went to visit him,

having been surprised at his sending us two companies of
Najibs as an additional guard, whom we admitted into the
garden with great reluctance, having no faith in them. He
then disclosed his plans.   He had secretly summoned
several Afghan and Patán chiefs, and induced them, in the
hope of plunder and reward, to assemble between three and
four thousand fighting men outside the city.   These were
in the middle of the night to surround and attack the
mutineers, giving no quarter. 'After this work is done,'
quoth Avitabile, rubbing his hands and chuckling in anticipated triumph, 'I shall blow all my prisoners from guns.'
Away we went, and sent to the mouth of the Pass for a
hundred of old Skinner's men and fifty of the garrison of
Ali Masjid to strengthen ourselves.   The tempestuous
weather during the night, which was such that 'a child
might understan', the deil had business on his han',' prevented the Ulu tribe from assembling at the appointed hour,
and the attack did not take place until daybreak.   We
could see the fight dimly from the tops of our houses, and
our horses were saddled in case it should be necessary to
betake ourselves to the mountains.   The Sikhs retired from
their tents to a small gharri, and formed in and round it.
Their discipline and the better quality of their arms and
ammunition put them almost on a level with their numerous
assailants, who, true to their nature (the idiots !), stopped
after the first rush to plunder the tents, where also they
found and cut to pieces some unfortunate Sikh women.

   "Both sides suffered severely, for the troops fought
with desperation.   The mutineers lost three hundred and
thirty, and the Afghans even more.   The ammunition of
the latter being expended, they at length retired, forming,
however, a sort of cordon round the enemy.   Before sunset the affair was over, and they were carrying away the
dead.

"'The Afghans,' said Avitabile, 'killed them with pleasure, for every man had a hundred rupees in his girdle, so the Afghans gladly cut off his head and took the rupees. If I had not done this, the whole garrison, who were waiting to see what would happen, would have mutinied in the night, and plundered and burned everything.'"

While matters were thus progressing, the Najibs had begun to twist their moustachios and talk of the infamy of the Governor letting loose murderous banditti upon the regular Government soldiers, for, in spite of the Najibs being Musalmans, a common *esprit* binds them to the other troops. Avitabile consequently listened to the overtures now made by the Kashmiri Regiment for peace. Perfect submission was offered, but he kept them in suspense several days. Mackenzie continues :—

"To-morrow (14*th June*) they are to be finally dealt with. As they are coming into the city, I trust the Najibs will not make common cause with them, especially as they told Avitabile they would march on the Vaziri Bagh, and seize Mackeson. Luckily these fellows have been kept from communicating with their comrades on the other side of Attok by the tremendous inundation which has, within the last ten days, spread death and ruin far and wide. About four months ago an earthquake upset a great hill into the bed of the Indus among the mountains. The first effect was to make the Indus fordable some distance above Attok. We heard that the still accumulating mass of waters was running about among the hills doing much damage and seeking an outlet. At last the dyke itself has partially given way, and the besom of destruction has swept the land. The extent of the damage and the loss of life cannot be ascertained, but upwards of one hundred thousand men, women, and children are supposed to have perished from the immense extent of very populous country over which this inland sea still rolls.

"30*th June.*—To our astonishment at Peshawar the news of Avitabile's having let loose the hill tribes on the Sikh troops was approved of by the Maharaja Sher Sing. He was enabled to do this openly, owing to the absence of the bulk of his mutinous troops, whom he had bribed to take leave and visit their homes. He went so far as to exhort the chevalier to go on with his good work and dis-arm the discomfited troops, who, wholly panic-stricken, had already restored the money extorted from him previous to the attack, accepted their proper pay, and agreed to go into the Euzufzai territory. At first they refused to give up their arms, and again all was in suspense; but Avitabile said to them: 'Submit entirely, give up everything which belongs to the king, or by sunset I will cut you into small pieces;' and he imitated the action of chopping them up. The sun was nearly down, and, perceiving that a second engagement with overpowering numbers must ensue in case of nonconformity, they were afraid, gave up their arms— sabres, tents, everything. They were marched out and disbanded, and then actually begged for a guard to escort them to the river! The present army will on their return from furlough become more *yaghi* (rebellious) than ever."

Just as a sort of tranquillity had been thus established Mackenzie was again prostrated by severe fever, and feeling his honour no longer at stake, he left that sink of disease the Vaziri Bagh, in the last day of June, and proceeded to Kabul, beginning to breathe freely directly he had reached the cooler atmosphere of Peshbolák.

"Here, in the district of Jellalabad, to Macgregor's [1] great credit, cultivation is increasing wonderfully, and the in-

---

[1] The late Major-General Sir George H. Macgregor, K.C.S.I., then Political Agent of the district of Jellalabad.

creased security of life and property gives much satisfaction
to the well-disposed.   The population abhor the idea of
being under Shah Shujah, and are sick at the very idea of
Dost Muhammad, rejoicing in being subjects of the 'Sahib
log.'   This is not humbug, but a fact, which I have had
excellent opportunities of ascertaining."

CHAPTER XII.

KABUL AND KOHISTAN.

(July to October 1841.)

" L'homme propose mais Dieu dispose."

ON the Indian principle that if a thing has to be done you must do it, with or without previous training, Mackenzie was, on his arrival at Kabul, put in charge of the Commissariat of the Shah's troops, continuing at the same time Political Assistant to the Envoy. As usual, whatever his hand found to do he did it with his might, and learning that the mortality among the camels was enormous without any unusual work, he obtained leave to purchase 500 yábus, the stout packhorses of the country, to supply their place, "an experiment," he remarks, "which ought to have been tried long ago, for Government lost upwards of 35,000 camels during the war of 1838-9, and I know that within the last month, out of a batch of some 2500, 800 have demised. Many die from eating a poisonous plant something like foxglove. It is odd enough that, while the camel from India eats this greedily, that of Afghanistan sturdily refuses to touch it. How comes this difference of instinct in the same animal? I believe the poison is unknown in India.

"A gallant Kazilbash gentleman (Ali Reza Khán) worked under me in the Commissariat. One day he brought me a Turkoman horse to look at, a dark bay with black points, not quite fourteen hands and a half, but what I may call the very pemmican of a powerful high-bred English hunter. He told me the animal's history, viz. that when Dost Muhammad, after we had driven him out of his country, fled to Bokhara, the treacherous Amir (the same scoundrel who afterwards murdered Stoddart and Conolly) cast him and his followers into prison. Arrangements, however, were made for the old chief's escape and that of his friends. Dost Muhammad was a big heavy man, and consequently the best horse of the party was provided for him. To baffle pursuit they pressed on with very little intermission, and accomplished a distance of 200 miles by the evening of the second day, the gallant steed in question having required neither whip nor spur, while the other horses were much exhausted. Shortly after this the Dost surrendered to Sir William Macnaghten, and my Kazilbash friend obtained possession of the horse, which, out of gratitude for my kindness to him, he let me have at the very reasonable price of £30."

Ali Reza Khán remained Mackenzie's staunch friend to the end of his days, and, as we shall see, was the main instrument of the release of the prisoners.

During his residence at Kabul, Mackenzie formed a friendship with Lieutenant Michael Dawes, a young officer who had already distinguished himself in Abbott's Battery, and who was a most consistent Christian. He had met Mackenzie for the first time at Sir William Macnaghten's at Jellalabad, and was very much struck with him. Some months after, at Kabul, Dawes was on a committee for purchasing horses, when Captain Mackenzie came into the tent exclaiming: "I've lost it! I've lost it!" Somebody asked, "What have you lost?" and he explained that he had wished to purchase a Persian and a Pushtu Testament at a sale, but some one had already bought them. Dawes said: "If you will allow me I shall be very happy to give you one of each." Mackenzie begged to pay for them, but this Dawes would not allow. Mackenzie said, "Well, you are a very generous fellow ; I'll come and breakfast with you to-morrow ;" and thus their intimacy commenced. Dawes was greatly interested in the Jews, and was at this time engaged in superintending the transcription of the Persian New Testament into Hebrew characters for the benefit of the Jews of Central Asia, who always write Persian, but in Hebrew letters. When Dawes left Kabul this edition was made over to Mackenzie and afterwards plundered, but it is not probable that any were destroyed.

In this work he employed two very remarkable brothers known as Mulla Musa and Mulla Ibrahim, Jews of Meshed, who had accompanied Abbott, Shakespear, and Arthur Conolly on their perilous journey through Turkistan to Bokhara, Khiva, and even into the Russian territories. They were both, like so many Asiatic Jews, men of remarkable personal beauty ; Musa a perfect Judas Maccabæus. The younger brother, Ibrahim, had just returned from his last journey to Bokhara for the purpose of communicating with Colonel Stoddart ; and a cousin of theirs, Ephraim, was soon after sent thither on a similar errand, and was murdered by the atrocious Amir. This work of transcribing the New Testament aroused a strong desire to know the truth of it, especially in the elder brother, a man of extraordinary vigour of mind and body, in earnest in everything he said or did. This disposition was kept alive by frequent conversations with Michael Dawes, who, when he left Kabul, made over the New Testaments which remained to Mackenzie's charge, he having already become acquainted with the two brothers. On one occasion Dawes entered an assembly of Jews at Kabul, and after talking to them, begged them to read the 53d chapter of Isaiah. The eldest of them did so, and then explained to his brethren how Christians applied this chapter to Christ, and they seemed to agree in the Christian interpretation. The greatest obstacle to their reception of Christianity was that they, in common with most Orientals, looked upon it as a system of idolatry, never having known any but Romanists, Greeks, etc. It was with surprise that they found that Dawes, Mackenzie, and some others were neither wholly indifferent to all religion nor worshippers of "Bibi Miriam" (the Virgin) and other saints. All these friendships proved most valuable and important to both parties.

Not long after his arrival at Kabul, Mackenzie experienced another of those remarkable deliverances from death which marked his career. Strolling early one morning into the garden of the Yábu Khana, a mulberry grove attached to the fort in which he lived, he recognised a bull-dog belonging to his friend Captain Troup, and called to it "Nettle, Nettle!" but it took no notice. A moment after it was clinging like a leech to his right arm with all a bulldog's tenacity. He saw at a glance that it had gone mad, and squeezed its throat with his left hand until it let go its hold, and then, holding it at arm's length, he succeeded at last in throttling it. It was a struggle for life, the creature snapping alternately at each hand, and he was almost exhausted when, to his relief, its head dropped, and it swung lifeless in his desperate grasp. He said afterwards: "I never saw anything so hideous as that dog's head, his jaws reeking with blood and foam, his mouth wide open, his tongue swollen and hanging out, and his eyes flashing a sort of lurid fire; the said head, although held at arm's length, being in very uncomfortable proximity to my face." Many natives were present, but were too startled to give any assistance. It had previously bitten two Sepoys, and Captain Mackenzie, having sent in vain for the Residency Surgeon, cauterised their wounds with hot iron and his own with caustic, which left a circular scar nearly two inches in diameter.

Towards the middle of September, the wound being quite healed, and the danger of hydrophobia considered past, Mackenzie made a tour in the lovely valley of Kohistan. He writes :—

"Major Ewart, commanding 54th N.I., and Captain James Skinner, commonly called 'Gentleman Jim,' from his more than usually pleasing manners and cultivated mind, having leagued with me to urge Father Time into a trot, he having sauntered fearfully of late, we started on the 21st. The Envoy lent us six of the King's Guards (Hazirbásh), and we marched light. The valley of Kohistan is some forty miles long, varying from four to ten miles in width, bounded on the N. by the eternal peaks of the Hindu Khush (Hindu-killer), from the clefts of which the snow never disappears. The beauty of the prospect increased as we advanced towards our first halting-place, Karez-i-Amír.

"The wells of this country consist of a number of shafts, sunk at short distances from each other, communicating by subterraneous passages, through which the water is led to any distance, the volume increasing as they encounter fresh springs, which the Afghans are extremely sagacious in hitting on. This mode of conveying water requires immense labour, but no evaporation can take place. These shafts and passages are often very deep and capacious, and the tribes avenge themselves on each other by filling them up and breaking them in, blood-feuds constantly resulting. I am inclined to think the patriarchs may have dug similar wells, which would account for the importance attached to them.

"The chief was absent with Captain Henry Drummond,[1]

---

[1] Whose life he saved when the mutiny broke out.

who is employed by Government in looking for coal and iron, the first a most desirable object in a country so poor in fuel. Almost every Afghan fort consists of a square with a tower at each corner, the walls being built of huge masses of mud, some six or eight feet thick at the base, and perhaps three at the top, the main building varying in height from twenty to forty feet, and all being pierced with numerous loopholes for wall-pieces and matchlocks. In general, they have only one strong gate, and our mode of taking them is very simple. If a few rounds from a great gun do not do the office of a key, two covering parties keep up a rattling fire on the walls while an officer rushes forward with a bag of powder, which he nails to the gate, fires by means of a slow match, and gets out of the way as fast as possible. The gate being shattered, the storming party enter and slay the garrison if pugnaciously given. Here one of our camels, apparently in strong health, lay down and died in the most perverse manner.

"This village of Karez-i-Amír consists as usual of a cluster of forts, round which we rode in the evening, ascending and descending several beautiful highland dells whose sparkling streams were bordered with plane and mulberry trees, and weeping-willows. We alighted at the residence of the Khan, who was absent, and were welcomed by the *hakim* (doctor) in the garden and vineyard, where we came upon a little child of the great man (all the children here are perfect cherubs), who, being accustomed to play with Drummond, evinced no fear of the Feringhis, albeit many still believe that a roasted infant is a great delicacy among us. From the towers the womenkind gazed at us with intense curiosity ; but politeness forbade our even looking their way openly. The great men and the inhabitants of cities are very jealous of their women, but among the mountains greater freedom obtains. If a

European travels in a native dress, he has frequent opportunities of seeing women unveiled; but even the distant
vision of an unadulterated Feringhi is the signal for all
females to drop their veils, and turn their faces to the wall,
over which they frequently climb with all the agility of
fear.

"Next morning started towards Istalif. Having a guide,
and trusting to the sure-footedness of our Turkoman nags,
we wandered on among the romantically beautiful glades
and dells of the Koh-dáman (skirt of the mountain), an
intricate and rugged path, leading among the richest vineyards and orchards, forming quite a forest of apple, pear,
quince, pomegranate, and mulberry trees. Overhead
gigantic plane and walnut trees, such as are hardly seen in
Europe, completely excluded the rays of the sun, and ever
and anon a sudden descent revealed to our delighted eyes
the flashing waters of some impetuous rivulet, bounding
with new-born energy from the mountain side.

"Thus we wound our way to Kohdara. The tempera-
ture of the different valleys of the Koh-dáman varies so
much, as to create a difference of weeks in their fruit
seasons, and to make it absolutely necessary to cover up the
vines during winter, in some, which are perhaps not more
than three miles from others, where the trees can be left bare
with perfect impunity; and yet there cannot be a difference
of fifty feet in the level of these places. We were met by
the chief, Khojah Mir Khan, attended by a host of armed
retainers. The heads of villages are paid for keeping up a
certain number of followers to act as police, but who are
also necessary for their personal safety, on account of the
inveterate blood-feuds which exist. Khojah Mir Khan has
suffered considerably from his hereditary enemies, and
doubtless has himself committed many atrocities in his
time, although his mild and venerable appearance would

scarcely argue him a remorseless shedder of blood.   In this
country the word 'Tarbur,' signifies both cousin and
enemy or rival, and practically the two significations are
always united.   The Tarbur of this man, named Saif-u-din,
was, when we first entered the valley in hostile guise,
viz. last year, chief of Kohdara, and, being a partisan of
Dost Muhammad Khan, opposed us vigorously.   After
thrashing our opponents, Sir Alex. Burnes's policy was
always to inquire who were the most powerful and inveterate cousins, whom he immediately installed in the
possessions of the discomfited.   In this case he found that
Saif-u-din had, besides shooting the two grown-up sons of
Khojah Mir Khan, caught one of his wives in a lonely
place playing with her child.   Snatching the infant from
its unhappy mother, he deliberately cut off its head, which
he threw in her face ; so that we are sure that no league
can be entered into between these two loving relatives.
Saif-u-din had just escaped from confinement, and his cousin
was in great alarm, which perhaps contributed to the zeal
with which he pressed us to spend a day with him.   Passing
through the village, many a friendly 'salam alekum' and
'khush amedid'('Peace be upon you' and 'You are welcome'),
greeted us, uttered with profound gravity and dignity by
small boys and ragged serfs, as well as by the 'rish-safed'
of the place.   The last class, literally the 'white-beards,'
are in every Afghan, and perhaps in every Oriental village,
looked up to with much reverence, and their opinions weigh
greatly in all the 'jirgas' or councils.   Our host had
chosen our resting-place with infinite taste.   Carpets and
cushions had been laid under the spreading branches of
some large trees at the top of a vineyard, which, sloping
down the sunny bank and intermixed with peach and other
fruit trees, presented an immense profusion of grapes of
every hue and kind.   Beyond and around, the gorge and the

sides of the little valley were covered with similar gardens. A number of small forts and towers, whose brown turrets, peeping out from the deep green foliage, made a beautiful landscape. Farther down was the highly-cultivated plain of Kohistan, with its groves and hamlets, bounded by a chain of bare and rocky mountains, rising ridge over ridge until the summits appeared to mingle with the clouds. Enormous trays of all kinds of fruit were placed before us, the attendants kindly peeling the fresh walnuts and almonds for us with their fingers. The personal habits of these good people being filthy in the extreme, it required a great effort on our part to swallow the proceeds. Skinner and I succeeded ; but it was in vain that I exhorted Ewart to open his mouth and shut his eyes, his disgust being doubled by the extra courtesy of a very grimy personage, who, perceiving that the major's head was resting on a stone, took off his turban and placed it beneath as a pillow. I gave a pocket-knife to a little son of the Khan, which pleased the father, and transported the child, who tormented everybody to admire the Feringhi's present. An elder brother looked quite discomfited at being left out, which induced Ewart to make him a similar present, and then the true nature of the savage showed itself in the boy's cunning tricks to obtain something else. I complied with his hints to give him some gunpowder, etc., which so emboldened him that at last, in a roundabout speech, in which he showed great power of cajolery and flattery, he asked me to give him my carbine, and remained quite unabashed, only laughing at my refusal. We were annoyed at the Khan's pertinacity in refusing payment for the food with which he supplied both man and beast in our little camp ; but it was a point of honour with him, as is generally the case in this country. Not only must the guest's wants be freely supplied, but, if necessary, blood must be shed for him. And yet, in the case of a

feudal enemy, eating bread and salt together is frequently
no protection from treachery. Near the Khan's fort are
still the blackened remains of another, sacked and burnt by
our troops last year. Its surrounding vineyards, now the
property of a 'cousin,' contrasted strangely in their fresh
beauty with the desolation of their former master's home.
Wherever we strolled we were pressed to enter the different
gardens by their owners, whose hearty hospitality could
only be satisfied by our eating some fruit, and carrying
away enough to stock Covent Garden. By this time grapes
had become a burden to us. One reverend senior encouraged
us by protesting that if the juice of his grapes made us
tipsy he would hold our horses, and was delighted when I
endeavoured, in wretched Persian, to return his banter.
This is in truth a fruit country. A beggar receives a melon
or a huge bunch of grapes, a visitor always brings an offering of fruit, and a religious man, saying 'In God's name
an oblation,' forces an apple into your hand. For many
months of the year the poorer people live on bread made
of dried mulberries ground into flour—a sweet food enough,
but heating. Next day rode on towards Istalif, through
similar scenery. Came upon some most lovely spots, looking as if they were the abodes of innocence and peace.
The few inhabitants we met apparently saw Europeans for
the first time in their lives. One lump of a lad climbed up
into a tree to observe us more accurately, and readily
entered into the joke when we laughed in his face. We
observed that the weavers sat on the ground with their feet
in a hole dug for that purpose. Primitive enough. Reached
Farzá. Rather a large assemblage of forts, on an eminence
clothed with large trees, a considerable mountain stream
rushing past. Here eight of the Maliks (chiefs) are Afghans,
and four Parsiwáns or descendants of Persians. As we
descended towards the stream a crowd of people came

running up to us in so tumultuous a fashion that our horsemen apprehended an attack, especially as one man seized
Ewart's bridle. The mystery was explained by the leader,
a stout young Afghan, dashing his turban on the ground
and scattering dust on his head, uttering at the same time
the most lamentable cry. It appeared that his brother had
just been murdered. It was evident that he was of a fighting race, for his shaven head was seamed with sabre cuts,
which is the case with every Afghan's head I have yet
inspected. We refused to meddle in the matter, or even to
turn aside to look at the body, recommending him to convey
the murderer, whom they had seized, to Kabul to be judged
by the Vazir, who would fine him forty tomuns, about £80.
Until the price of blood is done away, as many respectable
natives have averred to me, assassination must continue.
During our ten days' tour we fell in with five murdered
men, to say nothing of a poor fellow who came to me with
a bad musket-shot in the shoulder, to whom I gave a note
to one of our surgeons in Kabul, who has since reported
that he is doing well. Nearing Istalif our *ballad* (guide),
Aliverdi Khan, insisted that we should not pass his tower
without bringing good luck on it by alighting. We did so,
and I shall never forget the taste and beauty of the arbour
in which he had spread a carpet for us. It was under a
huge old mulberry tree, among the branches of which
clustered quantities of white and black grapes, the walls of
this luxurious retreat consisting of rose bushes, thickly
intertwined with jessamine. It is upon the huge verdure-
less mountains which towered up behind us that the famous
Kabul rhubarb grows. There also roam both wolves and
bears, as also an animal, half-sheep, half-deer, whose venison
is equal to that of the fallow deer.

"I had already remarked our entertainer, Aliverdi Khan,
as a most respectable soldierly old man. He recognised the

Turkoman horse I was riding as the one on which the Dost
had effected his escape from Bokhara, and was much affected.
He proved to be the very man who had contrived the escape
of the ex-Amir, and was, with the exception of the guide,
the sole companion of his flight.   This worthy old soldier
held the situation of Mír Akhor (Master of Horse) in the
service of the Amir; in which, indeed, he had passed his
life, and to whom he remained faithful to the last, having
sustained a gallant part in the last battle fought by his
master, that of Parwán Darra, where the Bengal cavalry
behaved so ill.   Of these Aliverdi spoke with bitter contempt, but made no boast of his own exploits.   So far,
however, as I can learn, it was he who led the charge which
proved so fatal to our officers, whose men had basely
deserted them.   The respect I involuntarily paid him, and
my possession of the animal that had stood his old master
in good stead at a pinch, quite won the old man's heart,
and I was unable to prevent his always holding my stirrup
while mounting and dismounting; and on one occasion
when he saw me thrashing the beast for nearly breaking
my neck by his obstinacy, he rode up and remonstrated.
He has refused many offers of good service under the Shah,
and is now most anxious, having settled the affairs of his
family, to be allowed to join the Amir in his exile in India,
and die in his service.

"From the height we had attained it was curious to see
the tops of the houses covered with grapes, drying into
raisins.   Those for exportation are the Kishmish, a small
white grape without seeds, and the Munaker, a long red
one, as big as small plums.   Approaching Istalif we stumbled
upon the two most magnificent camels I ever saw—one
(black) from Bokhara, and the other (white) from Samarcand;
both covered with that fine long hair of which the cloth
called Shutri is made.   I did not think it possible for camels

to be so majestically beautiful. How shall I describe Istalif! We pitched in a small grove on the summit of a high narrow ridge, the southern slope of which was adorned by gardens and vineyards, while the northern aspect, steep and un-garnished, save by a few giant plane trees, fronted the town ; which, like Syra in Greece, rose, terrace over terrace, up the face of the opposing hill, flanked by vineyards and orchards, and surmounted by a grove of trees, embosoming the shrine of a favourite Muhammadan saint. When the town is illuminated on a dark night on great occasions the effect is, I am told, extremely beautiful. It being bright moon-light, the good old chief, Khalifa Ibrahim Khan, regretted he could not gratify our curiosity. He paid us a visit, and deputed his eldest son, a personification of Tony Lumpkin, to wait on us during our sojourn, which task he performed with great zeal. It was impossible to bring our loaded camels up the steep road, and their burdens were conse-quently, under Tony's superintendence, brought up on men's shoulders. One strapping fellow discovered, after depositing his load, that it was a box of *wine*. He was somewhat discomfited at this, and at the laughter of his companions ; but Tony brought back his good humour, not by a *douceur*, but by, of all things in the world, throwing his arms round his brawny neck, and kissing him ! In the vineyards are eighteen different kinds of grapes, all excellent. I measured one of a kind called the *didu-i-gao* (cow's eye), and found it to be four inches and a half round by three and a half ! As we inspected the above-mentioned shrine, one of the superstitions attached to which is that no man can count the plane trees planted round it (and certainly we all failed in making our numbers agree), I saw one of our followers was leaning over a tomb. I asked him whose it was ; and he replied : 'That of my father, murdered by Dost Muhammad.' Indeed, most of our questions as to who

burnt that village, or who murdered the father of this man
and the brother of that, were answered by, 'Dost Muhammad.' And yet his last battle against us was fought by
these very people ; who, when he was in power, were always
in rebellion against him, and whom, he declared himself, he
was obliged to crush, as he would scorpions. A young
Persian, named Jáfir, son of Sohrab Khan, one of the king's
tax-gatherers, a perfect Master Slender, with a mincing gait
and soft voice, was anxious to show us his residence. His
garden contained peaches such as I have never seen, which
these uncivilised people rudely shook from the tree as we
would crab-apples, whereas their delicacy and flavour entitled
them to be plucked only by the fair hands of the pride of
her sex, an English lady. Friend Slender, sitting opposite
to me under our leafy canopy by a bubbling rill which
emptied itself into the fountain by which we lay supine
('Tony' lolling next me, and carving flowers with his long
thumb-nail on the rind of a pomegranate), reminded me of
the custom of his pleasure-loving race of placing tame
nightingales on the dewy sod close to the gushing waters,
whose soft murmur invariably awakens the soul of melody
within the 'lover of the rose.'

"Istalif contains three thousand houses, and yields a
revenue of thirty-five thousand rupees. On leaving it a
relation of the chief's accompanied us for a couple of miles.
The propitious spot he chose for saying farewell was at a
small mosk, erected in memory of the victory of Ali Sháhi
Mardán over a dragon, whose body is still shown hard by.
This is a mass of stone somewhat like a dragon, from which
flow the tricklings of a mineral spring of reddish colour and
saltish taste. None but an infidel, however, would deny
that these are the blood and tears of the still agonised
monster. Passed unnumbered flocks of a colony of wandering Ghaljais, whose black tents dotted the downs. As

the heat increased we gladly found ourselves among the wooded glades of 'Istarghitch,' the elders of which place besought us to alight and refresh ourselves, which we did, although we could not stay breakfast according to their hospitable wish. This vale would be equal to Istalif in importance but for the blood-feuds which for years past have caused a fearful annual destruction of life and property. Halted at Laghmán. The Political Agent, Eldred Pottinger (the hero of Herat), had gone to Kabul to impress upon the Envoy that, unless strong measures of prevention were speedily taken, a rise in Kohistan was imminent, and our means of defence quite inadequate; but his assistant, Captain Charles Rattray, gave us a hearty welcome. The fort affords good quarters, and the adjacent garden and vineyards are large and pleasant. The cantonment, Charekar, is about three miles off. The commanding officer, Codrington, an old brother cadet, with a brother of my friend Broadfoot, joined us in the evening, and old stories kept us up till late. In the morning we rode to Khoja-se-yárán, a remarkable spot, high up in the western range, where Codrington had prepared breakfast. Hard by is the mound celebrated in the memoirs of Sultan Baber, on which he and his warriors sat drinking wine and admiring the glorious prospect before them. Had an excellent view of Ghurband, Parwán Darra, the scene of our defeat,[1] and all the northern part of Kohistan, which Vigne the traveller pronounced infinitely superior to anything he had seen in Northern Italy. In the afternoon, Rattray being our cicerone, we started for Muhammad Tráki, the residence of a chief called Malik Saif-u-din, situated at the junction of three rivers. Rode through Charekar, close to which are the tombs of Dr. Lord and Lieutenants Crispin and James Broadfoot,

[1] By Dost Muhammad's men on the 2d November the previous year, 1840.

killed in the unfortunate Parwán Darra affair : they looked
shabby enough memorials. Thence our road lay east through
extensive meadowlands of soft and springy turf, with an
admixture of bog here and there, in which two of our horsemen stuck fast for a time. Passed several farmhouses
which, but for the high walls enclosing them, would have
looked very English. Crossed the above rivers a dozen
times, so much do they turn and wind. In all the current
is very strong, and during the summer they are unfordable
from the melting of the snow. Observed what we took for
flocks of wild duck, which proved to be only 'graven
images' of the bird of wood and clay moored in the water
as decoys, close to which the sportsmen lie in ambush. Had
Rattray not warned us we might have furnished the Afghans
with a good joke against us by letting fly at these mockeries.
It was late before we reached the fort of Malik Saif-u-din,
by whom we were clamorously welcomed. Although past
eighty, he is active and vigorous as a man of fifty, his fair
complexion and light gray eyes giving him the look of a
European. He never ceased talking ; his fair speech, however, being sadly at variance with the deep lines of cunning
and cruelty in his otherwise still handsome face. A tent
had been pitched for us immediately in front of his fort,
with a distant view of the Nijeráo valley, the people of
which are hostile to us, and give shelter to all offenders,
and where the leading man of all Kohistan, Mir Masjdi,[1] our
most active opponent during the war, now is. Although
crippled with wounds and dependent for his daily bread on
the chiefs of that valley, he refuses to submit to the Shah.
Being esteemed a very holy personage prevents his suffering
from want, superstition doing the work of charity. My
baggage did not arrive until next morning, so 'my lodging

---

[1] Two months later this man raised the standard of insurrection to
overturn the Shah and expel the British.

was on the cold ground.' Again on horseback early, under
the direction of our patriarchal host, in the direction of the
Rez-i-Rawan (running sand), distant about three miles.
During the ride Saif-u-din pointed out to us a grave, orna-
mented with a flag, as a sign that the faithful were to pray
and make offerings there. 'That,' he said, 'is the grave
of my father-in-law. I killed him shortly after my marriage,
as his head was full of wind,'—meaning that he gave himself airs. The Rez-i-Rawan is perhaps one of the most
curious objects in the world. It is a very steep bank of
sand, running up a mountain to the height of some three
hundred yards. The sand is extremely fine, and is supposed to be unfathomable. If a hole of any depth be dug
in it, in the course of a few hours all is smooth and level
again. On the plain below an annual fair is held, when
many persons perform the feat of ascending to the top,
which is by no means easy from its steepness and the
yielding nature of the sand, into which the leg sinks to the
calf, the foot slipping back at each stride. The sand displaced by the climber runs rustling down, creating a sound
like the distant dash of waves on the seashore, which,
when a multitude ascend and the wind blows strongly
against the face of the bank, resembles the loud clash of
cymbals. The natives assign this to supernatural agency,
and say that Friday, the Musalman Sabbath, is the most
auspicious day for hearing the wonderful music. Whatever
sand may be displaced from the top is always blown back
again by the strong winds which eddy round the base.
There is a similar hill in the neighbourhood of Mount Sinai,
of which Lieutenant Newbold of the Madras Army has
given an account, with like sounds and legends. Taking off
our boots, I and my comrades struggled up. The feat
cost me half an hour's exertion, although those who are
accustomed to it can do it in less. The rocks beyond are

limestone, whose sharp angular surface forbade our further
ascent with bare feet. We made boys race down. One
accomplished the distance in thirty seconds. After the toil
of ascending, the sensation of running down is delightful.
A petty chief of our party while bounding down pitched
forward on his head, which sinking deep in the sand, his
heels remained up in the air for a few seconds in the most
ludicrous manner. His own people were convulsed with
laughter, but he preserved his good humour, although the
force of the shock made the blood gush from his nose. We
then visited a famous cave, said to be the tomb of the great
saint, Khojah Muhammad.[1] Here the horse-shoe of the
saint was shown us. It is of stone, square, and big enough
for a camel. Found my baggage all safe. A rascally
Afghan chaprási, had been the cause of its being left out
all night, by which my Hindu servants were exposed both
to the cold and to ill-treatment from the boors, who had
beaten them. This and a lie from the delinquent provoked
me to cudgel him, the surrounding Muhammadans standing
astonished to see a káfir[2] make one of the Faithful 'eat
blows.' I detected an Afghan in a most unusual act of
gallantry for one of his creed. He was actually carrying a
woman across a stream on his back. Her veil slipping off,
discovered that his devotion certainly did not arise from
her beauty. In the afternoon we witnessed a novel mode of
fishing in the river below, for which clear water is the most
favourable. A dam of wicker-work had been thrown half
across the river, causing a strong rush of water towards a
small platform near the side, in which was a hole so contrived as to remain dry, the fish falling into it, and the
water passing through more wicker-work. A great number

---

[1] The old faqir living at this tomb, having received some kindness
from Lieutenant Haughton, strongly recommended him to *spend the
winter in Kabul.*   [2] Infidel.

of people waded down the stream towards this, frightening the fish by splashing, and spearing those within their reach. In both ways we caught an immense quantity. Saif-u-din's 'cousin,' Ahmed Khan, is the great man of all this part of the country. His father having slain his brother-in-law, Saif-u-din's father, he came to visit us in the open during the fishing, not choosing to trust himself near the stronghold of his enemy. I saw him go up to a petty chief, one of whose men his people had killed during the night, and pat him on the back, inquiring after his health with the affectionate concern of a father. A strange people !

"We had a visit from Malik Khojah Abdul Khálik ('The Chief, the Descendant of the Khalifs, the Slave of God '), formerly a desperate rebel. Conscious of his iniquities, although he did not know that we had received information that day that he was in full communication with the outlaws in Nijeráo, he had previously sent to know if he would be welcome, he is very handsome, and one of the most gentlemanly persons I have seen in this country; but he was far eclipsed in looks by a young Nijeráo chief who accompanied him. His beauty was quite supernatural. All the Khojahs call themselves descendants of the first Khalifs, and they and the Saiads are reverenced in the most absurd manner. This villain is thought too holy for this world, and they relate that his grandfather was a man of such sanctity that, when he had occasion for a horse, he used to put his saddle on any given wall, which immediately ambled gently on with its precious burden. During the night an attack was apprehended from the people of Durnámeh, a small upland valley where the inhabitants are very poor, pay no taxes, and supply themselves from the plain with the necessaries of life gratis. Our Malik[1] thought

---

[1] *Malik*—(lit. "a proprietor ")—a petty chief.

their design was surely to slay and plunder us, and made a great fuss arming and collecting his people; but our opinion was verified by its turning out a mere marauding party. We were awakened during the night by the firing, but the rogues were soon driven off. It was so cold that we were delighted at not being obliged to get up. In the morning crossed the river to the ancient city of Bágrám, whose ruins indicate former wealth and splendour, covering considerably more ground than the present city of Kabul; but not even a tradition exists as to its prosperity or its decay. Here Mr. Masson collected, I am told, upwards of twenty thousand ancient coins and relics, many of the former of course Greek. There is scarcely a house in Afghanistan which is not built of mud or of small sun-dried bricks; but in these ruins baked bricks are found of an immense size, such as cannot now be procured. The site of the citadel and part of the city wall are still conspicuous. Saw no signs of human beings throughout this little Babylon save some of the black-tent Ghaljais.[1] These people are here called 'Kuchigis' (Marchers). Tending their flocks and plundering are their only occupations. It is impossible to conceive a finer combination of wood, water, meadow green, and mountain gray, of fertile beauty and savage grandeur, than the view from this place.

"Returning to Laghmán, we rode to Kárabagh, some twelve miles. I was sorry to part from Rattray, who is a most amusing pleasant companion.[2] He told me that, travelling once with his present escort of horsemen at sun-

[1] Ghaljais or Ghalzais, or Ghiljves, lit. "sons of thieves"; the former is Afghan pronunciation, the second right.

[2] Not one of these pleasant fellows had more than two months to live. Lieutenant Charles Rattray was treacherously murdered on the 3d November; Captain Codrington killed on the 5th; William Broadfoot fell with Burnes, to whom he had just been appointed Secretary, on the 2d November.

set, the hour of prayer, he stopped and begged that he
might be no hindrance to the performance of their religious
duties. 'You surely do not take us for clowns or pedlars,'
said they; 'we are soldiers, and never pray!' 'Indeed,'
added one, 'I have only prayed twice in my life; once a
thief took advantage of it to steal my saddle, and the other
time a favourite horse got loose and damaged himself, which
has determined me never to do anything so foolish again!'
Kárabagh consists of ten or twelve forts, surrounded by
well-cultivated fields, orchards, and vineyards. The chief,
a portly old gentleman, came forth to meet us, and supplied
additional guards during the night on account of the Ghaljais, encamped at a short distance, of whose ravages he
complained bitterly, especially as the Vazir would not allow
him to execute any prisoners he took. Next morning,
while strolling through his gardens, we spied certain buildings which turned out to be a wine-press. The good man
being fairly convicted of making wine, which however he
persisted in calling 'grape juice,' frankly showed us the
process. It was rude, the vats being of clay, in which the
liquor was purified by a kind of chalky marl. It was afterwards boiled, poured when cold into goat-skins, and sent
to Kabul, where the faithful drink it secretly, fearing the
law. He said that after keeping two years, the flavour improved, which proves that it has body. I have drunk it at
Sir Alexander Burnes'; it tastes like small Madeira.

"30*th Sept.* 1841.—A ride of twenty-two miles brought
us into Kabul. In a solitary spot a miller betrayed the
customs of his country by refusing to allow me and my
men to assist him in arranging a sack of flour on the back
of a restive yábu, thinking we meant to steal it. On our
arrival at home, I found that the hounds of war had been
let slip into Zurmat, and that my kind friend the Envoy
had been appointed Governor of Bombay. The departure

of Sir William and Lady Macnaghten is a great loss. I
have watched him closely since my arrival in Afghanistan,
and am convinced of his worth, both as a public servant
and a private gentleman. As I do not choose to give up
the political line, and no situation is at present vacant here,
I shall return next month to Peshawar. Before next hot
weather *many things may occur* to help me out of the
scrape."

He deeply felt his sad and solitary Sundays at Peshawar, and said they were worse than those in captivity,
when Pottinger and Eyre both sought religious conversation.

Yes, it was all "quite settled." Sir William was to
start for Bombay, accompanied by General Elphinstone,
whose increasing suffering and helplessness from fever and
rheumatic gout had compelled him to resign his command.
George Lawrence was to be the Governor's Military Secretary; Sir Alexander Burnes, to his great satisfaction, was
to be the new Envoy; and Mackenzie was to revert to his
political appointment at Peshawar. The Envoy and
General were to start on the 3d October, when suddenly
the news came that the Eastern Ghaljais had risen *en
masse* and blocked the road to Jellalabad. *Ce qui arrive,
c'est toujours l'imprévu.*

CHAPTER XIII.

(October 1841.)

" La politique c'est le drame de l'homme qui s'agite, et de Dieu qui le mène."—Quoted by MADAME DE SÉVIGNÉ.

THE hounds of war had indeed been slipped in Zurmat, and they were to course the whole country. About two months previously the Envoy had applied for five additional regiments, but Burnes said : " If we cannot keep the Shah on his throne with one European regiment and his own contingent, the sooner we leave the country the better ;" and in an evil hour persuaded Sir William to withdraw his request, just two days before the rebellion broke out. Burnes was quite right in his alternative, but wrong in thinking the first half of it a possibility. Afghanistan is a poor country, and yet the Government of India were always insisting on economy, and requiring that it should pay its own expenses. Now the revenues were not sufficient to furnish an adequate income for the Shah, and also to pay the stipends of the chiefs ; and as the Envoy, a man of extreme delicacy of feeling, was unwilling to mortify Shah Shujah by requiring him to retrench, the stipends of the chiefs were cut down. Some of these stipends had been restored, some granted for the first time on the restoration of Shah Shujah, for good service done to him ; and Burnes had formally guaranteed them to the chiefs of Kohistan in

1839. They were paid either by a deduction from the
land-tax due by each chief, or by an order on the tax pay-
able by some turbulent district, which he had to levy, and
which would not otherwise have been paid at all; so that
the grant, though valuable to him who levied it, was of
little or no value to the Shah's Government. In return,
they maintained a sort of militia, and the Ghaljai chiefs
kept the passes open, and were answerable for outrages.
There were, for instance, four thanas or posts in the Khurd
Kabul Pass under four different chiefs, each of whom kept
up supplies for the use of our troops. Sir William reported
that the chiefs "acquiesced in the justice of the reduction;"
but, on the contrary, they considered it a direct breach of
faith. The whole deficiency amounted to only £14,000;
and this attempt at economy was the main cause of the outbreak and all its subsequent horrors!

The Envoy said that the instructions of the Supreme
Government left him no alternative; but Mackenzie was of
opinion that Sir William's training as Secretary to Government prevented his being sufficiently independent, and that
he should have refused to carry out so suicidal a policy.
He had strongly remonstrated against it, but he had become
quite weary of the manner in which his representations were
treated, and therefore gave way. A man in authority at so
perilous an outpost requires indomitable firmness, should
be an absolute pachyderm as to reproaches, and be at all
times willing to sacrifice his position rather than his well-
founded opinions. Such obstinacy is the most valuable
service he can render to the State.

There were also other grievances: one, which the Envoy
admitted to be well founded, was a new rule making the
chiefs responsible for robberies by Eastern Ghaljais, where-
ever they might be committed, instead of limiting their
responsibility to their own jurisdiction; another was the

extreme pride of Shah Shujah, which made him most unpopular. He kept his daughters unmarried, rather than
bestow them on the greatest chiefs ; and would make the
most powerful men in the country wait for hours before
admitting them to his presence. His government, thanks
to British power, was too strong and regular to be acceptable to these turbulent chiefs. They had now got a master
instead of having a chief, obliged to overlook their excesses
in return for their support. It was the difference between
an autocrat and a parliamentary leader.

The British incurred all the odium of constant interference, and yet effected no real amelioration in the state of
the country. We should have done either more or less.

Dost Muhammad was not beloved, but he had a strong
party. He was feared by all and hated by many, especially
by the lower classes. He ruled by craft, setting chief against
chief, and stirring up blood-feuds. In his youth he had
been notoriously vicious, but when he became Amir he
went through a ceremony of repentance (Toba), and began
to enforce outward morality. General Haughton says :
"Shah Shujah was an angel of light compared to the Dost.
He was a man of considerable ability, an Arabic scholar
and a poet, well acquainted with Persian literature, speaking Persian perfectly, and Hindustani with ease, besides
his mother-tongue Pushtu ; yet, strange to say, the court
language on public occasions is Turki ! Everything said to
the Shah in Persian was repeated to him by his Master of
the Ceremonies in Turki, and he replied in the same manner,
—a curious reminiscence of the time when Afghan kings
reigned from Bokhara to the Indian Ocean, and from
Meshed to Sirhind."

Charges have been brought against our army of seduc-
tion and carrying off women, as if this had aroused popular
fury. These charges were only part of a systematic attempt

"to blacken our character and to prejudice the populace against us," just as such monstrous inventions as the use of torture by Madras magistrates and the burning of the wounded at Istalif have been circulated for party purposes by some who might have known better. Not one specific case was ever brought forward ; had it been, it would have been promptly redressed by the Shah, the Envoy, and the General, for the discipline in prevention of any outrages upon the natives of the country was from first to last most severe. The women of Kabul and Kandahar had long borne a most unfavourable reputation among their own countrymen, and whatever the morality of our troops (of whom the British formed only one tenth), it may be safely affirmed that there was nothing to which the Afghans would object, and no such thing as interference with the peace of any native family. The districts most hostile to us were those in which (like Kohistan and the Ghaljai country) no troops had ever been quartered.[1] True, some of our officers married native women, chiefly widows, some before the Kazi, according to Muhammadan law (under which all marriages are dissoluble at pleasure); but this, however blameworthy in the Christian Englishman, could bring no disgrace on the wife. Such marriages were generally with the full consent of her kindred, and viewed with no disfavour by her countrymen. One of the latter complimented an officer who had formed such a marriage with the observation, "Now you have rendered yourself respectable,"— bachelors being ill thought of by Muhammadans. The fearful vengeance taken upon some of these poor women was only the usual savage mode of dealing with the family

---

[1] The Shah complained of seeing women riding towards the cantonments. Our numerous Musalman troops had brought their wives with them, who all adopted the " burkha " or Afghan muffler, and of course these women were seen.

of an enemy. If they burnt a young Afghan lady of some rank (a most beautiful girl of eighteen) alive, cutting the throats of all her servants, because she was the wife of a captain in our service, they did the same to the wives and children of our faithful adherent Ján Fishan Khan. Neither was there any general hatred to us as Europeans. On the contrary, the two races generally liked each other; there were many instances of personal friendship and confidence, and in more than one instance Afghans of rank saved the lives of British officers by hiding them in their own zenanas.[1]

The whole country round Kandahar, about three hundred miles west of Kabul, always had been hostile to us, but the Envoy took a sanguine view, and reported Afghanistan as "quiet," Burnes confirming him in this opinion, though many of our officers and men had been attacked and wounded close to cantonments. Both officers and men were openly insulted in the city even by the shopkeepers, and the whole demeanour of the people was that of anticipated triumph in the destruction of the English. Among other outrages, Captain Waller was wounded by the pistol-ball of an assassin, Dr. Metcalfe escaped being cut down only by the speed of his horse, a private was found barbarously murdered on the highway, and Brigadier Shelton having refused the usual night-guard of Sepoys to the Horse Artillery in his camp, an Afghan deliberately walked into one of the tents, pistolled a fine young trooper who was lying asleep, and escaped.

Macnaghten had plenty of warnings. Pottinger went into Kabul in September to point out the great danger arising from our gross breach of faith in cutting down the stipends of the chiefs and from the insufficiency of our military force, but, as he bitterly complained, was treated as an alarmist.

[1] Women's apartments; from *zan*, a woman.

Mackenzie had recorded his opinion a year before that the situation in Afghanistan was "alarming," adding "our gallant fellows in Afghanistan must be *reinforced, or they will all perish.*"

Early in October a faqir informed the Envoy of the treachery of certain chiefs, advised him to be more careful of his person, and to put the cantonment in a state of defence. About the same time three Ghaljai chiefs suddenly left Kabul and blocked the Khurd Kabul Pass, cutting off our communication with India, so that the journey of the Envoy and General was necessarily deferred, for a fortnight or so, as they supposed, but in reality it was for ever. The Shah shared Macnaghten's strange delusion as to the unwarlike nature of the Eastern Ghaljais. Macnaghten and Burnes both spoke with contempt of the insurrection. George Broadfoot, an intimate friend of Burnes, says "his views were, except in details, those of Macnaghten, and he was nearly as blind to what was passing round him."

A Ghaljai, much attached to Captain Henry Drummond, told him that some of the chiefs were meeting every night in Kabul, planning to join the Ghaljai insurrection; and that he himself had seen donkey-loads of powder and shot pass through his village, sent by the chief to the Ghaljais. Drummond warned Burnes on the 13th October, and the latter informed the Envoy that his Persian writer, Mohun Lal, could procure the Kurán to which the conspirators had attached their seals, so that their names might be known. Most unaccountably, the Envoy took no notice of any of these warnings, and Burnes did not like to interfere further.

In the meantime it was necessary to open the Khurd Kabul Pass at once, but as usual there was the chronic deficiency of carriage, so that it was not till the 11th of

October that Her Majesty's 13th could join the rest of the force at Butkhak, ten miles from Kabul. Broadfoot's newly-raised corps of sappers was so short of officers that Colin Mackenzie rode out with the 13th to assist his friend. Early on the 12th the force marched under Sir Robert Sale. His Brigade-Major, Captain Hamlet Wade, relates : —"Did not see a soul until nearing the Tangi (narrow gorge). Sir Robert directed some companies to ascend as flankers, and had hardly given the order when we were saluted by a heavy volley, and Sir Robert was unfortunately severely wounded, the ball fracturing the leg. I got a rap on the ankle. I could not help admiring old Sale's coolness. He turned to me and said, 'Wade, I have got it,' and then remained on horseback directing the skirmishers, until compelled from loss of blood to make over command to Dennie."

This truly formidable defile is in some places not fifty yards wide, the rocks rising almost perpendicularly on both sides to a height of five hundred to six hundred feet. Besides occupying these heights the enemy had thrown up a sanga, or barrier, at the narrowest part, flanked by a strong tower. Behind this they lay in wait, picking off officers in particular. Broadfoot was away reconnoitring, so that Colin Mackenzie was the only officer with the Sappers, who, with Dawes' two guns, two companies of Her Majesty's 13th, and two of the 35th N.I., formed the advance-guard under the command of Captain Seaton.[1] The 13th and 35th, as flanking-parties, gallantly struggled up the almost inaccessible heights to dislodge the enemy. Mackenzie and Dawes entered the gorge to carry the sanga. As they did so, the enemy from the crags above poured in such a tremendous storm of bullets that a number of the Sappers were knocked over, and the rest, abashed by the

---

[1] Afterwards Major-General Sir Thomas Seaton.

novelty of the thing—never having been fairly under fire before—halted and then gave ground. Mackenzie was left alone, but by standing firm, the special mark for the Afghan sharp-shooters, and at last rushing to the front waving his sword and cheering, he succeeded in rallying the corps, and they then won the pass. Dawes and his guns were in some danger when Mackenzie with the Sappers rushed up breathless to his rescue. Michael Dawes met his grasp with a cordial smile, the only man, Mackenzie said, except Broadfoot, whom he ever saw wear a natural smile in battle.[1]

After about half an hour the approach of the main body enabled Captain Seaton to push on, running the gauntlet to the end of the pass, when the enemy abandoned their position. Our skirmishers had everywhere got possession of the heights, and our Afghan auxiliaries under Ján Fishan Khan crowned the mountains and displayed their banners on the summit.

Broadfoot afterwards wrote :—

" To make you know the value of what Colin Mackenzie did would need a description of the place and circumstances, than which, to one unskilled to drive the pen, it were easier twice to force the pass. Chance threw on that corps and Dawes' guns the part of the affair on which all turned, namely, the forcing the pass itself, the part of the ravine strengthened by works, and intended to be defended by the enemy. The party attacking was so weak, and so completely unsupported, that all depended on uninterrupted success. Hesitation or confusion would have caused the attack to fail, and that would have risked a fearful disaster. Mackenzie commanded in a way few officers could have done ; the success was rapid and complete, and the day was

---

[1] Michael Dawes was the chief means of preserving our army at Chillianwala in 1849. After the action Brigadier Godby rode up to him and said : "Captain Dawes, I am happy to have this opportunity of thanking you for saving my brigade." Just after, Sir Walter Gilbert came up and roared out : "Dawes, thank you for saving my division !"

gained. Unquestionably great was the credit due to him. Dawes showed the coolness he ever showed."

Dawes used to say that circumstances which appeared most terrible at a distance lost their terror when they came to pass, and that grace and peace of mind were given when most needed. Major Wade records: "This is the severest service we could be sent upon, and nothing but the determined pluck of the officers and men gained us the day. Mein of ours dangerously wounded, losing part of the brain. The ball was extracted on the spot; it had split into two parts, one entering the brain, the other running along under the skin to the back of the head."

It is a curious fact that Broadfoot's Sappers, though incessantly engaged, bearing the brunt of every action, standing firm when all others, European and natives, shrank from the fight, were never even mentioned in the despatches. General Sale was in his litter wounded, and the report of Captain Seaton, who commanded the advance guard, was never published or even forwarded. Broadfoot says: "It would have flatly contradicted Colonel Dennie," who succeeded Sale in command. He characterises the military operations as "far more serious than was expected, and instructive as showing that even against Afghans *no rules of military science can be neglected with impunity.*" [1]

Mackenzie remained with the force left at Khurd Kabul. Dawes mentions their joining in prayer together, and also that on the 14th they were all under arms nearly the whole night. On the 15th Mackenzie was summarily recalled to

[1] Broadfoot thus describes his corps of 600 Sappers:—"300 Hindustanis—brave; 200 Ghurkas—braver; 100 Afghans and Hazáras—heroes. And all from emulation beyond their several unmixed countrymen." Three companies, some of whom fought under Mackenzie during the siege, perished at Kabul.

his political duties at Kabul, having gone out without "leave or license." Thus he first led the advance to Jellalabad, and then returned to share the disasters of the Kabul force.

Sale had returned with the 13th to Butkhak. Major Wade relates :—

"Our officers on picquet distinctly saw the enemy moving off towards Kabul, which proved the chiefs there to be in league with them ; but the Politicals consider this 'quite a mistake.' On the night of the 14th October we had a fine recruit brutally murdered on his post by some blackguards who crept close to him. He was shot close to a faqirs' garden, and the belts and accoutrements were found in their house in the morning. Yet Sir William Macnaghten has requested the General to order the faqirs' immediate release, as they are *most respectable people*, and identified by our friends as such. Shame ! Friends indeed ! we have not one in the country."

General Elphinstone told the Envoy the chief faqir ought to be sent back to General Sale's camp, and there hung. Sir William replied that, in the excited state of feeling against us, it would be highly impolitic. However, during the siege of Jellalabad, this faqir came there begging. He was recognised by a soldier in the 13th L.I., named Collins, an Irishman of extraordinary gallantry, but a great ruffian. He lifted the faqir's cloak, and (strange to say) found his comrade's wings on the man's shoulders ; whereupon he took him by the scruff of the neck, put him into a deep pool close by the bastion, and quietly drowned him like a dog. Major Wade heard of it from some natives, and called out the guard. Sure enough the man's body was there. He inquired how it had happened. They all said : "We don't know, Sir ; we didn't see anything."

Sale sent his sick and wounded into Kabul, and, after long waiting for want of carriage, marched again on the

22d, and was strenuously opposed. On the 24th, at Tezin, Captain G. H. Macgregor, Political Agent with the brigade, found that the principal Ghaljai chiefs, with seven hundred followers, were in a fort two miles from camp. He at once saw that the conspiracy was far more extensive than had been suspected; and, feeling that they had been treated with injustice, he made overtures to them. They proposed an interview, and thinking to conciliate them by showing confidence, he rode over, accompanied only by Captain Paton, a Persian writer, and an orderly. The Ghaljais were astonished by the boldness of the two officers in coming quite unprotected. Some proposed attacking them; others said: "No; there would be too great a contrast between their conduct and ours." Some of the Ghaljais told Mackenzie afterwards that Paton's gallantry on this occasion made them grieve when they heard of his being killed.[1] The visit, however, had no good result.

It was a very singular thing that the troops found the contract *hoosa* (chopped straw) unburnt at each stage in the pass. Had it not been for this, the cattle must have starved. When the brigade halted at Gandamak on the 30th for orders, they had lost two hundred and fifty killed and wounded since they left Kabul. That Sir William must have been to a certain extent aware of the dangerous temper of the people is evident from his lenity to the faqir murderer; yet when Mackenzie reported to him that Akbar Khan had arrived at Bamián, he refused to believe it, although the merchant who brought the news had seen him there with his own eyes.

Mir Masjidi, whom Mackenzie mentions as then a refugee in Nijeráo, marched for Kabul on the 30th October, which he would certainly not have ventured to do if he had

_____

[1] In the Khurd Kabul Pass on the 8th January, having previously lost an arm.

not received intimation of the intended rising. There cannot be a doubt that it had been long planned, though it burst upon us like the springing of an unsuspected mine. Whether Burnes really believed in the tranquillity of the country it is difficult to say ; he was certainly anxious for the departure of the Envoy, and he probably thought that he himself could put everything right. Calling on Sir William Macnaghten on the evening of the 1st November, he congratulated him on the peaceful state of affairs. But that day his own Afghan servants came to entreat him to leave his house in the city and go into cantonments, saying his life would be endangered if he remained. The two Broadfoots had often remonstrated with him for remaining in so unprotected a situation. Táj Muhammad, a Bárakzye, one of Dost Muhammad's own clan, went at dark to put him on his guard, telling him the conspirators were then assembled. Burnes sent a spy, who reported that it was not so. This spy was a notorious rogue and professional forger, and Táj Muhammad was only abused for his pains. That very night Aminullah Khan joined the conspirators, of whose meetings Captain Drummond had warned Burnes more than a fortnight before. Aminullah was originally the son of a camel-driver, but by dint of his talents, bravery, and cunning, rose to be one of the most powerful nobles in the country. The Amir, Dost Muhammad Khan, feared and suspected him so much as to banish him to Kandahar. He possessed the whole of the Logar Valley, and could bring 10,000 men into the field. Old, palsy-stricken, and almost speechless, he was still powerful. Being one of the first to join Shah Shujah, he was, by the influence of Burnes and Sir William Macnaghten, reinstated in his estates, and showed his gratitude by entering into a conspiracy to murder both. On joining the plotters he at once said : "Now, you have invited me here, and I have sworn on the Kurán; here is my advice: "Everything we do is made known to Burnes; take courage, therefore, and *lose no time.* Attack the káfir at once in his house before he can know our plans." This was done.

Early the next morning, 2d of November, William Broadfoot was breakfasting with Burnes. Mackenzie, who had been for six months in charge of the executive Commissariat of the Shah's troops, and had just made it over, was rejoicing at the accuracy of his Commissariat accounts, in which he took no delight, and was busy despatching his baggage to cantonments, where he intended to sleep, preparatory to marching on the morrow with the Envoy and General to Peshawar.

Very early that morning the Vazir Nizám ud Doulah, a very noble-looking man and perfect gentleman, had made an effort to save Burnes. He went in person first to the conspirators, where he was treated with disrespect, and from whom he escaped with difficulty, and then to Burnes, and endeavoured to prevail on him to accompany him to the Bála Hissar (the Royal fortress), or, if not, to go at once into cantonments; but all in vain. Burnes is said to have answered roughly: "Do you come here to teach me my duty?" As he was leaving, the Vazir said: "See, here are some of Aminullah's people already collected to attack you; if you will allow me, I shall disperse them." Burnes replied: "No; the Shah has sent for you; go at once." The Nizám ud Doulah accordingly rode away.

One can only account for Burnes' infatuation on the principle, "*Quem Deus vult perdere prius dementat,*" which applies to almost every act of that disastrous period. Burnes ordered his gates to be closed, but the house was surrounded by Aminullah and his people. At first there were not above 300, but they were soon joined by hundreds eager for plunder and blood. The Kotwal

(mayor) of the city, whom Burnes had turned out of his
office, brought wood and set fire to the gates.　Sir Alexander addressed the mob; his brother Charles was shot
dead by his side.　His small guard of Sepoys and those on
duty at the Treasury gallantly fought until killed at their
posts.　A messenger who brought the intelligence into
cantonments was not believed, and when the noise of firing
was heard, Macnaghten still made light of the matter, and
thought it would subside.　Shelton was sent with a force
to the Bála Hissar, which commands the city, but did nothing.　The Shah had immediately despatched the Nizám
ud Doulah with one of his regiments to assist Burnes.　He
found the gateway in flames, and the whole mob of the city
in arms.　After a stiff fight, the Vazir was driven back,
losing 100 men.　One of the Shah's sons, Prince Shahpur,
a most gallant lad of sixteen, then brought up reinforcements, forced his way to Burnes' house and beyond it.
But all was then over.　Burnes' body was lying in the
street hacked to pieces, and the last remaining Feringhi,
William Broadfoot,—the bravest of the brave, of rare
courage, both moral and physical, and as generous as brave,
—after a desperate resistance, had been shot down with the
faithful Sepoys.[1]　Thus perished three able and gallant
officers, and not a hand was raised by their own countrymen to rescue or avenge them.　Rescue was probably impossible.　George Lawrence recommended that two regiments should at once be thrown into the city, and that
Shelton's strong brigade should force their way in from
the Siah Sung Hills.　But the General and some others

---

[1] It was the first anniversary of the day on which his gallant
brother James fell foremost in the cavalry charge at Parwán Darrah, his
gold-banded cap glittering, as Ján Fishan Khan described it, until
nearly through the mass of the enemy, then several columns of smoke
arose, and he fell under a volley.

were haunted by baseless apprehensions as to the security
of the cantonment if even the smallest force were detached,
and the answer was that no troops could be spared, that
every house in the city was a fortress, and that Lawrence's
counsel was "insane!" The bodies of William Broadfoot[1]
and young Burnes lay in the street for days; but Naïb
Sherif, a very rich and clever old man, a great *bon vivant*
and boon companion of Sir Alexander Burnes, had the
courage to take up Burnes' body (for which he is said to
have paid a large price), threw it into his own well, which
was reckoned the best in Kabul, and which he filled up to
the top before morning. He also saved two of Burnes'
clerks, and was finally obliged to forsake his country on
account of his attachment to us, leaving landed property to
the value of £20,000, though he was still rich from the
treasures he brought away with him. He was the Deputy
of Khan Sherin Khan, the chief of the Kazilbashes, who
were all favourably inclined to us. He had a nickname for
many of the officers, and always called Mackenzie Shah-i-
Feringhi, King of the Franks.

"Shah Shujah disliked Burnes personally[2] on account
of a certain brusquerie of manner. The chiefs hated
Burnes as the man universally believed to have guided

---

[1] George Broadfoot learnt some particulars of this tragedy from the
Afghans, and wrote to his family:—"I feel myself quite changed by
William's death. That loving heart, that sound judgment, and calm
determined bravery, would indeed have made me grieve bitterly for the
loss of such a man, even had we not been children of the same parents,
and passed together the years of our infancy and early affections and
hopes. Poor Burnes, on William being wounded, knelt beside him
and wept bitterly; and well he might, for there lay dying a friend such
as few public men can hope to have."

[2] Mackenzie was of opinion that he knew something of the conspiracy, and hoped it would free him from Burnes, and be the means
of retaining Macnaghten, but he was perfectly aware that he was
entirely dependent on British support.

the British into Afghanistan. They alleged that he did not
behave to them with proper respect, and Jabbar Khan, who
had greatly befriended him in his former visit to Kabul,
deeply resented the systematic neglect with which he was
treated. Burnes thought himself popular among the lower
classes; but it is doubtful if he was so, though he certainly
had their real interests at heart, even more than his own
political advancement. The leading men regarded him as
the chief agent in introducing that system of order which
was utterly repugnant to them. The reproach which they
cast on him, of unbridled licentiousness, was an after-
thought."

Broadfoot says :—

"The Mullahs, and the mob they lead, detested Burnes from
his making light of all religions, which he was imprudent enough
to think they relished, because they laughed at his jokes. On
the other hand, they hated Macnaghten, because he had with
impure hands touched the Kurán, and read the glorious book,
without being thereby converted ; which, in my own case, a
Mullah, to the dismay of my men, pronounced the worst of infidelity. In this respect there is no pleasing them, and it is
foolish to seek to do so, further than by abstaining from offence.
Macnaghten was a little angry when I told him about my
Kurán, saying they never showed that feeling to him !"

Burnes had, in reality, strongly advocated our alliance
with Dost Muhammad, of whose anxiety for our friendship
he was convinced ; but ambition led him to carry out the
opposite policy of Government, and this cost him his life.

Drunk with blood and plunder, the whole population
took up arms, and rushed forth to seek further success.

Mackenzie was living in a fort just outside the city.
The story of his defence is best told in his own words :—
"The kilá or fort of Nishán Khan, in which I was besieged

in the breaking out of the Kabul insurrection, contained the
Shah's commissariat, and the quarters of Brigadier Anquetil,
with a guard of one havildar and twenty men. On the
south the Kabul river flows between the Kazilbash quarter
of the city and the fort. Close to the latter, on the north,
is a large grove of mulberry trees, called the Yábu Khana,
in which was a guard of six sawárs and, by chance, a detachment of a jemadar and ninety-five men of Captain
Ferris' Jezailchis, as also sixty of the Shah's sappers (Broadfoot's). These last were encumbered with a host of women
and children, brought up from their native country with
them, by the express orders of the Supreme Government.
The house of Captain Troup, capable of a tolerable defence,
is about forty yards to the east, while the large tower,
occupied by Captain Trevor and his family, lies across the
river to the south-east, distant about seven hundred yards,
and was perfectly defensible. It was important to maintain
our ground until the arrival of what we hourly expected, a
regiment from the cantonment, whose presence would have
immediately decided the wavering Kazilbashes in our favour,
and would have cut off all communication between the
insurgent population of Deh-i-Afghan and their rascally
brethren in the Murád Khana. Spreading far beyond the
Yábu. Khana, in the direction of cantonments, and circling
round the west of the fort, down to the river's edge, are
walled gardens and groves, which afford excellent cover to
a lurking enemy, who were enabled to come, without much
danger, to within a few yards of my defences.

"Early on the morning of Tuesday, the 2d of November,
as I was preparing to go into cantonments, intending to
accompany the Envoy on the following day down to
Peshawar, it was reported to me that an alarming riot had
taken place in the town. Brigadier Anquetil and Captain
Troup had gone out on their usual morning ride, and while

awaiting their return, I caused all the guards to stand to
their arms.   Suddenly a naked man stood before me,
covered with blood, from two deep sabre-cuts in the head
and five musket-shots in the arm and body.   He proved to
be a sawár of Sir W. Macnaghten (sent with a message to
Captain Trevor), who had been intercepted by the insurgents.   This being rather a strong hint as to how matters were
going, I immediately ordered all the gates to be secured, and
personally superintended the removal of the detachments
in the Yábu Khana, with their wives and families, into the
fort.   At the same time I caused loopholes to be bored
in the upper walls of Captain Troup's house, in which were
a naik and ten Sepoys.   Whilst so employed the armed
population of Deh-i-Afghan came pouring down through
the gardens, and began firing on us.   I threw out skirmishers ; but, in order to save the helpless followers, we
were obliged to abandon all the tents and baggage.   In
covering the retreat, one of my men was killed and one,
—Alidád Khan—badly wounded, while about five of the
enemy were killed.   The whole of the gardens were then
occupied by the Afghans, from which, in spite of repeated
sallies during the day, we were unable to dislodge them ;
on the contrary, whenever we returned into the fort, they
came so near as to be able, themselves unseen, to kill and
wound my men through the loopholes of my own defences.[1]
The canal was cut off during the day, and so closely watched
that one of my followers was shot while trying to fetch
some water; but we fortunately found an old well, the water
of which was drinkable.   Towards the afternoon, having
no ammunition but what was contained in the soldiers'
pouches, I communicated with Captain Trevor, who still

---

[1] In one of these sallies, one of his garrison being shot down from
a loopholed wall held by the enemy, Mackenzie and two jezailchis
rushed forward under a sharp fire and brought in the wounded man.

held his tower apparently unmolested. Even *then* Khan
Sherin Khan, the chief of the Kazilbashes, and four or five
other Khans of consequence, among them the leaders of the
Hazirbásh regiments, were with poor Trevor, earnestly
expecting that some decided measures on the part of the
British would justify them in openly taking our part.
Trevor despatched my requisition for ammunition *at least*,
if not for more effectual assistance. It arrived safely in
cantonments, the distance not being more than a mile and
a half. Captain G. St. P. Lawrence immediately volunteered to convey all needful supplies to Mackenzie if he
might have the loan of two companies. This gallant offer
was *refused*. Our troops were kept idle, and our outposts
abandoned to their fate. Shortly after our spirits were raised
by the apparent approach of a heavy cannonade with volleys
of musketry [1] from the direction of the Murád Khana, and
by the flight through the gardens of the multitudes who
were assailing me towards Deh-i-Afghan, from which quarter
crowds of women and children began to ascend the hill,
evidently in expectation of an assault from our soldiery.
But these cheering sounds died away, and it was in vain
that we strained our eyes looking for the glittering bayonets
through the trees. My besiegers swarmed back with shouts,
and it required much exertion on my part to prevent
despondency amongst my people, which feeling had been
strongly excited by the confirmation of the rumour of the
murder of Sir Alexander Burnes, his brother, and Captain
Broadfoot, by the sight of the smoke from his burning

---

[1] This proceeded from the 37th N.I., under Major Griffith, who
had been summoned back from Khurd Kabul. They made a most
orderly march, though hotly pursued all the way through the pass and
up to the city, and brought off all their wounded and baggage, although
unfortunately they had no less than five thousand registered followers!
Their loss was very trifling.

house, and by the intelligence that the treasury close to
Burnes' house had been sacked and the guard slain. In the
evening I served out provisions from the Government stores.
The attacks continued at intervals during the night, and we
had most disagreeable suspicions that the enemy were under-
mining our north-west tower. At early dawn we sallied out
to ascertain this, but were driven in again after finding our
apprehensions too well verified. There is much dead ground
about all Afghan forts, on which it is impossible to bring
musketry to bear, and the towers can always be undermined
in the absence of hand grenades on the part of the besieged.
To meet this attempt we sunk a shaft inside the tower, and
I placed four resolute men on the brink, ready to shoot the
first who should emerge. The extent of the fort required
all my men to be on duty at the same time, and some now
began to·wax weary. The cheerfulness of the remainder
was not improved by the incessant howling of the women
over the dead and dying. As a trait of Afghan character,
I must mention that whenever the Jezailchis could snatch
five minutes to refresh themselves with a pipe, one of them
would twang a sort of rude guitar as an accompaniment to
some martial song, which, mingling with the notes of war,
sounded very strangely.

"In the middle of this day (3d November), to my great
grief, I saw the enemy enter Captain Trevor's tower, and a
report was brought by two of his servants that he and his
family had all been killed, which, though untrue, had a bad
effect on my men.[1] Our ammunition had now become very

[1] Captain Trevor and his party walked to the cantonments, some
of the children being carried by the Hazirbash, Mrs. Trevor going on
foot through the river. On the road a blow was aimed at her by an
Afghan. A Hindustani trooper by her side saved her by stretching
out his bare arm. The hand was cut off by the blow, yet he continued
to walk by her with the blood flowing from the stump until they
reached the cantonments—an act of true heroism. My store-sergeant,

scarce, in spite of my having husbanded it with the greatest care. The scene of plunder going on in Trevor's house was evident from our ramparts; and the enemy, taking possession of the top, which overlooked my defences, pitched their balls from their large juzails with such accuracy as to clear my western face of defenders, and it was only by crawling on my hands and knees up a small flight of steps and whisking suddenly through the door that I could ever visit the tower that had been undermined. On one of these visits the sentry told me there was an Afghan taking aim from an opposite loophole. I looked through our loophole, but could not see him. As I moved my head the sentry clapped his eye to the slit, and fell dead at my feet with a ball through his forehead. The guard from Captain Troup's house now clamoured for admittance into the fort; and as Mr. Fallon, that gentleman's writer, called out to me that they were ready to abandon their post, I let them in, barricading my own door with sacks of flour. Against the door and small wicket on Brigadier Anquetil's side I had already piled heaps of stones and large timbers.

"In the afternoon the enemy brought down a large wall-piece[1] against us, the balls from which shook the upper part of one of our towers, alarming the Jezailchis. This disposition to despair was increased by the utter failure of ammunition. Captain Ferris had sent in his indents to Kabul six months before for his whole regiment. The ammunition not being supplied, both the detachment under

Smith, lived with his wife in Trevor's tower. He remained behind for an instant to secure a bag of rupees which he had saved. He was met by a crowd of Afghans, who made a rush to seize his bag; he shot the foremost assailant dead, and was immediately cut to pieces. He was a very brave man and a good non-commissioned officer, and his poor wife an excellent, kind, and most faithful creature. She acted as Mrs. Trevor's servant, and died of fever shortly before our release.

[1] A long gun too heavy to hold, made to rest on the wall.

Hasan Khan, who had come to fetch it, and the main body of the regiment at Peshbolák (half-way between Lálpura and Jellalabad) were left almost defenceless. The Afghans also brought down quantities of firewood and long poles, with combustibles at the ends, which they deposited under the walls of the Yábu Khana in readiness to burn down my door. Some sawárs who were stationed on Brigadier Anquetil's side of the fort now broke into a sort of half mutiny, and began pulling down the barricade against his gate to endeavour to save themselves by the speed of their horses. This I quelled by going down amongst them with a double-barrelled gun. I cocked it, and ordered them to shut the gate and build up the barricade, threatening to shoot the first man who should disobey. They saw that I was determined, for I had made up my mind to die, and they obeyed. In the evening I was quite exhausted, as were my people, having by that time been fighting and working for nearly forty hours without rest. Indeed, on my part, it had been without refreshment, as eating was impossible from excitement and weariness, and my absence for five minutes from any part of the works disheartened the fighting men. Added to this, my wounded were dying for want of medical aid.

"Abandoned, as I evidently was, to almost certain destruction by my own countrymen, my Afghan followers remained staunch to the last, in spite of the most tempting offers if they would betray me. Hasan Khan more than once pretended to listen to the overtures of the enemy in order to lure them from under cover, and then sent his answer in the shape of a rifle ball. When at last we had scarcely a round of ammunition left he came to me and said : ' I think we have done our duty ; if you consider it necessary that we should die here, we will die, but *I* think we have done enough.' I therefore yielded to his representations and those of Mr. Fallon, who had also rendered me valuable assistance throughout, and prepared for a retreat. This we determined should take place during the early part of the night, at which time, it being the fast of the Rámzán, the enemy would be at their principal meal. I ordered the jezailchis to lead, and to answer all questions in case of encountering a post of the enemy. The wounded were placed on what yábus I possessed (abandoning everything in the shape of baggage),[1] and followed next in order with the women and children, I myself bringing up the rear with my few regulars, who, I fondly imagined, would stick by me in case of a hot pursuit.

"Hasan Khan's anxiety for my safety was great, and he tried much to persuade me to accompany him and his Jezailchis in the van of our little column, which of course I could not do, the post of honour being in the rear. We were to avoid the town, to follow the course of the small canal above mentioned, and afterwards to strike off by lanes and fields in the direction of cantonments. A night retreat is generally disastrous, and this proved no exception to the rule, for, notwithstanding my strict order that all baggage should be left behind, it being very dark, many of the poor women contrived to slip out with loads of their little property on their shoulders, making their children walk, whose cries added to the danger of discovery. Going among the women to see that my orders for leaving everything were obeyed, a young Ghurka girl of sixteen or eighteen, who had girded up her loins and stuck a sword into her kamerband, came to me, and throwing all that she possessed at my feet, said: 'Sahib, you are right; life is better than property.' She was a beautiful creature, with fair complexion and large dark eyes, and as she stood there with

---

[1] The only thing he saved out of all his property was a little pocket Testament given him on leaving England.

her garments swathed around her, leaving her limbs free, she was a picture of life, spirit, and energy. I never saw her again, and fear she was either killed or taken prisoner on the night march.

"Before we had proceeded half a mile the rear missed the advance, upon whom a post of the enemy had begun to fire. All my regulars had crept ahead with the Jezailchis, and I found myself alone with a chaprási and two sawárs in the midst of a helpless and wailing crowd of women and children. One of these women, not being able to carry both her child and her pots and pans, had put down the former, who was consequently crying at the top of its lungs. I drew my sword and thumped her soundly with the flat of it until I made her take up her child, and thus I had it in my hand when I was attacked immediately afterwards.

"Riding on alone along a narrow lane to try and pick out the road, I found myself suddenly surrounded by a party of Afghans, whom at first I took to be my own Jezailchis and spoke to them as such. They quickly undeceived me, however, by crying out, 'Feringhi hast' (Here is a European), attacking me with swords and knives. Spurring my horse violently, I wheeled round, cutting from right to left. My blows, by God's mercy, parried the greater part of theirs, and I was lucky enough to cut off the hand of my most outrageous assailant.

"My sword went clean through the man's arm, but just after, I received such a tremendous blow on the back of the head that, although the sabre turned in my enemy's hand, it knocked me almost off my horse. The idea passed through my mind—'Well, this is the end of my career, and a miserable end it is, in a night skirmish with Afghans.' But then came the thought that all was right. I commended my soul to God, and became insensible, hanging on the saddle by only one foot, but I did not let go the bridle.

How I was rescued from that fearful peril I know not, but the next thing I remember is finding myself upright in the saddle in advance of the enemy, the whole picket firing after me. I passed unhurt through two volleys of musketry. The picket pursued, but I soon distanced them, crossing several fields at speed, and gaining a road which I perceived led round the western end of the Shah's garden. Proceeding cautiously along, I found to my horror my path again blocked up by a dense body of Afghans. Retreat was impossible, so, putting my trust in God, I charged into the midst of them, hoping that the weight of my horse would clear the way for me, and reserving my sword-cut for the last struggle. It was well that I did so, for by the time I had knocked over a heap of fellows—for they tumbled over one another—I found that they were my own Jezailchis. If you ever experienced sudden relief from a hideous nightmare, you may imagine my feelings for the moment. After wandering about for some time, and passing unchallenged by a sleepy post of the enemy, we reached the cantonments, which, but for Hasan Khan's prudence, sagacity, and true-heartedness, few, if any, of our party would have succeeded in doing. During the night many stragglers of my party, principally followers, dropped in.[1] From first to last I had about a dozen killed and half as many wounded.

Among the errors which led to our heavy downfall that of omitting to strengthen my post was one of the worst. Every Afghan of intelligence has confessed that if I had been reinforced by a couple of regiments we should have

[1] Jacob had started wearing a Persian lambskin cap of his master's. In crossing the shallow stream, Mackenzie recognised this cap floating on the water, and supposed his faithful follower was killed. He had been knocked off his pony, but reached cantonments on foot not long after his master.

remained masters of the city. That General Elphinstone was personally anxious for my safety was shown by the warmth of his reception of me."

George Broadfoot summed up the affair in a few sarcastic lines :—

"Colin Mackenzie, too, was in the outskirts of the city in an old fort. For two days he fought, and then cut his way to the large force, who did not seem able to cut their way to him, bringing in all his men and the crowd of women and children safe, himself getting two sabre wounds. A more heroic action never was performed. The unhappy women and children have *since* perished or gone into slavery, because 5000 men could not do what he did."

Mackenzie was publicly thanked for this service by the General and the Envoy.[1]

Mackenzie had been brought into close relations with Broadfoot's Jezailchis by leading them in the Khurd Kabul Pass. He was now brought into still closer relations with some of Ferris' regiment, who attached themselves to him

---

[1] *A Report drawn up by the Honourable Charles Hay Cameron, Member of Council, by direction of Lord Ellenborough, Governor-General of India, on the Kabul disasters in* 1841-42, *thus records it :—*

"On the night of the 3d and 4th November 1841, Captain Colin Mackenzie of the 48th Madras Native Infantry came into the cantonments. From the commencement of the insurrection he had with distinguished gallantry resisted the reiterated attacks of the enemy on Brigadier Anquetil's quarters, into which he had thrown himself. He maintained his position there until his ammunition was expended and his defences ruined. He then abandoned his baggage for the purpose of bringing off the women and the wounded on his baggage-cattle. By very skilful arrangements he forced his way through the investments both of his own castle and of the cantonments, and brought his charge safely into the latter. I resist the temptation which I feel to dwell upon this exploit as the solitary instance of signal and complete success which interrupts the continuity, and relieves the gloom of this long series of disasters."

with a devoted loyalty and affection which could not be surpassed. Up to the time of the outbreak only some friendly greetings had passed between him and them as they lay for six weeks encamped in the garden of the fort in which he lived. Long afterwards he said to Hasan Khan : " What made you come and fight for me when I was a stranger to you ?" " You came out and called on us to come," was Hasan Khan's reply. The confidence he showed in them appealed to their sense of honour ; but we must surely acknowledge the Divine Hand influencing the hearts of these men, and "turning them whithersoever He willed."

On his return to cantonments Mackenzie combined his duties as Political Assistant to the Envoy with the command of his gallant Jezailchis, who displayed the most devoted heroism. They were active in every engagement and sortie during the siege, being engaged almost daily, and were often the only troops out skirmishing. Numbers of them fell, a few departed to their own homes when Mackenzie was seized at Sir W. Macnaghten's murder, the remainder stuck to him until he was given up as hostage, and ten or fifteen rejoined their regiment on the return to India, where they were disbanded with a gratuity of a year's pay. During the time when Mackenzie was beleaguered in the fort of Nishán Khan they not only refused to listen to the repeated proposals of the Afghans outside to deliver him up to their vengeance, and thus insure their own safety, but throughout the siege of cantonments they laughed to scorn the most tempting offers from the chief to induce them to join the cause of Islam against the káfirs, invariably bringing the letters to Mackenzie.

A word on Jezailchis may not be amiss. They are so called from their jezails, or long rifles. The Afghans are perhaps the best marksmen in the world. They are accustomed to arms from early boyhood, live in a chronic state of warfare with their neighbours, and are most skilful in taking advantage of cover. An Afghan will throw himself flat behind a stone barely big enough to cover his head, and scoop a hollow in the ground with his left elbow as he loads. Men like these only require training to make first-rate irregular troops. Irregular corps have very few European officers, so that everything depends on the personal qualities of the commandant and his power of enforcing obedience and winning the attachment of his followers. Fidelity to their leader is the main tie they recognise.

Captain Ferris had raised one body of Jezailchis, who had distinguished themselves, and Broadfoot raised another, generally known as Broadfoot's Sappers, being trained for that work. These having seen their first action as a regiment in the Khurd Kabul Pass under Mackenzie, afterwards covered themselves with glory on the march to and during the siege of Jellalabad. In raising this corps Major Broadfoot took the advice of a very shrewd Afghan, by name Gul Shah, called "the murderer," because on one occasion he assigned as a reason for refusing to recruit in a certain village that he had slain three men there, for whom he had not yet paid the price of blood. This man advised Broadfoot not to take respectable men well-to-do in the world, but men of broken clans, ruined, houseless, and with no other resource, like those who joined David in the cave Adullam. He took Khaiberis, Euzufzais, Házarás, Hindustanis, but principally the Euzufzais, who also formed the majority of Ferris's Jezailchis, and are certainly the most faithful and gallant of all the mountain tribes to the north of the Indus, the Házarás ranking next in virtue. These last are principally Shiahs, and their being mixed up with the others, who are almost all Sunis, acted as a safeguard against general combination. One of Broadfoot's men was a young Házará, quite a lad, of not more than five feet four, who had fought against us at Bamián. He then enlisted, and soon distinguished himself so much that the officers gave him the name of "One in a hundred." He was wounded at Jellalabad, and, while just limping about, some promotions were made. He asked Major Broadfoot for the rank of naik (corporal), and the latter said to him, half in fun: "Pooh, you are a mere boy." He answered, "You never found me a boy in the day of battle," whereupon Broadfoot gave him the rank, to the great delight of all his comrades.

The discipline of these corps was of the most elementary kind, and indeed resolved itself into the very first principles of obedience—love and fear; personal attachment to a leader, the strongest motive with all half-civilised people; together with a clear perception that it will be the worse for them if they disobey him. Mackenzie's Jezailchis used to come and lean on his shoulder or put their arms round his neck in speaking to him, as if he had been one of their own countrymen. Rigid as he was in matters of principle, he adapted himself at once to foreign ways and customs, and was therefore always a favourite with foreigners of every country. He had not only great facility in acquiring languages, but he was so impressionable and sympathetic that he involuntarily adopted the very tone and gestures of the people he was among. He spoke Persian fluently, but, as a good Persian scholar who had lived at Ispahan declared, with "a *horrid* Afghan accent;" and any one who knew him well could have told without hearing a word whether he were speaking in English, German, or Persian by the characteristic gestures he used with each.

Though accustomed to the strict military discipline of the Madras Army, and at times amazed at the lax system which prevailed in Bengal, he saw at once how inappropriate the former would be to these rough and ready mountaineers, and always distinguished between what was essential to obedience and what he unceremoniously styled "red tape." He therefore encouraged his men to sing and talk on their march, and if they behaved ill he slapped their faces. Once two of them got so angry with one another that they drew their swords. Mackenzie sprang between them and cried: "Here, kill me if you want to kill anybody." The one in front of him, a very handsome young fellow, was so transported with rage that he put his head over his commander's shoulder to continue his abuse of his comrade. Mackenzie seized him by the ear, slapped his face, shook him, and then squeezed him as hard as he could, until Hasan Khan, hearing the noise, came out and belaboured both combatants with his whip till he had quieted them.

Mackenzie won and retained the attachment of all the men he ever led by never sparing himself, and by his warm-hearted sympathy with them. An instance of this may be given. Alidád Khan, one of his mountain escort, had accompanied him to Peshawar. When quite a lad he had distinguished himself in action against the Sikhs, and had received a tremendous sabre cut across the face, which nearly destroyed the sight of one eye ; but, in spite of this gash, his expression was quite beautiful. In getting the women and children into the fort he was shot through the leg. Mackenzie applied a field tourniquet of his own, but had neither the means nor the time to dress the wound ; the tourniquet was left on for nearly fifty hours, and when they reached cantonments the limb was quite numb. Alidád was placed in the hospital, which was under the superintendence of the Mission Surgeon, the same who had a few months before neglected, to Sir William Macnaghten's intense indignation, to attend Mackenzie himself when bitten by a mad dog. This man neglected the hospital, low fever came on, and Alidád died of it. His uncle and other relations who happened to be in Kabul, knowing the high esteem his commander had for him, came to fetch the body, and Mackenzie followed it for about 200 yards from the gate of the cantonments into the very midst of a crowd of Ghaljais, all of whom, however, respected his person, and forbore offering him the least molestation.

CHAPTER XIV

(November 1841.)

"If they are only well handled, and in each effort exert *all* their strength, they will deliver themselves."

GEORGE BROADFOOT, *2d Jan. 1842.*

NOTHING could be worse than the position of the cantonment. Major Abbot, the Chief Engineer with Pollock's Force, in his report speaks of "the extreme faultiness of the position. The cantonment appears to have been purposely surrounded with difficulties."[1] Some better positions were objected to by Sir W. Macnaghten on behalf of the Shah; and the actual site was sanctioned by Sir Willoughby Cotton, who of course was responsible for it. When that remarkably intelligent non-commissioned officer Sergeant Deane pointed out the ineligibility of the spot he was checked by Sturt for going beyond his province. The unnecessary extent of the cantonments was as great a blunder as their position, and they were also in an un-

---

[1] One objection to marching our whole force into the Bála Hissar seems to have been unknown; but General Haughton, who was quartered there in 1840-1, found that the wells were constantly drained before the day was out, even with a garrison of only two thousand men. There was an external supply from a small watercourse, but in the event of a siege that would most assuredly have been cut off.

finished state. Sir Willoughby Cotton roughly refused
Captain Skinner's earnest request for a place *within* the
cantonments for his Commissariat Stores.

On making over the command to General Elphinstone,
Sir Willoughby said to him : "You will *have nothing to do
here, all is peace !*"

General Elphinstone immediately saw its defects, and
generously offered to buy a large portion of land at his own
expense, so as to remove the enclosures and gardens which
offered shelter to an enemy within 200 yards of our ramparts, but his offer was declined. He, however, threw a
bridge over the river, which was of great importance.
Similar incredible folly to that which placed the magazine
at Delhi in the midst of the city, placed the magazine and
commissariat stores at Kabul outside our cantonment. The
magazine was at first put in its proper place, the fortified
palace called the Bála Hissar, but from this it was early in
April moved, to please the Shah, by direction of Sir W.
Macnaghten in the face of Sale's remonstrances. Strongly
attached as Mackenzie was to the Envoy, he considered
him much to blame for interfering in military matters,
never consulting the commanding officers, and consequently
making constant and egregious military blunders, as in this
case. For instance, he requested Shelton to suspend firing
from the Bála Hissar in the first week of November as the
inhabitants complained of the "annoyance!" He also
frequently checked the fire from the cantonments, to the
great mortification of the garrison, in order to "expedite
negotiations." A stronger man than General Elphinstone
would not have allowed this, and probably with a stronger
man the Envoy might not have attempted it.

General Elphinstone was a most gallant, accomplished
soldier, high-minded, courteous, and considerate to all,
greatly beloved by those who served under him, but lacking

in decision. The command had been forced on him by Lord
Auckland, and he blamed himself bitterly for having been
ever persuaded to accept it. Mackenzie never forgot the
lesson that duty requires a man to refuse employment for
which he is unfit; and when, during the Mutiny, a young
officer declined an appointment for which a severe accident
had disabled him, evidently with much reluctance and
many misgivings lest he should be accused of "hanging
back," he highly commended his moral courage, and recalled
the unfortunate case of General Elphinstone.

Few things are more pathetic than a private letter of
the General to his kinsman Lord Elphinstone, written in
trembling characters with the left hand :—

"CABUL, 26th July 1841.

"MY DEAR ELPHINSTONE,—I have been prevented writing to
you by almost incessant severe illness since I came here. I
arrived on the 30th April, and on that day had an attack of
fever followed by rheumatic gout, which laid me up till the
24th May, when I got about for fourteen days ; but on the 6th
June I was again ill with fever, followed as before with gout
and rheumatism, by which I have been confined frequently to
bed ever since, and with little prospect of recovery. I am
worse to-day than a month ago. My right wrist is so painful I
cannot move it. . . . I have it now in wrist, knee, and ankle,
and, if ordered by the medical committee, I shall apply to Lord
Auckland to be relieved. I shall deeply feel being obliged to
give up a command I should have liked had I been possessed of
health to perform its duties, but it is one requiring great activity,
mental and bodily. My stay would be useless to the public
service and distressing to myself."

The General after this became even worse. He did
resign his command, and was on the point of leaving the
country. Even in this state of extreme weakness and
suffering, when energy would have been almost beyond

human powers, his personal gallantry never failed. No one exposed himself more fearlessly or more frequently during the siege and even on the retreat.[1]

But in spite of our defective position, Mackenzie was strongly of Broadfoot's opinion that "if we had had a single General fit to command, no disaster would have happened at Kabul." The want of such a leader as either Pollock or Napier was our ruin. Shelton, though personally brave, showed himself an incompetent officer. He did nothing but object. His mind was set on getting back to India, and he discouraged the troops by advocating retreat from the first. After our disasters he evinced open hostility to his unfortunate General, and avowed his intention of throwing all the blame upon him. In a memorandum written a short time before his death, the General thus describes Shelton's behaviour :—

"His manner was most contumacious. He never gave me information or advice, but invariably found fault with all that was done, canvassed and condemned all orders before officers, frequently preventing and delaying carrying them into effect. He appeared to be actuated by an ill-feeling towards me."

Brigadier Anquetil was taken ill : Colonel Oliver was a croaker. There was no one to whom the General could make over the command.

Early on the 4th of November a force, reckoned at 15,000 men, issued from the city, threw a garrison into the Fort of Muhammad Sharif, and occupied the Shah Bágh (King's Garden), so as completely to cut off the commissariat fort, held by Ensign Warren and 100 men, from the cantonment.

[1] It is a curious fact that Lord Auckland did his best to repeat his error in appointing an invalid, by twice urging General Lumley to take the command, for which he afterwards selected Sir George Pollock ; but Lumley had the wisdom to abide by the decision of his medical advisers, who pronounced his health unequal to the task.

It was therefore necessary to take the enemy's fort and to succour Warren, who reported that he was very hard pressed. Instead of this being done at once, a conference was held that night at the General's, of which Vincent Eyre gave a graphic account in a letter :—

"The Envoy, Captain Boyd, and others, advocated immediate action. I considered that my standing in the service did not entitle me to obtrude my opinion, until the General suddenly accosted me, and leading me into his private room, asked what I thought he ought to do. He reminded me of the severe loss sustained in the sally that very day, and said that he could not bear to contemplate such a frightful loss of life. I replied that in a case of such desperate emergency soldiers must be prepared to sacrifice their lives, and that such secondary considerations should not be weighed in the balance against a measure involving the safety and honour of the whole force. He walked about the room for several minutes in great agitation, urging again and again the same objections, and receiving the same reply. At length he opened the door, and called in Major Thain and Captain Grant. The General had an unfortunate habit of flying from one subject to another, it being impossible to keep his attention fixed to an argument for any length of time. Observing this propensity, and seeing the necessity of bringing him to a speedy decision, I proposed that he should abide by the opinion of Lieutenant Sturt, Garrison-Engineer. He eagerly jumped at the idea, as releasing him from the burden of responsibility, and bade me go to that officer at once and state the whole case. This was done, but the whole night was lost by indecision."

Eyre continues :—

"I believe the General had an insuperable repugnance to nocturnal expeditions, and could tell of numberless instances where they had failed in Europe. It was an inconceivable trial to one's patience to be doomed to listen to such stories at this serious crisis, when every moment was of infinite value. No one could tell an anecdote better, and, unfortunately for us, he had one always ready, even at the most unseasonable time. It was broad daylight before the troops were ready, and then Ensign Warren marched in, having been obliged to abandon the fort, the enemy having set fire to his gate, and thus all our stores were lost."

Ensign Warren[1] was a man of cool, determined courage, who said little, and always went about with a couple of bull-dogs at his heels. When the Sepoys lost heart he could hardly keep them within the fort. One of the Afghans daringly planted their standard over the gate, Warren coolly walked up, though the enemy's marksmen were within thirty yards of him, all aiming at his body, tore down the standard, and returned with only one wound.

Mackenzie had come in on the night of the 4th. On the 6th he and his Jezailchis were again at work. The fort of Muhammad Sharif was taken by assault; but, in order to recover the Commissariat fort, which was not yet more than half emptied, it was necessary to drive out the enemy from the King's garden, the gate of which adjoined it. Lieutenant Eyre with his guns drove the enemy from the north side of the garden. Mackenzie with his men found an opening on the west side of it; they crept in and cleared that part of the garden, defeating quadruple their own number; but, not being supported, were obliged to retire with a loss of fifteen killed out of ninety-five. Eyre likewise was unsupported, and thus the Shah Bágh was lost. Eyre left a 6-pounder gun under Mackenzie's protection, while he himself joined a H.A. gun which had no officer with it. Large numbers of the enemy now filled up the Shah Bágh, and stealing up among the trees close to the high walls towards the 6-pounder, kept up so hot and precise a fire as to render its removal absolutely neces-

[1] He fell on 10th January in the Tangá Taríki.

sary. Captain Mackenzie had been joined by a party of H.M.'s 44th, with whom and a few of his own men he endeavoured to cover the operation, which was extremely difficult, it being necessary to drag the gun by hand over bad ground. Several of the Shah's gunners were killed, and many of the covering party knocked over, the gun being barely saved. "The Jezailchis," says Eyre, "under the able direction of Captain Mackenzie, were forward to distinguish themselves on all occasions."

Mackenzie relates an instance of the fine temper of his men under trying circumstances :—"Towards the end of this day one of the Queen's 44th Regiment, in spite of the difference of dress, chose to mistake one of my poor fellows for an enemy, and deliberately shot him dead. Great was the indignation of Hasan Khan and his comrades; but, on my explaining the nature of the mistake, they frankly forgave the European the offence, which among themselves, although an accident, would have created a blood-feud. Again, within the cantonments, a Jezailchi was wounded by a Sepoy in a quarrel. Revenge was determined on, and the consequences might have been disastrous, had I not interfered, and represented to the wounded man that my good name was concerned in his passing over the insult. No Christian could have behaved better, and when I endeavoured to force on him a sum of money he steadfastly refused."

On the 9th November Shelton was recalled from the Bála Hissar to assist the General, but he brought neither help nor comfort, openly talking of retreat. Colonel ——, though a very brave man, was one of the worst of the croakers. On Mackenzie asking him one day how he was, he replied: "Pretty well in body." "Well," said Mackenzie cheerfully, "that's always something in these hard times." Colonel —— turned to him with the most lugubrious countenance and uttered the words, " Dust to dust." Just after this rencontre, Mackenzie met Lieutenant Bird, always known as " Willie Bird," who was as gentlemanly, amiable, and handsome as he was brave. To him he related what had passed, when Bird answered, alluding to Colonel —— extreme corpulence : " What can you expect of a man who is all *run to body ?* "

H.M.'s 44th were in a most unsatisfactory condition. At the Envoy's urgent desire an attempt was made on the 10th to storm the Rikábáshi fort, within musket-shot of our works on the north-east, whence the enemy poured in a very annoying fire, killing our artillerymen at their guns. Their jezails carried much farther than our muskets, and they never throw away a shot. Missing the gate, we blew open a small wicket, into which Colonel Mackerell, Lieutenant Bird, and a handful of men forced themselves. Some Afghan cavalry charged the troops outside, and there was a scene of *sauve qui peut.* Major Scott and the other officers of the 44th in vain exhorted their men to charge, not a soul would follow them save a private named Steward, who was promoted for his gallantry. Shelton stood firm, and twice rallied the fugitives under cover of the great guns from the cantonments and the fire of Mackenzie's Jezailchis from the north-east angle of the walls. Colonel Mackerell and the whole party within the fort were slaughtered, except Lieutenant Bird and two Sepoys, who retreated into a stable, the door of which they barricaded with logs of wood. When at last they were discovered by the triumphant Afghans, Bird and his now solitary companion, a Sepoy of the 37th N.I. (the other having been struck down), maintained as hot a fire as they could, each shot taking deadly effect from the proximity of the party engaged ; and thus they stood at bay for upwards of a quarter of an hour, having only five cartridges left when they were rescued. Our troops found the pair " grim and lonely there," upwards of thirty of the enemy having fallen by their unassisted prowess. Our loss was not less than 200 killed and wounded. The capture of two guns on the 13th was our last gleam of success.

Two days after, Major Eldred Pottinger and Lieutenant J. C. Haughton came in from Charekar. Pottinger was the Political Agent in Kohistan, stationed at Laghmán, a fort about three miles from the unfinished barracks of Charekar. The latter post was held by Captain Codrington and his regiment of Shah's Ghurkas, most of them mere lads (half of whom had only been six months in the service), along with his second in command, John Colpoys Haughton, who had not yet been five years in the army, but had served throughout the campaigns of 1838-41. They all knew that mischief was brewing; but, although Pottinger felt the general insecurity of our position, he had no positive information, and was at this very time endeavouring to induce the neighbouring chiefs to attack the disaffected in Nijeráo, little dreaming that our stubborn foe, Mir Masjidi, far from being in Nijeráo, had been for two days twenty miles in his rear at Ak Serai, cutting off his communication with Kabul! Pottinger had sent a written assurance through his assistant, Captain Rattray, to Captain Codrington that he should have " at least twenty-four hours' notice of any move on the part of the disaffected." The garrison of Charekar was ready to march at an hour's notice, and could have left their women and children in one of Pottinger's four castles at Laghmán, but they were without any carriage whatever, even for spare ammunition or provisions, both of which were of course indispensable. It was the business of the political authorities to provide means of transport, as the military had no communication with the native officials save through the political officers. On the 3d November two servants of Haughton's started to go to Kabul, but returned with the news that the road was blocked by rebels. Codrington rode over to carry this intelligence to Pottinger, who had heard nothing of it,[1] and Haughton, the senior of the three young ensigns with the regiment, had to go and bring off his commanding officer after a sharp skirmish, in which the enemy suffered severely. In the meantime Rattray had been treacherously slain. The next morning Haughton, with two hundred men and a 6-pounder, carried ammunition and stores to Pottinger, who was unable to make a sortie to meet them. The enemy closed in on all sides in most formidable array, apparently not less than four thousand strong. The little force was frequently obliged to halt in close column to resist the enemy's cavalry, who were only kept in check by the gallantry of Mr. Haughton, who, by constantly loading and firing his gun, with the help of a couple of faithful men, covered the rear, and brought the detachment back, though with heavy loss and with Ensign Salisbury mortally wounded. That night Haughton had to repair the trail of the gun with his own hands. There were no wells in Kohistan, the water was turned off from the canal by the enemy, and all that could be obtained was from a few little pools.

After dark, Major Pottinger, Dr. Grant, and most of the Ghurkas effected their retreat from Laghmán, all Pottinger's Afghan escort having deserted except some Heratis and seven or eight men from Peshawar. The rest of the Ghurkas with him did not return for two or three nights. Haughton had been constantly looking out for them, and

---

[1] A most short-sighted piece of economy was forbidding presents, or limiting them to so paltry an amount that they were considered as an affront. This was one main cause of Pottinger's ignorance of what was going on.

such was his joy at seeing his own men again that he
hugged them as if they had been his children. Pottinger,
who had no military authority at Charckar, volunteered
to take charge of the guns, but the very next morning
was severely wounded, and from that time confined to
his bed. Codrington fell a few hours later, and Haughton
succeeded his beloved friend in command. Captain Codrington drew up a report speaking in the highest terms
of Haughton's gallantry and skill, but it never arrived.
The walls of the barracks were about 8 feet high, commanded on all sides. The garrison could only get water
by desperate sallies, and could not bring in any store of it,
and they had to make up ammunition for the guns, firing
even lengths of chain. Haughton never slept, and yet he
held out eight days after he was in sole command. One
curious device known to the Japanese was of great use,
they put up curtains so as to prevent the enemy taking
aim at the men behind them, and as the Afghans will not
throw away their shot at random, it stopped firing on that
side. Learning what had happened at Kabul, Haughton
felt it his duty to hold out to the last, to prevent his
besiegers from joining the foes of the Kabul garrison. Not
only were they attacked daily, but drums were kept beating
for hours, and night was made hideous by a large body of
the peaceful inhabitants, who were compelled to shout
" Dum i Chár Yár,"[1] and other war cries, for the sole purpose of wearing out the garrison. On the 11th half a tea-
cupful of water apiece was served out to the fighting men
only, and so great was their suffering that they insisted on
their commander measuring it out himself to ensure a fair
distribution, though, being Hindus, every man forfeited his
caste by drinking from the hand of a European. The cattle

---

[1] "The life of the four Friends," i.e. the four companions of
Muhammad.

had been entirely without food or water since the 6th, and Haughton's own allowance was one small cup of tea daily. Fully one-eighth of the garrison had been killed, two hundred were lying wounded, the remainder were utterly worn out, and on the 13th Haughton had to inform Pottinger that there was nothing left but to try and reach Kabul. In this every one fully concurred.

The gunners, who were Musalmans from the Panjab, had hitherto fought well. Some of them now deserted, and, to curry favour for themselves with the enemy, the whole of them joined in a plot, treacherously attacked their commander, severing all the muscles on one side of the back of his neck so that his head hung forward, cut off his right hand, inflicted severe wounds on the right shoulder and left arm, and then made their escape in a body. The enemy attacked on all sides. Pottinger had himself carried from his bed to the gate, and Dr. Grant, aided by a couple of the men, so vigorously worked the 18-pounder that the foe was repulsed. At night the doctor amputated Haughton's right hand, immediately after which they started, Haughton being held up by a man on each side of his horse, with a cushion under his chin to support his head. It had been arranged that, to avoid a crush at the gateway, one-half of the garrison should leave by the front gate and the other by the postern wicket. They were to meet on the parade-ground, where the postern party waited for the other in vain. Dr. Grant went back to bring them up, but they had taken the direct road to Kabul, which not one of them ever reached. Pottinger urged his party on as the only chance of life. After about twenty miles through byeways they missed Ensign Rose and the men, and at last none remained with them but a Ghurka Munshi mounted, Haughton's orderly Mán Sing and a sutler on foot, and Pottinger's bull-terrier who was too tired to bark. Haughton was so weak from loss of blood that he slipped off several times, hurting himself severely. In vain he entreated Pottinger to leave him to his fate. This Pottinger would by no means do. He bade Haughton sleep, and himself searched for the path. Then they pushed on, and reached Kabul, forty miles as the crow flies, at early dawn on a cold wintry morning (15th of November). Haughton was lifted off his horse, and his wounds dressed in the guard-room. So utterly exhausted was he that he felt that he could not have gone ten yards farther to escape immediate death. He was then lodged with Vincent Eyre, and always said that he owed his life to Mrs. Eyre's extreme kindness and care.

The enemy did not discover the retreat of the force till long after daylight, owing to the heroism of the bugle-major, who, being too severely wounded to leave, crawled up to a bastion and sounded the morning bugle as usual, as if the regiment were still present. Most of the wounded were slaughtered that day, and numbers of these gallant little Ghurkas were sold into slavery.

When Pottinger's urgent request for assistance reached Kabul on the 6th November, Mackenzie (who had arrived two days before) immediately volunteered to carry ammunition if they would grant him two hundred horse. He would have made a forced march by night, so as to reach Charekar early the next morning. Even so small a body of cavalry would have been invaluable, but the offer was utterly refused (like that of Captain Lawrence to relieve Mackenzie), and these gallant men left to perish. This disgraceful desertion of their brother soldiers by those at the head of five thousand men, not then beleaguered, is incomprehensible.

Major Pottinger, who knew pretty well what heroism was, and who was by no means given to excess of laudation, wrote to Mr. Haughton's father, 29th May 1842 :—

" No language that I am master of is sufficient to express my admiration of the fortitude and resolution your son showed. . . . Before Captain Codrington, his commanding officer, died, he requested me to make special mention of him to the Government, and to represent to Sir William Macnaghten that his conduct had shown him well fitted to command the regiment. The wounds he received there was not time to dress before we marched, so that he had to bear up against their pain for two nights and a day."

When a little better, Haughton was informed that a second amputation was necessary. He consented, and at an early hour the whole of the hideous apparatus was laid out in his room. But it was the 23d November, in the very midst of the battle of Behmaru. There he lay hearing the guns, but no one came to tell him what was going on, and it was not till near three in the afternoon that the doctors made their appearance, and the operation, from which he suffered intensely for twenty months afterwards, was performed.[1]

Immediately after the outbreak, the Envoy had recalled

---

[1] In those days rewards and honours were as sparse as they are now profuse. Besides, Lord Ellenborough seemed actuated by personal spite against the prisoners he abandoned. Haughton therefore got neither reward nor thanks for his heroic defence at Charekar. He did not even get credit except among his brother officers who knew the facts. He has since distinguished himself as Governor of the Andaman Islands, Commissioner of Assam and then of Cooch Behár. His care and sympathy for the wild tribes, his skilful subjection of the independent Garrows, his thorough work as a District Commissioner, place him in the first rank of Indian officials. His reward has been the smallest possible—C.S.I. After General Pollock's advance Haughton collected about 165 of the survivors of his regiment, who were distributed among the Ghurka corps in India. Mán Sing served under George Broadfoot, and was afterwards pensioned and received the order of merit. But of the 140 women and children belonging to the corps not one was ever heard of. Probably all were sold into slavery.

Sale against General Elphinstone's advice. Sale summoned a council of war, 10th November, who were unanimous that it was impracticable to obey. As usual, the owners of our hired carriage had deserted with their animals, the force was short of ammunition, the whole camp equipage was destroyed, there was no longer a single depôt of provisions on the route, the carriage of the force was insufficient for one day's rations, and the three hundred sick and wounded must have been sacrificed. He therefore pushed on to secure Jellalabad, the Shah's regiment of Jánbáz deserting to a man. Sale occupied the town late on the evening of the 12th November. The General highly approved Sale's decision, which secured our communications with India, although he earnestly besought succour when it arrived from Peshawar, adding "*nous sommes dans un péril extrême.*" The Envoy's opinion was that we ought to hold on as long as possible, and that a retreat would teem not only with disaster but dishonour.

Some decision should have been formed and adhered to. We should have made up our minds either to hold out or to march at once for Hindustan, taking the Shah with us. If we resolved on the former we should either have occupied the Bála Hissar at whatever cost, or we should have done everything to remedy the defects of our position, levelling every fort which commanded the cantonment, taking the offensive and laying in stores. But *nothing* was determined on. We were destroyed for want of resolution. Conolly, Mackenzie, and Eyre strongly urged the occupation of the Bála Hissar, but they were ignorant of the scarcity of water. The Shah was eager for it, and was able to hold out there for four months after we left. Mackenzie was of opinion that even if we had been obliged to shut out part of the camp-followers, they would have met with a less miserable fate than dying in the snow after being driven to cannibalism, especially as we should have commanded the city. War is an encounter with difficulties, but if two thousand men could hold out five months with ruinous defences at Jellalabad, five thousand could have held out at Kabul *if* they had had a leader.

But Shelton set his face against the movement and it was given up. The boldest *kasids* (messengers) could no longer be tempted to convey intelligence to Jellalabad, several having been tortured and put to death by the enemy. Three of Mackenzie's Jezailchis volunteered for that duty and performed it with success, although one of them was beaten almost to death on suspicion of his errand.

Hasan Khan also gave fresh proof of his gallantry. The quarter-master sergeant of the Shah's 6th got drunk, and sallying forth into the village of Behmaru was there slain. To kill a drunken man is looked on, even by these habitual homicides, as disgraceful, such a person being, in their opinion, under the protection of temporary insanity, an infirmity which claims the reverential forbearance of all eastern nations. Directly Hasan Khan heard of the catastrophe he marched boldly into the village with two or three of the Jezailchis, upbraided the murderers with a breach of religion, and brought in the corpse.

From one end of the siege to the other this famous jemadar was beset by offers from the chiefs of reward to any amount if he would change sides. These letters, sealed by the principal insurgents, he always brought to Mackenzie, and scoffed at all their overtures. He generally contrived to obtain correct information as to what was going on in the city, where some of his clan resided. Sir William Macnaghten and General Elphinstone often expressed the highest opinion of him, and the former promised him the highest rewards his influence could command.

On the 23d November a force under Brigadier Shelton at-

tempted to take the village of Behmaru whence we drew our
supplies. There is a hill not half a mile from the north face
of cantonments, and the village lies between the cantonment
and the hill. Instead of carrying the village immediately,
when it could have been taken in five minutes, Shelton
formed his troops in squares on the brow of the hill without shelter, refusing to allow a stone breastwork to be
thrown up. Here he kept them for seven hours exposed
to a severe and galling fire from the enemy, who swarmed
out of the city and soon amounted to between 10,000 and
15,000.

Contrary to standing orders only one gun was taken out,
so that in a short time the vent became too hot for the
gunners to serve. The cavalry were placed where they
could not act. Three times the face of the square had to
be made up, and was composed of H.M.'s 44th and the 37th
N.I. *mixed*. No wonder the men lost heart ! About 7 A.M.
the fire of the enemy was so galling that Lieut.-Colonel Oliver
endeavoured to induce a party of his own regiment, the
5th N.I., to follow him to the brow of the hill to keep it
down. Not a man moved, and it was only after that brave
officer had gone forward himself into the thickest of the fire
saying, "Although my men desert me, I myself will do my
duty," that about a dozen were shamed into performing
theirs. Mackenzie, who had been requested by the Brigadier
to act as his A.D.C., having called for volunteers from
H.M.'s 44th for the same purpose, only succeeded in per-
suading one man to follow him. This man's name was
Pollock, by trade a shoemaker. Between 10 and 11 A.M.
our ammunition was almost expended, the men having
moved out at 2 A.M. were faint from fatigue and thirst,
no water was procurable, while the number of killed and
wounded was swelled every instant. Large bodies of the
enemy endeavoured to cut off the supplies of ammunition

coming from cantonments, and the litters in which a few of the wounded were sent in. They were, however, checked by a party of our troops stationed in a mosk, and by Mackenzie's Jezailchis (who were for the day under the command of Captain Trevor), and who lined some low walls and watercourses.

In vain Shelton endeavoured to induce the men to charge bayonets. Several officers advanced to the front and, to encourage the men, actually pelted the enemy with stones. Most conspicuous were Captain Macintosh and Lieutenant Laing, who were almost instantly killed, Captains Colin Mackenzie, Colin Troup, and Leighton.

Mackenzie received a bullet in the left shoulder, which made him very faint. A sergeant was helping him off the field, when, feeling better, he returned to his work, and found poor "Bob," his charger, had been wounded while he was off his back. Several cavalry officers, both European and native, behaved most gallantly. It was about this time that H.M.'s 44th were attacked by a body of Afghan horsemen, whom they received with a volley when quite near. When the smoke cleared not a man or horse had been touched! The 44th, having no confidence in their weapons, fled. Not so Lieutenant Macartney; he snatched up a musket, waited till two Afghan horsemen were close upon him, then shot one and received the other upon his bayonet.

With great difficulty the officers rallied the fugitives behind the second square. They again advanced and found the bodies of Macintosh and Laing, and those of two Horse Artillerymen, who had perished while vainly endeavouring to defend their gun, which was now regained. The front ranks of Shelton's square had been literally mowed down, and most of the artillerymen, who performed their duty in a manner beyond praise, shared the same fate.

Mackenzie, feeling convinced, from the temper of the troops and the false position of the force, which could not now be rectified, that success was hopeless, and defeat, in its most disastrous shape, fast approaching, proposed to the Brigadier to effect a retreat while it was in his power to do so with comparative impunity. Shelton's reply was : "Oh no ; we will hold the hill some time longer."

On Shelton's refusal to retire, Colonel Oliver, who was a very stout man, remarked that the inevitable result would be a general flight to cantonments, and that, as he was too unwieldy to run, the sooner he got shot the better. He then exposed himself to the enemy's fire and fell mortally wounded.

Major Kershaw was gallantly defending one edge of the hill, when Brigadier Shelton sent Mackenzie to say the Major had better fall back on him. Kershaw replied that the Brigadier had better retire upon *him*, as otherwise the whole village would fall on the rear of our force. At last the Brigadier ordered this to be done ; but at that moment the Ghaljais broke the square, and an utter rout ensued. Mackenzie had galloped back, but could not at first find Colonel Shelton in the crowd, and, seeing the column begin to waver, he shouted : "Mount, Troup, mount directly." Captain Troup did so. The column broke and ran. In vain the officers shouted "Halt !" Mackenzie saw Colin Troup pass him on his galloway like a flash of lightning. He dashed into cantonments, got the mountain train gun, which had been repaired, and was bringing it and a fresh body of infantry to fire upon the pursuers when he was stopped by a staff officer.

Major Kershaw's party were all but annihilated. Colonel Oliver's body was found with the head and a hand cut off, and most of the wounded were miserably cut to pieces. The pursuit was in some degree checked by a gallant charge of one troop of cavalry and a sharp discharge from the Jezailchis.

"With heroic devotion our poor decrepit General came out and placed himself at the head of some cavalry who had rallied, yet he could not induce them to charge." [1]

Sergeant Mulhall and six gunners, sword in hand, awaited the advance of the foe, and it was not till they saw themselves alone in the midst of thousands that they dashed at full gallop, cutting their way down the hill, and managed to bring their gun through the enemy safely to the plain, where, only three of them being alive and they desperately wounded, they were obliged to leave it, and contrived to reach cantonments to the great joy of all who had witnessed their gallant conduct from the walls. Sir Wm. Macnaghten promised to bring Sergeant Mulhall to the notice of the Government, but neither was destined to survive.

Mackenzie often said that he never knew such a band of heroes as the 1st troop Bengal Horse Artillery.

By this time Captain Trevor had returned to cantonments, thinking the Jezailchis were coming with him; but, on the contrary, Hasan Khan posted them behind a low wall midway between the foot of the hill and the ramparts, and, allowing the mass of the fugitives to pass them, they poured in a hot and destructive fire on the pursuers, loading and firing as deliberately as if they had been smoking pipes.

Mackenzie relates that on his return from acting as A.D.C.:—"Finding my own men so well employed, I remained with them. The Afghans continued to shower a perfect hailstorm of balls on the flying troops, cutting to pieces all the wounded within their reach. It was then that a wounded Sepoy, who had fallen about a hundred yards from the position I held, waved his arm for help. Instantly three of my gallant fellows sprang over the wall, and dash-

[1] Sir G. St. P. Lawrence's *Forty Years in India.*

ing almost into the midst of the enemy, seized the wounded man by the legs and arms and brought him safely in. One of the three was shot down, when another of the band rushed to his assistance and brought him under cover on his back."

When at last Mackenzie reached the room where Eyre —whose hand had been shattered the previous day by a bullet—was lying, it is no wonder that he looked haggard and exhausted. The ball was cut out of his shoulder by Dr. Metcalfe,[1] and the wound, being merely a flesh one, quickly healed.

There is a tragical story of one of the officers who fell on this occasion. Two or three days before, he was standing in front of a very low rampart when a ball came singing along. He did not move an inch, and it just passed him. Some one asked why he did not cover himself behind the rampart. He turned round as pale as death, and with clenched teeth said : " I only wish it had been through my brain." His wish was fulfilled at Behmaru ; he fell dead, and all the blood rushing to the forehead, it became quite black.

Shelton's incapacity neutralised the heroism of the officers, and went far to extenuate the conduct of the men, who had lost all confidence in so incapable a leader. Their spirit was gone, and discipline had almost disappeared.

Conolly, accompanied with Ján Fishan Khan, the only chief who adhered faithfully to Shah Shujah, came in to urge the retreat of the whole force into the Bála Hissar. Shelton vehemently opposed this measure, and the General, considering our position untenable, advised negotiation. The chiefs demanded our unconditional surrender, and that

[1] A son of Sir Charles Metcalfe, who had been Mackenzie's travelling companion from Bombay to Calcutta ; fell at Gandamak, 13th January.

we should give up Shah Shujah and his family. Mackenzie suggested the answer—"death was better than dishonour, we put our trust in the God of battles, and in His name we bid them come on,"—which was at once adopted by the Envoy.

On the 5th December the enemy completed the destruction of the bridge which they had begun on the 24th. Shelton and Mackenzie had both urged the General to protect it, and Mackenzie had volunteered to do so by occupying a small fort, consisting merely of four walls, close to it. The General consented, when Lieutenant Sturt persuaded him not to do so as there was "no danger." Mackenzie talked to Sturt for half an hour on the subject, but he was obstinate ; consequently nothing was done, and the enemy carried off part of the bridge and burnt the remainder.

Mr. Baness, the Greek merchant, came to Captain Mackenzie and entreated him to prevail on General Elphinstone to give him a dozen or fifteen men, and he would go out and drive off the Afghans; and then heaped imprecations on Elphinstone, Shelton, and all concerned.

On the 8th December the Envoy officially asked the General's opinion whether we ought to negotiate. The General assembled a number of the officers, and Sir W. Macnaghten, who was not present, was handled somewhat severely.

On this Mackenzie rose and expressed his disapprobation that a military council should be made the arena of personal abuse, more especially of a man who—he being in political employ—was his immediate head, and told them that instead of deliberating like bearded men they were behaving like a party of troublesome schoolboys. The General repeatedly called the disputants to order, but Shelton replied doggedly : "I *will* sneer at him ; I like to sneer at him."

It was at this time that Sir William Macnaghten wrote
to his brother-in-law, the Honourable J. C. Erskine [1]:—

"KABUL, 9th December 1841.

"We have now been besieged thirty-eight days by a con-
temptible enemy. . . . The military authorities have strongly
urged me to capitulate. *This I will not do till the last moment.*
. . . We have no energy or spirit here."

So great was the want of common sense that hundreds
of the enemy, armed to the teeth, were allowed to insinuate
themselves into the cantonments and to walk about spying
everything. A Ghaljai drew his sword on Lieutenant Sturt
within a few yards of a loaded 6-pounder, because that
officer endeavoured to keep back the man's insolent comrades.

General Elphinstone frequently checked an effective fire
from the batteries for fear of "wasting ammunition," of which
we had an enormous quantity. So strictly were the sentries
forbidden to fire, that our camp-followers and friendly
Afghans were often robbed and even killed a dozen yards
from our walls, and the mess sheep of the 5th Cavalry were
captured within a hundred and fifty yards of the ramparts,
under the eyes of the whole garrison, even before we were
actually beleaguered.

Sir William was principally to blame for endeavouring
to buy off the hostility, first of one tribe then of another.
Had he confined his negotiations to one powerful clan—for
instance, the Kazilbashes—even this weak mode of defence
would have succeeded ; but the proceeding actually adopted
offered a premium to that tribe which should succeed in
rendering itself most formidable to us, and the prospect of

---

[1] Mr. Erskine (now Lord Erskine) was subsequently deprived of his
appointment by Lord Ellenborough for publishing Sir William's letters
and vindicating his character, but immediately restored by the Court
of Directors.

bribes was the means of detaining the eastern Ghaljais around Kabul when they would otherwise, according to their custom, have dispersed to their homes.

Shelton had from the very first been bent on a retreat, and Brigadiers Anquetil and Chambers now joined him in countersigning the General's opinion that no other step could be taken.

The Envoy, therefore, accompanied by Captains Lawrence, Mackenzie, and Trevor, met the chiefs on the plain on the 11th December, and made an agreement that the British should evacuate Afghanistan, and that they should be unmolested and furnished with supplies on the road. Trevor was given over as a hostage, though, as Mackenzie remarked, Sir William ought to have demanded hostages and not given them.

On the 14th the Bála Hissar was evacuated by our troops. Forage had for many days been so scarce that the horses and cattle were kept alive by paring off the bark of trees, and by eating their own dung over and over again, which was regularly collected and spread before them, while the camp-followers had no other food than the flesh of the animals which died daily from starvation and cold.

The chiefs refused to furnish either provisions or forage until we had given up all the forts around the cantonments. This was done on the 17th, bringing tears of shame and indignation into the eyes of some of our officers. Truly—

> "Woe awaits a country when
> She sees the tears of bearded men."

The severity of the weather increased, and a heavy fall of snow the next morning was a new enemy which never left us.

Hasan Khan, Mackenzie's jemadar of Jezailchis, repeatedly warned Sir William of the likelihood of a fatal termination to his hazardous interviews with the Afghan chiefs, and entreated to be allowed to be present with a handful of his men, pledging himself to secure the Envoy's safety. He argued that surely he was a better judge of the intentions of his own countrymen than Sir William could be, and that among them no dishonour was attached to what we called treachery. But it was of no avail.

On the 20th the Envoy, accompanied by Lawrence and Mackenzie, had another interview with the chiefs, who now demanded our 9-pounder guns. This the Envoy at once refused, and returning to cantonments, urged the General to march out boldly and meet the rebels in the field, as he felt sure we should beat them.

Another stormy conference took place on the 21st, and Captains Conolly and Airey were given up as hostages for our immediate retreat, Captain Trevor being sent back at the earnest request of his poor wife, who little knew what would be the result.

Three times the Envoy and his staff had risked their lives by going out to meet the chiefs, and three times, although on one occasion at least in imminent peril, they had returned in safety. Colin Mackenzie himself relates what followed.

CHAPTER XV.

"He shall deliver thee in six troubles : yea, in seven there shall
no evil touch thee. In famine He shall redeem thee from death ; and
in war from the power of the sword."—Job v. 19-20.

"For many days previous to the fatal 23d December the
poor Envoy had been subjected to more wear and tear, both
of body and mind, than it was possible for the most iron
frame and the strongest intellect to bear without deeply feeling
its effects. He had fulfilled all the preliminary conditions of
the treaty with the insurgents by evacuating the Bála Hissar
and the forts near cantonments, whereas the Khans had in
no one particular adhered to their engagements. Bad faith
was evident in all their proceedings, and our condition was
a desperate one; for, as Sir William had ascertained by
bitter experience, no hope remained in the energies and
resources of our military leaders, who had formally protested that they could do nothing more. Beset by imbe-
cility on the one hand, and by systematic treachery on the
other, the unfortunate Envoy was driven to his wits' end,
and forgot in a fatal moment the wholesome rule he had
laid down for himself, of refusing to hold communication
with individuals of the rebel party. Late in the evening
of the 22d December Captain James Skinner, who, after
having been concealed in Kabul during the greater part of

the siege, had latterly been the guest of Muhammad Akbar, arrived in cantonments accompanied by Muhammad Sadiq Khan, a first cousin of Akbar, and a Loháni merchant one of our staunchest friends. During dinner Skinner jestingly remarked that he felt as if laden with combustibles, being charged with a message from Muhammad Akbar to the Envoy of a most portentous nature. Even then I remarked that the Envoy's eye glanced eagerly towards Skinner with an expression of hope ; in fact, he was like a drowning man catching at straws. Skinner, however, referred him to his Afghan companions, and after dinner the four retired into a room by themselves. My knowledge of what there took place is gained from poor Skinner during my subsequent captivity with him in Akbar's house. Muhammad Sadiq disclosed Akbar's proposal, which was, that the following day Sir William should meet him and a few of his immediate friends, the chiefs of the Eastern Ghaljais, outside the cantonments, when a final agreement should be made ; that Sir William should have a considerable body of troops in readiness, which on a given signal were to join with those of Akbar Khan and the Ghaljais, assault and take Mahmud Khan's fort, and secure the person of Aminullah. Muhammad Sadiq signified that for a certain sum of money the head of Aminullah should be presented to the Envoy ; but from this Sir William shrunk with abhorrence, declaring that it was neither his custom nor that of his country to give a price for blood. Muhammad Sadiq then went on to say that, after having subdued the rest of the Khans, the English should be permitted to remain in the country eight months longer, so as to save their credit ; they were then to evacuate Afghanistan as if of their own accord ; that Shah Shujah was to continue king, and Akbar to be his Vazir ; and, as a reward for Akbar's assistance, the British

Government was to pay him thirty lacs of rupees (£300,000) and four lacs of rupees (£40,000) per annum during his life! To this wild proposal Sir William gave ear with an eagerness which nothing can account for but the supposition, confirmed by many other circumstances, that his strong mind had been harassed until it had in some degree lost its equipoise, and he not only fully assented to these terms, but actually gave a Persian paper to that effect written in his own hand. So ended this fatal conference, the nature of which Sir William communicated to none of those who on all former occasions were fully in his confidence—viz. Trevor, Lawrence, and myself. It seemed as if he feared that we might insist on the impracticability of the plan, which he must have studiously concealed from himself. All the following morning his manner was distracted and hurried in a way that none of us had ever before witnessed. It seems that Muhammad Akbar had demanded a favourite Arab horse belonging to Captain Grant. To avoid parting with the animal, Grant fixed his price at the exorbitant sum of 5000 rupees; but, determined to gratify the Sirdar, Sir William sent me to Grant to prevail upon him to take a smaller sum, but with orders that if he were peremptory the 5000 rupees should be given. I obtained the horse for 3000 rupees, and Sir William appeared much pleased with the prospect of gratifying Akbar by the present. After breakfast, Trevor, Lawrence, and myself were summoned to attend the Envoy during his conference with Akbar Khan. I found him alone, when, for the first time, he disclosed to me the nature of the transaction he was engaged in. I immediately warned him that it was a plot against him. He replied hastily, 'A plot! Let me alone for that, trust me for that;' and I consequently offered no further remonstrance. Sir William then arranged with General Elphinstone that the 54th Regiment, the Shah's 6th, and two guns should be held in readiness for immediate service."

(Captain Lawrence says :—"As we were leaving, General Elphinstone met us and expressed some fear of treachery. Sir William answered : 'If you will at once march out the troops and meet the enemy, I will accompany you, and I am sure we shall beat them.' The General replied, shaking his head : 'Macnaghten, I can't ; the troops are not to be depended on.' These were the last words which ever passed between them.")

Mackenzie continues : " It betrays the unhappy vacillation of poor Elphinstone that, after Sir William had actually quitted the cantonment, the General wrote a letter, which never reached him, remonstrating on the danger of the proposed attack, and strongly objecting to the employment of the two above regiments. About 12 o'clock Sir William, Trevor, Lawrence, and I set forth on our ill-omened expedition. As we approached the Siah Sang gate, Sir William observed with much vexation that the troops were not in readiness, protesting, however, that desperate as the proposed attempt was, it was better it should be made, and that a thousand deaths were preferable to the life he had lately led. After passing the gate he remembered the horse for Akbar, and sent me back for it. When I rejoined him, I found that the small number of the bodyguard who had accompanied him had been ordered to halt, and that he, Trevor, and Lawrence had advanced in the direction of Mahmud Khan's fort,[1] and were awaiting the approach of Akbar and his party, who now made their appearance. Close by were some hillocks, on the farther side of which, from the cantonment, a carpet was spread where the snow lay least thick, and there the Khans and Sir William sat down to hold their conference. Men talk of presentiment; I suppose

---

[1] " Exact distance, 350 yards from our rampart."—H. M. Lawrence.

it was something of the kind which came over me, for I
could scarcely prevail on myself to quit my horse. I did
so, however, and was invited to sit down among the Sirdars.
After the usual salutations, Muhammad Akbar commenced
business by asking the Envoy if he was ready to carry into
effect the proposition of the preceding night. The Envoy
replied : 'Why not ?' My attention was attracted by an
old Afghan acquaintance of mine, formerly chief of the
Kabul police, by name Ghulam Moyan-ud-din. I rose
and stood apart with him, conversing. I afterwards
remembered that my friend betrayed much anxiety as to
where my pistols were, and why I did not carry them on
my person. I answered that, although I wore my sword
for form, it was not necessary at a friendly conference to be
armed *cap-à-pie*. His discourse was also full of extravagant
compliments, I suppose for the purpose of lulling me to
sleep. At length my attention was called off from what he
was saying by observing that a number of men, armed to
the teeth, had gradually approached the scene of conference,
and were drawing round in a sort of circle. This Lawrence
and I pointed out to some of the chief men, who affected
at first to drive them off with whips; but Muhammad
Akbar remarked that it was of no consequence, as they
were in the secret. I again resumed my conversation with
Ghulam Moyan-ud-din, when suddenly I heard Muhammad
Akbar call out, ' Bigír ! bigír !' (seize ! seize !), and turning
round, I saw him grasp the Envoy's left hand, with an
expression on his face of the most diabolical ferocity.
Sultan Ján laid hold of the Envoy's right hand, they
dragged him in a stooping posture down the hillock, the
only words I heard poor Sir William utter being 'Az
baraí khudá !' (for God's sake !). I saw his face, however,
and it was full of horror and astonishment. I did not see
what became of Trevor, but Lawrence was dragged past me

by several Afghans, whom I saw wrest his weapons from
him.   Up to this moment I was so engrossed in observing
what was taking place that I actually was not aware that
my own right arm was mastered, that my urbane friend
held a pistol to my temple, and that I was surrounded by
a circle of Ghaljais with drawn swords and cocked juzails.
Resistance was in vain, so, listening to the exhortations of
Ghulam Moyan-ud-dín, which were enforced by the whistling
of divers bullets over my head, I hurried through the snow
with him to the place where his horse was standing, being
despoiled *en route* of my sabre, and narrowly escaping divers
attempts made on my life.   As I mounted behind my
captor, now my energetic defender, the crowd increased
around us, the cries of 'Kill the káfir' became more
vehement, and although we hurried on at a fast canter, it
was with the utmost difficulty that Ghulam Moyan-ud-dín,
although assisted by one or two friends (especially by a
merchant named Mirza Bawudin Khan), could ward off
the sword-cuts aimed at me, the rascals being afraid to
fire lest they should kill my conductor.   Indeed he was
obliged to wheel his horse round once, and, taking off his
turban (the last appeal a Musalman can make), to implore
them for God's sake to respect the life of his friend.   At
last, ascending a slippery bank, the horse fell.   My cap had
been snatched off, and I now received a heavy blow on the
head from a bludgeon, which fortunately did not quite
deprive me of my wits.   I had sufficient sense left to shoot
ahead of the fallen horse, when my protector with another
man joined me, and, clasping me in their arms, hurried me
towards the wall of Mahmud Khan's fort.   How I reached
the spot where Muhammad Akbar was receiving the gratula-
tions of the multitude, I know not; but I remember a
fanatic rushing on me and twisting his hand in my collar
until I became exhausted from suffocation.   I must do

Muhammad Akbar the justice to say that, finding the Ghaljais bent on my slaughter, even after I had reached his stirrup, he drew his sword and laid about him right manfully. My conductor and Mirza Bawudin Khan pressed me up against the wall, covering me with their own bodies, and protesting that no blow should reach me but through their persons. Pride, however, overcame Muhammad Akbar's sense of courtesy when he thought I was safe ; for he then turned round to me, and repeatedly said, in a tone of triumphant derision : 'Shumá mulk-i-má me-giríd !' (*You'll* seize my country, will you !). He then rode off, and I was hurried towards the gate of the fort. Here new dangers awaited me, for Mulla Momin, fresh from the slaughter of poor Trevor, who was killed riding close behind me, stood here with his followers, whom he exhorted to slay me, setting them the example by cutting fiercely at me himself. Fortunately a gun stood between us, but still he would have effected his purpose had not Muhammad Shah Khan[1] at that instant come to my assistance with some followers. These drew their swords in my defence, the chief himself throwing his arm round my neck, and receiving on his shoulder a cut aimed by Mulla Momin at my head. During the bustle I was shoved forward into the fort, and immediately taken to a sort of dungeon, where I found Lawrence safe, but somewhat exhausted by his hideous ride and the violence he had sustained, although unwounded.[2] Here the Ghaljai chiefs, Muhammad Shah

---

[1] Muhammad Shah Khan Ghilzai, Akbar's father-in-law, who had great influence with him, a man of insatiable avarice and ambition, and one of our most able and bitter enemies.

[2] Mackenzie afterwards described his feelings :—" At Sir William Macnaghten's murder a hundred swords were raised against me, but I felt myself completely in the hands of God, and that not one could touch me without His permission, and whatever was His will would be right."

Khan, and his brother, Dost Muhammad Khan, presently
joined us, and endeavoured to cheer up our flagging spirits,
assuring us that the Envoy and Trevor were not dead, but,
on the contrary, quite well. They stayed with us during
the afternoon, their presence being absolutely necessary for
our protection. Many attempts were made by the fanatics
to force the door to accomplish our destruction. Others
spat at and abused us through a small window, through
which one fellow levelled a blunderbuss at us, which was
struck up by our keepers and himself thrust back. At last
Aminullah made his appearance, and threatened us with
instant death, saying : 'We'll blow you from guns ; any
death will be too good for you.' Some of his people most
officiously advanced to make good his word, until pushed
back by the Ghaljai chiefs, who remonstrated with this
iniquitous old monster, whom they persuaded to relieve us
from his hateful presence, exclaiming, 'Don't say such
things ; they are your guests,' (Mahmud Shah's fort belonging to Aminullah). During the afternoon a human hand
was held up in mockery at the window. We saw that it
belonged to a European, but we were not aware that it was
really the hand of the poor Envoy. Of all the Muhammadans assembled in the room discussing the events of the
day, one only, an old Mulla, openly and fearlessly condemned the acts of his brethren, declaring that such
treachery was abominable, and a disgrace to Islám. At
night they brought us food, and gave us each a posteen[1] to
sleep on. At midnight we were awakened to go to the
house of Muhammad Akbar, in the city. Muhammad Shah
Khan then, with the meanness common to Afghans of rank,
robbed Lawrence of his watch, while his brother did me a
similar favour. I had been plundered of my rings[2] and

[1] Sheepskin cloak.
[2] Some months after an Afghan brought these rings for sale to

everything else previously by the under-strappers. Lawrence was mounted behind Muhammad Shah Khan, and I behind another. Leaving the fort, we passed through a large portion of the town unchallenged, the streets being as silent and deserted as a city of the dead. Reaching Akbar's abode, we were shown into the room where he lay in bed; he received us with great outward show of courtesy, assuring us of the welfare of the Envoy and Trevor, but there was a constraint in his manner for which I could not account. We were shortly taken to another apartment, where we found Skinner, who, being on parole, had returned early that morning. Doubt and gloom marked our meeting, and the latter was fearfully deepened by the intelligence we now received, of the base murder of Sir William and Trevor. Skinner informed us that the head of the former had been carried about the city in triumph."[1]

Sir William always wore an emerald ring said to have belonged to Muhammad himself. The words "Mustafa, the last of his race" were engraved on it in the square Arabic characters, and this was on his hand at the time of the murder. He had won rank, fortune, and honour for himself, and left none to inherit them.

Trevor had acted as both civil and military assistant to

Badiabad. Jacob, who had concealed a little money about his person, bought them, and gave them to Mrs. Eyre to keep, saying: "I give them to my master; he wear them, and they take them again."

[1] An Afghan account of the murder, contained in a very accurate intercepted letter from Muhammad Sadiq to his uncle at Kandahar, thus relates the circumstances:—"The Sirdar at last said to the Envoy: 'Come, I must take you to the Nawab's.' The Envoy was alarmed, and rose up. Muhammad Akbar seized him by the hands, saying: 'I cannot allow you to return to cantonments.' The Sirdar wished to carry him off alive, but was unable; then he drew a double-barrelled pistol from his belt, and discharged both barrels at the Envoy, after which he struck him two or three blows with his sword, and the Envoy was thus killed on the spot."

the Envoy. Besides the onerous task of reforming Shah Shujah's cavalry, which brought upon him the hatred of a very influential section of the Afghans, Captain Trevor had been selected by the Envoy to inquire into and report on the revenue throughout Afghanistan, with a view to amending the abuses which prevailed. These duties he unflinchingly performed, and thereby incurred the deadly enmity of many Afghans of rank, whose peculations he had brought to light. Among them, that of Mulla Momin, who had been collector in the district of Zurmat. Captain Trevor having been seized and disarmed, was being carried off on horseback when Sultan Ján, who had just arrived from Bokhara, and whose mind had been inflamed against Trevor by the dissolute and disappointed military men above alluded to, rode up, and exclaiming "Hamin sag Trevor hast" (this dog is Trevor), cut at him with his sabre. This gave the vindictive priest, Mulla Momin, the much longed-for opportunity, and falling upon the disarmed and helpless officer, he and his followers cut him to pieces.

"We of course spent a miserable night. At last Lawrence lay down on the floor to sleep, and Skinner gave me half his small charpai or truckle-bed. The next day we were taken under a strong guard to the house of Nawab Zaman Khan, where a council of the Khans was being held. Here we found Captains Conolly and Airey, who had, some days previously, been sent in as hostages for the performance of the treaty. A violent discussion took place, in which Akbar bore the most prominent part. We were vehemently accused of treachery and everything that was bad, and told that the whole of the transactions of the night previous had been a trick of Muhammad Akbar and Aminullah to test the Envoy's sincerity. They declared that they would now grant us no terms save on the surren-

der of the whole of the married families as hostages, all the
guns, ammunition, and treasure. At this time Conolly told
me that the Envoy's and Trevor's bodies had been hung up
in the public bazar, or chauk, and that it was with the
greatest difficulty that the old Nawab Zaman Khan had
saved him and Airey from being murdered by a body of
fanatics, who had attempted to rush into the room where
they were. After an immense deal of gabble, a proposal for
a renewal of the treaty was determined on, and Skinner,
Lawrence, and I were marched back to Akbar's house,
enduring *en route* all manner of threats and insults. Here
we were closely confined in an inner apartment, which was
indeed necessary for our safety. That evening we received
a visit from Akbar, Sultan Ján, and several others. Muhammad Akbar exhibited his double-barrelled pistols to us
which he had worn the previous day, requesting us to put
their locks to rights, something being amiss. *Two of the
barrels had been recently discharged*, which he endeavoured in
a most confused way to account for, by saying that he had
been charged by a havildar of the escort, and had fired
both barrels at him. Now, all the escort had run away
without even attempting to charge. The only man who
advanced to the rescue was a Hindu jemadar of Chaprási's,
a noble Rajput named Ram Sing, who was instantly cut to
pieces by the Ghaljais. He made this defence without any
accusation on our part, betraying the anxiety of a liar to be
believed."

On Christmas Day, as they were eating a pillau which
had been brought to them, Mackenzie suddenly turned
deadly pale and fell back in a kind of swoon. His friends
jumped up in alarm. "Poison" was their first thought,
and very little more of that pillau was eaten. "After every
one had left their cell Skinner mounted on his bed, and,
from a hole in the wall, drew forth a bottle of Madeira

which Sultan Ján had privily brought in under his chogah and given to him with a mysterious air. Two evenings or so afterwards he brought a bottle of brandy in the same way, and expressed a great desire to see an Englishman drink a glass of brandy, thereby inferring that so profane a liquor had never gone down his own throat. We took pains to inform him that English gentlemen did not take brandy in this fashion, but only a little now and then for the good of their health.

"Sultan Ján, Akbar's first cousin, was remarkably handsome, proportionately vain, and much given to boasting. We fell into conversation on the comparative merits of British and Afghan soldiers. Sultan Ján professed that he desired nothing better than to have a dozen before him, that he might show them what an Afghan *shamshiri* (warrior) was ; whereupon we both declared that we desired nothing better than to form part of any twelve British soldiers opposed to two or three dozen Afghans with Sultan Ján at their head !

"During these dreary days we were enlivened by our friend Skinner's account of his marvellous escape on the morning of the 2d November. About 7 A.M. Mr. Baness, a Greek merchant, who had lately arrived from Delhi with supplies of English goods, rushed into his house, advising him to go at once to cantonments, as a large crowd had assembled and were making a disturbance. Skinner immediately dressed, and, while waiting for his horse, his servant burst in saying the mob was approaching. He had just time to disguise himself as an Afghan and escape through a side door into the area of an adjoining dwelling when the mob broke into his own. His neighbour was grateful to him for kindness shown to several members of his family ; and his mother, a little old lady, in defiance, not only of great personal danger, but of every prejudice of a

Musalmani woman, came forth into the midst of the affray, and seizing Skinner by the hand, called him her son, and drew him into her house, thus screening him from pursuit by his murderous assailants. She then thoroughly disguised him by putting a bhurkah, or woman's veil, over his head. From this place of concealment he heard the mob plundering his house and uttering many curses at not finding him within. He remained with this family a month, treated with the utmost kindness as one of themselves ; and though repeated search was made, they never betrayed him, and only delivered him over to a servant of Aminullah Khan's when Skinner himself insisted on the measure, fearing that his further retention would ruin his protectors. Even then this kind family would not give him up until they had extorted solemn promises that his life should be spared. During the time he resided with them the daughter of his hostess used to sit by him for hours listening to his stories of his own and other countries, and deeply interested in all he told her."

Henry Drummond was saved in a similar manner by Usman Khan, the chief of Karez-i-Amír, and these facts are sufficient to confute the notion of bitter hatred and distrust of Europeans as such.

Captain Lawrence relates :—

" Early on the 26th I was summoned to the house of Aminullah Khan. Mackenzie, seeing me look grave at so portentous a summons, prepared to accompany me, but I declined his generous offer, thinking we should neither of us rush heedlessly into danger, but each take his own turn as circumstances might require. It was no wonder that both of us felt a shrinking from appearing in the presence of such a monster of cruelty as Aminullah Khan."

Lawrence was, however, very well treated, and had an opportunity of confuting the charge that the Envoy had

offered a price for Aminullah's head.[1]   He was sent back
to cantonments on the 29th.

Mackenzie's narration continues :—"Skinner and I remained in Akbar's house for a week, during which time
we were civilly treated, and conversed with numbers of
Afghan gentlemen who came to visit us.   Among others,
Muhammad Shah Khan Ghilzai showed his real feelings,
anger, as well as wine, being a revealer of truth.   'You
think,' cried he, 'that your troops will get safe to Jellalabad.   If there was no one else to intercept them, I and my
friends would do it.'   He then broke out into invectives
against the faithlessness of the British, and instanced the
reduction of his salary, saying it made him despised by his
clan as one whom the ruling powers ill-used and contemned,
adding : 'You broke your word to us on this point, so how
could we trust you on any ?   You might have finished by
sending me off to London !'

"Other Afghans described Akbar as boasting to the
Ghaljais of having slain the Envoy, and Pottinger's Munshi,
Mohan Bir, who had escaped with him from Charekar,
came direct from Akbar's presence to tell us that the Sirdar
had begun to see the impolicy of having murdered the
Envoy, which fact he had just avowed to him, shedding
many tears either of pretended remorse or of real vexation
at having committed himself.   On several occasions Muhammad Akbar personally and by deputy besought Skinner
and myself to give him advice as to how he was to extri-
cate himself from the dilemma in which he was.   Meanwhile negotiations had been brought to a head, for on the

---

[1] "That Mohun Lál offered a reward for Aminullah's head appears
probable ; but he never asserted that it was with Sir William's knowledge or sanction.   Such a course would have been abhorrent to a man
of the Envoy's high religious principles and unswerving rectitude."—
(G. St. P. Lawrence.)

night of the 30th December Akbar furnished me with an Afghan dress (Skinner already wore one), and sent us both back to cantonments.

" At the time of the murder, though two regiments had been warned for duty, and several officers distinctly saw through their field-glasses two bodies lying on the ground where the meeting took place (which must have been those of the Envoy and his brave jemadar), nothing was done. Not a man was sent even to ascertain the truth, and Major Pottinger in vain urged the General to lead the troops, who were inflamed with fury and indignation at what had occurred, to attack the city, which in their then temper they would no doubt have stormed and carried. Pottinger, though still suffering greatly from the wound in his leg, was obliged as Senior Political Officer to act in Sir William's place. He formally protested against renewing negotiations or doing anything which would bind the hands of Government, strongly objected to paying the £140,000 promised to the chiefs by the late Envoy, and maintained that the only honourable course was either to hold out to the last at Kabul, or to force our way at once to Jellalabad; but the General and the three senior officers, with Captains Bellew and Grant, were unanimous against him, and the hero of Herat was obliged to do what he abhorred.

" Macnaghten had special powers which died with him, and on his death the General's authority was acknowledged by all as supreme. Pottinger acted solely as the General's *go-between* with the Afghans, and signed the treaty in soldierly obedience, knowing full well that he would be held responsible for that which was the work of others. Treasure, guns, and more hostages[1] were made over to the chiefs.

---

[1] Captains Henry Drummond and Walsh, and Lieutenants Warburton and Webb, were sent to join Conolly and Airey. This was looked

Haughton, the gallant defender of Charekar, suffering fright-
fully from his wounds, was sent with the other sick and
wounded into the city, under solemn promises of protection
on the part of the chiefs."

This was the position of affairs when Mackenzie returned.   The Shah and other well-wishers sent urgent
warnings of treachery, but all in vain.   There was scarcely
any food, no forage, and so scarce was fuel that they had
to break up furniture, and Lady Sale relates that her last
meal at Kabul was cooked with the wood of a mahogany
dining-table.   But Mackenzie said : "Though we were all
starving and eating horse and camel, we could have marched
into the Bála Hissar, and held out for a year.   In a fortnight the tribes would have melted away."

There was a strong fortress commanding the town,
capable of receiving the whole force, and nothing would
induce the commanders to occupy it.   All foresight, one
may say all common sense, still more all decision and
energy, seemed to be taken from those in authority.   Individual acts of heroism are recorded on every page of the
memoirs of this disastrous time, but the public acts produce
a feeling of incredulous astonishment.

Speaking of the projected retreat, Broadfoot wisely
says :—"In every military measure, advance, halt, or
retire, fight or refuse, a man should have some clear
motive, some end to gain.   What is here their end?"   He
adds, as to the difficulties of a winter march :—"Nothing
is impossible with forethought, due preparation, and calm
obstinate courage.   But these are *all* wanting here ; gallantry and right-heartedness we have, but not the nerve to
look the very worst in the face, and, by preparing, meet it
unshaken."

upon as such desperate service that 2000 rupees a month were guaranteed
to any officer who would undertake it, but this money was never paid.

Many of the troops saw what should have been done ; all knew they were being sacrificed by the incompetence of their leaders, and this destroyed discipline, energy, and hope. The heathen expressed the fact that men doomed to destruction are deprived of ordinary wisdom, and the believer humbly recognises that it is "the Lord who giveth wisdom to the wise" (Dan. ii. 21).

The Kabul force originally consisted of about 5000 fighting men :—

> 1st Troop Bengal Horse Artillery.
> Half of Backhouse's Mountain Train.
> 5th Bengal Light Cavalry.
> Four squadrons Irregular Horse.
> Her Majesty's 44th.

Five Native Infantry Regiments, viz. :—

> 37th and 54th Bengal N.I.
> 4th Ghurka and 6th Hindustanis of the Shah's force.
> Three companies Broadfoot's Sappers.
> Ninety-five Ferris's Jezailchis.   12,000 camp-followers, *besides* women and children.

CHAPTER XVI.

THE RETREAT.

(January 6-13.)

"The Greeks and Romans would not have recorded in heroic verse the death and defeat of their fellow-countrymen. But the Goths, firm in their faith, with a constancy not to be shaken, celebrated those brave men who died for their religion and their country! What though they had been defeated, they died without fear, as they had lived without reproach, and they left no stain on their names."

COLERIDGE.

MACKENZIE had by this time lost his two best chargers. He relates :—"Our communication with Sir Robert Sale was at length completely cut off when the chief of the Jabbar Khail (the most lawless robber tribe in Afghanistan), who was secretly on our side, offered to carry a despatch to Jellalabad, provided that we furnished him with a horse that could do 120 miles through the snow in one night! Mine (the one which had belonged to the Dost), was selected. The despatch arrived safely, and I never saw my Bucephalus again. Do you think he is now enjoying himself with unencumbered back, forgetful of the rein, in the clover-fields of Pegasus?"

The other, a chestnut named "Bob," which he had complained of for "compelling him to do horsebreaker in front of Shelton's brigade," was by no means of a docile character. Riding out to the Khurd Kabul Pass in October his master lost temper with him for bucking and bounding, gave him a severe cut, and in so doing, hit one of the pistols in his belt, which went off, the ball just skimming outside his own leg.

"Bob" was taken at the Envoy's murder, and the last his master saw of him was with his head up in the air, his feet firmly planted in front of him, resisting with all his might the Afghan who was endeavouring to lead him away, exciting a charitable hope that he would surely throw whoever attempted to ride him.

Major Pottinger then gave Mackenzie the good horse which had brought himself in from Charekar, and which carried his new master throughout the retreat; for retreat had been resolved upon. Those in command were blinded; those who saw clearly could do nothing to avert it. Broadfoot wrote from Jellalabad on the 2d January 1842:—

"If they attempt to capitulate or retreat the Afghans will probably inveigle them into the passes and then attack them, and heavy indeed would be their loss, without cattle, fuel, or food, assailed night and day amidst the snow. . . . The whole country will rise."

And so it did. Having resolved to retreat, this is how they did it.

On Thursday the 6th January the troops began their fatal march. There were about 4500 fighting men (of whom less than 700 were Europeans), and alas! at the very least, 12,000 male camp-followers, besides women and children. It was evidently impossible either to protect such a mass or to maintain order among them. They were a most serious clog upon the movements of the troops, who, by themselves, could have pushed their way onwards by forced marches. No wonder Vincent Eyre exclaims: "It is devoutly to be hoped that every future Commander-in-Chief of India will prevent a force employed on field-service from being ever again afflicted with such a curse.". Deep snow covered the whole landscape, and the cold was intense.

At 9 A.M. the advance began to move out. An hour after a chief sent to beg the march might be delayed, as his escort was not ready to accompany them. The troops were kept standing in the snow half the day. At last the General was persuaded to order Shelton with the main column to move on; but he then changed his mind, and wished to countermand him. Mackenzie saw that the garrison, which was half-in half-out of cantonments, would be ignominiously butchered by the enemy who were swarming around, firing on our men, who were becoming quite disorganised. He therefore galloped off in defiance of the General's entreaties, "Mackenzie, don't—don't do it," and conveyed the order to Shelton to resume his march. About five in the afternoon the Sepoys of the rear-guard, having manned the walls for eleven hours without food, with the thermometer below freezing point, at length left the cantonments. Before they did so Lieutenant Hardyman, 5th Light Cavalry, and fifty men were stretched lifeless in the snow. The camp-followers mixed themselves up with the troops and threw them into utter confusion. Thousands of Ghazis (fanatics) set fire to the cantonments and committed every kind of atrocity; while scores of our worn-out people sat down in despair to perish. Mackenzie always remembered, as one of the most heartrending sights of that humiliating day, fixing his eyes by chance on a little Hindustani child, perfectly naked, sitting in the snow, with no father or mother near it. It was a beautiful little girl about two years old, just strong enough to sit upright with its little legs doubled under it, its hair curling in waving locks round the soft little throat, and its great black eyes, dilated to twice their usual size, fixed on the armed men, the passing cavalry, and all the strange sights that met its gaze. And instead of being able to take up this poor little native of a tropical climate and cuddle it in his arms, and give it warmth from his own body, he was obliged to leave it there to die. Many other children as young and innocent he saw lying slain on the road, and women with their long dark hair wet with their own blood. If an Afghan boy of twelve had passed it, he would have drawn back the infant's head and amused himself with cutting its throat. The Afghan children were seen stabbing with their knives wounded grenadiers, one of whom, the day before, could have put a dozen of those children's fathers to flight with his bayonet. He used to say that the greatest honours a sovereign could bestow could not compensate for the horror and misery of beholding such scenes.

The rear-guard under Colonel Chambers did not reach camp at Bágrám, a distance of only five miles, till two the next morning. The cold became more intense, and many died of it. Captain Lawrence says :—"The silence of the men betrayed their despair and torpor, not a voice being heard. In the morning I found lying close to my tent, stiff, cold, and quite dead, in full regimentals, with his sword drawn in his hand, an old gray-haired conductor named Macgregor, who, utterly exhausted, had lain down there silently to die."

Some of Mackenzie's Jezailchis had gone to their homes when he was seized at the time of Sir William's murder, never expecting to see him again; but about twenty, who with Hasan Khan, still faithfully adhered to him, suffered but little from the bitter cold owing to their systematic way of proceeding. They first cleared a small space from the snow, covered it with their sheepskin coats, then laid themselves down in a circle closely packed, with their feet toward the centre, with all the remaining coats laid over the whole party. Mackenzie declared that by this means he felt scarcely any inconvenience from the cold. The Shah's 6th Infantry deserted *en masse;* but this was caused by despair, not by fanaticism. They were disarmed, and never trusted by the Afghans.

7th January.—No order was given, no bugle sounded. The force moved off in a mob of troops, camp-followers, and cattle, without the faintest semblance of order or discipline. Scarcely half the Sepoys were fit for duty. Anquetil's brigade now formed the rear-guard, and was furiously attacked. Owing to the crowded state of the road it was impossible for reinforcements to get to him.

The troops under Shelton gallantly kept the enemy in check for more than an hour. Akbar Khan, who had been sent by the chiefs to escort the force to Jellalabad, insisted on their halting at Butkhak, only ten miles from Kabul, just at the entrance to the Khurd Kabul Pass, promising to supply food, forage, and firing.

Mackenzie relates :—" The last night that I spent in the snow, January 7-8th, was in a little tent which dear Jacob got put up for me, I know not how. Pollock, a soldier of the 44th (the one who volunteered to follow me at Behmaru, where he got a ball in the thigh, the wound of which was not yet healed), lay close to me on one side for warmth, and Major Scott of the 44th coming in, I asked him to lie down on the other. He said he could not, on account of the intolerable pain of his feet, which were frost-bitten. He sat in a chair which happened to be there. I had two bottles of port, and admonished him to take some, which he did, and I believe that was the last wine he ever drank, for his body was afterwards found stripped and the chest cut open." Two nights' exposure to the frost "had so nipped the hands and feet of even the strongest men as to completely prostrate their powers and incapacitate them for service ; even the cavalry, who suffered less than the rest, were obliged to be lifted on their horses. In fact, only a few hundred serviceable fighting men remained."[1]

Shah Shujah had entreated Lady Macnaghten and the other ladies to take refuge in the Bála Hissar, but they had declined. Captain Lawrence had offered to take charge of the ladies and children with the late Envoy's escort, who behaved extremely well, but on the second day the bearers of the palanquins and litters were so thoroughly exhausted as to be unable to proceed. Most of the poor ladies were therefore packed into kajáwahs (panniers) slung on each side of a camel, though some of them were invalids, and Mrs. Anderson's baby was only five days old when she started. On the morning of the 8th the Afghans were gallantly charged by the 44th under Major Thain, showing that under an able and judicious officer they could yet redeem their reputation. Muhammad Akbar now insisted on Major Pottinger, Captains Lawrence and Colin Mackenzie, being delivered up to him as hostages that the force would not march beyond Tezin, until tidings should be received that Sale had evacuated Jellalabad. The General ordered them to go, which they did about eleven, and found the Sirdar at breakfast on the hillside. Finding they had been almost without food for the last two days, he invited them to eat with him, at the same time depriving them of their firearms. From their position they witnessed the march of the remnant of the army as they entered the "Jaws of Death," the fatal Khurd Kabul Pass. It is about five miles long, an impetuous mountain torrent dashing down the centre. This had to be crossed and recrossed about twenty-eight times. It is supposed that three thousand souls perished in that pass.

"Lieutenant Sturt, Lady Sale's son-in-law, was mortally wounded near the end of the defile, and would have been left on the ground to be hacked to pieces by the Gházis but for

[1] Eyre's *Narrative*, p. 226.

the generous intrepidity of Lieutenant Mein of the 13th,"[1] who, although dangerously wounded in the head, went back and stayed by his friend at the imminent risk of his life, until Sergeant Deane[2] of the Sappers came to his assistance, and helped him to drag poor Sturt on a quilt through the remainder of the pass. They then set him on a miserable pony, and brought him into camp.

Towards the end of the pass the hills close in considerably, at this part the Afghans had erected on each side small stone breastworks, behind which they lay, dealing out death, with perfect impunity to themselves.

Those ladies who were on camels could do no more than crawl along at the slow rate of about two miles an hour. How can we sufficiently admire the behaviour of the Hindustanis who unflinchingly remained at their posts, and led the camels through the murderous fire!

Mrs. Vincent Eyre was the first lady who cleared the pass, owing to her horse taking fright and running away with her. Captain Anderson's eldest girl and Captain Boyd's youngest boy fell into the hands of the Afghans. Neither of these poor babes was five years old; they had been placed in camel-panniers, the boy with his mother on one side, and the girl on the other, under the charge of Mrs. Mainwaring, a young merry girl, whose husband was

---

[1] Eyre's *Narrative*, p. 227.

[2] "To Sergeant Deane the army (while in cantonments) was very greatly indebted for his great exertions in getting in grain. He is very superior to his present station in life, and the fluency with which he speaks Persian enables him to pick up information, and to go about at times in disguise for the same purpose. Sergeant Deane's wife, a very handsome Persian woman, whom he had formally married before the kázi (judge), was taken by force during the captivity, and married to a younger brother of Muhammad Shah Khan. Whenever he enters her presence she salutes him with her slipper. It is only within a few days that she has been told of Deane's death. She appears to have been sincerely attached to him."—*Lady Sale's Journal.*

at Jellalabad; although she had an infant ten weeks old of her own in her arms, generously volunteered this charitable office, seeing that Mrs. Anderson had another child, a baby, to take care of. The camel on which the above little party were was shot; it lay down, leaving its helpless freight a stationary mark for the bullets of the Afghans. A Hindustani sawár took Mrs. Boyd on his horse and carried her through in safety. The kind-hearted Mrs. Mainwaring was nearly meeting a more wretched fate. She had just contrived to dismount with her own infant from the fallen camel, when an Afghan horseman rode up, threatening her with his sword, and desiring her to give him the shawl she wore. While she was urging some vain remonstrance, a grenadier Sepoy of the 54th contrived to force his way to her rescue, and discharged the contents of his musket into the body of the Afghan. He then gave his arm to his fair *protégée* and supported her failing steps to near the exit from the pass, where, poor fellow, he fell by a bullet from one of the stone breastworks.

Several of the ladies and children owed their lives, under God, to the manner in which Hasan Khan and the remnant of the strangely-devoted little knot of Jezailchís brought them through this vast "Glen of Slaughter."

In the meantime the hostages were taken by Akbar and some Ghaljai chiefs, in the midst of about thirty horsemen, on the track of the retreating force. Sultan Ján asked Captain Lawrence if he had a sword, adding : "Well, then, *use it* if any man comes too close to you."

Akbar and Sultan Ján rode on professedly to stop the firing, but Pottinger said : "Mackenzie, *remember* if I am killed that I heard Akbar Khan shout 'Slay them' in Pushtu, though he called to them to stop firing in Persian."[1]

The Gházis became so threatening, demanding that the

---

[1] This was well known among the Afghans.

hostages should be given up to them for a sacrifice, that
their guard made them take shelter under some overhanging
rocks, where they remained unnoticed until the evening.
A poor Irishwoman was brought to them whom Sultan
Ján had rescued from a Ghaljai who was about to cut off
her fingers to get at her rings, one of which was rather
tight, although her condition at the time should have
entitled her to any man's pity. She was a Mrs. Bourne,
wife of a private of H.M.'s 13th, and was so stupefied with
fear and cold that Captain Lawrence could hardly rouse her
sufficiently to hoist her up behind Mackenzie on his horse.
They wrapped a sheepskin coat around her, tying the
sleeves of it in front; but it was only with the greatest
pains he could keep her petticoats from riding up, a point
on which he was especially anxious on account of the
Afghans, who little considered the difficulty of riding
astride in a decorous fashion. On their way they found a
poor soldier stripped of everything but his trousers, with
one arm cut off. Mackenzie begged Sultan Ján to stop, and
tried to lift him on a horse. The poor fellow said, "No
use, sir; it's no use; let me die;" and so they were obliged
to leave him. Poor Mrs. Bourne was nearly dying with
thirst, and cried every now and then: "Och, Captain dear,
for the love of God get me a dhrink of wather!" A heavy
blinding snowstorm came on, and Mackenzie felt her licking
up the snow as it fell on his shoulder. Little Stoker (son
of a private in the 13th), a child of two years old, was
taken from his dead mother, a very fine young woman, all
covered with her blood, and placed in Mackenzie's arms. A
wounded soldier of the 44th and Captain Boyd's little boy
were brought to them by Akbar's orders, and Captain
Lawrence carried the former behind him on his horse.

Towards evening the hostages were conducted along the
fatal pass, and came upon one sight of horror after another.

All the bodies were stripped. There were children cut in two. Hindustani women, as well as men—some frozen to death, some literally chopped to pieces, many with their throats cut from ear to ear.[1]

The hostages and their escort arrived in the evening at a little fort of which the owner was absent, and, on Sultan Ján (one of their greatest chiefs) asking admittance, the occupants not only refused, but on his insisting, knocked him down and belaboured him as he lay on the ground. He took it with marvellous coolness, and came back saying: "See how these fellows have treated me!" They had the prospect of passing the night in the snow, when an old man came out and acted as mediator; moved partly by representations of the necessity of the case, partly by threats of what should be done to them hereafter, they at length opened the gate. Mackenzie says:—"I saw curious female faces peeping out of sundry nooks, and, the rest of the party having gone on in front, I said: 'For the love of God, give this woman a little water.' There was a little bustle within, and they brought water and a lotah to drink out of. Just as she had done, a rude Afghan came up and gave me a push. With some difficulty I restrained myself, though I still had my sword by my side, and said: 'One cannot let a woman die for want of water.' We

[1] Lieutenant Greenwood describes the scene which met the eyes of Pollock's force on the following September:—"On entering the Khurd Kabul Pass we were all struck with the utmost astonishment. The other passes were as nothing compared with this almost impregnable defile. The dead of General Elphinstone's army lay in heaps. In some places they seemed to have been mowed down in whole battalions. Although eight months had elapsed they had been preserved in the snow, and their ghastly faces seem to call upon us for revenge. At the narrow defile called Tangi the road was completely choked with dead bodies, and the stench in such a confined passage was absolutely insupportable."

then, guards and all, went into the inner room, a good-
sized one, with a fire in the middle of it. Lawrence and I
pulled of little Stoker's shoes and stockings, dried and warmed
them, and made him nice, and then put him to sleep.

"We all lay down with our heads close to the ground
to avoid the smarting, blinding smoke. At midnight they
brought in sheep's tail boiled in water, and half-baked
indigestible bread, which we dipped into the broth. Poor
little Stoker ate a mouthful or two, but he was quite exhausted with terror and fatigue.[1]

"Little Boyd lay snug under George Lawrence's posteen,
and Mrs. Bourne (who was a perfectly respectable, well-be-
haved woman) crouched down a little apart from the circle of
men."[2] That night the unfortunate remnants of the force
bivouacked in the snow at Khurd Kabul, only four small
tents remaining. In one of these with thirty other persons poor Sturt, suffering agony, lay dying, Lieutenant
Mein going to and fro all night to bring water from the
stream to assuage his dreadful thirst. The thirst of the
whole party was so great that the poor ladies eagerly drank
the blood-stained water, which was all they could get.

Kabul is upwards of 6000 feet above the sea-level, but

[1] "He was subsequently placed under the charge of Mrs. Wade (the
infamous half-caste wife of Sergeant Wade), but, it being discovered
that she was in the habit of beating him cruelly, he was taken from
her, but died at Bamián just before the deliverance of the captives.
The last time Mackenzie saw him he was lying on the ground covered
by a soldier's ragged cloak, moaning his little life away. It is a comfort to think of the tender arms of the Good Shepherd waiting to receive the little lamb, who had found this world such a rough one."

[2] "She was confined about two months after at Badiabad (the only
bad confinement of the four which took place among our party), when
Mrs. Eyre and Lady Sale were both kind to her. Her baby died at
Shewaki, but she herself lived to rejoin her husband, when the officers
of the regiment gave her a little tent, and did all they could to make
her comfortable."

the pass rises all the way, and Khurd Kabul is 1200 feet higher. It snowed all that night, and the wonder is that any survived. H.M.'s 44th only mustered 100 files, the Native Regiments about 60 files each.

Sunday, 9th January.—A large portion of the troops and camp-followers moved off without orders at 8 A.M. They all saw that their only chance was in pushing on as fast as possible; when, therefore, having gone a mile, they were recalled by the General at the request of Muhammad Akbar, they were filled with despair. Mothers threw their children from them in utter desperation, and the general feeling was that there was no hope left. Towards noon Captain Skinner came to urge the General to accept Akbar Khan's offer of protection for the ladies, children, and wounded officers. The Sirdar promised to escort them down safely. The extreme suffering of mind and body the poor ladies had undergone since the 5th was apparent in their worn and grief-stricken faces. Many of them had tasted nothing but a little dry biscuit during those wretched days, and their thirst amounted to agony. Some had been carried from their beds to start, and were in their night-dresses, and almost all had lost everything they had in the world. The General expressly ordered the married officers to accompany their wives, and intended that all the wounded officers should also be sent over; but in the confusion only two were able to obey.[1] After the ladies were delivered up to Akbar Khan, less than a dozen Jezailchis remained alive. Muhammad Hasan Khan therefore obtained permission of a senior officer, and betook himself with two of his men to the mountains, to provide if possible for the safety of his family.

[1] "Lady Sale insinuated that the married officers abandoned their posts of their own accord. It was by General Elphinstone's express order. Eyre and Waller were wounded."—C. M.

All Akbar's promises of supplies were unfulfilled, and on Monday the 10th the march was resumed. After Khurd Kabul there is a series of tremendous defiles as far as Gandamak. The Afghans crowned the heights and a general massacre took place, in which the Native Infantry were totally destroyed. By evening the force consisted of only 300 men, fifteen officers having fallen since morning. In the midst of this scene of desperation and horror, Mr. Fallon, a Government clerk, saw a soldier of the 44th deliberately shoot an officer off his horse. It was determined to push on by night by a short cut to Jagdallak. The last gun was abandoned, and with it Dr. Cardew, who had been lashed to it in the hope of saving him. He was found dead by the Afghans the next morning.[1] The remnant of that band of heroes, the 1st Troop Bengal Horse Artillery, faint and wounded, had been hewn in pieces while endeavouring with their remaining strength to cut the spokes of their guns.[2] Sergeant M'Nee was the last man who remained, and though severely wounded, managed to spike the gun before he was taken.[3] From thence through the dangerous pass of Jagdallak on the 11th it was one continued conflict.

Akbar Khan now professed his inability to restrain the Ghaljais, whom he had been urging on. The heroism

[1] Dr. Cardew was one of those "fighting doctors" for which the Indian army is famous. He was conspicuous throughout the siege for his zeal and gallantry, and became a great favourite with the soldiery in consequence.

[2] The conduct of the 1st Troop should never be forgotten. An officer writes from Jellalabad, 15th May 1842:—"Gallant and honourable men can scarce restrain their tears when they describe the conduct of these noble men. Mackenzie, a prisoner on parole from Akbar's camp,—every inch a soldier and a gentleman,—entreats not to be talked to on the subject, as he cannot command his feelings. I feel quite honoured in being in the same service with such heroes."

[3] His conduct throughout the captivity was excellent.

of the little band of survivors, among whom Shelton distinguished himself, was all in vain. The General, as a point of honour, steadily refused to lay down arms. On arriving at Jagdallak the little force took up a position behind the ruined walls of a small fort. The General called all the officers to "form line and show a front." At that moment Captain Grant, Assistant Adjutant-General, received a wound in the face which broke his jaw. This was so far from quelling his spirit that, up to the final massacre at Gandamak, he was among the foremost to encourage his companions in arms to fight manfully while they had life and limb. Being at length rendered powerless by wounds in both arms, he ordered an artillery sergeant who had lost his own weapon to draw his sword and rush yet once again on the miscreant Gházis, which the poor fellow did, and, after maiming several of them, himself received a mortal wound.[1]

"The worn-out troops, with no other sustenance than a little raw flesh of some gun bullocks, no other drink than snow, now threw themselves down for a short respite; but their vigilant foes poured in a destructive fire on them as they lay. Captain Bygrave, therefore, with Lieutenant Macartney, M.N.I., and about fifteen or twenty of the 44th, sallied forth to drive the enemy from the heights or perish in the attempt. Unflinchingly they charged up the hill, the enemy retreating before them in the greatest trepidation."[2]

In the evening (Tuesday, 11th January) Captain Skinner, who had been continually passing to and from Akbar to the General, brought a request that the latter would meet the Sirdar at a conference, with Brigadier Shelton and Captain Johnson. Akbar received them hospitably, and assured them that food would be at once supplied to the famishing troops.

---

[1] Private letter of Vincent Eyre. [2] Eyre's *Narrative*, p. 244.

For the first time since the 6th they had a quiet sleep. The next morning the General in vain demanded the necessary escort to enable him to rejoin his force, declaring he preferred death to the dishonour of being separated from them ; but Akbar treacherously held him fast. On this the General wrote to Brigadier Anquetil: "March at once ; there is treachery." Early in the morning (12th January) Major Thain and Captain Skinner rode out, expecting to learn the result of the conference. A Ghaljai, Sir Biland Khan, passed Major Thain, who was in advance, went close up to Skinner, and shot him through the face. He was carried within the enclosure, and died in a few hours.[1]

[1] Mackenzie, in a letter dated 11th May (during his second visit to Jellalabad), thus describes his friend James Skinner :—"My affection and esteem for your brother increased daily as I became more intimately acquainted with his noble nature and amiable qualities. His perfect knowledge of the language and people of Afghanistan, combined with his influence among all with whom he came in contact, from his acknowledged integrity, persuasive and gentlemanly manners (for he had more tact in his intercourse with Afghans than almost any man I ever met), must have raised him to high position had he lived. Skinner's employment in the Commissariat being in abeyance, he acted as Political Assistant to Major Pottinger, and when that distinguished officer was given up as a hostage he appointed Skinner to act for him. To Skinner all our ladies and children and several wounded officers owe their lives, he having induced the Sirdar to demand them of General Elphinstone, and having persuaded the General to comply. Besides exposing himself most gallantly to the unceasing attacks of the enemy, he several times nearly lost his life while endeavouring to open negotiations with Akbar Khan to ensure the safety of the troops ; indeed, the Sirdar remonstrated strongly with him for doing so, entreating him to remain in his camp. I saw James Skinner on the 10th of January at Khurd Kabul for the last time alive, I being a hostage in the Sirdar's hands. On the 14th of January I passed his corpse with much emotion, and heard with pleasure the next day that the Sirdar had caused it to be decently interred, a solitary instance of respect towards his fallen enemies extorted by his involuntary admiration of valour, wisdom, and integrity,—sentiments I have heard Akbar express frequently when Skinner's name was mentioned."

"The whole day was spent by the troops under a galling fire ; sally after sally was made, but again and again the enemy returned to worry and destroy.   Late in the evening it was resolved to push on at all risks, leaving the sick and wounded to their fate."[1]

"About three miles from Jagdallak they arrived at a barrier formed of branches of the prickly holly-oak, well twisted together, about six feet high, and, although many officers and men fell victims to the frantic fanatics, yet at length the united exertions of horses and men forced the barrier down.   The remainder of the 44th were again put into something like order by Captain Bygrave and other officers.[2]"

About 300 of all colours crossed the barrier.   They fought with desperation, and sold their lives dearly.   Brigadier Anquetil and eleven other officers fell at the barrier.   Captain Dodgin of the 44th, a most powerful and active man, who had only one leg, killed five Afghans with his own hand before he was slain.[3]

Those who passed the barrier struggled on until near Gandamak, moving at the rate of two miles an hour, much delay being caused by the anxiety of the poor fellows to bring on their wounded comrades.   As morning dawned on the 13th it was seen that they only mustered about twenty muskets.   The senior officer was captured, "the

---

[1] Eyre's *Narrative*, p. 248.   [2] Wade's MS. Journal.

[3] Lieutenant Greenwood describes the Jagdallak Pass nine months after :—". . . it was impossible to avoid treading on the dead, who were lying in hundreds on the road, the caves on either side were also full, and the bodies were in such a state of preservation that the features of several were recognised as those of old friends by the officers and men.   This pass was in some places not more than ten feet broad. The Afghans had, of course, removed their own slain ; but Akbar himself admitted that 5000 of his people had fallen in the pursuit of General Elphinstone's force."

rest made a resolute stand on a height and drove the enemy
so fiercely down that the Afghans took up their post on the
opposite hill and marked off man after man, officer after
officer, with unerring aim. Parties of the enemy rushed
up at intervals to complete the work of extermination, but
were as often driven back by this dauntless handful of
invincibles.[1]

> ' But those who fought that dreadful day
>   Stood few and faint, but fearless still,' "

until almost every man being wounded, a final onset of the
enemy, sword in hand, completed their annihilation of our
army after eight days of such misery as few troops have
endured except on the retreat from Moscow. Half a dozen
mounted officers made their way somewhat farther, but
Dr. Brydon alone reached Jellalabad.

---

[1] One circumstance relating to the 44th is worthy of mention.
Major Hamlet Wade was in the habit of keeping a journal. He was a
cheerful vigorous man of sense and action, not the least given to fan-
cies, yet he notes under the date, Kabul, 7th July 1841 :—" Sir Robert
Sale inspected the 44th this morning. The colours of the regiment are
very ragged, and when they passed in review I was suddenly startled
by what I took to be a large funeral procession. What put such a
thing into my head I know not, as I was thinking of very different
subjects. I cannot help recording this, it has made such an impression."
This is very striking when one thinks of the after fate of this regiment.
One can only adopt Hamlet's saying —

> "There are more things in heaven and earth
>   Than are dreamt of in your philosophy, Horatio."

CHAPTER XVII.

CAPTIVITY.

"Ah, freedom is a nobil thing,
 Freedom makes man to have lyking,
 And he that aye hath livet free
 May not well knaw the miserie—
 The anger na, the wretchit doom,
 That's couplit with foul thraldom."
Barbour.

THE captives in the power of Akbar Khan consisted of two sets of hostages—those given over in December before leaving cantonments,[1] and Major Pottinger, with Captains Lawrence and Colin Mackenzie, given up on the 8th January; the prisoners (most of them, like General Elphinstone, Brigadier Shelton, and the ladies, detained by treachery), the invalids left at Kabul, and a few captured on the retreat.

On the morning of Sunday the 9th January Pottinger, Lawrence, and Mackenzie were ordered to mount, their horses having been kept saddled and unfed the whole night. Mackenzie carried the wounded private behind him, and Lawrence poor Mrs. Bourne, who showered blessings upon them for not leaving her among these savages as Sultan Ján proposed. After an hour's ride they came to the Khurd Kabul Fort, where Akbar Khan received them very courteously. In the evening Captain Skinner, as we have seen,

---

[1] Captains Conolly, Airey, and Drummond; Lieutenants Warburton, Webb, and Welsh.

returned with the ladies, their husbands and children, several wounded officers, and Mackenzie's Christian servant Jacob, who, after his master was given up, had attached himself to Mrs. Eyre. The joy of Captain and Mrs. Boyd at finding their lost child in Captain Lawrence's arms may be imagined. Lady Macnaghten and Captain Lawrence, from the number of servants attached to the mission, saved most of their property, as did Mrs. Trevor. Lawrence placed his at the service of everybody who was in need, cut up his flannels for the children, and remarks :—"The arrival of my baggage afforded me the great gratification of supplying the gentlemen with many necessary articles of apparel."

Many of the Hindustani servants faithfully stuck by their masters, but numbers of them died from frost-bites or fever. Most of the ladies hid themselves to avoid seeing Akbar, whom they look upon with abhorrence in spite of his courtesy and fine speeches ; but when he asked Lady Macnaghten in grave mockery to forgive him for the murder of her husband, she said she did, and offered him her hand,—his being, as it were, red with her husband's blood ! She afterwards made Captain Lawrence give him the murdered Envoy's riding-horse.

On the morning of the 11th the ladies were packed in kajáwahs, and the whole party started for Tezin, the officers being cautioned to use their swords and pistols in case of attack from the bloodthirsty Gházis who thronged the road. Their hearts were torn by the awful spectacle of the mangled bodies of their late comrades. Captain Lawrence relates :—

"I recognised the body of the venerable old subahdar of the Envoy's escort, Appambal Singh, lying on the road by the side of his dun horse. It was told me that the Afghans offered him his life if he would go over to them. 'No,' replied the grand old soldier ; 'for forty-one years I have eaten the Company's salt, and I will now show myself ready to die for them.'"

On the 12th the captives marched from the fort at Tezin, taking with them a few privates who had been saved by some of the chiefs, among them Miller, a servant of General Elphinstone's, and M'Glynn, a poor simple Irishman who, being wounded and too lame to keep up with the others, was about to give himself over to certain death by lying down in the snow, when Colin Mackenzie came up. M'Glynn told him he should die if he were left behind, which was self-evident. Mackenzie made him mount behind himself, and his gallant Turkoman carried them both up places fit only for a mountain-goat. When the good horse could no longer carry double, Mackenzie got off and walked, though suffering greatly from his foot, which was frost-bitten, making M'Glynn get into the saddle and rest his legs by using the stirrups.[1]

They reached the Fort of Sarubi, sixteen miles from Tezin, that evening, and were joined by Dr. Magrath and three privates. The doctor, who was wounded, owed his life to an Afghan, who recognised him as having shown kindness to some of his sick friends at Kabul. The party were thus furnished with medical aid, of which many of them were sorely in need. The Afghan remedy for frost-

---

[1] This poor soldier lived with him throughout most of their captivity, and did all he could to show his gratitude. Captain Mackenzie made room for him in the little apartment where he himself lodged, and he messed with Jacob. Although a Roman Catholic, he was always present and most earnest and attentive at their daily Bible-reading and prayer, which Mackenzie conducted. The latter took pains to instruct him, and when they parted M'Glynn seized his hand and wept as if losing the only friend he ever had. He took his pension and remained behind in Calcutta, but there was reason to hope that the good seed had fallen into good ground. It is satisfactory to know that the gallant horse also survived, though when he reached Firozpur he was in such a state of disease from a twelvemonth's starvation, that his master left him with Mr. Clerk, under whose kind care he completely recovered.

bites, consisting of a cold poultice of cow-dung and water, proved most efficacious.

Captain Lawrence writes :—

" We had this night to bivouac on the snow, and, by surrounding the ladies and children with Lady Macnaghten's trunks and my own, we formed a slight shelter for them from the piercing wind ; and with some tea and sherry which she and I had saved, we passed the night with less suffering than we dared anticipate."

" 13th.—Marched for Jagdallak through the same scenes of suffering and death as the two previous days. From among the miserable survivors I contrived this day to save two—one a subahdar of the 37th N.I., whom I took up on my horse ; and the other an old Hindu treasurer of Captain Bygrave's, whom I induced a good, feeling Afghan to carry behind him on his horse. Hundreds of miserable Sepoys and camp-followers were huddled together on each side of the road. They begged us with the most heartrending supplications to assist them, but, alas ! no aid could we afford ; and indeed they were beyond human help, for the Afghans having stripped them, the greater number were, from the effects of the frost, quite incapable of moving. Besides which, we were surrounded by a guard of Akbar's retainers.

" Passing by the ruined enclosure at Jagdallak, within which the remnant of the force had sought shelter, we beheld a spectacle more terrible than any we had previously witnessed, the whole interior being one crowded mass of bloody corpses."

(Here they found Akbar Khan encamped, and learned that General Elphinstone, Brigadier Shelton, and Captain Johnson, were prisoners in his hands since the previous day.)

"During the whole of these trying marches I felt truly proud of my countrymen and women ; all bore up so nobly and heroically against hunger, cold, fatigue, and other privations as to call forth the admiration even of our Afghan guards." [1]

14th January, Jagdallak. — Akbar Khan carried off his prisoners at sunrise over a difficult pass, and after a fatiguing journey of ten hours, during which they only made twenty-four miles, they were refused admittance into the Fort of Katz, and had again to bivouac in the open air, a cutting wind blowing strongly. The next day (15th) they crossed the Kabul river, which was up to the girths of the horses and extremely rapid, Akbar and Sultan Ján themselves carrying over two of the ladies behind them. Unmeasured abuse and threats were heaped upon the captives by the inhabitants of the forts and villages near which they passed.

One ruffian nearly frightened poor Mrs. Mainwaring to death. She had unfortunately fallen from her pony, and was seated by the roadside with her baby in her arms crying, when Captain Lawrence overtook her, put her up again, and rode by her till they rejoined the column. After a march of sixteen miles they were lodged in the town of Targhari, where a great number of Hindu merchants resided. These showed much kindness and compassion to the captives, and many of their own poor countrymen found a refuge at this place, and received daily food from them. The next day (Sunday 16th) they halted, and for the first time since leaving Kabul were able to join together in Divine worship — a melancholy, but deeply impressive service, interrupted by the tears and long-drawn sobs of some of their number. The town was so hostile that Akbar dared not let his prisoners stay. They marched the next morning under a strong escort. Akbar and Sultan Ján saw every one of the captives start, and then closed up behind them, thus preventing an attack from the fierce

[1] *Forty Years in India,* by Lieut.-General Sir G. St. P. Lawrence.

Ghaljais who swarmed around. At last, at 2 P.M., they reached Badiabad, a new and strong fort in the valley of Laghmán, belonging to Muhammad Shah Khan Ghilzai. There Akbar left them at first in charge of a consummate rogue named Musa Khan, who defrauded them of their supplies, and twice stole one of Lady Macnaghten's favourite cats for the sake of the reward of twenty rupees which she offered for its recovery. He was, however, soon succeeded by Mirza Bawudin Khan, who, though rough in manner, secretly befriended the prisoners.

There is no doubt that Afghans and Europeans get on much better together than Europeans and Hindustanis. The Afghans are an extremely hardy, bold, independent race, very intelligent, with a ready fund of conversation and pleasantry which renders them very agreeable companions.

At Badiabad the captives remained eleven weeks, to 10th April. There were only five rooms for the party, so that from five to ten ladies or officers occupied each. The soldiers who were able to move were located in a stable. In a small shed lay a poor lad about sixteen, a son of Sergeant Wade, whose extremities had mortified from frost, and whose agony was beyond description, until in about a week death relieved him. In the same shed also lay a fine young soldier of the 44th, with both his legs broken by a gun-shot, whose sufferings were most acute. The sick soldiers used to send for Captain Mackenzie to read to them. Among others he visited the sergeant-major of the ———, who was in a dreadful state from his wounds mortifying, and read the Scriptures to him and his comrades. It was almost impossible to breathe in the underground place in which they were. The unfortunate sergeant-major, a very handsome, fine soldier, had enlisted in consequence of having committed murder, and died a dreadful death. Mackenzie kept poor M'Glynn in his own room, and carefully tended him. Captain Waller, Mr. Riley, Mr. Fallon, and good Jacob, were his other companions. Conductor Riley and his wife were very superior people, he being a gentleman's son who had enlisted. They were likely to be confounded with the poor privates, as the Afghans only understood the two classes of officers and "white men;" and some of the ladies gave themselves great airs towards Mrs. Riley, which was not only most unfeeling but absurd. Captain Mackenzie therefore chose to live with them that he might be useful in raising their station, for which they were most grateful.[1] As for Jacob Augustine, Mackenzie said he never saw such a fellow. As a servant he was invaluable, full of resource, a capital cook, and always on the look-out to promote his master's comfort. Every one who knew Mackenzie knew Jacob, whom he called his "man Friday." When out skirmishing he would often find Jacob with a carbine close to his heels. "Jacob! what are you doing here? Go back directly!" was shouted in vain. Five minutes after Jacob would be at his master's back again. He behaved in all respects as a truly Christian man. Once, however, he was, when alone, caught by the Afghans, and threatened with instant death unless he repeated the Muhammadan profession of faith—"There is no God but one, and Muhammad is the prophet of God." Taken unawares, he did so. He went at once to his master, and confessed what he had done; but for many days his anguish of mind was great at having, for fear of death, denied his Lord. Many of our soldiers did the same without feeling the sin of it; but the Hindus in general staunchly refused to save their lives by becoming Moslem.

Public worship was regularly conducted every Sunday by Lawrence and Mackenzie in turns. Jacob had picked

---

[1] Mr. Riley afterwards received a lieutenant's commission, and was Commissary of Ordnance at Delhi.

up a Bible and two prayer books, the former marked
with the name of Private Thomas M'Dowell, 13th Light Infantry, who, poor fellow, must have perished on the retreat.

A copy of John Newton's *Cardiphonia* had been given to
Mackenzie on leaving England by her who afterwards
became his wife. This, with all his other property, had
been abandoned in the Nishán Fort; but some time after
an Afghan came into cantonments offering books for sale,
and this among them, with a large stain of blood upon it.
Mackenzie pounced upon it, and bought it for two rupees;
it was a great source of reading to the captives.

The last time Mackenzie saw his own watch Muhammad Akbar asked him to wind it up. He did so, sorely
tempted to give it one turn too much and break the
spring, but refrained and courteously handed it back. The
Afghan gentlemen are extremely sensitive to courtesy,
having excellent manners themselves. Mackenzie was
therefore most punctiliously polite, "hypocritically so," as
he used to say with a laugh, which made him a favourite
with them. So was Captain Bygrave, but Akbar could not
bear that "grim and grumpy hero Pottinger." Their severe
trials, and the close intimacy in which the prisoners lived, of
course brought into full relief all their good and evil qualities. Conventional polish was a good deal rubbed off and
replaced by a plainness of speech quite unheard of in good
society. For example, Mackenzie himself was so provoked
by an exhibition of callous selfishness, combined with an
attempt to make him the medium of telling Akbar a downright falsehood, that he told the culprit "he wouldn't marry
her if there was not another woman in the world, and that,
except an Irish perception of fun, she had not a single good
quality that he was aware of!" After so outrageous a
speech, it is not surprising that she complained to the other
ladies that "Captain Mackenzie was becoming quite unbear-

able." Though compelled to occupy the same room at night the most perfect propriety was observed, the men of the party " clearing out," as they expressed it, early in the morning, and leaving the ladies alone. They used to relate with much amusement that on one occasion a knock was heard at the door of the court where the gentlemen were washing themselves. "Don't come in," cried they; "we are not dressed." "Never mind," was the old lady's reply, "it's only *me !*"

Captain Lawrence was entrusted with the arduous task of dividing whatever food, money, or cloth was supplied by the Sirdar, and found it quite impossible to give satisfaction. At last he made over the thankless office to a committee of three, and not even the request of the ladies could prevail on him to be a member of it. Mrs. Eyre, having but one gown, begged a lady who had trunks full to lend her another. The answer was, she could not spare any !

At the end of January Bawudin Khan brought 1000 rupees from Muhammad Akbar, which Captain Lawrence distributed, giving fifty to each officer and widow and dividing the rest among the European soldiers ; besides a parcel of chintzes, longcloth, needles, and thread for the ladies and women. The gentlemen twisted the soft cotton into thread by rolling it in their hands. Mrs. Eyre, having but one needle, commissioned Captain Mackenzie to persuade Lady Sale, who had eight or ten, to spare her one or two ; but, though he never exercised greater diplomacy in his life, he was unsuccessful. Needles and pins being so precious, Mackenzie contracted a habit, which he retained all his life, to the amusement of his friends, of picking up every stray needle or pin he could see.

But if some of the captives were selfish, some were very generous, like young Mrs. Mainwaring, who, on receiving a box of useful articles from her husband at Jellalabad,

most liberally distributed the contents among the other
ladies, who were much in need.

His fellow-captives describe Mackenzie as the life of the
party, keeping up their spirits by his trust in God, and
enlivening them by many a joke. On one occasion he
volunteered to tell the ladies a story. As he had a special
gift for narration, they all eagerly listened, and he began,
in nursery fashion : "Once on a time there was a young
lady who pre-tend-ed to be ve-ry good in order to get a
hus-band. And when she had got a hus-band she was not
very good. Was that right ?" "*No!*" roared all the men,
who were drawn up behind him. They asserted that the
ladies were quite confused, because each felt that that was
what she herself had done, which accusation the fairer half
of the company strenuously denied.

Several of the other captives were no whit behind
Mackenzie in indomitable spirit and cheerfulness. He
himself reported of George Lawrence that he was "ever
cheerful and never despairing." But in Mackenzie's case
this was united with so intense a feeling of the disgrace to
our arms, and of the peril to our women, as to make outward
liveliness more the result of duty than of natural feeling.
A letter of his to George Broadfoot gives some glimpses of
his state of mind. In forwarding copies of Mackenzie's
letters, Broadfoot says :—"The other prisoners wrote often,
but very great caution was necessary, as all letters were
sent open and translated to Muhammad Akbar by a Delhi
college student with him. The first letters received were
from some of the ladies and full of praises of their treatment. One or two from the men were in the same strain ;
but they contrived to give us a hint that the praises were
compulsory, and that we must do likewise to ensure the
delivery of our letters. Alas ! we know but too well the
real story. You will observe the religious tone of Colin's

letter. It is not more so than his letters and conversation on all occasions. He has been very religious for several years—ever since his wife's death."

"BADIABAD (in the valley of) LAGHMÁN,
30th January 1842.

"MY DEAR GEORGE,—The receipt of your letter yesterday sent a gleam of sunshine on my path, which has lately been most dark and gloomy. Many sincere thanks for your affectionate sympathy, as also for your generosity in sharing your little property with me. The clothes were most acceptable, as they will enable me to keep at bay the vermin which have almost devoured me. I am pretty well again. My frost-bitten feet have almost recovered, one place only continues to slough, and in that the inflammation is checked. My heart is almost broken by the fearful calamities and sufferings of my friends, who have been so remorselessly butchered. In writing later I hope to relate the dreadful tale. You say the conduct of the chief has been *noble.* It is well. I know not how this captivity may end ; but my firm trust is in God, who has hitherto so miraculously preserved my life. Our party bear up wonderfully. The ladies' demeanour reflects infinite credit on them, and the poor children prove the truth of the saying, that God tempers the wind to the shorn lamb. That you, my dear and much valued friend, are alive, and, I trust, well, is a great comfort to me. Give my love to all friends, especially Dawes and Champion. . . . Thank God, my faithful friend Jacob has escaped unhurt, and is zealous and assiduous as ever. Give Bode [1] his salam. Give me news of yourself and of all I love.—Affectionately yours, C. M."

On the 19th of February the monotony of captivity was very unpleasantly diversified by a tremendous earthquake. An unusual degree of heat and stillness pervaded the air. Eyre relates :—"At 11 A.M. we were suddenly alarmed by a violent rocking of the earth, which momentarily increased

[1] Broadfoot's German servant.

to such a degree that we could with difficulty maintain our balance. Large masses of the lofty walls that encompassed us fell in on all sides with a thundering crash; a loud subterraneous rumbling was heard, as of a boiling sea of liquid lava, and wave after wave seemed to lift up the ground on which we stood, causing every building to rock to and fro like a floating vessel. Most providentially, all the ladies with their children made a timely rush into the open air at the commencement of the earthquake, and entirely escaped injury. General Elphinstone, being bedridden, was rescued by the intrepidity of his servant Moore, a private of H.M.'s 44th, who rushed into his room and carried him forth in his arms. The poor General was greatly beloved by the soldiery, of whom there were few who would not have acted in a similar manner to save his life."

G. St. P. Lawrence relates:—"The whole party assembled in the centre of the court near a low building, when suddenly the entire structure disappeared as through a trapdoor, disclosing to us a yawning chasm. The stoutest hearts quailed at the appalling sight."

A tremor in the earth was perceptible throughout the remainder of the day, and the Afghans were, for the time being, overwhelmed with terror. Brigadier Shelton had quarrelled with almost every one of the prisoners except Mackenzie, with whom he happened to be sitting on a bench on the roof of the house when the shock took place. He looked round fiercely to see who was shaking his bench. Mackenzie cried, "It's an earthquake, Brigadier!" and, calling to Lady Sale, made for the stairs, which were cracking and falling about them, and, by God's mercy, they all reached the bottom in safety. In the evening Shelton came up and said: "Mackenzie, I want to speak to you." "Very well, Brigadier." In a solemn tone, to make him feel the enormity of the offence: "Mackenzie, you went downstairs *first* to-day ; " to which the latter coolly replied : " It's the fashion in an earthquake, Brigadier. I learnt it among the Spaniards in Manilla ! "

An old Munshi named Nadir Beg from Delhi, formerly attached to the Kabul Embassy, had accompanied Mackenzie from India. He and his son, Bahádar Beg, a boy of scarce twelve years of age, inhabited an upper apartment in one of the lofty corner towers of the fort. The poor old man was completely bedridden from frost-bites, and when the walls began to totter and the roof momentarily threatened to fall in, he called aloud to his son to save himself by instant flight; but he nobly refused to leave his father's side, declaring that, if it were God's will, he would perish with him. Although the room above them fell in with a crash, and their own roof partly gave way, they escaped uninjured, and survived to return to their own country together. The old man was justly proud of his son, and loved to dilate on his heroic conduct. Shocks of earthquake recurred for many days after, sometimes almost hourly.

The state of General Elphinstone called forth the strongest sympathies of every one, with the exception of Brigadier Shelton, who openly avowed his intention to cast the whole onus of blame on his unhappy chief. Officially, of course, the commanding officer was the responsible person ; but, considering the General's bodily sufferings and infirmities, his second in command was really far more so. Captain Eyre mentions in a private letter :—

" Although we all, as much as possible, studied to avoid the discussion of late events in the General's presence, still remarks would occasionally creep out unguardedly, that grated terribly on his wounded spirit ; and on one occasion he was stirred up almost to frenzy by a conversation he unfortunately overheard, and which made him passionately declare to a friend who strove to comfort him that no one could blame him more than he blamed himself. On another occasion he was bitterly lamenting the folly he had committed in forsaking a happy home in his infirm state of body to seek 'the bubble reputation' in a distant land, and he most affectingly concluded his self reproach by applying the lines from Gray's *Ode* to himself—

> "Ambition this shall tempt to rise,
>   Then whirl the wretch from high,
>   To bitter scorn a sacrifice
>   And grinning infamy."

At the beginning of March all the unfortunate Hindustanis who had been crippled by the frost, and were consequently suffering excruciating torture, were dragged out of the fort to perish. This was believed to be by order of the owner of the Fort, Muhammad Shah Khan Ghilzai; for Mirza Bawudin, though compelled to obey, readmitted several of them at night, and Lawrence having appealed to Akbar Khan, remonstrating against this cruelty, those who had remained within reach were let in again.

This illustrates the savage hardness of heart of the Afghans; though, remembering the atrocities which have been committed in European warfare, and that even in our own times, under Pelissier, the French retained so much of the barbarian as to suffocate a number of Arabs in a cave, we cannot say that this characteristic is peculiar to them. The poor frost-bitten servants were, in Akbar's opinion, "totally useless, and their maintenance very expensive, therefore he ordered them to be sent away!" It is to Christianity alone that we owe the idea that helplessness is a sufficient claim for help, whether in man or beast.

The Afghans were perfectly aware of the strong affection which knit Mackenzie and Broadfoot together, and Gaffur Khan, one of the most able of the chiefs, who was partly for us and partly against us, now told the latter that his determined and virulent hostility against the Afghans, and his unsparing use of the sword, would destroy Mackenzie. Broadfoot turned upon him and said : "Gaffur Khan, you know that if I were ordered to attack Badiabad, and had to blow open the gate, and if I knew that Mackenzie was on the other side and must be blown to atoms, I would apply the match with my own hand." The chief replied : " I *know you* would ; and there are but three Feringhis in Afghanistan who would do the same—you, Captain Havelock, and Mackenzie himself." "And yet," as Mackenzie once said, in speaking of the superiority in affection of strong natures over weak ones, "Broadfoot's tenderness for me was something *absurd.*"

Mackenzie's correspondence with Broadfoot was for some time interdicted ; at last the following arrived :—

" *27th March.*

"MY DEAR GEORGE,— . . . I am not to blame for not having written to you lately, as our late custodian told me a note to your address could not possibly be conveyed. I received all your, and Orr's, and Cunningham's gifts, of which I kept part, distributing the rest. Many hearty thanks to them and yourself. Pray say all that is kind to them and my other friends for their most acceptable letters. To Dawes I feel especially grateful for his unceasing and truly Christian kindness to my poor friend Champion, of whose death I heard with mingled feelings of regret and joy,—the latter arising from my knowledge of the manner of his end. . . . Up to this point we have constant shocks night and day. All are in good health ; the wounded are recovering, and so are the frost-bitten. My feet are quite well. I am anything but downhearted as to myself ; but I confess I am still most anxious about our women, children, and wounded, in case of any unadvised resolve on the part of 'the head and front of the offending,' and my thoughts are melancholy enough when I look back ; but God's will be done, and I think I can say : 'Though He slay me, yet will I trust in Him.' I was really gratified by the recollection of my friends the Sappers; say so to them. [Our men sent him all sorts of kind messages.—G. B.]   Some of your poor fellows used to fight under my command, and right well did they behave in divers sharp encounters.   Alas! alas! where are they now?   God bless and prosper you.—Ever yours most affectionately,

" C. M."

Broadfoot adds :—" We have great hopes that the Ghaljais will not permit Akbar to murder or carry them off, but retain them to make peace with us.   Akbar is of a violent temper, and, when Governor of Jellalabad, noted for cruelty and treachery, even among Afghans."

In the middle of March Akbar was wounded by one of his own servants, and Shah Shujah murdered.   General Sale having defeated Akbar on the 7th April, capturing his camp and guns, the chiefs proposed putting all the captives to death; but Akbar would not hear of it, probably fearing reprisals on his own family, who were in the power of the British in India.   He determined, however, to move them from Badiabad to a place at a greater distance from the British force at Jellalabad.   Just before starting Muhammad Shah Khan plundered Lady Macnaghten and Captain Lawrence of everything of value he could find,— her shawls and jewels being estimated at from £10,000 to £15,000.   On the 11th April the poor privates were left behind, and the rest of the party marched off, meeting Akbar on the road, who spoke frankly of his defeat and of the gallantry of our men, which nothing could exceed, old Sale being conspicuous at their head on his white charger. Captain Lawrence remonstrated with the Sirdar for exposing helpless women and children to so much hardship, and exhorted him to send them at once to Jellalabad, as such a step would redound to his credit.   Unluckily Muhammad Shah Khan came up and seated himself by Akbar's palki. On hearing Lawrence's proposal, Muhammad Shah Khan turned to him with a diabolical look and said : "So long as you can ride, you *shall* ride ; when you cannot, you shall walk ; when you cannot walk, you shall be dragged ; and when you cannot be dragged, *your throats shall be cut.*" Lawrence jumped up, exclaiming : "Muhammad Shah Khan, warriors don't talk thus to men whose hands are tied." Both Akbar and Muhammad Shah Khan then apologised ; but it was a glimpse of the real savage nature of the latter. Poor General Elphinstone was much exhausted by the fatigue, and seemed sinking into the grave. Captain Lawrence says :—"He told me repeatedly he wished and even prayed for death, as, he said, sleeping and waking, the horrors of that dreadful retreat were before his eyes. We all felt deeply for him, and tried to soothe and comfort the old man ; but it was of no avail, as he was evidently heartbroken, and repeatedly expressed deep regret that he had not fallen in the retreat." Day after day they marched till they encamped outside the fort of Sarubi, where they remained four days, so that they enjoyed a quiet Sunday on the 17th. On Tuesday, 19th, they marched sixteen miles to Tezin, though it poured the whole day. They were all drenched to the skin. Mackenzie and Eyre passed the night in the stable with their horses, the rain dripping over them till morning. This day's exposure was the death-blow to General Elphinstone. He was brought into a room with a fire where Muhammad Akbar and his father-in-law Muhammad Shah Khan, held a conference with Pottinger and Lawrence, and the chief determined to send an officer to General Pollock to negotiate. "The Sirdar proposed to send Captain Mackenzie as a person he trusted would act with justice towards him and his party, as well as for the English."—(Pottinger to General Pollock, 20th April 1842.)

"*20th April.*—It poured all day, and a severe shock of

earthquake made the ladies rush out of the fort. Mrs. Waller, who had travelled sixteen miles the previous day cramped up in a kajáwah on a baggage-camel in the dreadful weather just described, gave birth to a daughter—the fourth birth since they left Kabul.   Fearing a rescue of the prisoners, all except the General, the Wallers, Eyre, Pottinger, Mackenzie, and Dr. Magrath, were marched off at sunrise on the 22d to the valley of Zjandeh.   There was still plenty both of ice and snow.   Somewhat later those left behind were hurried off to a small fort two miles higher up the valley of Tezin.   In the confusion Mrs. Waller with her two children seemed to be quite forgotten. Captain Waller, who could not speak Persian, applied to Mackenzie, who went to Akbar Khan and represented to him how shocking a thing it was to leave a lady and two children to have their throats cut.   An old kajáwah was found and strung on a pole ; the young mother and her baby were packed into it, and carried by two Afghans, and sustained no material injury.   The General, though so weak as to be unable to stand, was made to ride the whole way, propped up by a man on either side.   He did not survive many hours, dying that same night.   Vincent Eyre records that he "exhibited a measure of Christian benevolence, patience, and high-souled fortitude which gained him the affectionate regard and admiring esteem of all who witnessed his prolonged sufferings, and who regarded him as the victim less of his own faults than of the errors of others."

CHAPTER XVIII.

*"What a tragic history is this we are making! but yet how noble a struggle to be engaged in! Enough to make men of women."—
Letter of Major George Broadfoot.*

IT is necessary to diverge a little from biography to history to give some idea of how it fared with the garrison of Jellalabad, who were far more disadvantageously placed than the force at Kabul; and then to sketch the action taken by the Government of India, and the indomitable firmness of the General who, in spite of obstacles on every side, vindicated our national honour and rescued the captives from lifelong slavery. If any of the details appear tedious, it must be remembered that, as credit has been both unfairly claimed and unjustly withheld, these details are necessary to make it clear how great a debt of gratitude is due by his country to the honoured memory of George Pollock, and, next to him, to that of George Broadfoot.

It was with difficulty Sale had reached Gandamak,[1] two marches from Jellalabad. George Broadfoot says:— "From the 9th of October we have fought every step of the way." On the 10th November Sale received the Envoy's summons to return to Kabul. As we have seen, a Council of War decided that it was impracticable to do so.

---

[1] Sale had returned to Butkhak on the 12th October, and remained there eight days. On 20th, being reinforced, rejoined the force at Khurd Kabul; 22d, Tezin; 26th, with difficulty got to Gandamak.

He pushed on to Jellalabad by the 13th. He had only one day's provisions; the place was open on all sides, with excellent cover for the enemy up to the very walls, and he had only 2000 men to defend an *enceinte* of 2300 yards. The very next morning they were closely invested, but they sallied forth and routed the foe, who suffered severely. After this they were left quiet for a fortnight, during which time supplies came in fast. The whole force set to work to make the place defensible. They made temporary parapets with packsaddles, built bastions, destroyed cover, broke down forts, dug trenches and a huge tank, made roads, barracks, cattle-sheds, fascines, fuzes, and a flour mill, and worked without intermission, except when fighting, till the middle of February, with Christmas day for their only rest. They routed the enemy again on the 1st December; and Turábáz Khan, the Chief of Lálpura, rendered most essential service by bringing in money from Peshawar.

Major Hamlet Wade writes:— "Our communications have been cut off on all sides, and the only mode of sending a letter is by enclosing it in wax, which the kasid secretes on his person."

On the 9th three horsemen brought the official order from General Elphinstone for the evacuation of Jellalabad, in accordance with the treaty made by Sir William Macnaghten, which Pottinger, though strongly opposed to it, yet thought it his duty to sign. Broadfoot as usual discusses principles, he wrote to Mr. Prinsep :—

"Nor can they include us in any convention. A General, not the absolute ruler of a State, can only capitulate for those under his own orders, for the instant he capitulates he ceases to command—abdicates, *ipso facto*—all authority over all not in the same straits as himself. He yields to force; those not subject to that force are not bound to yield to commands he, no longer a free agent, is compelled to give."

Major Wade's journal reflects the feeling of the garrison: —" Thank God ! they return with our refusal to comply."

"On the 13th January, about one o'clock, a horseman was observed from the direction of Kabul. It turned out to be Dr. Brydon.[1] Treachery of the enemy and supineness on our part have finished the tragedy."

Broadfoot, thinking that neither the General nor the Political Officer, Major G. H. Macgregor, rightly estimated his position, begged Captain Havelock to represent the true state of things to the General, and to tell him that if he were not prepared to defend the place to the last extremity, he should retreat that night while it was still possible. The General resolved to stand his ground. But on the 21st they received the distressing intelligence of the repulse of Wild's force at Ali Masjid. A Council of War of the five commanding officers of Corps was summoned. Sale avowed his opinion that they had nothing to hope from Government, and that he agreed with Macgregor that we should accept the terms which Akbar offered for the evacuation of the country. The General and Macgregor stated that they were resolved to yield, and to negotiate for a safe retreat. Happily there was one indomitable spirit who was determined to resist. This was George Broadfoot. The Council was of so stormy a character that Broadfoot proposed an adjournment, that the members might have time to cool down. As they went out Colonel Monteath told Broadfoot that he, too, considered it their duty to hold out. At night Broadfoot visited Captain Havelock, and found that he fully agreed with him, though he disapproved of the warmth of his language. Broadfoot therefore wrote down all he had to

---

[1] Dr. Brydon was severely wounded. "His collectedness in trying circumstances, and his caution and accuracy of memory, are remarkable." — (G. Broadfoot).

say, and read it at the next meeting, when Havelock expressed his entire concurrence, though he had no vote.

Macgregor, who was the chief speaker, urged that Government had abandoned them, referred to his own experience of men in high places,[1] and expressed perfect confidence that the Afghans would observe *this* treaty. Broadfoot denied that Government would abandon them, and maintained that even in that case they were bound *by duty to their country,* no matter how the Governor-General in Council might treat them. He also strongly maintained that no obedience was due to a superior officer who was no longer a free agent, and that General Elphinstone, as a prisoner, was only entitled to command those in the same dilemma as himself.

But the council agreed to treat for surrender, Captain Oldfield being the only member of it who sided with Broadfoot in voting against any treaty to evacuate the place.

Broadfoot proposed to demand all our captives before starting ; Sale and Macgregor opposed this, as it might prevent the present terms from being carried out, and said they would be restored to us at Peshawar. After a sharp discussion between the three, Broadfoot's proposition was lost. He then proposed that if we were to evacuate the country it should be done as a military operation without the knowledge of the enemy, by fighting our way; but neither could he carry this point. After the voting Broadfoot could not forbear "congratulating them on the figure they would cut if a relieving force should arrive just as they were marching out," whereupon Dennie stoutly declared that in that case he would not go. Broadfoot replied : "We should make you ; faith must be kept !" The messengers returned to Akbar, but next day the ditch round the works was begun. This greatly raised the men's

---

[1] As A.D.C. to Lord Auckland.

spirits, which were depressed by seeing Councils assemble without knowing what had been decided on. The cheerful manner in which all the garrison worked incessantly at the defences did them the greatest credit, Broadfoot being the engineer.

The prospects of the garrison were anything but bright, but their resolution did not fail. Major Wade writes :— "All hope, I think, is cut off, and here we must die like soldiers, sword in hand. The unfortunate camp-followers come tumbling in—fifteen yesterday, and two to-day. *9th February.*—Followers every day coming in. We have only one hundred and fifty rounds of ammunition per man. This is a bad prospect; but I trust in that Almighty Providence that has hitherto so wonderfully aided us."

In due time an answer from the chiefs arrived, requiring that all the chief gentlemen should put their seals to the agreement as a proof of their sincerity. Broadfoot had not been idle in arguing with his friends on the subject, so that when the council of war reassembled, and Sale and Macgregor urged the officers to affix their seals, a good many supported Broadfoot's view, that this suspicion of their sincerity entitled them to break off the negotiation. General Sale used strong language about their opposition, and such high words followed that they adjourned for an hour, and met again in good humour. Colonels Dennie and Monteath and Captain Abbott had now come round to the conclusion that they should hold on, and a letter proposed by the two Colonels, which practically put an end to the negotiation, was adopted by all; Sale consenting to be guided by the opinion of the council, and Macgregor alone "hoping they would not have cause to regret having refused the terms he could now get for them." The messenger was sent back to Kabul, and the very day after they had thus proved their manhood, "kasids came in from Pollock saying that the 3d Dragoons, etc., are on the way to join him, and that his instructions are on no account to allow this garrison to be forced to make a disastrous retreat; so we are not to be deserted, thank God!"[1]

Akbar, finding there was little hope of carrying Jellalabad by arms, had just blockaded it, but a most unexpected trial was at hand. They were rejoicing at the news of succour, when an hour or so after all their defences were ruined in a moment by the same earthquake so severely felt by the captives. "It brought down the house. This was followed instantly by a more severe shock, and the frightful roar under our feet, crashing of houses falling, and darkness from the dust caused thereby, I shall never forget. It was awful in the extreme."[2] This tremendous convulsion threw down a great part of the defences of Jellalabad, and laid the place completely open to the enemy. "Sir Robert has determined on repairing the walls and still standing on here in preference to retreating, I am happy to say."

"*Feb.* 20.—By night yesterday the exertions of the officers and men had made the place proof against surprise, Broadfoot and his sappers being foremost in repairing the defences. We sleep fully accoutred at our alarm posts." Brigadier Monteath had been going his rounds, his two orderlies were the only men killed, and he himself was buried in the ruins. General Sale, hearing of the mishap of his companion-in-arms, rushed to the rescue, and, in his honest zeal, laid hold of the Brigadier's head, which was the only part of him visible. Monteath, though a man of talent, information, and an excellent soldier, was a great dandy, and took most particular care of his wig, which he oiled and dressed throughout the siege with great tenderness and pains. No sooner did he feel some one tugging at his head than he awoke to consciousness and cried : " Let

[1] Wade's Journal.   [2] *Ibid.*

go my head!" Sale, in his joy at finding he was alive, tugged ten times harder, whereupon the Brigadier exclaimed in wrath : "Who is the scoundrel tugging at my *hair?*" which speedily caused his gallant old friend to let go.

The journal continues :—"Earthquakes daily for some time, and the enemy commenced a system of almost daily attacks on our foragers and the fort itself. By the 28th February the defences had risen like magic, and in many places stronger than before."

"17th March.—The advisability of attacking Akbar was mooted yesterday by Broadfoot and Havelock."

On the 24th March the enemy made a bold attack, but were routed by Broadfoot, as he quaintly expressed it, "in a manner which prevented their ever returning," and it is said they despaired of success from that time. Broadfoot was severely wounded in the body.

"1st April.—Our men captured a flock of 500 sheep and goats, a most valuable prize." When these were divided among the troops, the 25th Native Infantry said meat was not so necessary for them as for their white brethren, and requested that their share might be given to the 13th, between whom and themselves there existed a romantic friendship which ought not to be forgotten.

Sale, though as brave a soldier as ever lived, had a singular dread of responsibility ; but urged by Broadfoot and Havelock, and authorised by a council of war (which falsified the old saying that "a council of war never fights"), he—having armed and embodied about 1200 of the camp-followers—sallied forth at daybreak on the 7th April with 1800 men (almost the entire garrison), and routed Akbar at the head of fully 6000. Akbar fled early.

Broadfoot, who was unable to stir owing to his wound, writes with his usual modesty :—

"I was able heartily to rejoice that my misfortune brought

conspicuously forward one of the best officers in the service, Captain Havelock of the 13th, who that day, to the public advantage, took my place."

"10*th April.*—Grain is coming in abundantly.

"16*th April.*—This morning General Pollock marched in and encamped on the Kabul face. We had four months' English news to receive."

The heroism of the garrison could hardly be surpassed, and as they had nothing but water to drink, their discipline, good conduct, and healthiness were most remarkable, but they did not *relieve themselves* as has been sometimes asserted. They held out nobly, and gloriously defeated the enemy, but they were under 2500 men, and could neither get down to Peshawar nor advance to Kabul. That Pollock relieved them is proved, not only by the opposition he encountered in the Khaiber (though at the head of a force at least four times the number of the garrison), but by the words of Sale's own despatch.[1]

The heat at Jellalabad from the end of April was tremendous, 105° to 110° in the shade. Everbody who could do so lived in underground chambers called ty-khánás. Broadfoot dates a letter "from my den six feet under ground."

There were several remarkable men in the garrison of Jellalabad. First, the gallant warm-hearted old General himself, who, as everybody knows, was Colonel of the 13th Queen's. At one time the state of that regiment was very bad. After the fearful mortality in Ava it was recruited with the refuse of all the jails in London, and was in a frightful state of insubordination. One officer was shot, so were several non-commissioned officers, and threats

[1] "The relief of the place was effected by the victorious advance through the Khaiber of the army under Major-General Pollock, C.B." —Sale's *Despatch*, 16th April 1842.

of assassination were constantly sent to Colonel Sale. The gallant veteran used to come on parade the next morning with the letter in his pocket, and give the order to load with blank cartridge. "Present—fire," sitting all the time on horseback in front of them, and then say: "Ah, it's not my fault if you don't shoot me!" The regiment was brought into order by severe punishment. For some time perhaps as many as four culprits in the morning and four in the evening would receive up to eight hundred lashes each for crimes such as attempting to stab an officer; and when they came out of hospital the smallest sign of insubordination, such as an impertinent reply, was visited by three hundred lashes, after which discipline they became like lambs, or, as one of their officers said, "mere babies, you could do anything with them," and their noble conduct at Jellalabad is a matter of history.

Sale was beloved by all, men and officers alike. Captain Hamlet Wade, when quite overworked by having to act as Quartermaster-General besides his own duty as Brigade Major, comforts himself with the thought: "But it's a pleasure to serve old Sale."

Nothing could induce Sale to behave himself as a General should do. He used to ride about two miles ahead of his troops in spite of all remonstrances, and in action would fight like a private. Wade, who loved him like a son, used to reason with him, and, in cool moments, he would allow that it was wrong to do this; and, previous to the next engagement, would say: "Now, Wade, I'll play the General to-day; I won't expose myself." Shortly after, on returning from some message, Major Wade would find him in the very thickest of the fray, and, when it was over, would go up to him and, touching his hat, say in a sneering way: "How well you kept your promise, sir, to-day!" to which old Sale would answer: "Never mind; it's all right."

Major Wade added : "It made me so angry to see him exposing himself."

On one occasion Sir Robert Sale's life was almost despaired of. He was bled and leeched to excess ; the next day he rested, but the third he mounted again, and was on horseback the whole day. During the siege he was in the habit, like many of the officers, of taking his gun to the ramparts and firing at the enemy. This was very useful, as it checked the fire of the Afghans and saved the scanty ammunition of the garrison, as we could not afford to let the sentries return shots. On these occasions Sir Robert was attended by an Irish orderly, who flattered him most grossly, which the old General could not endure. There were therefore constant skirmishes between them to the great amusement of the force. When the General shot half a dozen yards wide of the man he had aimed at, the orderly would cry : "Ah, Gineral, now, wasn't that a beautiful shot ? Sure, you nearly did for him !" to which came the gruff answer : "You lie ; I didn't."

The suspense about the fate of the prisoners was most trying to Sale's affectionate nature. He would sit for hours without speaking, thinking of his wife and daughter's fate ; and yet in public he was always full of confidence and spirits. He was sitting one day with Major Macgregor in sad silence, when tears began to flow down the veteran's cheeks, and he wept like a child. Some alarm occurred—he was up in a moment, cheering and encouraging everybody.

In a private letter Broadfoot says :—"The best soldiers among the elder officers are Sale and Colonel Monteath of the 35th N.I., a soldier one likes to be under before the enemy. We must then go low down for good officers, and first comes Captain Havelock of the 13th. It is the fashion to sneer at him. His manners are cold, while his religious opinions seclude him from society ; but the whole of them together would not compensate for his loss. Brave to admiration, imperturbably cool, and looking at his profession as a science."

Havelock was as good a soldier as he was a Christian, as stern to himself as he was to others, who rose every morning two hours before any one else that he might have uninterrupted leisure for prayer and the study of God's Word. If the march was at six he rose at four, if at 4 A.M. he rose at two. Henry Lawrence describes his "reading and praying much as on parade in a little chapel in the town to about forty soldiers and a dozen officers—a good soldier and a good man—the best of both probably in camp."

All the artillery officers Broadfoot pronounces above the average — two (Captains Backhouse and Dawes) greatly so; and names Captains Abbott and Paton and young Monckton Combes, Sutherland Orr, and Frank Cunningham as "fine, gallant, intelligent lads."

There was also George Macgregor, the Political Assistant, whose name was dreaded throughout the district, and who, when his political duties came to an end by General Pollock's arrival, reverted with ardour to his work as an artillery officer. And there was George Broadfoot himself, whose rare military genius made him the engineer of the garrison, whose iron firmness of character refused to entertain the thought of surrender when almost every one else pronounced it unavoidable, who was perhaps the greatest student of the art of war we have ever had, and whose extraordinary energy alike of body and mind deserved the words which Colin Mackenzie inscribed on his tomb:—
" The foremost man in India and an honour to Scotland." [1]

[1] The whole account of the Councils of war at Jellalabad is taken from Major Broadfoot's notes of them given by Havelock to Mackenzie. Havelock compared them with his own memoranda and pronounced them "so correct that it was unnecessary to attach any remark."

We must now recall the course of events in India. The invasion of Afghanistan in 1838, as in 1880, was the act of H.M.'s Ministers. In 1850 Sir John Cam Hobhouse, President of the Board of Control, confessed : " The Afghan war *was done by myself ;* the Court of Directors had nothing to do with it."[1] It was done "entirely without the privity of the Court of Directors." The reason alleged was " the inveterate hostility " of Dost Muhammad to the British, and the letters of Burnes laid before Parliament were so garbled by Hobhouse (Lord Palmerston being Foreign Secretary) as to make it appear that Burnes had reported this hostility and had recommended the war. This was exactly contrary to the truth. Burnes gave proof that Dost Muhammad was "entirely English," that he had asked succour from Russia because we refused it, that he showed him an autograph letter from the Emperor Nicholas full of promises, and that he was most anxious for our alliance. Lord Auckland disapproved of Burnes' negotiations, and recalled him. Burnes pointed out the impolicy and even the injustice of attacking Dost Muhammad ; and although, misled by personal ambition, he afterwards advised the best way of acting against the Amir, yet up to the last he expressed his hope that it would not be necessary. Dost Muhammad said : "I have not abandoned the British ; the British have abandoned me." When Burnes was aware of the falsification of his letters, he sent home the true copies. Lord Stanley honourably gave them publicity, and the fraud was exposed by Mr. Baxter twenty years after, in the House (19th March 1861). On the British Government remonstrating with Russia, the Emperor disavowed his Envoy Vicovich, who is said to have shot himself. A most disgraceful amount of falsehood on both sides !

---

[1] Evidence before the Official Salaries Committee of the House of Commons, 1850.

But although Lord Auckland was the willing instrument of H.M.'s Ministers in the unprovoked invasion of Afghanistan, and although he entirely misapprehended the difficulty of setting up Shah Shujah, who had scarcely any adherents, yet it should be ever remembered that, after the outbreak, he did all that was done. The whole of the force with which Pollock made his victorious march was sent up by Lord Auckland; not a man was added to it by Lord Ellenborough. On the first intelligence of the insurrection —*i.e.* before the end of November[1]([a])—a force of 4000 men under Brigadier Wild was on the march to Peshawar; but the Commander-in-Chief, Sir Jasper Nicolls, detained the Horse Artillery, which should have accompanied it, at Firozpur,([b]) in spite of the Governor-General's request. Sir Jasper, who had justly opposed the invasion of Afghanistan, was now unwilling to risk troops when it was necessary to succour their comrades. Brigadier Wild was therefore sent up *without guns*, the Commander-in-Chief being of opinion that "guns could be of no use in a pass."([c])

Early in December Lord Auckland recommended the despatch of a second brigade, including H.M.'s 9th Foot, under Brigadier M'Caskill, and wished Wild to advance through the Khaiber.([d]) Wild, whom Henry Lawrence calls "that ill-fated and ill-used officer," was required to make bricks without straw. He had no European troops and no guns; the Sikhs were in a state of mutiny, and refused to lend their guns. He was ordered to replenish the magazine, Treasury, and Commissariat at Jellalabad, but he had no carriage, and no Cavalry but one troop of Irregulars, was short of ammunition, and his Native Troops—all young soldiers—were scared by the dangers of the Pass, and were tampered with by the Sikhs.

[1] Blue Book, from Governor-General, 2d December 1841, p. (a) 13; ([b]) p. 111; ([c]) pp. 73-4; ([d]) p. 79.

The fort of Ali Masjid, about fifteen miles from Peshawar, and five miles from the mouth of the Khaiber Pass, was beleaguered. Wild was persuaded to send two regiments to its relief (15th January). They made a successful night march, piloted by Mackeson, but the provisions remained behind. Wild started to relieve them, but his Sikh auxiliaries mutinied and marched back to Peshawar, where Avitabile closed the gates against them. His own Sepoys, under heavy fire, huddled together in confusion and dismay, suffered severe loss; the Brigadier was wounded; the garrison at Ali Masjid was starved out and had to fight their way back; and the Sepoys returned to Peshawar more disheartened than ever.[1](d) "Few officers," says Henry Lawrence, "have been worse treated than the gallant and unfortunate Wild. As brave a soul as ever breathed, he was driven broken-hearted to his grave."

(e) Lord Auckland then ordered up a third complete brigade on 21st January; hastened its march on 28th. The Commander-in-Chief refused Clerk's and Mackeson's demands for more artillery and infantry, because he "thought no force now sent forward would be of any use in supporting our troops during their *retreat*."(f) The news of the destruction of the Kabul force reached Calcutta on the 31st January, and the Governor-General immediately reiterated his order for the despatch of a third brigade, adding also a tenth company to every regiment. As Lord Auckland was about to lay down office, he wished to prepare everything so that his successor could advance or retreat as seemed best. He referred the question of the reconquest of Afghanistan to the home authorities, but thought all that could be done at once was to withdraw the garrison of Jellalabad in safety; but he never lost sight of the captives, and his final instructions to General Pollock

[1] (d) Blue Book, p. 69; (e) pp. 91-124; (f) pp. 116-117.

(24th February 1842) run thus :—"You will consider it *one of the first objects of your solicitude* to procure the release of British officers and soldiers, and their families, private servants, and followers." He gave full power to the Commander-in-Chief, and to Generals Pollock and Nott, to act according to their discretion, conferring supreme political as well as military authority in Afghanistan on the two Generals. Kaye is decidedly hard upon Lord Auckland for expressing in his private letters a fear that we might be obliged to fall back on Firozpur; but all that he did was manly and wise.

General Pollock had been most judiciously selected by Lord Auckland himself, who was determined to have an officer of the Indian army. Pollock received his appointment on New Year's Day, overtook M'Caskill's brigade, and found, on reaching Peshawar on the 5th February, 1800 men in hospital, the troops disheartened, and a very insubordinate and unmilitary spirit in some of the officers. Major Pottinger wrote :—"Some of the worst officers in the army have been sent with General Pollock."[1] A captain of the 53d N.I. declared openly at mess (his colonel and major being present) that he would do his best to prevent any Sepoy of his company from again entering the Khaiber. Henry Lawrence was snubbed by Government for reporting the dangerous and unsoldierly language used by some of the officers. The Hindus of four out of the five regiments refused to advance. They had all been enlisted for service in India, and could not go beyond the

---

[1] Broadfoot wrote at the time :—"As to the down-heartedness of the native troops after Wild's defeat; it happens in all armies, none more subject to it than our European troops. I have seen it to a distressing extent, and when Colin comes he will tell what he has seen. Troops of every nation depend upon their officers, and these much on the leader. No fear of the natives if the *Europeans* keep right ; *above all, the officers.*"

Indus without losing caste.   A very able Hindu gentleman,
thoroughly loyal to the British, traced the mutiny of 1857
in a great measure to the Afghan campaign.   He said it
was a direct breach of faith to take Hindus out of India.
Practically they were compelled to go for fear of being
treated as mutineers (as the 34th were for refusing to go to
Sind), but the double pay they received by no means com-
pensated them for losing caste.   Those who survived had
to pay heavily for re-admittance to caste on their return
to India.   Sometimes no sheep being procurable, beef
was served out under the name of "red mutton."   The
men pretended not to know what it was, but of course
beef was an abomination to the Hindu.   The Sepoys mis-
trusted the Government from that time forward, and were
always fearing that their caste would be destroyed, besides
which our disasters taught them that Europeans were not
invincible.

At this time delegates from Wild's brigade held nightly
meetings endeavouring to form a combination among all
the Native Regiments to refuse to advance.   The sight of
the miserable and maimed camp-followers who daily arrived at Peshawar, and who had lost limbs from the frost,
and their accounts of their treatment by the Afghans, added
to the unwillingness of the troops.   With mutiny and constant desertions among the Sepoys, and in the presence of
a large inimical force of Sikhs, it was impossible for the
General to exercise discipline.   He therefore wisely took
no notice of what he could not punish, though we may
fancy the self-control it must have cost him, with his fearless devotion to duty, to suppress his scorn of such craven
conduct.   He set to work with his usual indomitable
patience to put things to rights, visited the hospitals, spoke
to and cheered the men, showed them they were cared for
by supplying them with worsted gloves, stockings, and

other comforts, and thus gradually restored confidence.
He had to resist the exhortations of the garrison of Jellalabad on the one hand, and of all India on the other, calling
upon him to advance. Had he attempted to do so, the
consequences must have been ruinous. As the Commander-
in-Chief, in reporting to the Horse Guards, justly observed :
—" Any precipitancy on the part of a general officer panting
for fame might have had the worst effect." Not only were
the garrison at Jellalabad unable to understand why first
Wild and then Pollock delayed advancing to their relief,
but the General dared not give the true reasons, until they
suggested his writing in rice water as they had iodine.
Then at last he was able to tell the true state of affairs.
Major Wade notes :—" 23d *March.*—Yesterday a letter
from Pollock. It looked to all intents and purposes a
clean sheet of paper, and was put into a Kurán by the
kasid. The four regiments of Brigadier Wild's command
have got into such a state of funk that they have
refused to advance, and Pollock says he feels sure that if
he ordered them to move they would throw down their
arms and go back bodily to India. He must therefore
'await the arrival of more white faces to restore confidence.'" He was very short of ammunition and very
short of carriage.[1] He cut down the baggage of the army,
beginning with his own, to the scantiest limits, and on the
arrival of H.M.'s 3d Dragoons and a troop of Horse Artillery on 29th March, determined to push forward without
waiting for H.M.'s 31st Foot, which was only a few marches
behind. Mr. Clerk's extraordinary tact and firmness had
at last brought the Sikh Government to a sense of their
duty as auxiliaries, and they rendered valuable service in

[1] Broadfoot speaks of "the wretched way in which the force was
equipped and provided. Not a thought seems to have been bestowed
on the nature of the country or the probable operations of the force."

keeping open our communications. Henry Lawrence was invaluable at Peshawar, Mackeson no less so. The General, having issued the most carefully-planned orders for the advance, went round himself to every commanding officer the night before starting to make sure that his orders were fully understood. These arrangements were pronounced "perfect in conception and complete in detail," and were admirably executed.

The force marched on the 5th April, Colonel Taylor and H.M.'s 9th leading. The front and rear of all the three columns consisted of companies of the 9th, next to whom came the 26th N.I. The Sepoys, being now backed by Europeans, and having confidence in their General, "behaved nobly, vying with their European comrades." Ferris' Jezailchis (under Ferris and Richmond Shakespear) "excited the delight and admiration of all." Pollock showed the "use of guns in a pass" by dispersing the enemy from behind the Sunga and the heights above it with showers of shrapnel.

After severe fighting, and having restored our faithful ally, Turábáz Khan, to his own territory *en route*, the force reached Jellalabad on the 16th, and were played in by the band of the 13th to the tune of "Eh, but ye've been lang o' coming." They found the garrison, to their surprise, "fat and rosy," though they had fed on camel and horse flesh. Major Smith says :—"The walls of Jellalabad were manned by the garrison as we passed to our encamping ground, and when the salute was fired and returned, a loud and thrilling cheer burst forth to welcome us. It was a most exciting scene. Rarely, indeed, have so many hearts beat happily together as throbbed at that moment in the ranks of the relieving and relieved. I trust that many, too, felt it to be an occasion of deep solemnity, and lifted up their grateful thoughts to the Almighty."

This was the first time that the terrible defile of the Khaiber, twenty-eight miles in length, had ever been forced by arms. Timur Lang and Nadir Shah at the head of their enormous hosts had bought a safe passage through it from the Afridis. Akbar the Great in 1587 is said to have lost forty thousand men in attempting to force it, and Aurangzeb failed to get through. One of Pollock's greatest difficulties arose from the desertion of the camel-men with their animals, which compelled him, even after he had marched, to leave part of the ammunition behind. He placed on record a protest, which has apparently been lost sight of since, that the present system of hiring camels is "most ruinous as regards efficiency, and that *no force* beyond the Indus ought to be dependent on it." He recommended that "only purchased camels, and Sirwáns [1] whose houses are in our provinces, should be employed."

Meeting the General, Broadfoot emphatically says :— "General Pollock is superior to any General I have yet chanced to meet in these regions."

Having, during his enforced detention of two months at Peshawar, surmounted all obstacles from those under his command, General Pollock had now a more arduous trial of his firmness and patience from those in authority over him.

Lord Ellenborough had arrived on the 28th February, and within the first week consulted Mr. Prinsep and Sir William Casement, members of Council, about *countermanding* the 3d Brigade sent forward by Lord Auckland.[2] He was, however, induced to issue a spirited proclamation, and wrote to the Commander-in-Chief that "the release of the prisoners . . . is deeply interesting in point of feeling and honour" (15th March), and that "the release of the last Sepoy is as essential as that of the first European;" but

---

[1] Camel-men.   [2] Stated on the authority of H. T. Prinsep, Esq.

this was a mere hot fit, speedily followed by a cold one. He had no sooner got away from his Council, going up to Simla alone, than, on hearing of the surrender of Ghazni and the repulse of Brigadier England near Quetta, he (on the 19th April) ordered Nott to evacuate Khilat-i-Ghiljye, and to withdraw as soon as possible from Kandahar to Sakar, and Pollock to return to Peshawar, if it could be done without injuring the health of the troops, which was to be his sole consideration.

In the meantime Colin Mackenzie arrived in camp on the 25th April, after a most perilous journey, with proposals from Muhammad Akbar, and furnished the General with invaluable information as to the state of the country and the amount of opposition he might expect. In consequence the General reported to Government on the 28th :—"I believe there is not a soul to oppose us between this and Kabul."

Mackenzie came again to camp on the 8th May, and the General showed him the orders he had received in *quadruplicate* to retreat, and abandon the prisoners. An advance was no less perilous to them, but Mackenzie strongly urged that "no consideration for the prisoners should stand in the way of vindicating British honour." The Commander-in-Chief had (29th April) reiterated the Governor-General's orders to General Pollock "to withdraw every British soldier from Jellalabad to Peshawar." Pollock was not to delay on account of the prisoners at Badiabad "unless they were actually on their way to camp," adding "those at Kabul cannot, I think, be saved." On this General Pollock wrote a noble remonstrance (13th May), plainly saying :—"Our withdrawal at the present moment would have the *very worst effect*. . . . We *cannot disregard* the release of the prisoners . . . our remaining here or a few marches *in advance* is essential to uphold the character of

the British nation."[1]   But Pollock did more.   He did what
not one in five hundred would have done.   He immediately
wrote to Nott *on no account to retire* (as he had been
ordered to do) *until he should hear again from him.*   The
General said subsequently :—"I felt that to retire would be
our ruin.   The whole country would have risen to destroy
us.   I therefore determined on remaining at Jellalabad
until an *opportunity offered for advance.*   Stopping Nott for
a few days, after his receipt of orders to retire, was perhaps
a very bold step.   If it had not succeeded I knew that I
might lose my commission ; but I felt pretty certain that
if we worked together in earnest the game would be ours.
And I wrote accordingly to Nott to halt until he should
hear from me.   He had made, I think, two retrograde
movements, and replied that he would wait until he heard
from me again."[2]

Never was there a more noble act of disobedience.
Nelson's blood was up when he put his glass to his blind
eye, and refused to see the signal to cease firing; but
Pollock persevered calmly in practically refusing to obey
an ignominious order, though reiterated by Lord Ellenborough and repeated by the Commander-in-Chief.   He felt
that beyond and above all civil and military authority was
his duty to his Queen, his country, and his God.

Stout old General Nott was disgusted at the order to
retreat, but considered that as a soldier he had no choice
but to obey.   He therefore brought off the garrison of
Khilat-i-Ghiljye, which had been gallantly defended for
months by a mere handful of men under Captain John

[1] It is a very remarkable fact that this letter, so honourable to the
General, was suppressed and excluded from the Parliamentary Blue
Book, and only unearthed by the inquiries of Lord Palmerston and
Lord Lansdowne.   The history of this discreditable affair can be found
in the *Life of Sir G. Pollock*, by Lieutenant C. Low, p. 303.

[2] *Life of Sir G. Pollock*, p. 297.

Halkett Craigie, and into which he was just about to throw
succour.   He had remonstrated with Government, and now
gladly obeyed Pollock's instructions, declaring himself
"prepared to advance" should the Governor-General change
his mind.

Lord Ellenborough took no notice of Pollock's letter or
of Nott's advice that Jellalabad should be retained, except
by repeating his refusal to allow Pollock "to remain beyond
the Khaiber;" and Mr. George Clerk having expressed his
opinion that General Pollock would "*not abandon either the
British captives* or *the position he holds at Jellalabad*," Lord
Ellenborough got into such a fright that he reiterated the
orders of 29th April lest Pollock "might possibly have
been *misled into adopting*" Mr. Clerk's view, and "regrets
that he had not retreated to Peshawar directly after relieving Jellalabad!"

General Pollock concealed these orders to retreat from
every one.   But the secret leaked out through the Commander-in-Chief's staff at Simla.

It would be tedious to enumerate the repeated orders
sent to General Pollock to withdraw; but he had *determined
to remain* until he could advance, and his patient firmness
was at last rewarded.   Such a storm of indignation was
raised both in India and at home at the thought of abandoning the prisoners, and Her Majesty's Ministers so strongly
disapproved of it, that Lord Ellenborough was obliged to
wriggle out of his resolution to do so.   On the 4th July he
hit upon the highly ingenious device of giving Nott the
option of *retreating in advance*.   He declared that the withdrawal of the British armies was the first object of Government, but allowed Nott to retreat *via* Kabul on his own
responsibility; which was like ordering a retreat from York
to London, but allowing the commander to "retreat" by
advancing to Edinburgh!   On one point, however, the

Governor-General was determined. Nott was by all means to bring away the sandal-wood gates from Ghazni! This he did, and this comprises the exact amount of Lord Ellenborough's share in the success of the campaign.

By this time his Lordship entirely ignored the Commander-in-Chief, and wrote to the General direct. His letter reached Nott just in time. The day was named, and the force told off for the retreat when (20th July) Nott received it, and immediately determined to retire a portion of his army *riâ* Ghazni and Kabul. Pollock was also allowed to "support Nott," though the Governor-General did not anticipate he would march to Kabul, and actually authorised him to exercise his discretion by ordering Nott to retire by Quetta, even though he should have begun his march towards Kabul!

Pollock eagerly seized the responsibility thus thrown upon him. He felt the full benefit of being unshackled and allowed to judge for himself, and despatched five messengers in succession to Nott, who gladly availed himself of what Pollock called "the glorious temptation." Before the end of June, owing to the untiring exertions of Mr. Robertson, the Lieutenant-Governor of Agra, and of Mr. George Clerk, the Governor-General's Agent at Lahore, a great number of ponies and mules had, at Pollock's suggestion, been purchased in Upper India and the Panjab, and he was thus enabled to move.

Early in July, Colin Mackenzie being at death's door from fever, Akbar Khan sent Captain Colin Troup to General Pollock, but the negotiation had now become a farce, as Pollock was resolved to do nothing to prevent himself from advancing. The General demanded the surrender of all guns and trophies, but offered an exchange of prisoners without reserve, including of course the Dost. This, however, was beyond Akbar's power. Troup was sent back the next day accompanied by George Lawrence, whose brother Henry tried in vain to persuade him to let him return in his stead.

All this time Pollock stood alone, bearing the opposition of the Governor-General without support or sympathy from any one, keeping his own counsel, knowing it would be ruinous to let any one guess the orders he had received. He seems never on any occasion to have called a council of war, but to have eagerly accepted the full responsibility of his post. He had sent Sale to Fattiabad, two marches in advance, and, on hearing from Nott, made known on the 16th August his intention of marching to Kabul. Though the heat was terrific the enthusiasm with which this most unexpected order was received was unbounded.

They marched on the 20th almost without baggage, three or four officers in a small hill tent, while "that chivalrous soldier Broadfoot, ever foremost in devotion and duty, offered to take on his sappers without any tents at all."

Pollock's force consisted of only 8000 men. After his first engagement at Gandamak he was obliged to leave two H.A. guns, with both cavalry and infantry, at that place, from want of baggage-cattle. All the camp-followers were compelled to carry eight days' supplies, the fighting-men three. After loading the commissariat camels to their utmost carrying capacity, the General ascertained that the mounted troops had in their kit a spare pair of pantaloons apiece, on which he ordered the legs to be filled with grain and carried by the men in front of them on their saddles. This is not the place to recount the splendid achievement of forcing the passes. The General, who was now as ardent and eager as the youngest ensign, himself forced the village of Mamu Khail at the head of a wing of the 9th, amid the cheers of the whole army.

Every success was followed by the submission of neighbouring chiefs, and by plentiful supplies pouring into camp. On the 13th September he defeated Akbar in the tremendous Tezin Pass, and then marched unopposed to Kabul, which was reached on the 15th. The next day the army marched through the city and hoisted the British flag on the Bála Hissar under a royal salute. So admirable was Pollock's discipline, that not a house or an individual was injured either in going or returning.

Thus it is evident that it was Lord Auckland who despatched the force with which Kabul was occupied and the captives released; and that to General Pollock alone that advance and release are due, because, although Nott gladly co-operated with him, he would not have resisted the Governor-General's orders as Pollock did. The Commander-in-Chief was passive, Lord Ellenborough opposed to all that was done, and it was owing to Mr. Clerk that a useful body of Sikh auxiliaries accompanied the army and kept open our communications, and to him and Mr. Robertson that the General was furnished with the scanty supply of baggage cattle, without which he could not have stirred.

Lord Hardinge wrote to Sir Frederick Pollock, the General's brother:—"*The whole merit of the advance from Jellalabad to Kabul is due to Pollock.*"[1]

---

[1] The march to Kabul, only 103 miles from Jellalabad, took nearly a month. It was so difficult, that 10 miles often took from 12 to 24 hours. Pollock marched 20th August; reached Gandamak 23d; defeated Ooloos at Mamu Khail 24th; back to Gandamak on 30th; 7th September to Surkháb; 8th, routed Ghiljyes at Jagdallak; 10th, Seh-i-Baba; 11th, Tezin; 13th, forced the passes to Butkhak, routing Akbar, who had 16,000 to 20,000 men; 15th, Kabul.

CHAPTER XIX.

COLIN MACKENZIE'S EMBASSY TO JELLALABAD.[1]

(April to May 1842.)

To return to the captives. The story of Colin Mackenzie's embassy to Jellalabad was told by himself. "We were now in Muhammad Khan's fort at Tezin. Major Pottinger had long been endeavouring to persuade Akbar to send one of the captives to Jellalabad to treat with General Pollock, thinking that this measure would at least delay the explosion, which he hourly expected, of the pent-up fiery passions of the chiefs (who were irritated beyond measure by their disgraceful defeat, on the 7th of April, by Sir Robert Sale before Jellalabad), which might have proved highly dangerous, if not absolutely destructive, to us. But, as the Afghans always endeavour to deceive, they never give another credit for good faith. However, at the end of April (the 23d, the day on which General Elphinstone died), Akbar seemed more inclined to listen to Pottinger's proposal. His own fortunes were at that time in a very low condition; not only had he just been defeated by General Sale, but his followers had dwindled away, the faction against him at Kabul, headed by his uncle Zemán Khan, was daily increasing in strength, and General Pollock

[1] These reminiscences were written by Captain Mackenzie at the repeated request of his wife. He said: "But for the wish to gratify you, they would in all probability have perished with me."

was apparently advancing to devour him. All his efforts to induce the people to oppose our troops were fruitless, added to which he was troubled by an unhealed and painful wound in the arm, which increased his depression of spirit. At this time General Elphinstone was suffering from violent dysentery. We had no medicine left. I had a lump of opium in my waistcoat pocket, and that had given him some relief, but at last the opium was done, and we could get no more. The only thing I could think of was a pomegranate, which we boiled, and made a very strong bitter drink, which appeared to do him some good; but nature was exhausted, and he sank rapidly. I offered to read the prayers for the dying to him—he assented, but said he would change his apparel. He called his servant,—'Moore, I wish to wash;' and added (showing how he was reduced): 'Bring me that blue shirt which Captain Troup gave me.' It was done, but he then sank into a stupor, so that I could not read to him. Ghulam Moyan-ud-dín (the man who saved my life at Sir William Macnaghten's murder) came to me to know if it was true that General Elphinstone was dying. I took him into the recess where the General was gasping out his life, and when he saw the old chief stretched on the floor dying in such misery he appeared a good deal affected. Akbar was informed of it, and expressed his regret and his sorrow that he had not followed Pottinger's advice by sending the General to Jellalabad, where he would have had medical assistance; but he had never believed in the General's extreme danger until too late. He promised, however, to send his body if he died, and declared his intention of sending one of us on a mission to General Pollock. Akbar and the chiefs then consulted who should be sent, and they all pitched upon me, for they had got into their heads that I was a Mullah, and they thought that I would come back. Well, Akbar gave me his instructions, and Pottinger gave

me his. Dost Muhammad Khan, the Ghaljai, had a long
private conversation with me, in which he endeavoured to
engage me in his own peculiar interests, without much
reference to those of Akbar, concerning whose *nasib* (fate)
he appeared more than doubtful. He also repeatedly asked
me if I would come back, and was quite unable to understand the reasons which I told him would induce my return.
By the way, when I did come back, he frankly avowed that
he never expected me, and ridiculed the idea of a promise
being binding under such circumstances. Akbar did expect
that I would keep my word, but he felt by no means sure
that I should do so alive, and plainly gave me warning of
the danger before I started. He only asked me once if I
intended to return, and was quite confused when I answered:
"Are you the son of an Amir, and ask me, an English
gentleman, such a question?" Akbar's propositions were
that the British General should treat with him as the
acknowledged head of the Afghan nation; that there should
be an exchange of prisoners, including all on each side;
that the British should retire from Afghanistan; and that
General Pollock should give him a handsome *douceur* in
money. In case of these arrangements being effected, he
stated that he should be glad to enter into an alliance with
the British, both offensive and defensive. This was his
public message given openly, but in secret he desired me to
ascertain if a private arrangement could not be made to the
effect that General Pollock should insure an amnesty to
him and his followers for the past, and that the British
Government should bestow on him a large *jaghir* (grant of
land). In this case he said that he would willingly act
as Pollock's lieutenant, and assist him in reconquering
Afghanistan. In fact, I believe that, but for his fear of
acting in direct opposition to his father-in-law, Muhammad
Shah Khan, who was decidedly the most talented and

energetic of our enemies, Akbar would at this time have openly gone over to our side, always presupposing that Pollock would have pledged himself for his personal safety, and a decent provision for himself and family. Most of the prisoners were under guard in the valley of Zjandeh, distant nearly ten miles. Pottinger, the Eyres, Wallers, Dr. Magrath, and my faithful Christian servant, Jacob, were with me. All, except Pottinger, whose spirit never quailed, and whose courage, moral and physical, was always found equal to any emergency, looked on me as devoted to almost certain destruction ; and, indeed, several of the Afghan chiefs, knowing the character of the country through which I had to pass, did not attempt to conceal the unfavourable nature of their anticipations.

"At this time the poor old General died. The last words he said were (one likes to remember the very words of a dying man) to his servant Moore : 'Moore, lift up my head, it is the last time I shall trouble you.' He did so, weeping bitterly, for he was very much attached to his master. I went and took leave of the poor old General's remains, and kissed his hand, but I shed no tear, though my heart was very full.

" I was to start immediately. I rode a horse of Lady Sale's ; they wanted me to take my own saddle, but as the European fashion of it would have betrayed me instantly, I asked for an Afghan one, and never saw *my* saddle again. That night Sultan Ján led me out of the fort. My *posteen* (sheepskin cloak), which was full of vermin, had the sleeves so battened together by the rain that I could not force my arms in, but he soon solved the difficulty by cutting off the ends of the sleeves with his sword. I found that I was to be under the charge of a noted robber, named Batti Dusd, *i.e.* Batti the thief ; for this man was a sort of Rob Roy among the Ghaljais, and

had contrived to ease Sir Robert Sale during his unquiet
march to Jellalabad of some hundreds of camels, all of
which he resold to the General in his extremity. Our party
consisted of two horsemen of Akbar's, and three of Batti's
own men, who were, like himself, on foot. Leaving the
fort, we turned to the right, and, crossing the valley, we
struck into the defiles of the mountains which separate the
valley of Tezin from that of Zingáneh ; there we edged
away to the north-east, forcing our way up the bed of a
mountain torrent, which reached every now and then to the
breasts of our horses, over huge boulders of stone that
made it all but impassable, until we came to a small cascade
up which it was impossible to go. The horsemen began to
abuse Batti for bringing them such a road ; he declared it
was a very good one, and told me to dismount and follow
him. The precipice on the right was wholly impracticable,
and he took us up a goat-path on the left, where I cannot
sufficiently wonder at the horses being able to follow. The
exertion was tremendous. As soon as I found myself alone
with Batti, and discovered that he could speak Persian, I
began to make friends with him. He abused the horsemen
for a couple of milksops. He himself was the finest
specimen of a wiry athletic mountaineer I ever saw; he was
nothing but bone, sinew, and muscle, an Ahmedzye, about
thirty years of age, and never appeared in the least fatigued
or out of breath in surmounting hills, to which Ben Lomond
is a joke. In going up this tremendous ascent not even
his nostril was expanded. In toiling up these places he
generally put his heavy matchlock behind his back, with
the ends resting on the inside of his elbows, and marched
up of course without using his hands, and often singing a
Pushtu war-song. At last we worked our way up to the
snow, which was still more dangerous from its extreme
slipperiness, and from our track sloping on one side towards

the torrent at an angle of about forty-five degrees. The exertion was so great that in spite of the cold wintry wind the perspiration streamed off like rain. Even the Afghan horsemen declared they had never seen such a road. Here and there we saw a little mountain fastness perched on some " bad eminence," standing in strong relief against the sky, which we passed with as little ado as might be. At the top of this stupendous pass we came among the most magnificent cedars and pines of from eighteen to five-and-twenty feet in girth, with their giant branches tossed abroad horizontally, as if defying the elements ; the effect of these forest Titans in the moonlight was more grand and romantic than can be described. At the very summit of the pass a long pole is planted in the ground, with a white flag on the top, on passing which all good Muhammadans stroke their beards and utter a prayer. The name of the pass is Kharkhachár. The descent on the Zingáneh side is comparatively easy, but, drenched as I was with perspiration, I suffered much from the icy blast which seemed to cut through me. Our road at first lay along a narrow ridge from ten to twenty feet only in breadth ; the brightness of the now fully-risen moon scarcely enabling our eyes to penetrate the vast profound on either hand, especially on the right, where the gloomy depth of the abyss, of at least two thousand feet, darkened by the huge shadow of the opposing mountain, which rises abruptly ridge over ridge, until lost in the blue ether, dimly revealed through the boughs of the holly-oaks and cedars which fringed the descent, the flashing waters of the torrent beneath. On the left the gulf opened out in the direction of the pass of Jagdallak and its fatal barriers, where, still untouched by decay, lay the bodies of many of my brave comrades ; for there fell Anquetil, Chambers, Nicholl, Skinner, Macartney, Dodgin (who fought so desperately, though he had but

one leg, that the enemy were obliged to shoot him from a
distance), and many a devoted soldier besides; and there,
some four months previously, had I witnessed the deep
despair of poor General Elphinstone when he and his unhappy subordinate, Colonel Shelton, were entrapped by
their treacherous enemy.   Beyond, in misty outline, loomed
the savage hills of Tagáo, Nijeráo, and the Ushín tribes.
Buried in deep reflection, I loitered behind my guides, and
while memory brought the harrowing events of the past in
ghostly array before me, the future seemed shrouded in
uncertainty and gloom.   The consciousness of utter insignificance, however, which as usual was produced in my
mind by the contemplation of the mighty works of God
even in the material world, and my sense of weakness
and absolute inability in any way to control the progress
of events which were rapidly hurrying to a crisis,
fraught with safety or destruction to myself and my
fellow-captives, and with honour or dishonour to my country,
had the good effect of leading me for comfort, support, and
direction to Him whose arm is never shortened to uphold
and save all who put their trust in Him.   Well might I
say, 'Hitherto the Lord hath helped me,' and the thought
gave me courage.   Presently I was summoned to the front,
and, mounting my horse, we pressed on rapidly, it being
Batti's earnest desire that we should pass certain locations
of the Jabber Khail tribes, in whose country we now were,
if possible before daylight; for he frankly admitted to me
that he, an Ahmedzye, would be unable to protect me in
case of discovery from the fury of these wild men, who
acknowledge little more than a mere nominal allegiance
even to their own chiefs if any sacrifice of plunder or
bloodshed be involved thereby.   Our road became rougher
at every step as we plunged into deep ravines and wound
our painful way along ancient watercourses now dry, whose

beds consisted wholly of large pebbles rounded by the action of the torrents of former days, which bruised the feet of my unfortunate Cape horse in a lamentable fashion, especially after the loss of one of his shoes.

"Before we reached the valley of Zingáneh, we had to cross a shallow stream (whose pure sweet waters I shall ever remember with gratitude, for my tongue clave to the roof of my mouth, and then and on three subsequent journeys did it quench my thirst). We then ascended another chain of hills, lower indeed than those we had left behind, but very steep, rugged, and barren. The valley of Zingánch itself, at the point where we entered (with the exception of a narrow strip of land fit for cultivation, not more than sixty yards in breadth, and along which, on spots where a few mulberry trees gave a scanty shade, some families of the Jabber Khail Ghaljais had reared their miserable huts, or pitched their black tents), was merely a confused mass of rocks and rounded stones, through the midst of which the Surkh-áb river foamed and struggled. This river during the heats of summer is a dangerous torrent, being then swollen by the melting of the snow of the lower ridges of the mountains of Solomon, the highest of which, called the Takht-i-Sulimán (or throne of Solomon), forms a magnificent object in the distance, especially when seen in the broad daylight, as I afterwards did, from the top of the Kharkhachár Pass. Day beginning to dawn, Batti mounted my horse, causing me to ride behind him with my hands and face enveloped in the folds of my turban and sheepskin cloak, leaving my eyes scarcely as visible as those of the roughest Skye terrier. Of course I was smothered, but there was no help for it, as it was necessary that I should pass for a sick *urbáb* (or small chief) of Peshawar, sent by Akbar Khan under Batti's charge to his native place. In this guise we sneaked past those rural abodes of 'the gentle Afghan swains,' which it was impossible to avoid by circumbendibus. But the old Cape horse, who had fallen quite lame, now entered a vehement protest against the double burden imposed on him by standing still, and, when urged to proceed, kicking like fury. The Afghans laughed, but it was no joke to me, not being predisposed to mirth, and perched as I was upon the sharp ridge of the brute's backbone, so muffled up as to be unable to use my hands. Every jolt made me sympathise with Aiken Drum, who, as the old Scotch song informs us, 'rode upon a razor.' In good earnest, during the four or five hours' ride which followed, my position was one of downright torture. My feet being unsupported, felt as if a hundred pounds weight were attached to each of them (I suppose from the blood rushing into them and the consequent stoppage of circulation), and the pain in my limbs actually made me groan. Entering the Isárak Valley, one of the most extensive and fertile in Afghanistan, and possessed chiefly by the Jabber Khail (which clan, the most powerful of all the Eastern Ghaljais, is divided and subdivided into numerous tribes), we followed the course of the Surkh-áb (or 'red water'), which, after traversing these rich lands from west to east to within a few miles of Gandamak, takes a northerly direction, and finding a passage through a chain of low mountains, falls into the Kabul river at a place of the same name as itself. Our object was to reach Chinghai,—which in Pushtu means a high fortress (some twelve miles down the valley of Isárak and half-way up one of the mountains of Solomon, which bound the valley to the south),—which belongs to two brothers, principal chiefs of the Jabber Khail, viz. Sir Fráz Khan and Sir Biland Khan, the latter of whom arrogated to himself the truly Afghan distinction of having assassinated James Skinner. *En route* we met several

Ghaljais, whose inquiries concerning me Batti and his followers evaded by lying; but eluding their ominous curiosity was a great grief to me, as, in addition to the intolerable pain I was enduring, I had sedulously to muffle up my white skin, the least appearance of which would have been my death-warrant; and keeping my wide Afghan trousers from riding up to my knees was next to impossible. Some five miles before we reached Chinghai, as we tried to slip past a fort belonging to a small chief, who was so execrably diabolical as to be accounted a perfect ogre even by his own people, we were thrown into great consternation by being challenged and ordered to stop. Our consultation was brief and our actions decided. The two horsemen rode boldly up to the fort and asked for a pipe, while Batti, myself, and the footmen turned abruptly to the right. Several men pursued us, thinking our shyness suspicious, and overtook us just as Batti in desperation tried to force our jaded steed up a steep bank. Seeing them closing in upon us, I slipped off and made straight up the hill, paying no attention to the calls of our pursuers, whose course was arrested by our ready-witted guide, who succeeded in pacifying them and lulling their suspicions, my sulky inattention confirming the idea that I was one of themselves. At last we reached the foot of the mountain on which Chinghai stands, and crossed the Surkh-áb, there a deep and dangerous torrent, by a bridge not more than a foot and a half in width, and which bent and trembled under the weight of the horse that carried Batti and myself, for I had again mounted (*post equitem sedet*, etc.). We hoped to pass another fort close to the river unobserved; but just as we had forded a small stream, and were right opposite the gate, our horse fell, and I tumbled off into the midst of a crowd of ruffians who had rushed out at the cry of 'Strangers.' Worn out with pain and fatigue, and despairing of escape, I was on the point of dropping my disguise, and meeting my fate with as much fortitude as I could muster under such appalling circumstances, but it was only a passing temptation. By God's blessing I did not lose my presence of mind. The instant I abandoned my first desperate impulse life seemed doubly dear, and I confess that the imminent prospect of being murdered in cold blood, without one friend near, and without being able to strike a blow in my own defence, made me feel for the *first* time the anguish of mortal fear, notwithstanding the awful extremity in which I had twice before stood, when surrounded by the Afghans in cutting my way into cantonments, and again at Sir William Macnaghten's murder. I already felt by anticipation a dozen daggers clashing in my side, but I was upborne by strength not my own. I kept my sheepskin cloak wrapped closely round me, concealing my face, and staggered forward, like a man worn down by sickness. One of Batti's followers took the hint, and caught me by the arm as if to assist me, reviling the luckless horse which had played such a trick to so good a man. To my astonishment, the crowd gave way before me, and I emerged from what appeared to be certain destruction. Meanwhile Batti, who, as he afterwards confessed, had at first given me over for lost, was far from idle. Lest second thought should prove my doom, he commenced a most fluent harangue in Pushtu to his gaping audience, painting, in glowing colours, various imaginary successes lately achieved by Akbar over the hated káfirs and the rival faction at Kabul. Thus favoured, I continued my retreat unmolested up the steep pathway leading to Chinghai; but such was my fatigue that it was with difficulty I could drag one leg after the other, and not daring to look behind, lest the action should excite suspicion, for the first hundred yards I fully expected every

instant to feel a knife in my back. My relief was great
when the trampling of a horse announced the proximity of
Batti, who dismounted in my favour, and thus we reached
the fort. About a dozen horsemen were assembled under
the walls, to avoid whom was necessary, while Batti sought
Sir Fráz Khan. Our two horsemen mingled with the
others, whom I took to be some of the Jánbáz who had
deserted from us, and who continued to regard me with
looks full of distrust, so that I was glad to be led away by
one of Batti's men from so unwholesome a neighbourhood
to a platform a little way off. Here he admonished me to
lie down and keep myself covered up with my posteen. This
I did, and not knowing whether my enemies had departed
or not, I lay for nearly two hours on my face under a bak-
ing sun, with my feet drawn up like a hedgehog, for more
effectual concealment. My breath scorched my lips, and it
became a matter of doubt whether death by apoplexy or the
sword were preferable. At last a voice made me look up,
and I found myself alone with a strange Afghan, whose
sinister countenance was not at all improved by a large
claret stain over one cheek. This proved to be Sir Fráz
Khan himself. I told him I was dying of heat, whereupon
he led me into the family burying-ground (!), a pleasant
grove of fruit and plane trees on a gentle slope commanding a magnificent view of the whole valley of Isárak,
with its numerous forts and groves, which derives a rare
fertility, freshness, and verdure from the impetuous river
which intersects it, the roar of whose dashing waters, now
softened to a murmur, stole up the hillside with a soothing
influence. Overhead the birds twittered amid the thick
foliage, which cast a deeper shade of green on the soft fresh
grass on which I lay; a rivulet of water, turned by the
chief's order into a channel close by me, sparkled and
bubbled along, inviting frequent draughts while I laved

my burning hands and face. I was supplied with food—namely, milk and the bannocks of the country and a kaliun, and, divesting myself of all superfluous garments, I lay enjoying this transition from a real Papistical purgatory to a Muhammadan paradise, until I fell asleep.

"In the afternoon Sir Fráz Khan paid me a long visit. He was a middle-aged man, crafty and courteous, and much more dangerous than his brother, Sir Biland Khan. The latter was young, insulting and brutal, and hated the British, so that he could scarcely treat me with civility though I was his guest. Sir Fráz did his best to prove that he was the only Afghan who really entertained a genuine friendship for the English, that he had not participated in the revolt against us, and spoke of the massacre of our troops with abhorrence. In spite of his art, however, his real feelings peeped out sufficiently to mark the hypocrite and the villain, even if I had not known my man, and the master-passion of this most sordid of his covetous race (who are all perfect Catilines '*Alieni appetentes suorum profusi*') broke out in spite of himself when he denounced and reviled Macgregor on account of the pitiful presents he had received from that officer when Sir Robert Sale's force passed through Gandamak on its return to Jellalabad, on which occasion the knight—as most Englishmen will take him to be by his name—swore many a solemn oath of fidelity to us. Alack for our policy! Unnecessary profusion in the first instance has always been followed up by unwise parsimony, which again reacting, involves prodigious expenditure—in the present instance, unhappily, not only of treasure, but of human blood. Macgregor had no choice, for the Supreme Government most unwisely prohibited presents, or khillats, beyond a certain value,—at least, these were the instructions given by Sir William Macnaghten to his Political Assistants; but there is no doubt in my mind that a judicious generosity at that crisis might have detached Sir Fráz Khan and his powerful clan from the faction of Akbar Khan, and thus a different complexion would most probably have been given to subsequent events. My disinterested friend ended his harangue by endeavouring to make a treaty with General Pollock through me in his own favour, quite irrespective of the interests even of his own brother, Sir Biland Khan; and hinted that, under his auspices, the rescue of that portion of the prisoners who were in the valley of Zjandeh would not be very difficult. By the way, had this proposition been listened to, and he had really carried off the prisoners in question—thereby trebling the hardships, if not involving the destruction of the remainder—far from delivering them into the hands of the British Government, he would have undoubtedly kept them in pawn on his own account. Poor wretch! at the time I write his mortal remains rest in the pleasant burying-ground where I experienced his hospitality on this and a subsequent occasion; for he has since been murdered by his feudal enemy at the foot of the hill, whose unpropitious acquaintance I had narrowly escaped that morning. In the evening Batti Dusd took an affectionate leave of me, evidently glad to be rid of so unsatisfactory a charge, for although I think the peculiar notions of his race concerning the point of honour would have led him to die in my defence, he felt that the life of a true believer would in that case have been unworthily wasted. Honest Batti, if I may poetically call him so, was a man of extraordinary intelligence, and, like most of his countrymen who are distinguished for superior vigour of intellect, personally liked Europeans. Muhammad Shah Khan was an exception to the general rule, and of course the Mullahs and all under their influence, to use their own expression, longed to drink our blood. Not that the Afghans are generally a priest-ridden people. On the contrary, they openly despise both their spiritual guides and the Kurán itself, if these should stand in the way of the gratification of any particular passion.

"My guards were now two men of the Jabber Khail (Sir Fráz Khan's own clan), one Dost Muhammad and an Akhunzádeh, the latter having been selected on account of his known craft and reputed sanctity, the former as being an acknowledged bold and faithful villain, and both from their intimate connection with the greatest rascals in the country, of every clan and tribe, and especially with the Black Tent Ghaljais, several hordes of whom were known to lie on our route. The parting pipe was smoked, 'Bismillah' was the word, and I recommenced my pilgrimage, it being difficult to say whether I or my unhappy horse was the more stiff and indisposed for nocturnal rambles. Avoiding the track at the bottom of the hill, we pushed along a spur of the mountain, over very broken and dangerous ground, occasionally passing by a small fort with its hanging gardens watered by little mountain streams, along the banks of which grew the musk willow (Béd-i-mushk) in great profusion, filling the air with its charming fragrance. Edging down once more into the valley of Isárak, we followed it westward, and then struck off the direct road to Jellalabad, making as straight as possible for the Kabul river, leaving Gandamak on the left. You may imagine my feelings as I looked at the hill where British honour was finally quenched in the blood of the small band of gallant men, the remains of our betrayed troops, who had manfully struggled on thus far to be sacrificed almost within sight of the haven of safety ; for another march would have taken them clear of these fatal mountain passes into the comparatively warm and fertile plain of Jellalabad, where a few disciplined and brave men under good leadership might have easily held their own against any amount of the wretches who massacred the few stragglers who, under Captain Bellew, reached Fattiabad.[1]

Before dawn we stopped in a field of young wheat, and, after the free and easy fashion of the country, allowed our horses to feed *ad libitum*. Probably the excellent Akhunzádeh chose that particular field as belonging to some one whom he had formerly injured, that being, curiously enough, often a motive for increased hostility. Resuming our journey, daylight ushered us into a rather large camp of the Black Tent Ghaljais, of whose fraternity my guides were rather doubtful, and exhorted me, as I valued my life, to continue to act the sick urbáb. Most of the people were asleep, but we were challenged when half-way through by a man who fortunately proved to be an old friend of my guides, and in that capacity insisted on our smoking a pipe. Not perfectly trusting even him, the Akhunzádeh dismounted and himself presented me with the *chillam*, I holding a little aloof so as not to be recognised in the imperfect light as a Feringhi. These Black Tent Ghaljais are a very fine race of men physically—their women are of

---

[1] "It is beyond question that if Wild could have pushed his force of 4000 men through the Khaiber at the beginning of December, carrying nothing but three days' provisions in their haversacks and their ammunition, for which donkeys were available, Turábáz Khan would have received them with open arms and supplied all things needful. The march thence to Jellalabad was a hop, skip, and jump. This, combined with the news of the other brigades then actually advancing through the Panjab, whose numbers would have been quadrupled by rumour, would have taken the Khaiberis by surprise. Sale might then have retraced his steps towards Kabul. He ought, at any rate, on the first rumour of our evacuation of Kabul, to have marched to meet us certainly as far as Gandamak, after which there are no defiles worth speaking of on the road to Jellalabad. Doubtless these measures would appear very rash to many, but from those accustomed to Eastern warfare, and who know the country and people, I should expect a different judgment."—C. M.

corresponding outward form and go unveiled. They are
the freest of free mountaineers, and *de facto* acknowledge no
authority, human or divine. The strong will, powerful
arm, and hard heart are the qualities which can alone rule
these savage animals. Living continually in their tents of
coarse black woollen stuff (whence their name of *Khaneh par
dosh*, *i.e.* house upon shoulder), their habits are purely
pastoral, which signifies,—in spite of poets and would-be
philosophers,—a state of unmitigated and incredible wicked-
ness and immorality. They migrate from the borders of
the Panjab over the range of the Sulimán Mountains far
west into the country of the Hazárás, and back again,
choosing their pastures according to the season, and frequently having to fight with a rival clan for possession of
the same. Their blood-feuds are consequently innumerable,
and woe to all travellers and kafilas whom they meet who
do not possess some acknowledged claim to their forbearance. None but the more powerful clans dare to insult or
injure even individuals of these nomadic tribes, as, when
they unite for purposes of revenge, which they readily do
on slight provocation, they are extremely formidable, and
most savage in their reprisals. Shortly after my departure
from the Fort of Tezin, Akbar Khan despatched the corpse
of General Elphinstone, accompanied by one of that
lamented officer's servants (Private Miller of H.M.'s 44th[1]),
under charge of one of his principal officers and a guard,

---

[1] Miller was a Londoner, a man of great coolness and presence of
mind. On the retreat he was separated from the force, and found
himself at the top of a small hill, when an Afghan advanced to slay
him. Miller immediately brought down his musket, and presented
it at the Afghan (who speedily departed) but did not fire at him.
On coming down the hill Miller found himself in the midst of a crowd
of Afghans, who had seen the whole transaction, and who, probably
under the influence of some chief of more than ordinary humanity,
spared his life because he had spared that of their countryman.

towards Jellalabad, thinking to propitiate General Pollock by this tardy act of courtesy. Miller was disguised as an Afghan, and great pains were taken to conceal him from the observation of the people of the country. The evening of the first day's journey the party encountered a camp of these very Black Tent Ghaljais, who, discovering the nature of their errand, cut down the European, and dragging the corpse from the coffin, loaded it with indignities, and would have finished by burning it and completing the murder of the unfortunate servant, but for the strenuous remonstrances and entreaties of the escort and its leader, whom, however, they beat and maltreated, despoiling the officer of his turban and sword. This is an instance of their savage independence, and shows what would have been my fate had my disguise been penetrated. Some time afterward, when I happened to encounter my quondam guide, Batti Dusd, he exhibited me to his wandering companions (to whom he related the incident of my falling off the horse at the foot of Chinghai Hill) as a wonderful instance of the mercy of God, to which they all replied by stroking their beards and exclaiming : 'That was indeed a great miracle !'[1]

"Some three hours more hard riding brought us close to another camp of these vagrants, by which we glided without stopping to smoke the usual pipe, my guides, who seemed well known to the people, excusing themselves on the plea of haste. About the middle of the day we reached the Kabul river, where we stopped to rest and refresh ourselves as we best might, our fare being principally a stale bannock. While sitting on a stone in the bed of the river at some distance from my companions, an Afghan made towards me hastily, but observing my two guides he turned off and entered into conversation with them. He had discovered me to be a Feringhi, and to avoid unpleasant

---

[1] Batti, in describing him, used to say he speaks like a king.

consequences in case of his summoning his friends, we mounted and made the best of our way to Jellalabàd. The climate of the plain in the middle of the day was a trying change from that of the snowy mountain I had lately left, the thermometer ranging in the shade from 135° to 140°. The heat quite stupefied me, and by the time we reached the outlying picket of General Pollock's camp, which was after sunset, my horse could not have carried me another hundred yards, and I was (*Scottice*) *sair forfaughten*. A vidette challenged us, and we halted until the subahdar[1] of the party, accompanied by several troopers, came out to inspect and examine us. They would not believe that I was a European, so black and haggard had I become, until I laughed, when the old native officer at once recognised the Sahib. This picket was commanded by poor Captain Mellish of the Bengal Cavalry, who received me with great warmth, lent me his charger to carry me to General Pollock's tent, and promised to look after my poor worn horse and my companions." Major Smith, Deputy-Assistant Adjutant-General, writes :—"About dusk I was standing near my tent door conversing with Ponsonby when three Afghans rode up. We looked at them with some curiosity, and the foremost, accosting us, said to my astonishment in a very gentlemanly tone : ' Will you be good enough to direct me to General Pollock's tent ?' He proved to be Captain Colin Mackenzie. You will judge how eagerly we questioned him." "General Pollock and my old friend Macgregor were astonished at the sudden intrusion of such an apparition, and the latter claimed me as his guest. The news of my arrival soon spread through the camp, and I still remember with much pleasure the hearty sympathy and genuine kindness manifested by every officer and soldier in it to the best of his ability."

[1] Native captain.

Mackenzie arrived on the 25th April. Macgregor furnished him with soap, a clean suit of Afghan clothes, and, to his great comfort, with a clean turban of pure white muslin. His own clothes were a heap of vermin, and he admired the placidity with which Macgregor told his servants to carry them away and burn them at once. The constant exertions and hardships he had undergone throughout the siege of cantonments and his subsequent captivity had rendered him as hard as iron, so that Macgregor could not forbear expressing amazement at his strength.

When he came out of the tent dressed he found an immense crowd of the soldiers of the garrison, with their worn uniforms, sunburnt faces, and kindly eager eyes, staring at him as one almost alive from the dead. The affection with which he was received by Broadfoot's Jezailchis was quite overpowering. They rushed upon him, seized and kissed his hands, clung to his clothes, and even to his boots, as he sat on horseback. Many of them had fought under him, and the others were their brothers and kinsfolk. They immediately held a jirga, or council. On these occasions they sit in a circle, and the kaliun, or pipe, passes round to each man several times before any one speaks a word, then each gives his opinion. They agreed that Mackenzie Sahib must be very poor and very hungry, and therefore as the best way of showing their attachment these poor fellows actually made up a bag of rupees, and came to present it to him, with five sheep, as if to make up at once for past starvation. He took the sheep, and Broadfoot endeavoured in vain to make them understand that it was impossible he could take the money. They had no idea of there being any false delicacy either in offering or receiving money when it was wanted. Broadfoot at last settled the matter to the satisfaction of all parties by say-

ing : "You know this man is my brother. I have lost two
brothers in this war, and he is in the place of both. It is
my right to supply him with everything he wants, and I
cannot let any one else do it." This they understood at
once. Among them were some of his own band, who had
taken an opportunity of escaping from their captivity. He
says :—" Our mutual joy was great, and I raised some money
and offered it to them. Their spokesman, a fine young
Euzufzai, dashed the rupees on the ground, and exclaimed :
'Do you think we sought you out for this? No, our pay
is all we wish for.' And it was only by coaxing them that
I could persuade them to accept a 'Ziafat,' or feast of
welcome."[1]

Mackenzie found Broadfoot very weak, and suffering
greatly from his wound (splinters of bone and bits of cloth
continually coming out), and also from inflammation of the
eyes. In the evening Mackenzie dined at the mess of the
9th as the guest of General Pollock. The warmth with
which he was received was indescribable. Every man
would drink his health even if he had only a little arrack
and water, and Colonel Taylor (the second lieutenant-colonel
of the regiment), having two or three cherished bottles of
Madeira—the last of his store—brought them forth in his
honour. He stayed four days, and the regiment insisted
that he should be *their* guest also, and not only the General's.

Most of his time was of course spent in conferring with
the General, to whom he afforded most valuable information regarding Akbar's position, the situation and relative
power of the contending factions, the undefended state of
the roads and the perfect facility of an advance upon
Kabul by two routes, the urgent necessity for so doing,
requesting him in the name of the prisoners to look on the

---

[1] By the time Pollock arrived the Jezailchis were all in rags, having
been seven months without pay.

risk to them as a mere secondary consideration.[1] He told him that had Sale advanced on Kabul immediately after the victory of the 7th April he would have got every prisoner.

Pollock absolutely refused to treat directly with Akbar, but he sent a memorandum in Persian for his perusal, promising nothing save a ransom of £20,000 for the prisoners and personal safety for himself.

Colin Mackenzie left Jellalabad to return to captivity on the 28th April. When it was known that he could carry up a few little things for the captives, the commotion among the men was extreme. They would have given the clothes off their backs, but they had scarcely anything to send. It reminded him of the lines—

> " The rudest sentinel in Britain born
>   With horror paused to see the ruin done ;
>   Gave his last crust to feed some wretch forlorn,
>   Wiped his stern eye, then firmer grasped his gun."

Even some of the officers begged him not to return, looking on his destruction as certain, and the Afghans expressed unbounded astonishment at his doing so. Macgregor wanted him to stain his face, Wade at least to take pistols ;

---

[1] The General fully acknowledged this important service, and afterwards wrote to him :—" You came to my camp under difficulties and dangers which few would have encountered, and had you been discovered there cannot be a question as to the result, that your life would have been sacrificed. I recollect your anxiety when visiting me, that no consideration for the prisoners should weigh in the scale, if by so doing the British Government or the well-being of the army would be in any way compromised, as you deemed the honour of the British nation and the unsullied character of the British army paramount to every other consideration. This involved the advance of the troops to the capital, which you are aware that I advocated. Your view was so far correct that, under ordinary circumstances, my advance (which you also advocated) would have lost the prisoners, yourself among the number."

but he could not bear the idea if he were seized of being
found "painted." The men, who had never obtruded
themselves, but who followed him with eager eyes whenever he came out, kept out of the way with instinctive
delicacy the day he left, as did the officers. They did not
want to make the return harder for him, and could not
bear to see him go.[1]

Major Broadfoot wrote to a near connection of Mackenzie :—

"JELLALABAD, May 3, 1842.

"Colin left us in the morning of the 30th April, carrying
back General Pollock's answer to Akbar Khan, and the admiration for himself and fervent good wishes of all this force. His
conduct throughout has been most noble, and may fill with just
pride all connected with him. At Kabul, amidst the deepest
gloom, his spirit never quailed, and when all others ceased to
resist, he continued unceasingly, with his handful of Jezailchis,
to show the enemy that a remnant at least was still resolved, if
destroyed, to perish with honour. He was in excellent health,
and the Afghan dress which he wore became him well. He was
chosen for the mission by Muhammad Akbar, though another
officer volunteered to go. Truly rare indeed is the courage
necessary to execute such a task, and to do it, as he did, so
cheerfully and full of vivacity, that most men thought him
blind to the dangers before him, but, alas ! I knew he saw too
plainly ; but the thought of shrinking from performing his promise never found a moment's rest in his mind, and when many
(not I, as you may believe) urged him not to return, he treated
the proposal with good-humoured ridicule. We are all most
anxious to hear of his safe arrival. His road carries him, unfortunately, through districts filled with the most lawless and

---

[1] The men of every regiment he served with always showed him
the most lively sympathy and affection. In 1850, on his way to the
Dekkan, he fell in with the 9th Foot, then on the march. The men
crowded around him, and many an honest soldier's hand was stretched
out to grasp his with—"We know you, sir ! We know you !"

bigoted of the population, and filled too with a most hearty contempt for us. . . . My hope and my belief is, that Colin, though it may be difficult to conceal his journey now, as was done before, will be suffered to pass in safety, seeing that he is going *to* Muhammad Akbar, of whose hatred to infidels they are abundantly satisfied. Colin's adventures have been most romantic, and his preservation is a miracle. When Sir W. Macnaghten was murdered, Colin's life was saved only by extraordinary exertions on the part of a chief, Moyan-ud-dín Khan, who literally risked his own life to save him. This chief has all along been one of the most active and boldest of our enemies; between him and Colin, however, there is a strict alliance. Oddly enough, there is every reason to believe it was the very man who wounded me. He intimated as much to Colin, and gave so minute an account of the transaction that he must have been present. He performed the feat with a double-barrelled gun, the plunder of some unfortunate officer. For his care of Colin, however, I have sent him word that if ever he falls into the hands of the black káfirs (as my men are called) to seek me out and he shall be safe."

On the receipt of this message from Broadfoot, Ghulam Moyan-ud-dín at once replied by asking for some percussion caps. Mackenzie conveyed the request, and Broadfoot of course made him a present of some. Broadfoot continues :—

"I myself am known as the 'black-coated Feringhi,' from a velvet shooting-jacket of Colin's which I *borrowed* in Kabul, and, having worn eight months, shall never return. Regarding Colin there are many conjectures. That he is my brother is certain, but then his being Sir William Macnaghten's son is puzzling, seeing that I have no claim to that honour. The graver shake their heads at it as confirming some strange stories of the domestic manners of the káfirs, and doubtless conclude our expulsion indispensable to the preservation of Afghan morality, as there is little hope of our locking up our ladies as we ought."

Mackenzie reached Tezin on the 3d May. Muhammad Akbar was exceedingly dissatisfied with General Pollock's reply, in which he took no notice of any alliance with him. He flung the paper on the ground in a rage, crying, "This is nothing," and therefore sent Mackenzie back again after only seven hours' rest; but he never imagined that Pollock would defer his advance, and his real object in all these missions was to gain time to strengthen himself. Neither the Afghans nor the captives could guess the reason of Pollock's delay.

Pottinger writes to General Pollock, 3d May:—"I beg to apologise for the blotted state of my letter, as I have only time to write this while Captain Mackenzie is sleeping, preparatory to resuming the march."

On this second journey he was somewhat safer, as the wonderful history of the Feringhi's fidelity to his word under such circumstances had got wind, and, though incomprehensible to the Afghans, they were manly enough to admire it. Not many details are known of his second journey to and from Jellalabad. He arrived there on the 8th May, and stayed about three days. He was received with the greatest joy in camp, as they supposed he had succeeded in arranging the release of the captives. He was so harassed and worn-out, and had such incessant business with General Pollock to make him understand the exact condition of affairs, the whole country being in a state of anarchy and civil war since the assassination of Shah Shujah in March, that he had neither time nor inclination to write home. He only wrote a long letter to Major Skinner giving the details of his brother's murder. He was in the General's tent when an Arab arrived from Fattih Jung, who was then holding out in the Bála Hissar after the death of his father the Shah. He sent to say it was impossible for him to hold out beyond a month, as his ammunition was failing. General Pollock said : "Tell him that within three weeks my guns shall be heard in the Khurd Kabul Pass." But in this Pollock reckoned without the Governor-General. Fattih Jung held out for five weeks and then surrendered.

Mackenzie started on his return on the 10th May, and the garrison saw him depart with even greater despondency than before, looking upon his fate as now hopeless. He himself thought so likewise. He could only look up and trust in God. He thought to himself : "All seems dark, but it is God's will." And what a deliverance was granted to him and his companions in misery !

Broadfoot writes to a friend :—

"*18th May 1842.*

"Poor Colin Mackenzie, most noble Colin, 'the modern Regulus,' as Havelock truly styles him, has been in again on his fruitless mission. Heroism such as his may gild even defeats like ours. At Kabul he displayed the most chivalrous valour, and to him it is mainly owing that Sir W. Macnaghten, after the first shock, showed more resolution than the others. His coming in here, and then, with death staring him in the face, going back, even when Muhammad Akbar's conduct seemed to release him ; *above all*, the motives from which he did it, and the spirit in which he went, raise him to something more than the word hero can express, unless it be taken in its ancient and noblest sense, and then never was it more worthily applied."

Two days later Broadfoot writes again :—

"*20th May 1842.*

"Colin is, alas ! once more among the Afghans, whom, however—barbarous as they are—his heroism and virtue have filled with admiration. I have just been visited by some leading men of the tribes westward of this valley, who spoke of his self-devotion as, to them, incomprehensible. 'For,' said they, 'he is not deceived ; he is a wise man, and knows how Afghans

observe treaties, yet he goes back when he has it in his power to
remain in safety.' When Colin was last here we heard of Muhammad Akbar's going to Kabul.[1] Some, whose opinions are of
weight, doubted Colin's obligation to return ; but he would not
listen to this. My own opinion was that, as Akbar was not
bound to abstain from hostilities, Colin was not free to remain,
but I did think him entitled to remain till it was known
whether the excitement of this new war would render his present
escort insufficient to protect his passage, and, above all, to learn
whether the same cause had produced any popular outrage on
the other prisoners. Colin agreed, but urged, only too truly,
that delay on his part might provoke these outrages, and he
therefore departed. We have not yet heard of him, but there
has hardly been time even if he go only to Tezin, though he will
most likely have to go on to Kabul. Anxious about him we
cannot but be, yet I know the men with him are desirous to
protect him, and I believe them able to do so, for they are near
relations of the principal chief, and the esteem they perceive
Colin enjoys here has confirmed their opinion, already very high,
of his value as a hostage in their hands. These men fought
against us all the way from Kabul to Gandamak, and then,
returning to Kabul, fought there till they accompanied Muhammad Akbar to this place. They were a good deal with me,
being fond of talking of any affairs where they had chanced to
see any officer they remembered, and they one and all spoke of
Colin with unfeigned *wonder.* His defence of the fort, and
cutting his way after all to the cantonments, whose occupants
did not dare to go to him, and his brilliant valour to the last,
made them doubt his being of the same race as those who, alas !
but too often showed differently before them. 'Had he,' said
they repeatedly, 'been ruler the victory would not have been
ours ;' for they well know who did, and who did not, advocate
vigorous measures. They also spoke with reverence of his wisdom, for, said they : 'He speaks as kings and vazirs cannot speak.'"

---

[1] While he was negotiating, Akbar went to Kabul, rallied his
followers, and began to get the upper hand.

It is remarkable how Mackenzie's whole character impressed the Afghans, and how they spoke of him for years after. One officer said all knew him and all liked him. Another, soon after the Bolarum Mutiny, was amazed at a strange Afghan rushing up and seizing his bridle with the inquiry—"*How* is Colin Mackenzie?" Forty years after, an old subáhdar of the regiment he had raised related on returning from the Afghan campaign of 1878 :—"All those devils around Kabul know Mackenzie Sahib."

It was on this visit to Jellalabad that Mackenzie saw the order, dated 19th April, which Lord Ellenborough had sent in quadruplicate to General Pollock, requiring him to retreat and leave the hostages and prisoners, ladies and children to their fate, *i.e.* ignominious slavery and death,— surely the most disgraceful order ever issued by a Governor-General.

Poor General Elphinstone's body had at last arrived safe at Jellalabad on the 30th April, and had been buried with military honours.

Mackenzie left a short narration of one of his adventures on his journey back :—"I was accompanied by two brothers named Wali Muhammad and Shábudín, the former an astute and austerely religious personage, the latter fat, jovial, and undevout. With a view to their and my own comfort, on the day that I left Jellalabad (to redeem my parole with Akbar), I took with me a small basket of cold fowls, hard-boiled eggs, biscuits, etc., as we were pretty sure of getting little or nothing to eat for the first sixty miles or so. Starting in the middle of the day, by nightfall we reached a village where several of our poor fugitives had been basely tortured and murdered. Among these was Lieutenant S., one of the finest men in the army, remarkable for his personal strength, activity, and feats of manly daring. Sad to say, he and an extremely beautiful

Afghan girl had become so deeply enamoured of each
other that when our fatal retreat from Kabul began they
resolved that nothing but death should them part. And
truly it was so! There is no doubt that, humanly speaking, he could have reached Jellalabad in safety had he
consented to abandon her, but I do not believe such a
thought ever crossed his mind. To be brief, their over-
burdened horse at last sunk under them, they were seized,
carried into the village (which I still long to burn to the
ground), and there the brutal villagers, after stripping and
scourging him with whips, hacked him to pieces. The
poor girl was a witness to the torture and murder of him
whom she certainly regarded as her husband, but her life
was spared on account of her great beauty. They soon
fell to quarrelling about her, swords were drawn to establish
the right of possession, when, to put a stop to further
mischief, one of the leaders struck off her head. After a
couple of hours' heavy sleep on the bare ground I was,
although mortally tired, rather glad to be aroused and quit
of such an unhallowed place, on the outskirts of which we
had halted, for my guides told me fairly that they could
not have answered for my life had we ventured inside. On
we went during the remainder of the night and the following morning until near noon, shaping our course towards
the Sulimán range. By that time we had arrived in the
middle of a wild and savage defile, hemmed in by precipitous
cliffs of red sandstone, quite devoid of any kind of vegeta-
tion, and in whose gloomy solitude we apparently were the
only living things save a magnificent eagle, which was
soaring about a hundred yards over our heads—the very
emblem of majesty and power — vividly suggesting the
aptness of the Scriptural expression, 'taking refuge under
the shadow of His wings.' During the whole journey my
guides were nervously anxious about me, for they knew as

well as I that my life depended more on the caprice of those
whom we met than on their own ability to protect, and it
was in the hope of meeting no one that they had chosen
this route. We therefore decided to halt and take some
refreshment, and to allow our fagged horses to rest. We
eagerly unpacked our little basket, and we really were
'jolly under the circumstances.' But the munching process
was suddenly arrested by a very undesirable apparition,
viz. that of two most sinister-looking ruffians, armed to the
teeth, who seemed to have emerged from some crevice in
the rock. They slowly drew near, followed to our dismay
by another, and another, and another, until we counted
six or seven of those robbers, who in Afghanistan acknowledge no tribe, and whose hand is against every man. I
had no arms except a short native talwár stuck in my
kammerband for show, the smallness of whose handle pre-
cluded my using it. My cloak had been thrown off to sit
upon, the mufflings of my turban removed from the lower
part of my face, and I stood before our rascally visitors
a Feringhi confessed,—an infidel, to slay whom was possibly
profitable, and certainly meritorious. My guides whispered
hurriedly together, evidently holding their own lives as
well as mine dirt cheap, and were, as I saw, on the point of
buckling to like men, and thereby, considering the odds
against us, hastening our destruction. I saw at once that
diplomacy must be our weapon, and before the commission
of any overt act of hostility, while we sprang to our feet,
I ordered my companions to be quiet, and gave the saluta-
tion of peace and welcome to the intruders. Wali and
Shábudín at once apprehended my tactics, and the robbers
were courteously invited by all of us to sit down and eat
with us. Such fellows are always hungry, and, taken by
surprise, they did sit down. With hospitable zeal I supplied
them with the best of our provisions, and (hoping that the

Arab principle was in force among them) I officiously
pressed them to eat salt with the hardboiled eggs, of which
last article Afghans are inordinately fond, possibly on the
theory of the Scotch ploughman who gave me as his reason
for preferring cold crowdie to hot—'Ou, sir, it lies langer
on the stamack.' During the meal the conversation between
our forbidding guests and my guides was rapid and energetic. I could not make out the exact nature of the lies
with which the former were mentally crammed ; but I do
know that they crammed themselves with our provisions
until nothing was left for the remainder of our journey.
It appeared, however, that my party insisted magniloquently
on the fact of my being Akbar's guest and ambassador,
and, luckily for us, the marauders in some degree acknowledged the authority and prestige of Sir William Mac-
naughten's murderer. Moreover, good cheer, as well as
'refined learning,' 'softens men's manners and subdues
ferocity.' '*Emollit mores,*' etc.—What sayeth the Latin
grammar? Our uneasy meal having come to a close we
put a good face on the matter and prepared to go. No
opposition was offered, but, by way of experiment, the
robber spokesman, pleading extreme poverty, requested me
as a generous European to give them some rupees. I
looked at him with an air of astonishment, and my guides
with great volubility pooh-poohed the request as an absurdity,
it being evident, they said, that no man in my situation
could be furnished with money. So the rogues allowed
us to proceed on our way, and you may be sure that we
travelled for some time, as the Spaniard says, 'with our
beards on our shoulders.' "

The Fort at Chinghai was again Mackenzie's half-way
house on his journey, and Sir Biland Khan now escorted
him thence to Kabul. Both he and his brother told
Captain Mackenzie that their interview with MacGregor

after Sale had forced the Khurd Kabul Pass, determined them to resist the British to the death, as they saw our weakness.

He reached the valley of Zjandeh, an almost inaccessible place, many thousand feet above the level of the sea, to the south-east of the Tezin valley, on Sunday, the 16th May, and found most of his fellow-captives there. Akbar had despatched them to this out-of-the-way place for safety on the 3d May. The spring was only just beginning, and frost had just ceased. Muhammad Rafiq was now their keeper, a most kind and courteous jailer, who distributed all the money he had among his prisoners. The Afghans are a curious compound of good and evil qualities. Mackenzie used to say that they would share their last loaf with you, and yet if you left an Afghan nobleman in a room with ten rupees you would probably find five less on your return. Mackenzie had brought money, letters, and papers with him, which were eagerly welcomed. He had borrowed two hundred rupees from the Treasury at Jellalabad, which he spent in supplying the most pressing needs of his fellow-captives, chiefly those of the privates.[1]

He found that Captain and Mrs. Anderson had been agreeably surprised by the arrival of their eldest girl from Kabul. After she had been lost in the Khurd Kabul Pass she was taken by an Afghan horseman to the city. Conolly hearing of her had induced Nawab Zemán Khan to buy her for four hundred rupees. His family had treated her with the greatest possible kindness. She spoke nothing but Persian, though still understanding English, and had been taught to say: "My father and mother are infidels, but I am a Musalmani."

Mackenzie left the next day, 17th May, to join

[1] Which sum the Court of Directors, with full knowledge of the circumstances, afterwards made him repay.

Muhammad Akbar, who had carried Pottinger and Troup
with him to Kabul.

Fattih Jung, a son of Shah Shujah, had possession of
the Bála Hissar, and there was open war between him and
Akbar Khan, and between the latter and the Kazilbashes,
besides intermediate fights between Akbar and Nawab
Zemán Khan and between most other people. Ján Fishan
Khan, the staunch friend of the British, had been obliged
to fly for his life, his two sons having been slain in the
fight with Akbar.[1]

Akbar, who was besieging Fattih Jung, was in great
straits for want of money. The Supreme Government had
very properly refused to honour the bills for fourteen lacs
(£140,000), which had been given to the chiefs as the price
of the safe conduct of our Kabul force to Jellalabad. When
the bills were returned, a deputation of the principal chiefs,
headed by Muhammad Shah Khan, the most able and
unscrupulous of them all, came to Major Eldred Pottinger,
who was then confined in the lower part of the tower in
which Akbar was living, and required him to sign fresh
bills for the amount. He reasoned with them, and
endeavoured to show the utter uselessness of such a proceeding, but in vain, and they began to threaten him. He
well knew the atrocities of which Afghans are capable,
but threats only roused the indomitable courage of the hero

---

[1] He was a noble-minded chief, and remained steadfast to the Shah.
Immediately on the outbreak his forts and property had been destroyed.
Lady Sale relates that at the time they were beleaguered in cantonments the chief was ignorant of the fate of his family. "He only knows
that one young boy was burnt alive. He had one wife with him when
the insurrection broke out, and urged her to fly to Paghman (his
territory) for safety. The old chief told me her reply was worth a
lac of rupees: 'I will not leave you; if you fall, we die together; and
if you are victorious, we will rejoice together.' The Afghans afterwards took as many of his family as they could get,—wives, young
daughters, and children,—put them into a tower, and then blew it up."

of Herat. Fixing a stern, unflinching look on the savage chiefs, he said, very slowly and steadily : "Cut off my head, for I will never sign those bills." There was perfect silence for a minute or so, and then they all left the room to consult Akbar, who saw at once that there was no hope of bending such a man. So Eldred Pottinger gained the day.

Akbar, having sprung a mine under one of the towers of the Bála Hissar, made terms with Fattih Jung, acknowledged him as King, and installed himself as Vazir. Zemán Khan, finding himself unable to protect Conolly and the other hostages any longer, confided them to the protection of the Mir Waiz, or chief Mullah, who, after solemnly swearing that he would never give them up, sold them to Akbar for 400 sequins.

Mackenzie, Pottinger, and Troup lived with Muhammad Akbar at first in a small fort called Bin-i-Shahar, a little way out of the town, and afterwards in the city. Akbar used frequently to consult them. About this time he sent for Captains Mackenzie and Troup, and, having dismissed every one else except two most courteous gentlemanly old "Rish-safeyds" (white-beards), he asked their opinion as to the probability of General Pollock's advance to Kabul. Mackenzie endeavoured to evade replying by saying: "You can judge quite as well as I can ;" but Akbar pressed him very closely, saying: "Whatever is in your heart, tell it me." Mackenzie promised that he was not to be offended, and then, so well did he know Pollock's determination, that although the Governor-General's peremptory refusals continued for a month after this, he told Akbar plainly, to his great chagrin, that it was his decided opinion that Pollock would march to Kabul. Some one then proposed consulting Major Pottinger, to which Akbar angrily responded expressing his rooted dislike to Pottinger, calling him a hard, impracticable fellow, adding that he had no confidence in

him. Just then Major Pottinger, having heard of the conference, entered, looking as grim as ever. Akbar immediately
welcomed him in an extravagant manner, introducing him in
the most flattering way to the Rish-safeyds as "the great
Major Pottinger, the man in whom he placed the greatest
confidence, the defender of Herat, who had done so much
for Islam," and all this before the faces of the two officers
to whom he had just expressed his real sentiments!

The streets of Kabul were full of unfortunate Hindustanis begging for bread, which was daily served out to
them by Nawabs Jabar Khan and Zemán Khan. Numbers
of others had been made slaves (some sold to the Turko-
mans), and were never released. The civility of all classes
in and around Kabul towards the British at this time was
remarkable.

Akbar had moved his prisoners from Zjandeh to the
fort of Shewaki, three miles from Kabul, where the hostages were allowed occasionally to visit them, and where
they were joined at the end of June by the European soldiers who had been left behind at Badiabad since 11th
April. They had been robbed and starved in great measure at the instigation of the vile wife of Sergeant Wade (a
half-caste woman), who had left her husband and betaken
herself to the Afghan jailer, whom (*suadente diabolo*) she
stirred up in every way against the unfortunate prisoners.
Badiabad being very hot, they had suffered much from
fever. Sergeant Reynolds, who had a broken arm, died
of lockjaw; all were miserably thin and weak, Mrs.
Bourne's baby looked like a skeleton, and died a few days
after. Soon after, Akbar sent Sergeant Cleland and Gunner
Dalton of the Horse Artillery to join the captives. The
Afghans literally chopped many of our Sepoys into pieces
because they would not become Muhammadans, but many
of our English soldiers made the Musalman confession of

faith without the smallest scruple. Cleland and Dalton, however, proved worthy of belonging to that band of heroes the 1st Troop Bengal Horse Artillery. Akbar Khan had desired Sergeant Cleland to point some of the guns he had taken against the British at Jellalabad. Cleland positively refused. Akbar in a rage cried: "If you do not obey, you shall be put to death instantly." The brave soldier immediately began to strip off his jacket, and answered: "Very well, I am ready." Gunner Dalton did the same, and Akbar was so struck by their gallant behaviour that he saved their lives and commended them highly.

After Akbar's defeat by General Sale on the 7th of April, Cleland and Dalton were carried across the river with part of the fugitive Afghans. One of the party was a man of some rank, mortally wounded, who had evidently had some share in the murder of Sir William, for, as he lay dying all night in the tent they had pitched for him, he continually cried out to the murdered Envoy as if he were present. Gunner Dalton, who was sitting by his side, with a strange degree of savage humour kept on saying in a soothing kind tone of voice: "Ah, you may well cry out, for you are going to hell, my jewel;" and the Afghans, thinking he was praying for or pitying the sick man, patted him on the back, and called him a good fellow. Dalton was an Irishman, full of fun and frolic, even in the most desperate circumstances. He made himself a terror to the Afghans by feigning madness, of which they have a superstitious dread, thinking the insane inspired. Whenever the Afghans desired Dalton to do anything he ran at them, butting with his head like a ram, and bellowing and stamping with his feet. "Truly," said they, "he is an inspired man!"

CHAPTER XX.

"Blind mortals and blind moles, you neither of you know, as you go burrowing on, how near you are to light. But perhaps the moles know best. The incumbent soil must surely weigh less heavily as those persistent little paws, guided by God Himself, come within an inch of the upper air. But men's hearts seem meant to be heaviest just before the sorrow is lifted off."—HERBERT EDWARDES' *Life of Sir Henry Lawrence*, i. p. 131.

ABOUT the 1st July the excessive fatigue and excitement of his four journeys to and from Jellalabad, which Sir Robert Sale drolly characterised as "worthy of his gallant and philanthropic mind," together with the violent transitions of heat and cold to which he was exposed in crossing the mountains and then descending into the stifling valleys, coupled with previous hardships, and the acute mental suffering he endured from the disgrace of our arms and the massacre of so many friends and intimates, brought on an attack of typhus in its most virulent form, under which Mackenzie nearly sank. He had come out to visit his friends at the Shewaki Fort when he was taken ill, and was nursed with the greatest tenderness by the Eyres and also by the Rileys. When he became delirious he would take nothing except from Mrs. Eyre; but when she gave him his medicine and spoke to him in a soft voice, he contrived to make a hollow sound in his chest something like "Thank you." Mrs. Eyre had the luxury of a bed on four legs, which she gave up to him, sleeping on the ground herself. All hope of his recovery was given up, and Eyre read the *Prayers for the Dying* to him, but he was so weak that he could hardly hear anything. Jacob sat by his dear master with his eyes fixed upon him, tears streaming down his face and quite unconscious of everything else. Mrs. Eyre spent the last money she had in buying some chickens, which she made into broth, which revived him wonderfully. Mr. Riley used to sit up all night with him, and being a man of immense muscular strength would, when he got a little better, carry him in his arms and take him out into the fresh air. The fort was surrounded by rice-fields up to the very walls, and these sheets of stagnant water, together with low diet, brought attacks of the same disease in a somewhat modified form on many of the captives, poor Jacob included. Akbar Khan sent Dr. Campbell at their earnest request, but there was hardly any medicine to be had,—which, however, may not have been a disadvantage. Mackenzie being in this state, Akbar Khan despatched Captain Colin Troup to Jellalabad on the 10th July, offering to release the prisoners at once if Pollock would return to India. At the same time Major Pottinger wrote the following noble letter to the General :—

10th July 1842.

" At present I do not think it would be advisable to ransom us for money, as he (Akbar) is in want of that necessary ; and the name and character of the British must suffer in the opinion of our own subjects and soldiers in India, if we were to pay for the release of a few Europeans, while so many thousands of our native soldiery and camp - followers are reduced to slavery throughout this country, and many other poor wretches, deprived of their hands and feet or otherwise mutilated or diseased, are supporting their precarious existence by beggary. If these latter persons be not released many, if not all, must perish in the ensuing winter ; and it appears to me that Government will lay itself open to the odium of undue partiality if it release us by ransom."

He also recommends a proclamation threatening punishment if the ladies are withdrawn, and that letters should be written to the Hazárá chiefs and others, which would probably prevent the prisoners being carried off through either the west or north districts. He adds :—

"Muhammad Shah Khan is the right hand and head of Muhammad Akbar. He is our bitterest as well as our ablest enemy, and will be the last to submit to our sway. By reducing his castles and property in Laghmán you will cripple his means, and, it may be, oblige him to fall on his master for money. This will give opportunity for his enemies to undermine him, and certainly to weaken his influence." [1]

So little is now remembered of this self-denying heroic officer that it is impossible to omit such a letter. Vincent Eyre likewise wrote to his family in England :—

"The report that our army was going back to India without striking a blow seems incredible. Negotiations are going on for our release. God grant that they may succeed ! though we have no wish to be liberated at the expense of our country's honour."

Pollock offered an exchange of prisoners without reserve, including of course the Dost, but took no notice of Akbar's condition that we should retire from Afghanistan. Troup returned on the 27th and was sent off again with Captain G. St. P. Lawrence on the 29th ; but Pollock had just received permission to act on his own responsibility, and as he was preparing to advance, he would not make any terms. Akbar was furious when Troup and Lawrence

[1] Parl. Papers, No. 434.

returned from their perilous journey, and the captives were now in extreme danger. A short time previous Akbar was holding a council of chiefs, when Major Pottinger, who was, unknown to most of them, in an adjoining room, over-heard a Kohistani chief propose that all the English prisoners should be slain, on which Akbar got up in a rage and turned the man out of the assembly. Akbar now de-clared that if Pollock and Nott advanced he would send the whole batch of captives to Turkistan to be sold as slaves to different chiefs. Pollock wrote to Khan Sharin Khan Kazilbash, and other chiefs, assuring them of free pardon on condition of their preventing the removal of the captives from Kabul, and threatening, on the other hand, to raze the city to the ground in case of Akbar's threat being fulfilled.

In the meantime Conolly had come out to Shewaki to see his friends, and, like Mackenzie, was seized with virulent fever, under which he sank five days after on the 7th August. He was universally respected by the Afghans and greatly beloved by his brother officers. His influence had saved the detachment of sick and wounded left at Kabul under Lieutenant Evans, he had supplied them with money furnished by the two noble Arab Jews, Musa and Ibrahim, at great personal risk to themselves, and he and the other hostages had refused to avail themselves of several opportunities for escape from consideration for the detachment, who would have been exposed to the vengeance of the mob. Only three years had elapsed since Arthur, Edward, and John Conolly had arrived in Afghanistan with bright hopes and prospects, all three having been placed in political employment by their uncle, Sir William Macnaghten. Edward was shot through the heart in Kohistan in September 1841. He was a small man, mounted on a very large horse, yet, strange to say, he dismounted, turned an appealing look never to be forgotten on the friend next him, and fell dead. Arthur was at this time still languishing in the dungeon at Bokhara, and, when he wrote his last letter to John, they had been upwards of eighty days without change of raiment, eaten up by vermin, and Stoddart, a magnificent man, reduced to a skeleton. Both Stoddart and Conolly were accredited Envoys from Government, but Lord Ellenborough, instead of demanding their release as such, wrote to the tyrant of Bokhara pleading for them as "innocent travellers." This sealed their fate. Not long after both suffered martyrdom for their faith.

On the 12th August Major Pottinger with the five hostages,[1] who had been given over on the 29th December, and who had remained all along in the city, were now sent to join the other captives at Shewaki, Akbar giving the order—"Take away those dogs!" On the 17th a private, and Mrs. Smith, widow of Mackenzie's store sergeant (a most faithful, good creature), died of fever, and were buried next to Conolly, Captain Lawrence reading the service over them.

On the 23d, the very day Pollock reached Gandamak, Colonel Palmer and the eight other officers of the Ghazni garrison arrived at Shewaki, which seemed to them a small paradise after the close confinement they had endured; Colonel Palmer having even been tortured by a species of "boot" to reveal treasure which did not exist.

On the 25th August Akbar sent off the whole of the captives by moonlight towards Bamian except Captains Troup and Bygrave, whom he chose to keep with him; Mrs. Trevor with Captain and Mrs. Anderson being dangerously ill from

[1] Captains Walsh, 52d M.N.I.; Henry Drummond, 3d Bengal Light Cavalry; Lieutenants Jas. Airey, H.M.'s 3d Buffs; Warburton, Bengal Artillery; and Edward Webb, 38th M.N.I.

fever,—the latter quite unconscious,—were with the utmost difficulty allowed to remain, with Dr. Campbell to attend upon them. Mackenzie was still so ill that it was a question whether it was worth while to send him. He had, however, to start with the rest. The escort of 300 or 400 men was commanded by Saleh Muhammad, an ex-subáhdar of Afghan horse, who had deserted with all his men and joined the Dost at Bamián in 1840. The ladies now adopted the outdoor costume of Afghan women, consisting of a large white sheet with a burkha or veil completely concealing both face and figure. It would have been well had they done so previously, as riding unveiled exposed them to insulting remarks, which were most trying to the gentlemen who heard them. Mrs. Eyre was the only one who had previously consented to wear the Afghan veil.[1]

After a rough march of sixteen miles they were joined by a doctor, with fifty-seven Europeans of the sick detachment, Lieutenant Evans, H.M.'s 44th, and Lieutenant Haughton, both very ill. Charges were signed by every one of the sick soldiers against this doctor for having appropriated their scanty allowance to his own use, etc., etc. These were sent to General Pollock, but as Lieutenant Evans did nothing in the business, the doctor was never called to account for it.

26th August.—This day no food whatever was supplied to either man or beast. They marched through a most lovely country, "so distracted by blood feuds that the inhabitants scarcely dared to venture a few hundred yards from their own dwellings."

Bamián was one hundred and twenty miles distant, and they took about twelve hours to go from ten to fifteen

---

[1] Before this, when they wore turbans, several of the ladies used to send for Captain Mackenzie daily to put them on properly, on the plea that they were unable to do so themselves.

miles, starting at two A.M. each morning. One Sunday (the 28th) no tents were pitched, and the fever patients suffered greatly. They halted in a meadow, cold and damp, with many willows. Mackenzie and his little party, who always clung to each other, drew their rugs together, and lay as close as possible for the sake of warmth. In the morning Colin Mackenzie awoke with raging fever. He was slung as usual in a kajáwah on one side of a camel, with Mrs. Eyre, who was also very ill, on the other. The agony he endured during that tedious, interminable march cannot be told. The idea chiefly present in his mind was, " Well, I shall last ten minutes more." Ten minutes—ten minutes—went and came. At the end of the day he was still living, and was shot out of the kajáwah like so much rubbish, and where he fell there he lay. Poor Jacob was in dreadful distress about him. The next day, at the end of the march, Pottinger, Webb, and one of the doctors, carried him into a wretched little tent, and laid him on Haughton's rug. Some one—he thinks it was Dr. Berwick—had a little quinine in his pocket, which they made him swallow, and which had the best effect. Another had a little tea, which they made him drink. One day, when he was a little better, the bottom of his kajáwah came out just after starting. He managed with the strength of desperation to hold on until good Henry Drummond, who was coming along sick and sad on horseback, saw him, and made the camel-man stop. Captain Drummond supported his friend, and got him on his own saddle, where he was propped up the rest of the day's journey, while he himself took his place in the bottomless kajáwah, and clung on like a sailor in the shrouds, balancing Mrs. Eyre, until the end of that weary march. Henry Drummond was always one of the most kindly and affectionate of human beings. He had been employed by Government in searching for coal in Afghanistan, and even in this extremity he would hold forth on "coal formation" and persist in arguing about—the corn laws! to the exasperation of his fellow-captives.

They had now entered the Hazárá country. Mustafa Khan, a Kazilbash chief, had kindly prepared a quantity of small cakes, which he distributed with comforting words to the captives as they passed. The Kazilbashes were all along our secret friends, and would have joined us in a body if Mackenzie had been supported in his defence of the fort which adjoined their quarter of the city, or if we had shown any vigour or any ability to protect either ourselves or our friends. Being of Persian descent, they are Shiahs, or followers of Ali, and have therefore considerable influence over that half of the Hazárá tribe who hold the same tenets, and who inhabit all the neighbourhood of Bamián.

The hatred of the Sunis and Shiahs towards each other is even greater than that which they feel towards Christians, and the knowledge of these facts induced Pottinger, before leaving Kabul, to set to work a secret agency to seduce Saleh Muhammad by means of his clansmen the Kazilbashes.

On the 29th and 30th the prisoners endeavoured to bribe Saleh Muhammad with the offer of a lakh of rupees to effect their release, but he would by no means listen to the proposition, and treated them with great harshness. On the 31st Mackenzie felt for the first time that death would be a relief. Racked with fever, he was slung as usual on one side of a camel, and poor Mrs. Eyre, who was dreadfully ill, on the other. He said: "Her fortitude at last gave way, and how she did groan!" At length on the 3d September they reached Bamián, where Mackenzie and his little coterie were thrust into a sort of shed, in the inner apartment of which some Afghan shepherds had been living.

It was filled with lice and ticks, but by this time they had
become almost callous in their misery.   Another of their
company, Gunner M'Crae, succumbed to illness and fatigue,
and was buried on the 5th—the last milestone of our
march into Afghanistan.

At last, on Sunday the 11th September, the decisive
order arrived from Akbar for the instant march of the
prisoners to Kulum.   The Wali of Kulum had sent an
officer with two thousand men towards the frontier to
receive them, but, to the unbounded astonishment of most
of the party, Major Pottinger came to tell them that Saleh
Muhammad had offered to make them over to the British
on payment of twenty thousand rupees in cash, and one
thousand rupees a month for life.   Pottinger, Johnson,
Mackenzie, and Lawrence immediately signed a guarantee
to that effect, although, as Mackenzie wrote:—"We had
some misgivings that Saleh Muhammad only wanted
our names in writing as concerned in an attempt against
the Sirdar to betray us and ensure our destruction.   Nevertheless, the case being a desperate one, we agreed to run
the risk; and suspecting from our knowledge of the importance attached by Afghans to rank that he would require
also the names of Shelton and Palmer, these gentlemen
were requested to join in the bond of assurance.   Both
refused "lest they should implicate themselves with Akbar
Khan."[1]   All the other prisoners then joined in guarantee-
ing the amount in case Government should refuse to
sanction it.   The cause of this sudden change in their
jailer's views was the arrival the previous night of Said
Murteza Shah, a Kashmiri, the agent of Mackenzie's
staunch friend, Ali Reza Khan, the Kazilbash.

From the time of Akbar's return to Kabul after his
defeat by Sale, Ali Reza Khan had been obliged to take

[1] Pottinger's Report.

refuge in the Hazárá hills. Akbar offered a large reward
to any one who would bring him in dead or alive; but in
spite of all difficulties he still continued through his friends,
at very great personal risk to themselves, to supply the
British prisoners with clothes and money. A few days
after the departure of the main body of the prisoners for
Bamián, a brother of his informed Captain Troup privately
that Ali Reza had induced the Kazilbashes to seize Saleh
Muhammad's mother and family, and place them as hostages
for the safety of the captives in Ali Reza's own fort. Doubtless Pollock's letter made them the more willing to do this.
Captain Troup pledged himself that Ali Reza's agent,
Murteza Shah, should be amply rewarded. The latter then
gained over Saleh Muhammad's brother, and took him to
Bamián, with urgent letters from the Kazilbash chiefs to
their clansman. Mohun Lal, Burnes' Munshi, had found
refuge among the Kazilbashes, and was active in promising
rewards. Major Pottinger speaks highly of the great
courage and skill shown by Murteza Shah in the negotiation. Immediately the agreement was complete, Major
Pottinger appointed a new Governor of the province in the
name of the British Government, and dispensed presents
and promises to the Hazárá chiefs, who almost unanimously
declared in our favour. The prisoners then contributed
whatever money they could muster to provision the two
little forts they were in, in case of a siege. Among their
guards were ten Heratis who had served under Pottinger,
and who promised to be faithful to him, and an old servant
of his—ragged and wretched—who got reviled by the
Afghans for rendering many little services to the captives.
There were also two of Mackenzie's Jezailchis, who, to save
their lives, had been forced to take nominal service with
Akbar. Mackenzie says:—"Their secret kindness to me
was unbounded, although they begged me not even to

exchange a 'Salam Aleikum' with them openly. One of them was severely beaten, as far as I could make out, for his sinful leanings towards a káfir, but this did not in any way cool his zeal in my behalf." Among the Europeans there were only about twenty-four able-bodied men fit for service, while the guards numbered four hundred.

Pottinger wrote to inform General Pollock of the success of the negotiation; and Saleh Muhammad received a letter from Akbar ordering him to hurry away the prisoners, and to put to death all those who were unable to travel; at least he *said* he had received these orders, but he never showed the letter. On the 16th September, hearing that Pollock was fast drawing near to Kabul, and that Akbar had fled to Kohistan, Saleh Muhammad thought the time was come to march back. Sad to say, this their first march towards freedom was the last march of a poor private of the 44th, who died on the road. At night they had the joy of receiving a note from Sir Richmond Shakespear telling them he was advancing to their relief with seven hundred Kazilbash horse. The next day (17th September) they halted at noon, and sat down under the shade of the small fort of Kálu, when, about 3 P.M., the friendly banner of the Kazilbash was seen streaming in the air. Sir Richmond Shakespear galloped up, and was warmly greeted by those he had come to rescue. Only Brigadier Shelton was displeased because Shakespear had not reported his arrival *first* to him before noticing his grateful countrywomen and countrymen whom he first met. The need of exertion in the negotiations with Saleh Muhammad and the subsequent march had roused Mackenzie to action; but when Sir Richmond galloped up, and the cry "We are saved!" went round, illness reasserted its dominion, and he could not raise himself from the ground. He only said " Ah !" when he heard of Shakespear's arrival, and to the latter's hearty greetings, replied merely by giving his hand without a word; and when he saw Sir Richmond exchange turbans with Saleh Muhammad the only thought that passed through his mind was a lazy wonder "if Shakespear would be covered with vermin in the process."

None of the captives felt anything like the joy which might have been anticipated. Their captivity and preservation produced a strong religious impression on almost all the prisoners; but, strange to say, far less on the ladies than on the men. Eyre says:—"Even the most thoughtless among us could not fail to acknowledge in all that had befallen us the distinguishing grace and protecting providence of a merciful God." General Pollock had reached Kabul on the 15th, and immediately despatched Shakespear, who had volunteered to lead the Kazilbash horse to the rescue of the captives.[1] The General also sent ten thousand rupees to quicken the movements of our allies. Akbar had still a following of from one to two thousand horse, and might intercept the prisoners, while Sultan Ján, with upwards of ten thousand, was in full pursuit of them. Sir Richmond Shakespear therefore despatched an earnest request that troops might be instantaneously sent out to their support. They marched the next morning, 19th September, at 3 A.M., the Kazilbash chiefs supplying them with fresh horses. As they passed the fort of Mustafa Khan, he again regaled them with cakes, curds, and excellent tea, rejoicing at the fulfilment of the assurances he had given them on their sorrowful journey northward, that they would soon be at liberty. Mackenzie had continued exceedingly ill ever since July, but this day he could no longer sit on horseback, but

---

[1] This handsome and chivalrous officer seemed to have a peculiar vocation for rescuing captives, having previously delivered many unfortunate Russians from Khiva.

was obliged to lie on the ground unable to stir hand or foot. Vincent Eyre and Gunner Dalton, at the imminent risk of being cut to pieces by the Afghans, gallantly stayed by him till evening. Dalton, though suffering dreadfully—a 12-pounder having crushed his chest, so that the ribs lapped over each other—came and held his head in his lap, and nursed him like a brother.[1] Mackenzie related afterwards that at that time he suffered so intensely that he has absolutely roared, but not like poor Major Pottinger, who described his own outcry as "something between a roar and a whistle," and Mackenzie said it was so ludicrous that he laughed, and Eyre laughed, and they all laughed, excepting poor Haughton, who was far too ill to laugh.

In the evening the hospitable old chief insisted on escorting them in person into camp, the road being very unsafe, for they had just learned that a hostile chief with a thousand followers had reached Kálu a few hours after they had left, and would probably try to overtake them. In the meantime General Pollock sent orders to Nott, who had arrived two days after himself, to despatch a brigade in the direction of Bamián. Nott's own officers had already suggested this movement as they passed the road to Bamián on their way into Kabul, but that irritable and morose commander refused. "Government," he said, "had thrown the prisoners overboard, why then should *he* rescue them?" He therefore abused not only the officer who brought the order, but his cavalry escort, and wrote a strong protest against the proposed measure, professing, however, his willingness to obey a positive order. Pollock, who looked upon such a service as a privilege, and to whom the release of the prisoners was a matter very near both his heart and his conscience, answered with imperturbable gentleness that

[1] Poor Dalton died of dysentery the day after reaching India for want of the common comforts a sick man ought to have.

"it need not be done," and sent Sale instead, who started at night on the 19th September, marched twenty-four miles to Argandi, where he left his camp, and pushed on to the crest of the pass of Safed-Koh. There he left his guns and infantry, and taking the 3d Dragoons and 1st Light Cavalry met the captives and their escort, who had come about twelve miles since daybreak. All hearts were full, hardly any one could speak. Mackenzie himself could say nothing, but at last he went up to General Sale, and, after riding by him for about a quarter of an hour, found voice to say: "General, I congratulate you." The gallant old man turned towards him and tried to answer, but his feelings were too strong; he made a hideous series of grimaces, dug his spurs into his horse, and galloped off as hard as he could. The detachments of the 9th and 13th L.I. raised three hearty cheers for each of the ladies as she ascended the hill, and Backhouse's mountain train wound up with a royal salute. "A delay of twenty-four hours," writes General Pollock, "would have enabled Sultan Ján to overtake our people." They reached the camp at Argandi after a march of twenty-five miles, and next day, 21st September, passed through Nott's camp. His force were anything but pleased at losing the honour and pleasure of securing the captives, and many of the regiments turned out and gave Sir Robert three hearty cheers. Kabul was almost deserted; Burnes' house a heap of rubbish. They reached Pollock's camp at sunset amid the warmest congratulations, and found that the sick ladies and Captain Troup had been rescued at Shewaki by Ján Fishan Khan, and brought into camp on the 15th.[1]

---

[1] The whole number of Europeans finally released were—including the 10 hostages—20 officers (10 of them wounded), 10 ladies, 2 soldiers' wives, 22 children, 6 of the Bengal Horse Artillery, 38 of the 44th, 7 of the 13th L.I., and 2 clerks.

Ferris' Jezailchis showed Mackenzie a singular proof of affection. They all considered him as one of their own body, and brought him an offering of sheep, whose owners they had probably killed a few minutes before, and of rupees. But this time he satisfied them for not accepting the money, by saying that now he was free he was very rich. The few survivors of those who had served with him gradually rejoined their regiment.

Soon after the arrival of the prisoners in camp, General Pollock considered it necessary to send two brigades against Istalif, in consequence of the chief Aminullah being encamped there in great force, knowing full well that if allowed to remain unmolested he would harass and distress the rear of the army. Lord Ellenborough had named Captain Mackenzie for any political employment, and as General Pollock considered him "the ablest of the whole body," he "nominated him to a situation of great responsibility, in political charge of Prince Shahpur and a considerable body of Kazilbash horse, to co-operate with General M'Caskill in the reduction of the Kohistan Valley." Prince Shahpur was Shah Shujah's favourite son, the child of a noble Popalzai [1] mother and had, though a mere lad, shown his gallantry when leading a force to the assistance of Sir Alexander Burnes. He had watched for days beside the body of his murdered father, and when Akbar pillaged the women of the Royal household, had remonstrated with him, saying: "Do not take their little flour." Yet Akbar took it, and left them in actual want. Shahpur, although so young, possessed the intelligence and decision of a man of thirty. His "presence was expected to yield good results politically, but the state of feeling in the minds of the Kazilbashes and of the native portion of the force towards one another was not satisfactory. A smothered hate

[1] The clan of which the Royal house is the chief family

existed which required all Mackenzie's watchfulness and tact to prevent exploding. No collision took place."[1] Mackenzie's high-bred courtesy and delicate sympathy were here of the utmost value. Instead of the haughtiness and bad taste too frequent among Englishmen, he always behaved to the young Prince and the Kazilbash nobles as he would have done to men of the highest rank at home. This so won their hearts that he became the most popular man in their camp, and even the chief men used to offer him their own pipes to smoke. The young Prince always made him sit beside him, and conceived a real friendship for him. In an appeal which he sent in some years later for an increase of pension to Prince Shahpur as the representative of Shah Shujah-ul-Mulk, Mackenzie says:—" I beg to state emphatically that the conduct of Prince Shahpur throughout these important and successful operations was worthy of unqualified admiration, and that, on our hasty withdrawal from Kohistan, he did his best to persuade the Kazilbash chiefs to aid him in holding that district, in following up the victory we had gained, and, if possible, in securing the person of our arch-enemy Akbar Khan. But the Kazilbashes doubted our assurances of subsequent support, and announced their determination to return to Kabul with the British troops, on which the gallant boy Shahpur turned to me, and, almost with tears of indignation, exclaimed: 'The cowards forsake me!'"

For this service Mackenzie had to fit himself out with horses and arms as best he could with funds supplied by his faithful Jewish friends. But European clothes were not to be had; he therefore continued to wear the Afghan costume till he reached Calcutta.

Starting on the 26th September, General M'Caskill stormed Istalif on the 29th, after several hours' hard fight-

[1] Letter from Major-General Sir John M'Caskill

ing. It was a very strong place, but the enemy were driven from position to position. We took two guns and recovered an immense quantity of our Kabul loot. Aminullah fled early in the day.[1] During the assault the General's position was in an orchard, where he refreshed himself with the delicious plums of the country. On Mackenzie reporting to him that the place was entirely in our hands, he briefly said: "All right; take a plum." Mackenzie was in some peril from our own men, who took him for an Afghan. "If it hadn't been for your v'ice, sir, I should have put my bagnet into you," said one of the gallant 9th.

As is too frequently the case, our troops were most unjustly accused in the newspapers of cruelty and lawlessness at Istalif, and Englishmen have been found to believe that we allowed the Sepoys to set fire to the Afghan wounded—the fact being that when a man's clothes caught fire it was from the fuse of his own matchlock. Far from

---

[1] General M'Caskill wrote to Mackenzie:—"On making the attack you placed yourself by my side and made your services valuable to me, acting as one of my Staff, for which I had the satisfaction to express my approbation and thanks to you in Orders, as well as in the Report I made of that service. You and I know, though the superior authorities may not have yet known, that, but for that chastisement having caused the dispersion of the combined chieftains and their numerous followers, measures had been matured for rendering the retirement of our forces extremely harassing, which would have entailed on us a heavy loss. A whole nation was to have arisen against us as one man, and were to have assailed us in flanks and rear. What might have been our loss under such circumstances who can tell? We had an enormous train of cattle and exhausted artillery horses, besides numerous sick and followers, to protect in our defilings through rugged and formidable mountain passes, of which our active enemy well understood how to take advantage. For your part in this service you are, in my humble opinion, fully entitled to the Kabul Medal, and if I might be permitted to say further, a step of Brevet rank besides.— With best wishes and a very high opinion of your merits and deserts, Very sincerely yours,

(Signed)   "JOHN M'CASKILL."

such accusations being true, all the women and children
who had not fled, about five hundred in number, were collected together at the top of the city, where they were all
day long joined by stragglers. We set guards over them,
supplied them with grapes and water, and provided in every
possible way for their comfort until the evening, when we
sent them under the escort of a friendly chief to the place
where their routed countrymen had reassembled, and this act
of British humanity was gratefully acknowledged by the
Afghans. Shortly after securing the safety of the women,
Mackenzie met a grenadier of the 9th carrying something
very tenderly. "What have you got there, my man?" "A
babby, your Honour; I didn't think, Sir, as how it was my
duty for to kill it." "Kill it! no; give it to me." It was a
beautiful Afghan infant. He rode with it to the group of
women and offered it first to one and then to another. Each
answered: "It isn't mine." At last on an old woman rudely
refusing to receive it, he said sharply: "If you don't take
it and take care of it I will drag you away and throw you
into the midst of the troops." The hard-hearted old dame
yielded, held out her arms, and the creature's soft innocence
seemed to find its way to her heart.

The force next destroyed Charekar, which had been so
heroically defended by Haughton and his Ghurka regiment,
and where Mackenzie gathered up the bones of his brother
cadet, Captain Codrington, and had them buried, returning
to Kabul on the 7th October.

Shewaki and many other forts were burned, and, in spite
of General Pollock's orders, there was a good deal of indis-
criminate plundering. We ought to have remained longer
to have recovered more of our captive people. Hundreds
were left in slavery, even, it is said, some Europeans. Upwards of 350 men of the 27th N.I. joined Nott at Ghazni
alone, but before starting for India he made a general clear-

ance, expelling no less than 500 from the Bazar of the 16th
Regiment, not to speak of others, most of them destitute
Hindus who hoped to be allowed to return under our
escort. Pollock, on the contrary, carried with him about
2000 crippled Sepoys and camp-followers of Elphinstone's
army, whom he mercifully provided with carriage, appointing two officers to provide for them and to send them to
their own homes.

Fattih Jung, who had taken the place of his father the
late Shah, having escaped from the clutches of Akbar Khan,
fled to our camp, re-entered Kabul with General Pollock,
and reassumed his place on the throne. But the General
having carefully explained to him that the British Government would not interfere further with the government of
Afghanistan, and would not assist him, he and all the royal
family resolved to return to India with the army, Captain
Lawrence being placed in charge of the old blind king Shah
Zemán and the ladies. The party in favour of the Sadozi
family then raised Prince Shahpur to the throne. The
high-spirited lad willingly accepted the offer, though he
knew that the British would not support him. The General,
therefore, spared the Royal Fort, the Bála Hissar, and after
consultation with the Kazilbash chiefs, blew up the magnificent bazar where the mutilated remains of the murdered
Envoy had been exhibited. War, even under so mild and
just a commander as Pollock, is a terrible thing, and many
a guiltless and friendly Hindu and Kazilbash was involved
in the punishment which befel the blood-stained Kabuli.
Owing to Pollock's strict discipline supplies came in freely,
but Nott's Sepahis and followers were very unruly, plundering in spite of Pollock's warnings to Nott, and on the last
day the troops broke loose. The Hindu Sepoys, being
naturally most bitter against the Afghans, and maddened
by the sight of clothes and accoutrements, the spoil of their

unfortunate comrades, plundered and destroyed the greater part of Kabul, many of the poor Hindu merchants losing everything they possessed. Still there were no atrocities ; women and children were invariably respected, and General Pollock could truly assert that "none were killed in cold blood, and no troops ever conducted themselves with more forbearance under such unprecedented aggravations." To prevent any further mischief Pollock made Nott and the whole force march on the same day as himself.

Mackenzie had now to part from the young prince, to whom he had become so strongly attached. He was sitting by his side when Shahpur took his hand, drew a ring off his own finger, and, placing it on that of his friend, said : "I am poor, I have nothing but this, do not forget me !"

Within two months Akbar had carried everything before him, and the brave boy narrowly escaped with life, and has since lived in exile at Lodiana.[1]

A good bit of work had been nobly done, and although the army was hurried back to India by the Governor-General, leaving many of our unfortunate people in captivity, yet those who had distinguished themselves naturally looked forward to having their services acknowledged and rewarded.

[1] Mackenzie writes :—"The royal brothers being thus reassembled, part of the pension formerly paid to their father Shah Shujah (whom we for our own policy had carried back to Afghanistan at the sacrifice of his life), was divided among them, Teimur receiving 2000 rupees a month, and the stout-hearted and constant Shahpur only 400 for himself, his family, and the innumerable dependants who, hungry and naked fugitives from the vengeance of their countrymen, flocked to him as the last representative of the Duráni monarchy for food and raiment. Shahpur has a heart in his bosom, and in spite of rigid self-denial and economy, of which I am personally cognisant, he has not been able to avoid debt."

CHAPTER XXI

(1842-3.)

LORD ELLENBOROUGH issued a magniloquent proclamation ordering the evacuation of Afghanistan, dated Simla, 1st October 1842, at least twelve days before he could possibly have heard of the release of the captives.[1]

General Pollock marched from Kabul on the 12th October, and his column arrived at Jellalabad on the 22d without the loss of a man. He had "crowned the heights the whole distance, and had a strong rear-guard," whereas M'Caskill and Nott, who did not take these precautions, had several smart skirmishes, in one of which Nott lost sixty-one killed and wounded. Pollock had to exculpate himself to the Governor-General for the expedition to Istalif, and for not having marched sooner! Jellalabad and Ali Masjid were blown up, and again, thanks to Pollock's masterly precautions, he lost but two or three men and no baggage on the march through the Khaiber. He ordered that every camel that could not come on should be shot and its load burned. M'Caskill and Nott again suffered severely because not equally careful.

---

[1] "The date," says Stocqueler, "is particularly unfortunate for the Governor-General's fame, as it proves beyond all question that he had not made the release of the prisoners an indispensable condition of the evacuation of the country."

A very miscellaneous party accompanied the army, among them the noble-hearted chief Ján Fishan Khan, now, as he himself said, "only poor Said Muhammad," for, despoiled of his fertile lands in Laghmán, he was almost destitute. Many of his family had been slain; one young son had had his throat cut, though he begged hard for life, pleading that he was but a little child and could never have harmed any one; the remnant of his house went with him into exile.[1]

Mackenzie's small tent was crammed. "Jews, Turks, infidels, and heretics," were all welcome. Besides his faithful Jacob and Private M'Glynn, he had in one corner the two Arab Jews, Mullas Musa and Ibrahim, who had so faithfully befriended the captives, and in another his gallant jemadar, Muhammad Hasan Khan, for a great pleasure had awaited Mackenzie on the march. He had not dared to inquire for Hasan Khan, fearing to hear of the dreadful fate he antici- pated for him. He relates:—"On arriving at Gandamak, as I dismounted, I saw a wretched, half-naked man standing by my tent door. His bare feet were cut and bruised by the sharp stones, his beard matted, and his eyes hollow and sunk. This was all that remained of the most splendid specimen of Eastern chivalry I have ever known. He waited to see if I should recognise him, and then rushed into my arms, fell on my neck, kissed me, and burst into tears. My joy may be imagined. I led him into the tent, procured him refreshment, clothes, and a pipe, and then heard from him a detailed account of all his adventures and miseries, which he frequently interrupted to bless God for the miracle of my preservation, for at one time he had also given me up for lost. Though the presence of the British army at Kabul had freed him in some degree from

---

[1] Government afterwards gave him a jaghir (estate or fief) worth one thousand rupees a month.

the hot pursuit of the blood-hounds who had been so long on his traces, yet he failed in all his attempts to join us. Rendered desperate by our departure, he resolved to gain the shelter of the Feringhi camp or perish. He made his way across the most difficult and least-frequented tracts, travelling by night concealing himself by day, with scarcely any food, for he dreaded to claim the usual hospitality exercised by Afghans, and was on the point of falling in with our troops when he was seized by a band of robbers. Fortunately they did not know him, and therefore only plundered him of his arms and clothes, taking even his slippers. In this condition he arrived at General Nott's camp, where he was made prisoner on suspicion of being a spy, his arms tied behind him, and he was driven along the flinty road until his undefended feet were completely disabled. In fact, he narrowly escaped being put to death, as Nott's people were not rigidly ceremonious in dealing with Afghans, as I myself had several occasions of testifying; while, for want of a better, I still wore the costume of the country. Encountering an officer who knew him, he was at last released and directed to my quarters. I cheered him by reminding him of the 'Insaf' of the 'Kumpani Bahadur' (justice of the great 'Company'), and almost felt myself justified in engaging that Lord Ellenborough would delight to honour him. Instead, therefore, of going to Lahore to seek for service among the Sikhs, Hasan Khan shared my tent and my funds, and accompanied me to Firozpur."

All the captives suffered from depression of spirits, some of them, as Eyre, to a terrible degree. Some of the ladies dreamt of the horrors they had witnessed night after night for months after their release. But on the march, when they started sad and weary from sickness and fatigue, Sale used to put them all in good spirits. He would clear the way for himself, and if he saw any camp-followers on the road would dart after them, chase them in and out, bestowing unmerciful cracks on the crown on any he could reach, and then, his anger having all evaporated, would ride back again and join in the laugh at his own exploits.

After a month's halt at Peshawar, marked by a terrible outbreak of sickness in the force, Pollock marched for Hindustan. Avitabile had entertained the Generals and officers magnificently, and welcomed Mackenzie with the greatest joy, presenting him with a complete Persian dress and a Bible and prayer book ! In spite of the savage cruelty of his nature he now took leave of him with tears flowing down his cheeks, pressing him in his arms as if he had been his son.

The country between Peshawar and the Jelam is so shapeless and barren, and so intersected with deep ravines, that seen from a height it gives one an idea of chaos. Mackenzie took up a fellow-prisoner named Keane (a Horse Artilleryman who had been badly wounded) to help him across one of these streams. As they were struggling through it he remarked : "Och, sir ! this is a very con-thrairy country." Most unfortunately, in crossing the Jelam without sufficiently ascertaining the nature of the bottom, which was a quicksand, several poor fellows of the 16th Lancers were drowned. A trumpeter, mounted on a camel, floated a good way down, but as he continued to sound many calls, he was rescued. Another day Mackenzie was riding with the 3d Dragoons, when his Jewish friends came up to him in great excitement, having just recognised two London Jews serving as troopers in the regiment, who had hailed them in Hebrew as brethren. Musa and Ibrahim had long been employed in the dangerous service of convey-ing money to the English officers detached on missions in

Turkistan, encountering every sort of peril, privation, and fatigue. Their dealings with Government began by Ibrahim being sent across the desert from Persia by Colonel Shiel to our Envoy Arthur Conolly, and they had successively relieved the pressing wants of Lieutenant Richmond Shakespear at Khiva, and the unfortunate Colonel Stoddart at Bokhara (where their cousin Ephraim fell a victim to the ferocious Amir), and had received the handsomest testimonials from these officers. During the siege of cantonments they found refuge in the hospitable house of Vincent Eyre, who supplied them from his own table, and both before and after the retreat they contrived to convey information and money to the Envoy and to the captives at extreme risk to themselves. Akbar Khan at length seized them, screwed a heavy fine out of them, and imprisoned Musa for some weeks. His great peril drove him to prayer, and happily he had carried into his dungeon one of the Persian New Testaments, which he himself had transliterated into the Hebrew character, and which he studied with ever increasing interest. At last his friends succeeded in purchasing his freedom. He and his brother continued their assistance to our destitute officers after the release, and on our unexpected evacuation of the country were compelled to fly. During the march they occupied their spare time in comparing the Old and New Testaments. They were thoroughly versed in the old Scriptures, and so eager in their inquiry after truth, that even when Mackenzie was sleeping they would awaken him with many apologies to ask him to solve some difficulty or explain some prophecy. He was often astonished at their sagacity and the honesty of their reasoning on points of faith against which all their prejudices were enlisted. They frequently expressed their anxiety that their brethren in Central Asia should be able to ascertain the true cause of the degraded condition of Jews throughout the world, the true character of the Lord Jesus, and whether the Messiah were come, and frequently declared that until they had become acquainted with Dawes, Eyre, and a few other officers, they had always believed Christianity to be synonymous with idolatry, and that the Asiatic Jews, having only seen members of the Romish, Greek, and Armenian Churches, feel this idolatry an insurmountable barrier against the Gospel.

Instructing his Jewish friends was thus Mackenzie's chief occupation on the two months' march from Kabul. As they approached India, Mackenzie left the force at the Rávi, and hastened on to Firozpur, where a warm welcome awaited him from the Commander-in-Chief, from Mr. George Clerk, and all the General Staff of the Army, which welcome was promptly extended to Muhammad Hasan Khan on his history and merit being made known to them. Mackenzie never forgot the kindness and sympathy shown him at this time, especially by his hosts, Mr. and Mrs. George Clerk, and Lady Smith, Sir Harry's warm-hearted Spanish wife.

On reaching our frontier, the Satlej, Broadfoot indulged in humorous description :—

"We have been distributing medals which, with the gay ribbon, have thrown the garrison, and above all the men of the Sappers, into a very amusing state of joy. The latter worthy corps amused themselves till a pretty late hour last night with periodical cheers just so timed as to prevent each interruption to sleep being forgotten before another came, and, as it would have been cruel to interrupt them, I suffered patiently.

"Colin is better, but still very unwell, and he has amazed the people here I understand by a display of velvet and gold almost equal to Shah Shujah himself when in his glory. The ladies say he is 'a love of a man!' etc., etc., all which Colin takes meekly."

Lord Ellenborough, with his usual perversity, determined, in spite of Sir Jasper Nicoll's remonstrance to
reserve the honour of a public reception for the garrison of
Jellalabad alone, excluding Pollock, the General in command,
and his gallant force, who had relieved Jellalabad and
rescued the captives, and Nott's Division, which had co-
operated with Pollock. The Governor-General in person
superintended the painting of the elephants' trunks and the
erection of so ridiculous a triumphal arch, made of bamboos
and coloured cotton, and resembling a gigantic gallows, that
the soldiers marched under it with peals of laughter. On
the 17th December Sale and the Jellalabad garrison were
received by the Governor-General, the Commander-in-Chief,
and the Army of Reserve, with presented arms and a salute
of nineteen guns. On the 19th Pollock crossed the Satlej,
and was received by the Governor-General at the foot
of the bridge of boats, but there was no presenting arms
and no salute to greet either him or Nott and their
gallant soldiers. Then came honours and rewards. Lord
Ellenborough, so aptly named by General Churchill
"Brummagem Boney," was made an earl, as Lord Clan-
ricarde truly said in the House of Lords, "for successes
which had been achieved contrary to his opinions and
orders."

He inaugurated a period of "feasting, dancing, and
general junketing," but neither he nor any of his personal
staff paid the smallest attention to any of the hostages or
captives. Not even an aide-de-camp was sent to inquire
for the ladies, "the severity of whose sufferings had been
equalled only by the noble constancy with which they had
borne them," or to offer them any assistance !

Lord Ellenborough had imported all the violence of
English party spirit into India (a thing unknown before),
and he wished to place his conduct in strong contrast with

that of his truly honest predecessor, in which verily he succeeded. When Colin Troup laid before him the record of twenty-two years' good service, the Governor-General's answer was "that he could not be expected to provide for *the children of another Government !*"

The truth was that most of them, and certainly Mackenzie, had strongly disapproved of our intermeddling in Afghanistan ; but even so vain a man as Lord Ellenborough could not be wholly unconscious of the shamefulness of his own conduct, and he hated the brave men and helpless women whom he had tried so hard to abandon to life-long slavery.

As for General Pollock, whose forethought, consummate military skill, and indomitable firmness and valour made him probably the best General we have had in modern times, except the Duke and Sir Charles Napier, he got nothing but the Grand Cross of the Bath. He suffered for his noble but "unauthorised advance," and it was not till nearly thirty years after, when eighty-four years of age, that he obtained anything like adequate recognition of his great services.

The officers who had fallen into the hands of the enemy, excepting of course those who being hostages[1] were all the time on duty, had been by the Governor-General's orders placed under arrest on reaching Pollock's camp, and were now, as is usual in the case of prisoners, tried by court-martial. All were most honourably acquitted, except Shelton, who was found guilty of negotiating with the enemy for fodder for his starving horses. Pottinger's political conduct was brought before a Court of Inquiry, which pronounced that he had shown throughout "a degree of energy and manly firmness that stamps his character as

[1] Major Pottinger ; Captains G. St. P. Lawrence, Colin Mackenzie, Henry Drummond, and Walsh ; Lieutenants Warburton and Webb.

worthy of high admiration." In spite of this, however, no notice was taken of Pottinger, and the hero of Herat went away to China to die from the combined effects of his wound, of hardship, and of depression of mind and body. There can be little doubt that unmerited neglect hastened his death. Many others who had deserved well of their country got neither rewards nor thanks, and among these the defender of Charekar.

As a matter of course the captives, who were in want of everything, applied for their pay. Mackenzie as a political officer was entitled to political as well as military pay, and also to compensation for loss of property. A hostage is *on duty*, and entitled to full military pay and allowances. To the amazement of everybody Lord Ellenborough personally denied his right to compensation because he was a political, denied that he was a political because he was a hostage, and finally denied that he, Pottinger, and Lawrence, were hostages, though they had been specially demanded as hostages by Akbar because they were political officers. To this Mackenzie answered that if they were not hostages they must be deserters and ought to be shot. Six months before, during his last mission to Jellalabad, he had commissioned Broadfoot to inquire whether, because of the general failure at Kabul, all who served there would be excluded from honours, and it is pleasant to see the zeal with which Broadfoot advocated his friend's case in writing to men in high office. He says :—

"Where one set of men cause the misfortune, and others diminish its extent or its disgrace by their courage and skill, the latter surely should, and I believe usually do, receive their reward. His defence of the fort is a *separate* exploit ; it was brilliantly successful. His conduct in the Khurd Kabul Pass was most distinguished."

But in spite of the highest testimonials from Pollock,

M'Caskill, etc., etc.,[1] Mackenzie was refused the Kabul medal and its accompanying *batta* (*i.e.* six months' pay), and it was only the pertinacious friendship of Lord Dalhousie, who applied for it three times, that procured it for him eleven years after (1853), although Lord Hardinge gave it at once to Hasan Khan for service under Mackenzie's command.

The Governor-General had assured both Ferris' and Broadfoot's Jezailchis that they would be entertained in the British service for life. Nevertheless, to their intense indignation, this promise was broken, and they were disbanded at Firozpur with a gratuity of a year's pay.

Three times did the Commander-in-Chief apply officially for pensions for some of Mackenzie's Jezailchis who had lost hands and feet in the snow. His Excellency did not obtain the common civility of a reply. It was not till five years after that Lord Dalhousie, on Mackenzie's representation, granted each of them full pay (seven to ten rupees a month for life). The services of Hasan Khan were in like manner treated with contumely. Vincent Eyre wrote, May 1843 :—"Hasan Khan is at Simla. Nothing has been done for him, and the poor man is in great distress. I purpose raising a subscription for him." At last, through Mr. Clerk's interest, a paltry pension of fifty rupees a month was given to the gallant jemadar, and subsequently Sir Henry Hardinge evinced his sense of his claims by increasing that sum to six hundred rupees a month. But if any

---

[1] Sir George Clerk wrote :—"Deploring as I constantly do the hatred and contempt in which our name as a nation is now held throughout Central Asia, I find some consolation in the knowledge that there also, in certain places, heroic acts of some individuals of our country have left a lasting impression of their admirable conduct among a brave people ; and I firmly believe that no one manifested a spirit, or performed deeds better calculated than yours to relieve the mortification felt for British disgrace in Afghanistan."

man ever deserved the Order of Merit, Hasan Khan is that man. During the Satlej campaign he joined the army with a small party of followers, armed and equipped at his own expense, and greatly distinguished himself. Just before the battle of Ferozshahar Major Broadfoot said to him : "You have done great things with Mackenzie Sahib; let me see what you will do with me." Although much distinguished by Lords Hardinge and Gough, the latter pronouncing him the bravest man he ever saw, he got no reward but the Satlej medals, at which he was much disgusted.

Nor did the two faithful Jews fare better. Arthur Conolly had given them bills on Sir William Macnaghten, but when they arrived at Kabul the cantonment was besieged, and Sir William gave them bills on the Government of India. On reaching Firozpur they presented these bills for payment; but Lord Ellenborough repudiated the debt, and refused to acknowledge any obligation towards these men, who had lost all by their noble fidelity to the British. Mackenzie was already sufficiently indignant at the treatment he and his friends had met with, but this last act of injustice was too much for his patience. For the last year he had lived as it were face to face with death. This had produced a habit of daring and recklessness that cared for no consequences. The Governor-General was nothing to him. Filled with indignation at Lord Ellenborough's contemptuous refusal of bare justice to men who had sacrificed everything for our sakes, his wrath exploded in a vigorous certificate, which he left with Musa and Ibrahim on going to England, strongly recommending them to the good offices of every British officer, and stating that Lord Ellenborough had refused them all compensation, "why, is between God and his lordship's conscience." In all simplicity the two Jews forwarded this with their petition to the Bombay Government. From thence it went up to the Governor-General, and then home. The Board of Control was furious. The Court of Directors, though generally friendly, called upon Captain Mackenzie (Christmas 1844) to explain his conduct. This he did by relating the manner in which Lord Ellenborough had behaved, which still further increased the wrath of the " authorities in the far West" *i.e.* the Board of Control. Mackenzie's staunch friend, Mr. W. B. Bayley, wrote to him most kindly, "with full recognition of the high value of his services, eminent military character, and of the cruel treatment he and others most deserving continue to experience from quarters which the Court of Directors cannot yet influence," but urging him simply to acknowledge the impropriety of an officer publicly condemning the conduct of the head of his Government. This Mackenzie consented to do, and received an expression of the regret of the Court that " so distinguished an officer" could have been guilty of so insubordinate an act.

This was the first official recognition that his services had been distinguished. It has been necessary to anticipate events a little in order to finish the subject.

In the meantime Mackenzie obtained sick furlough at Firozpur, took his Jewish friends with him to Lodiana, where he introduced them to the excellent American missionaries, Messrs. Newton and Porter,[1] and proceeded to

[1] They visited Mr. Newton almost daily for two or three months until they professed themselves fully satisfied that the Lord Jesus was the Messiah and the New Testament the Word of God. Still they stumbled at the doctrine of the Trinity and at the Godhead of the Lord, though they prayed daily in His Name, and declared that their only hope of salvation was through the merit of His atoning blood. After some time they went to Bombay, where Musa died. Mr. Pigott, the chaplain, wrote at the request of Ibrahim, and said:—" That although Musa continued to feel some difficulty about the Divinity of

Calcutta, much out of health and thoroughly sick at heart. He was cheered by the affectionate welcome of his brother James and his sisters-in-law, and embarked for England in March 1843.

the Lord Jesus, yet his sole dependence in death was fixed on Him. We can hardly say that the saving grace of God could not be extended to some who have to learn the oneness of the Son with the Father fully in the next world."

END OF VOL. I.

Printed by R. & R. CLARK, *Edinburgh*

www.ingramcontent.com/pod-product-compliance
Lightning Source LLC
Chambersburg PA
CBHW051525100726
47898CB00005B/1574